The Queen of Ruin

THE QUEEN OF RUIN

THE HANDIWORK OF RUIN: BOOK ONE

E.R. GRIFFIN

For Mom,
who read it first,
and then several more times.
Thank you for everything.

The Unnamed North
Vale
Noor
Whisper Sound
Akhratan
The Eye of Ei'ish
The Ridge
The Grey Sea
Rai'al
The Bay of Songs
Unladd
Godsfang Mountains

FIFTEEN YEARS AGO...

-Denmoor-

FAIRBORN MANOR STOOD quiet in the smoky dark. Nathy distrusted the calm. Silence was dangerous, because silence came before shouts, before fists, before slammed doors. But this silence was long, which was unusual. Unusual things were dangerous, too.

This quiet, this heavy cloak of uninhabited dullness, meant something big. His mom had gone away, his dad was off the bottle. And these unfathomable events, which made the house so quiet, made it unsafe.

It was time to leave. He had a job to do, anyway.

Nathy closed his rucksack, tossed it over one shoulder, and slipped out the door of the mudroom. He snuck around the side of the decaying manor house, following the overgrown grass to the road, his path bright. Both moons were up tonight, the big white glowing one and the feebly lit, lumpy one—the stolen moon, Pyrenee. *"They're the Sisters, brought back together at last,"* Mom had said once.

A lump rose in Nathy's throat.

Denmoor's streets were grubby and dark; the light from the streetlamps bled pathetic puddles of yellow across cracked heaps of pavement grown through by tree trunks and weeds. It was a bad place, and no place for a Rakashi kid. But if being Rakashi was standardly a danger on these streets, the Sisters paid him for his troubles in quick feet as he slipped along in the shadows.

Nathy paused at one of the trees which had urged its way through the concrete. Its leaves were thick-grown, its branches tangled. It would do. He climbed through the foliage and hauled himself up onto the roof of a bustling apothecary. He stayed low as he hopped along the close-packed buildings.

The streets below were crowded with night life. Nathy was too young to know what half these people got up to, but his intuition and talent for eavesdropping had effectively ruined any construct of innocence. He knew the hookers from the bookies from the hired guns just from scanning the people on the ground.

He dropped back to the pavement at a familiar old shop and shuffled inside, keeping his head down like his mother had taught him: No eye contact. Not with the Watchmen's eyes out there.

The shop smelled like a dozen strains of burning incense, and melted wax squares on hot plates wafted the scent of rosemary and pomegranate to the rafters. He stood on the other side of a long counter, propped his elbows on it, and waited. Time passed and the incense choked him. He fished a stray cigarette from his pocket and lit it in the fluttering flame of a cinnamon-scented candle.

"Nathy?" A boy, eleven years old like Nathy, with his same russet skin and black hair, appeared from a narrow door behind the counter and waved him forward. Nathy vaulted over the counter and followed his friend down a secret door in the floor.

"Mom's been worried," said Sinclair.

Nathy exhaled smoke. "Does she still have it?"

"Yeah, sure. Are you...I mean, your mom definitely said...?"

"I don't feel like repeating myself," Nathy said. The other boy winced.

They stopped in a basement cluttered with the wares and means of selling one's Sight—low tables with beaded tablecloths and crystal balls in dragon-claw stands, jars of salt (keeps the goblins out, or the ghosts, depending on who you're selling to), and tins of every kind of tea, each flavor endowed with foresight. For a price.

Nathy's eyes were immediately drawn to a woman wrapped in colored scarves. Birth gems glittered on her every finger. Madame San Clair's face looked like a newspaper left in the rain and scraped from the sidewalk. But for her age and wrinkles and the hideous warp of her features, Nathy felt nearly as warm from her eyes as he did from his own mother's. She waved him forward impatiently, and he hugged the many rolls of her waist.

"There's my little *jana-kal.*"

"My mom," Nathy said. "D'you—is she still—I mean, can you see if—"

It's impossible to fully ask a question you don't want the answer to. He stopped trying.

"I can hear her mind no more," said Madame San Clair, and her hand on Nathy's shoulder told him what he'd as good as known.

"That doesn't mean she's..." Sinclair said.

"It's okay," Nathy said. He didn't mean a syllable of that damn word, *okay*, like his mother dying had anything in common with those two pointless sounds brought together. But what did Dad say? Life is a stage, and you're in the play whether you like to act or not. "She's with the Sisters."

Something in his gut told him that would be the last lie he ever told himself; after that night, he would lose every trace of whatever unique ability it was that allowed living creatures to deny reality.

"Have some tea." Madame San Clair lifted a full cup from the small round table behind her. Nathy took it with a sneer.

"Do I have to?"

The glint in her eye said yes, yes he did. He drank and drank and winced on the last swallow, always the most difficult, and handed the cup back. She set it down and peered into it as the tea leaves settled and his future became bare.

"Oh dear," she said. "Oh, my poor *jana-kal*."

Nathy rolled his eyes. "What?"

"I see...yes, it must be...but..." She turned her globe-like eyes on him, then her table. She lifted a deck of cards and held it out to Nathy. "Shuffle."

He sighed, shuffled the cards, and handed them back. She drew the top card.

"Well?" he said.

She turned the card toward him, hand trembling with age and nerves. "The Hanged Man, reversed," she said.

The picture on the card showed a man tied to a tree, his arms splayed across branches, his head drooping to his bare and bloody chest. Somehow worst of all, the man was smiling, a grin splitting his bloody lips. Nathy took the card from her fingers and frowned at the image. Madame San Clair had drawn it upside down.

"And your cup," Madame Sin Clair said. She lifted it in her palm and Nathy peered inside. The tea leaves made a bumpy but unmistakable image—a man, apparently bound at the wrists and tied to a stake. His tiny pinpoint eyes ran with tea-stained water.

"What's it mean?" Nathy said.

"Deception," Madame San Clair said. "You are hard to see for, my *jana-kal*, but I can say this: a betrayal most grievous lies in your future. You will lose many, perhaps even yourself, to greed and lust and promises. Dark years lie ahead, Nathy."

"Well, don't go easy on me or anything," Nathy said. When she looked away, he slipped the card into his back pocket. "D'you have it? Her sword?"

Madame San Clair nodded once, solemnly. Nathy held out his hands. Madame San Clair placed a heavy blade wrapped in black velvet across his palms, perfectly balanced. He teetered under its weight, but steadied himself, tightening his shoulders. The blade itself was nearly as tall Nathy, five feet long at least. It wouldn't be easy carrying this thing around.

He peeled back the velvet—the blade let off a faint orange glow, like a candle, and was inscribed with Annanym. Most people couldn't read the old Elonni symbols, but Nathy knew these. Dad had taught him.

To bend the knee of God... Nathy grinned. "Neat."

"That's very dangerous now," Madame San Clair said. "Take care when—"

"Ow." Nathy examined the slit on his thumb, stuck it in his mouth. He tasted iron and his skin throbbed. He was a quick healer, but this wound only got more painful.

"Be careful!" Madame San Clair slapped Nathy's hand away from his mouth. "That blade is the single most deadly—"

"Yeah, yeah." He rewrapped the blade, set it on the ground, and drew his wand. He tapped the end of the wand to the blade, whispering Rakashi words, and smiled when the blade shrank, smaller and smaller until it looked like no more than a knife. He placed the shrunken weapon into the waistband of his trousers. "I need to find Mr. Barker."

He didn't like what he saw in her old eyes. It was judgment and sorrow together, a strange mixture, cold on his skin and sinking into his blood.

"I'll find a way myself," he said.

"Wait." She turned to the crystal ball set on her table and ran her hand along its surface. She murmured in Rakashi, and a thick cloud formed beneath the glass. Nathy peered into it, waiting. Nothing came.

"Where is he?" Nathy said.

"I...I can see him no more. It's like he's—"

"Dead?"

She shook her head. "It doesn't mean that."

She didn't sound so sure.

"Whatever. Can't be that hard to find somebody."

"My *jana-kal*—wait!"

"I'll be *fine*." He began to walk toward the stairs.

Madame San Clair reached for him and grabbed his shoulder. He had just turned his dark, annoyed eyes on her when she said another word which was nearly as damning and horrible as *okay*: "Smoke."

Smoke. Fire. That was their way.

"*What?*" Sinclair said. His face paled and his eyes watered.

Nathy clutched the hilt of the sword; the sweat of his palm made it slippery.

"Go," Madame San Clair said.

Nathy nodded once and started toward the stairs, only to backpedal at the sudden vicious stench coming from the upper floors. A wall of smoke and ash hit his eyes and tunneled down his throat. Despite the pain and obstruction, he forced himself to look. Smoke twisted down the stairs to meet him, heavy and dark.

"Is there another way out?" he choked.

Madame San Clair shuffled to an old trunk on the other side of the room and pushed it aside, peeling away the dust of the floor and revealing a small trapdoor.

"Sisters, don't let them have sealed it," she prayed. She lifted the trapdoor and gestured to her son and Nathy. Sinclair darted forward and into the trapdoor. Nathy didn't move.

"Come," Madame San Clair said. "Quickly!"

The basement roof collapsed, so rotted by flame it could sustain the weight of the shop above no longer. Nathy backed up onto the stairs. The flaming beams of the roof surged between them, barring Nathy's path. Madame San Clair, with

13

glistening eyes and a sea of fire between her and her *jana-kal*, sunk into the trap door and shut it behind her.

Nathy had little time to feel alone. He was suddenly smothered in a blanket, and he felt himself pulled up, up, up, and through an incredible heat. He was thrown down onto pavement sometime later, and the blanket was ripped away. He gasped for breath and looked around. Across the street from where he lay, Madame San Clair's shop burned from the top windows, the fire eating its way down like a snake consuming something bigger than itself.

A hand grabbed his upper arm. He swung around with a punch, but it was caught in another's palm. His captor was a girl, beautiful in a way Nathy was only just beginning to appreciate. She looked a little like a woman, yet still sort of like a girl.

"Let go," he said.

"Do you want to die?"

"Do you?"

She laughed like she had bells in her throat and pulled him away from the fire with annoying strength. She had white wings, extended like she'd just been flying. An Elonni.

He yanked against her grip; she ignored him until he twisted her wrist with unintentional vigor. She swung him around and slammed his back into a tree.

"You're Nathaniel Fairborn, aren't you?"

"Yeah." She had the elitist southeastern accent his father had and tried to hide. It took him a second, but he wasn't dumb—one look at the belt of weapons on her tiny waist and he put two and two together.

"You're a Huntress."

"Uh-huh."

"You work for my dad." He twisted his arm, trying to break her grip, but it only tightened.

"Not anymore," she said. "I'm here to help you." She dropped him and he landed like a cat on all fours. "Do you know who Roselyn Ruark is?"

He rose and brushed the knees of his trousers. "Should I?"

"Probably. He's been hired to kill you." She nodded toward the flaming scalp of Madame San Clair's shop. "That was him. Don't take it personally, he's just...efficient."

"Did he kill my mom, too?" Nathy said.

The pretty girl levelled her gaze at him and pursed her lips, considering, like she figured he'd either lash out or start crying; he planned for neither. "Yeah," she said. "That's what I've head, anyway."

Nathy stared at his palms and watched his fingers curl and make fists without his consciously doing so. "Roselyn Ruark, huh?" Knowing the killer's name—that somehow changed the game for Nathy, and *Roselyn Ruark* wedged into his memory and set up camp and promised to stay for a very long time.

"Well, then, I'll kill him."

"You're adorable," the Huntress said in a way that sounded like *you're stupid*. "Don't get in over your head, though, tough guy. Follow me."

He trailed the beautiful, ruthless Huntress through the grimy streets. She extracted a cigarette from a pocket and lit it. Her wings retracted and dissolved like light now that she had relaxed a bit.

Nathy watched the smoke curl from her cigarette and twist in the air. He shouldn't like smoke anymore, he realized, but hey. Some destructive things were pretty. "Can I have one?"

"You're too young."

He sidled up to her. "What's your name?"

She gave him a suspicious glare and said, "Isobel."

"And you helping me, huh?"

"I pulled you from a fire, didn't I?" she said.

"I meant, I dunno, I guess *why* are you helping me?"

"What kind of monster leaves a defenseless kid in a fire?" She smirked and pinched his cheek.

He pushed her hand away. "I'm not defenseless. I've been chosen to—"

She shushed him and held out her hand to halt his steps as a carriage rattled farther up the street. Isobel grabbed the front of Nathy's shirt and ducked into an alley with him. They crouched behind a heap of rubbish.

The snarl of wheels grew louder. A carriage tumbled into view, tugged along by a giant with a broad, flat nose and wide nostrils. He breathed like he had a cold, thick panting that steamed the air before him.

The carriage and the giant stopped, and the street was quiet. The extra moonlight from Pyrenee made the ground bright, brought the trees and lamps and all the mysteries of the dark, narrow streets out of obscurity.

A slender figure unfolded from the carriage, a man Nathy's father's age, with a thin, curled mustache and slicked black hair. Following the skinny man was a broader man with reckless blond hair. He had Nathy's face, aged and white but strikingly similar nonetheless. Nathy thought his heart pounded loud enough to hear.

"Come out, come out," the skinny man said. "You annoying little abomination."

"Roz," Nathy's dad said. "Shut up."

"What? He's a freak. You said as much."

"Watch what you say to me," Nathy's dad said in calm, disinterested tones.

Nathy sank down against the alley wall. That voice made his stomach hurt. That voice meant fists and nights without dinner. It meant cuts and lashes. When Dad was mad, things were bad. Nathy covered his ears, and the Huntress squeezed his shoulder. Her hand shook.

"What the hell are you doing, Fairborn?" she said below a whisper.

The two men were silent so long, Nathy began to think they'd moved on. He lifted his head—and cried out when a big hand snatched him by his long black hair and lifted him from the ground. Air whistled around his ears as he careened to hit the alley wall. His face rested on the rubbishy ground. He peeked at the unfolding scene with one eye.

The skinny man had Isobel on the ground, holding her wrists out above her head. His face was pressed against hers as he whispered something in her ear that made her scream in rage.

A fist connected with Nathy's stomach and his rucksack was torn away from him. His father shifted through the contents, throwing larger items to the ground. An old, cherished stuffed dragon bounced off the ground with a muted cry and landed by Nathy's feet. He didn't touch it. His dad stopped rummaging and threw the rucksack aside.

"Where is it?" Dad was so broad and tall he looked like a monster in the shadows, his yellow hair lit by the moons.

"Where's what?" Nathy said.

His dad kicked him in the stomach.

"Cooperate."

Nathy bit the inside of his cheek. "I don't know what you're talking about."

He endured another kick while Isobel's screams rose in his ringing ears. Ruark covered her mouth and with his free hand held her throat. She fought against his grip, even as she lost access to air with the tightening of his hand.

"Let her go!" Nathy said. He received another kick and curled in on himself. He reached for the toy dragon and took it into his arms. Its fur was musty and smelled like home, like incense and Mom's perfume. Across the alley Isobel screamed—they were really, badly hurting her, because of him.

Nathy pushed himself up, left the dragon on the ground, and tackled his dad's legs. He failed to even budge the bulwark that was Mortimer Fairborn, and stumbled backward. His dad cocked his head, curious.

"You don't want us to hurt her?" he said.

Nathy said nothing. His fists were clenched, and he felt his fingernails, sharp against his palms, little punishments for the pain he was causing this total stranger who'd only tried to help.

"Roz," Mortimer said. "Kill her in the next, oh, five seconds, if my son doesn't oblige my request."

Roselyn Ruark drew a knife. Nathy pulled the shrunken sword from his waistband and threw it like it burned him. It grew as it careened across the narrow space, lengthening into its true form. Mortimer caught it by the hilt, turned the blade this way and that. He smiled.

"Thank you, son." He drew the sharp tip against his thumb, as Nathy had done earlier. A line of red spilled and flowed down his skin. "You did the right thing."

"Make him stop it!" Nathy said. Ruark had the knife pressed to Isobel's throat; a blossoming patch of red filled the hollow of her neck.

"Roz, please stop," Mortimer said. "We'll take care of her later."

"Lunatics," Isobel said through her teeth and a mouthful of blood from her bitten tongue. She shoved Ruark off her, but Ruark grabbed her face and held it up for Mortimer's perusal.

"What should we do with our bad little girl, then, hm?"

Mortimer crossed to the other side of the alley. He placed the edge of the sword against Isobel's throat and tipped her chin up. She stared back, small breaths puffing through her nose, jaw tight.

"I'll deal with her later." Mortimer drew the sword back, leaving a thin red line across her throat. "Patriarch will be so disappointed. You might have been the best of all of us." His eyes flicked to Ruark's. "Throw her in the carriage. I need to speak with my son."

Ruark smiled slowly and rose, his arm wrapped around Isobel's throat. She jerked against him, twisting and throwing her elbows, but the Huntsman held fast. He whistled to the giant, who rose with a sad look at Nathy, and picked up the carriage. Ruark shoved Isobel inside, throwing a final punch as she lunged for the door.

"I'm going to find Mr. Barker!" Nathy shouted at his father's back. "He's going to kill you, all of you!"

Mortimer turned to his son with eyes that somehow looked friendly for one cruel moment. In the next instant, they clouded over with a threat. "William Barker is dead. It's over." He smiled faintly. "Come on, son. You still have a place with us. I'll forgive you for this night. But you've got to make the right choice. Now."

Nathy's muscles jumped, enticing him to run. He might make it; Mom had taught him a spell that would take him from one place to another, and what better time to practice? He got to his feet, fumbled for his wand, started to say the words—

Mortimer kicked him back and pinned him down with a knee to his stomach. He buried the tip of the sword into the corner of Nathy's left eye and dragged it down, scraping his cheekbone, flaying his skin.

"I was trying to do you a favor," Mortimer said, pressing the blade down harder into meat and bone. *"One eye to see truth. The other to blot out darkness."*

Nathy screamed and screamed, and when nothing, not even street sounds answered, he realized he was alone, more alone than even the moon, who at least had Pyrenee. He realized, then, that all the good things were just stories.

This was life.

Blood filled his vision, and he lost sight of the Sisters dancing above.

I

LONG MAY SHE LIVE

-*Hollows Edge*-

THE CANDLES STOOD in a circle, the Annanym was chalked to the floor, and the old book of prayers lay open at the right page. Lacey knelt before the ritual space and closed her eyes.

"*Hallas Elroi.*"

A feeling of summer's light rose from her core and rushed through her spine. Wings of light curled around her shoulders, blooming at last into ruddy feathers. She opened one eye and checked her bedroom door. She ought to have time before her stepfather came knocking.

Wind breathed through the cracks in the house, its cadence like a conversation heard from far away. The wordless tongues of nature had no syntax, used to lexicon; it was mere sound, absent of significance. And yet she felt she could almost understand what it said. Like she knew who was speaking through the wind.

"Dad?" She squeezed her eyes tight. "Are you there?"

Her stepfather told her disembodied voices were to be expected, that the old house was haunted. So close to the bogs, where ghosts were said to rise, it wasn't unlikely a spirit had been trapped in the wood.... Jonas Underhill boasted all the wisdom of a man who never left his village of birth and therefore knew the very woods and sky and every creature like the lines on his own palm.

Maybe it wasn't her dad speaking over the groaning winds. Probably just a passerby lost to the marsh. But if it was him...

She snapped her fingers above the wick of the nearest candle; a small fire burst between her skin and lit it. "*Ay myam—myamin?*"

She consulted the prayer book and squinted at the symbols. She knew so few Annanym, and nobody had spoken the old Elonni language they represented for millennia. She knew the beginnings of this prayer but little else.

"How long *is* this?" She sighed and set the book back in its place. Maybe she had Elrosh's attention anyway—and if he was God, well, shouldn't he be able to understand her? She lit the other candles with quick snaps. "Please...hear my request," she said, winging it. "I'd like to speak with someone passed. Please send me—"

Her door rattled in its frame, the warped wood groaning, as her stepfather's fist made contact.

"Wake up!"

Jonas. Lacey ripped the tattered blanket from her bed and tossed it over the candles and Annanym, remembering too late the tiny flames. Smoke hissed through the holes and a rank stench wafted forward.

"Girl?" Her door opened with a weary screech. Her stepfather loomed over her, huge and burnt from a summer spent in the sun, his face gray with stubble. His long, ragged hair was pulled back, but coming loose in greasy strands. A double-barreled shotgun hung at his back, and two nor'moles dangled from his belt, their long bodies gone limp.

"The hell is that?" He eyed the lumpy, simmering blanket.

"I...dropped my candle. And panicked. So, I tossed the blanket over it."

"How many damned candles did you light?"

"Oh, a few. It was..." She stamped her heel down on a growing ember. "It's so dark in the winter, y'know?" She smiled, the action less quelling than she'd hoped.

Jonas's scowl cut down to his jowls. "You'll cease whatever foolishness this is, girl. I've got you a job to do."

"What's that, sir?"

A smile creeped through the weathered folds of his skin. "You'll be witness for us today."

Lacey balked. "For an—an execution?"

"That's right."

"Why can't you go?"

"Don't question me. There's work enough here, and I'm already behind thanks to your laziness."

Hot, quick anger rushed Lacey's blood, but she didn't form a retort worthy of her stepfather's cruelty in time. He'd already turned and walked out the door.

"Just close your eyes when the sword falls," he shouted back. His short laughter drifted away with him.

THE SUN HAD nearly risen and spilled enough pale winter light to see by. Lacey stood in the knee-deep snow in her yard, cold despite her boots and old wool coat. But she stood frozen for another reason.

Hollows Edge carried a weight, its very air dense with lost potential and stagnation. Yet this was all of Lacey's world: Du'unsene Forest behind her, black and ancient and secret; the plowed white lane and its spokes of dirt roads before her; and the scattered town below the hill. The great, fat pines and the quiet, colorless winter made her bones ache.

Life seemed nothing, insignificant, from this little yard.

There was nothing to be done about it.

She followed the lane past a patchwork of thatch-roofed cottages and sunken farmhouses guarded by bare trees. A harvested and snow-buried cornfield stretched out beyond them.

The lane dipped downhill, into the village, which was little more than a sad smattering of shops, half of them shut up. Farther on stood a narrow stone church to the Old God on the edge of the marshes, empty most days thanks to dead fervor.

Lacey avoided the church generally; she'd found the Old God worshipped by the humans as irascible as any of the more popular ones, and much less fun in every other way. But she stopped there sometimes for the graveyard, to see her father. He lay in a distant, weedy corner, with the other village men fallen fifteen years ago in the War of Teeth, beneath a shared tombstone.

She didn't have time to see him today.

Lacey joined the morning bustle of the village. Each family had sent at least one witness to the execution, but most came as a unit, the spectacle more tempting than grueling work. Men with cold-pinked faces and women with chapped hands led bony children to the town square. Happy chatter drifted from mouth to mouth.

Lacey shivered as wind passed through the holes in her coat.

The gong of the clock tower throbbed in the distance...once...twice. The third ring was echoed by the hoots of the growing crowd. Applause crackled through the throng.

"Excuse me," Lacey said to a woman walking nearby. "Do you know what's happened?"

"Well, what I heard—" But her voice died as she turned to find it had been Lacey who'd spoken to her. The woman's mouth clapped shut.

"Mutt," she said, and pushed farther ahead.

Lacey drew her coat closer around her chest. "Cow."

Twenty years ought to have been enough time to grow accustomed to the human villagers' hatred. Lacey was mixed—human, thanks to her mother, but also Elonni by her father's blood. And the Elonni, despite their might bleeding from the capital city to every corner of the realm, had hardly earned the love of the mortal kinds.

Yet she didn't belong with the Elonni, either. She was weaker than they, dulled by her human blood. A mutt didn't belong anywhere.

She was the product of something that should never have been.

The crowd pressed around the gallows and rabbled as one while the low, cold voice of a preacher chanted over them, words in a dead language Lacey knew only from prayers. A collection of bat-eared, gunmetal gray bergfolk, only three-feet high and easily unseen by the distracted multitude, wound through the crowd nicking watches and coins. One neared Lacey, and she gave him a look.

"Elonni-girl," the bergfolk said, and bowed.

"Hey, Cuyler." She narrowed her eyes. "Is that my purse?"

Cuyler regarded one of a dozen coin purses fastened around his skinny waist with a string. "No, no, t'isn't yours, Elonni-girl. T'isn't right to be stealing from you."

Lacey held out her hand. Cuyler scowled and untied the belt. He dropped the little purse into her waiting palm.

"Thank you, Cuyler."

The bergfolk shrugged and rejoined his fellows. He slipped a wallet from a man's jacket as he went.

"Household," a voice barked too close to Lacey. She winced, turning to find the constable standing beside her.

"Household," he repeated, not bothering to look at her.

"Falk-Barker-Underhill."

He looked up at that, eyebrows raised. Lacey grinned.

"Oh. It's you." The constable checked a name from his parchment. "Underhill, then."

"I prefer Falk-Barker-Underhill."

"That's nice." He moved on without further comment.

Curiosity wedged into Lacey's mind. She could just hang back, let taller people blot out the gallows and the horror about to unfold. But part of her had to know, had to see who had been condemned. There hadn't been an execution in so long.

She squeezed between two men and got a clear view. The town's four Watchmen stood before the gallows, their bloodred uniforms stark against the gray landscape. Before them knelt a ragged man, facing the crowd, his head bowed and covered with a black cloth. One of the Watchmen stepped forward.

"Jacor Raymath, you are hereby sentenced to die, by the will of God and the wisdom of the Elderon."

A muffled laugh puffed against the black cloth. "Right," the prisoner said. Then, louder: "I die for a better world. Hail Annylon, Queen of Ruin! Long may she live."

The Watchman tore the cloth away, grabbed a fistful of the prisoner's hair, and yanked his head back.

Lacey didn't recognize the prisoner and had little chance to try and place him. Before she had fully registered the gold of his hair, the hate in his eyes, the stubble on his face, a sword emerged from his chest, right where his heart had once beaten. His blood filled the cracks in the cobbled road and carved a path through the snow.

Lacey wanted to close her eyes, but they instead followed the ruby trail back to its source, trying to understand how so much blood could be in one person. She had never seen someone die before. When she was a child, forced to follow

24

Jonas along to executions, she'd always shut her eyes. Now that she'd seen it, she couldn't look away.

The Watchman ripped the sword from the prisoner's body and sheathed it. With that one cold motion, he and his fellows dispersed. A villager nearby hummed the first bars of a hymn. The old women of the village joined him, their voices mixing with lyrics sung out of time as they knelt in the red snow. The slain man coughed blood, his paling cheek against the ground.

"Gets no easier to see death," said a voice beside her. She turned to find the preacher smiling down at her. He was somewhere in his sixties, tall and broad-shouldered with a severe, squared haircut. His suit was neat, stylish. And he gave off a certain aura, one of power, authority.

"You're Elonni," Lacey said.

He tipped his head, smiling. "So are you, from what I hear."

"What happened to the old preacher?"

"Ah. Brother Jerimiah passed away, I'm afraid. About a month ago. You'd know that if you attended services, my dear."

Lacey took a step back from him. "Did the Elderon send you?"

He quirked an eyebrow. "Why would you think that?"

"It's just, we've never had an Elonni preacher. Don't you worship Elrosh?"

"I do. And perhaps your village should, too." His eyes drifted toward the gallows, something heavy and strange in his gaze. "The humans seem to have lost their way."

She followed his gaze. The Watchmen had returned with a wheelbarrow and now loaded the dead man into it, each taking hold of a limb. "What'd that man do?" she said.

The preacher reached out a long, steady finger and placed it over Lacey's heart. "Sin starts here." His fingernail pressed into the worn fabric of her coat. "And spreads to every corner of our lives. I imagine he must've made one of our gods very angry."

Lacey pushed his hand away. "And sticking a sword through him fixed that, did it?"

The preacher laughed. "You're a fiery one, my dear. Watch that they don't find what's in your heart."

Lacey opened her mouth, but the preacher pushed past her and began his easy way back to the stone church on the far side of the village. He passed by the Watchmen, now lighting a gathered cluster of logs at the edge of the square. A tangle of smoke rose from the wood as a small fire crackled to life; the warm orange eye of the pyre burned across the distance, and soon the preacher was a shadow to its sun.

2

THE HUNTRESS

-Mondberg-

THE WOLF LAY curled on the slick cave floor, shuddering with snores, breath steaming white and dissipating on the frigid air. The creature was huge, its fur matted and ruddy. Nathy stepped further into the cave, eyes on the slumbering beast.

"Hey," he said.

The beast snored on. It's claws, chipped like used nails, scrabbled at the cave floor.

"Hey! Wake up." Nathy toed the creature's side. It didn't stir. He walked around to its rear and stamped his foot down on its pluming tail.

"Hey!"

The wolf yelped and scrabbled to its feet, spinning on him. Fangs dripped saliva, the manic sneer accompanied by a rumbled growl.

"Don't get excited," Nathy said, scratching the wolf behind the ears. It snapped at his hand.

"Bad dog." Nathy flicked its nose.

The wolf shook its head and sat back on its haunches. Its fir stirred as though disturbed by a light wind, and soon its flesh seemed to crack, shift, rearranging in a grotesque display of anatomy that left a kneeling, naked man in its place.

"You're late," Landon Woods said, rising.

Nathy looked away. "Put some clothes on."

"From what I hear, you like to look."

"You're not my type."

Landon lumbered off to the back of the cave where a limp rucksack waited. He was massive in his human form, a head taller than Nathy and broad through the shoulders. Nathy preferred the wolf.

Landon returned dressed in a thick bearskin coat. He tossed a scarf around his thick neck, smiling down. His yellow eyes were always a wolf's, glinting with an eternal hunger. "Glad you could make it, Ferrickek. Welcome to Mondberg."

Nathy gestured for Landon to lead the way, and they left the cave, coming out onto a thin stretch of shore. Huge drifts of sea ice skirted the coast and hung suspended on distant black waters reaching toward the rising sun. Old snow underfoot crunched as the two men picked along the sandless beach. The land was dead, gray-white and pearlescent, glowing under a late-rising sun.

"You're quieter than I remember," Landon said.

"I hate the cold." Even as he said it, Nathy slipped on the ice, grabbing uselessly at the air as he fell hard against the smooth beach.

"Watch it," Landon said with a wolfish grin. "The ice hides in everything."

"Yeah, I'll remember that," Nathy said. He rose and found grounding in the snow. He walked the coast slower than his companion.

In the distance, the frozen beach curled away, tighter and tighter against the jutting black-rock cliffs until it stopped entirely and gave way to the sea. A few small fishing boats left tied to the shore by thick ropes stood frozen to the water. They looked resolute, an unmanned armada. The coiled remains of a frost-caked fishing net clung to the beach. Abandoned spears and tankards for oil lay scattered.

Landon led Nathy away from the beach into the piled snowdrifts stacked opposite the waters, and they trudged through snow up to their waists. Soon, Nathy couldn't feel his legs.

"You know what she wants from me?" Nathy said. He wanted to distract himself from the sound of his teeth chattering in his skull, his veins pumping weakly toward his heart.

"Course."

"And?"

"I'm just here to deliver you, mate."

Beyond the high snow and through the bluster of ice, the first rambling outposts of a town emerged.

"They call that one the Point of No Return," Landon said, nodding to a ramshackle pub. "Best beer you'll ever drink, but the food is shit."

Nathy followed the other man past dilapidated buildings half-buried in snow. Huge wooden toboggans rested by every wilting clapboard home. In shop windows, spears, guns, and huge knives for skinning game—Landon glared at them with unease—beckoned tradesmen come with what money they had and invest in their particular brutality. The air stunk of oil and cooked fat. Mondberg was an ancient place, and somewhere in those distant snowy peaks rested rock temples and sacrificial stones. Yet here and now, it was nothing but a commercial port. The wolves were dead, mostly. Landon was one of the youngest of his kind, blood heir to a decimated pack.

As they neared the town's center, the tall, stone reach of the Watchmen's tower became visible. There were so few people left in Mondberg, Nathy wondered why they bothered with a guard anymore. Nobody knew about Landon and his pack, and otherwise the once-wolf town harbored only humans interested in hunting the rare artic creatures.

But the Elderon never was content with security; Albion Crane and his deadly paranoia reached across the realm, into even the smallest nocturne towns.

They stopped in the town's center. Nathy tore his eyes away from the structure in the very middle: a stake, black from use, the singed remains of rope around its base.

"If you think about it," Landon said, "in this weather, being burned alive isn't the worst thing that can happen."

Nathy half-smiled. "You have a point."

They stopped outside a pub. Its sign creaked wearily in the ice-wind. Flower boxes decorated the window sills on the second floor, and they were filled not with greenery, but snow. More goddamned snow.

"She's in there." Landon looked at him. "You'll at least hear what she has to say, right?"

"I'm more interested in the pay. So, yeah."

"Good. Always a pleasure, Nath," Landon said. His yellow eyes glinted, more canine than human. With a short nod, he turned and meandered through the town's square, vanishing at last into the flurry of snow carried off the ground.

Nathy turned back to the pub and, as his eyes fell on the door, it opened. A tall, slender woman, her blond hair bound in a loose braid, emerged, lighting a cigarette. She wore a suit and a wide-brimmed hat, a fur coat dangling from her shoulders.

The left half of her otherwise beautiful face hid behind a black leather mask, fasted across her forehead with a thin ribbon. The eye peering from the mask saw nothing, its iris gone milky and blind. Her good eye, blue and sharp, swerved to Nathy's face.

Isobel. He almost didn't believe he was seeing her again.

"Hey," he said when she didn't.

"So. You showed."

"I—" But before he could get another word out, she closed the distance between them, reached out a small hand, and pushed the shaggy black bangs away from his left eye.

"Hm." She nearly smiled. "It almost suits you, you know?"

Her eyes hung on the scar slicing down the left side of his face, squinting his eye and dragging at the corner of his mouth. She slid a fingernail along the gorge-like pattern, stopping at last at his lips.

Nathy brushed her hand away. "Yeah. Thanks."

"I can hardly believe it," she said, listing her head. "Nathaniel Fairborn in the flesh. After all these years."

"It's Ferrickek now."

Isobel shook her head. "You can't help your birth, Nathaniel. Your father could have helped himself, but, well...the past is past. Long past."

Nathy said nothing.

"Well. Come inside." She held the door for him, and he walked past, relieved at the close warmth of the pub. Men dressed in oilskin coats and brimmed hats sat along the bar, chatting over frothy mugs, their fishing equipment abandoned at their feet. Isobel led him to a table in the corner. She sat across from him and rested her chin in her palm.

"Beer? Whisky?"

"Yes."

She smiled at him like an indulgent parent and waved the bartender over. "Two whiskies. Dealer's choice. Thanks, darling." She tossed her hat onto the table, shrugged off the coat.

"Aren't you cultured," Nathy said.

"You're tense," she said, ignoring him. "Why?"

Their drinks arrived, giving Nathy a moment to wonder that himself. He liked Isobel. By all accounts he owed her his life. Not so long ago, they'd been on the same side. Before Nathy had decided he'd make his own side.

"I hear you started splitting your time between the Elderon and Flynn," he said.

"If you're worried that I'm secretly helping the Elderon—"

"I'm not," he said. "I'm worried that you joined up with Flynn after everything."

She sipped her whisky, her solitary blue eye never leaving his face. "And what reason has Flynn ever given you to not trust him?"

"That a serious question?"

She ran her fingernail lightly along the rim of her glass. "I know why you left, if that's what you're asking. I tend to think you're being unfair, but..."

Nathy downed his whiskey in a single shot. "What did you need from me, Izzy?"

"Right to business. Fine, then. Flynn has me on a special mission. My connections within Theopolis, and my...well, my skill set have become pertinent lately."

"What, you're Flynn's assassin now?"

"You're one to talk."

Nathy grinned. "It wasn't a judgment on *you*, Izzy."

She swirled her drink in its glass, the dark brown liquid catching the faint light from the window. "How about I get right to it? We'd like to hire you to find someone."

"Just find them?"

"And deliver them."

"But not..." Nathy dragged his forefinger across his neck.

"No. The opposite. We have a lead on the Monarch, you see."

"Oh, gods, this again?" Nathy ran his hands down his face, shaking his head. "No."

"You haven't heard what I have to say."

31

"I know what you'll say. And I don't have time to hunt down a person you don't even know exists, no matter what you're paying."

"We've found her. Rather, I did." She leaned back, her smile sharp and beautiful. "A prominent university professor in Theopolis has been hiding her all this time."

"She was in the capital?"

"Hollow's Edge. Little down a way south of here. We had someone there. Jacor Raymath. He'd nearly gotten to her." She looked away. "The Watchmen got to him, though."

"You lost another one on this? Gods, how many people have to die for Flynn's pipe dream?"

"That's the issue, then? You don't believe the Monarch exists?"

"It's a story. My mom used to tell it to me, and when I was little, it wasn't some mythical queen making me feel better. It was having my mom there to tell me a story. Then she died because some crazy people actually believe this shit."

Isobel leaned forward, lips slanted. "You think a bedtime story could inspire such fervor?"

"Every religion probably started the same way. People telling lies in the dark to sleep better."

Isobel's tiny smile bloomed. "So cynical."

Nathy ignored her. "So you found someone who you think is the right girl." He leaned back in his chair. "Why not go get her? Hollows Edge is, what, half a day by train?"

"She won't be there by then."

"So find her again. You did it before."

"We're running short of time. And a Rakashi mage has resources I don't have, wouldn't you say?"

"Is Jade busy?"

Isobel's neat, neutral expression was thrown, just for a moment, but Nathy caught it. "Jade couldn't find her."

"She's better than me."

"You'll just have to trust me," Isobel said, her voice edged with impatience, "that it has to be you."

Nathy shrugged. "What do I get from this?"

"Roselyn Ruark."

He leaned forward with such sudden ferocity, Isobel flinched, her hand going to her belt where a small dagger dangled in a scabbard.

"Roselyn Ruark?" Nathy ground out.

Isobel relaxed, her hand leaving the dagger. "As far as compensation, you can name your price."

"Go back to Ruark."

Isobel waved her hand lazily. "It's the same as it was when you left. He's still a Huntsman. And Commander Lately still has him assigned to capture the Monarch, if she ever shows. As far as enemies go, he's our biggest threat at the moment. So, your job is twofold: assassinate Ruark, and bring the Monarch back."

Nathy shook his head, the weight of the revelation hard in his gut. "You're paying me in revenge?"

She surprised him by laughing, a sound like wind chimes in a storm. "Revenge is for boys, sweetie. A silly game. Even so, when it comes to killing Ruark, I have to imagine you'll do it with more...well, *fervor* than other assassins."

Fervor didn't cut it.

He would enjoy this.

"Why now?" he asked.

"I don't know what you mean."

"You do," he said. "Four years ago, I was given a similar assignment. Until Artemis went in my place." He met her frozen gaze. "Flynn tell you about that?"

Isobel finished off her whiskey with a few delicate sips. She cleared her throat. "He did. I suppose he learned his lesson."

"Hard lesson." Nathy sighed. "Fine. You've got a deal."

Isobel nodded, crisp and businesslike. "Perfect."

"I gotta ask." Nathy levelled his gaze on her, braced himself. "You ever hear from my old man? Does he still hunt for the Elderon?"

She pressed her lips together, considering him, and shrugged. "I suppose it won't hurt to tell you. Mortimer has been underground since the war. He's...well, I guess you'd say he's got himself some peculiar habits. And friends. But he was always good at what he did. The Commander calls on him from time to time, clean up a few renegades here and there."

"What made him go underground?"

"It's possible to be too good at this job, Nathaniel. You ought to remember that."

Nathy looked off toward the pub's patrons, these men huddled close, cheeks going red with drink and laughter. The simplicity of their merry afternoon...did Mortimer ever join friends around a table, laugh and clink his glass to another's?

"You're much easier to get along with than he is," Isobel said now. "I suppose you have more of your mother in you."

"What happened to you?" Nathy asked. "After they took you away."

She tapped the rim of her glass with one perfect fingernail. "I think you can guess."

He tried not to stare at her ruined white eye, the mask hiding gods' knew what. She was just a girl when it happened. She had been so large in his memory, this powerful goddess ripping him from the flames, that he'd never considered she was barely older than he'd been.

"But you stayed," Nathy said. "You didn't leave the Huntsmen."

Her blue eye darted away; the milky eye hung sightless, watching nothing. "I didn't have anything to go back to. But now," she said, her voice strengthening, "I do have something. However you feel about Flynn...just know you're doing the right thing."

"Don't care. Just get me to Ruark. I'll bill you later."

"I think we'll get along, Nathaniel." She finished her whisky and rose, grabbing up her hat and dropping it onto her blond hair. "Come along. It's a day's journey by fulcan."

Nathy followed her out into the town square. Isobel motioned for him to halt, then issued a sharp whistle between her fingers. A great black bird launched from the roof of the pub and landed beside them, displacing snow in great gusts and crushing the stake underfoot. The few townspeople wandering outside yelped and backed away from the creature.

The beast's wide yellow eye burned like a second sun, eyeing Nathy with distrust. The bird was monstrous in size, the length of a modest home. A great black crown of feathers lined its eyes. Isobel petted the creature's beak, and it nipped at her affectionately.

"I am *not* getting on that thing, if that's the idea," Nathy said.

"Yes, you are. This is the fastest way to Theopolis."

"Not if I fall off and die."

"Nathaniel, are you afraid of heights?" She climbed easily onto the fulcan's back and offered a hand to him. "Just hold on tight."

He eyed the great black bird warily, but took her hand, and she yanked him up. Isobel settled onto the creature's broad neck, then patted the spot behind her. Nathy cautiously sank down, the beast's feathers warm through his clothes, vaguely comforting.

"So does it just—"

Isobel cut him off with a whistle, and with it the beast rose, beating its huge wings, and carried them into the cold white sky.

3

DR. POOLE

"HOW WAS IT?"

Jonas stopped forking hay into a feeder to leer at Lacey as she passed the barn. She shoved her hands deeper into her coat pockets and looked beyond him, to the two skinny cows wilting against their enclosures.

"Am I milking today?"

He spat, the bullet of saliva cratering the snow. "Later. Your mum needs ya."

Grateful to get away, Lacey turned toward the ramshackle farmhouse. The upper story seemed to sag into the lower, the whole thing warped and bent from wind and time. The top step of the porch was long gone, eviscerated by wood rot.

Looking too long at it carved the pit in Lacey's stomach deeper. It wasn't the hunger and poverty, the ugliness of their little lives played out on this grim stage. It was the knowledge that she had already reached the end of her story, that her life could not play out any differently than it had for the women who had walked these frozen grounds before.

She remembered the blood on the cobblestones, the absent gaze of dead eyes.

Maybe the slain man was lucky. He was dead, yes, but to get to that point, perhaps he'd had some great adventure.

Lacey had reached the door without consciously moving toward it. She'd dodged the rotted step, knowing exactly when to move. That was perhaps the most depressing part of it all: the automation of her consciousness.

"Mum?" Lacey called. She hung her coat in the hall and stepped into their cramped kitchen.

"Lacey, thank the gods." Aeyrin set aside a mixing bowl filled with pulpy, off-color dough and drew her daughter into

36

a hug. "I can't believe Jonas sent you to witness. Are you okay? Was it horrible? You look...fine." She frowned.

"It's okay, Mum. It wasn't...well, maybe it *was* the worst thing I've ever seen, but it didn't bother me so much." She shrugged.

Her mother's eyes were rimmed with shadows, her skin pale in the dim kitchen. Yet Aeyrin still somehow looked beautiful, her hair richly dark and her eyes a strange, yellowed umber. Lacey had taken on her father's coloring, pale as milk and ginger to boot.

"Well, I'm glad you're home. Someone's—well. Something has—um. You see..."

"Mum. What is it?"

"Nothing bad! Good news, actually." Footsteps thudded up the porch, capturing Aeyrin's attention. "That might be him now."

A tall, lean figure rushed into the kitchen, preceding the slamming of the front door. "I couldn't find her, Aeyrin, but I—oh. She's right here."

Lacey blinked. "Dr. Poole?"

A man on the younger side of middle age, Dr. Poole remained persistently handsome, his laughing hazel eyes curtained by unkept salt-and-pepper hair. His nose bent at the bridge, lending his gaze a hawklike quality.

"Surprise!" A grin dimpled his cheek.

Lacey, rising from her shock, hugged him around the waist. "What are you doing here? I can't believe you're visiting. Gods, why would you want to be here in the winter?"

Her godfather only ever came in the summer, when he took her on a weeklong trip to Theopolis. Those days were what little a farmgirl in the Northern Reaches had to look forward to. In all Lacey's memory, they hadn't strayed from tradition.

"That's the surprise." He held her by the shoulders and smiled down at her. "You look more like Will every day."

Lacey narrowed her eyes. "Most ladies don't want to hear they look like their fathers, Dr. Poole."

He waved her off. "It's just the hair. You've got all your mother's looks, too."

Aeyrin's face darkened with a blush. "You're not in the capital, Absolom. No need to charm the entire room."

Dr. Poole gave her a smile and a shrug, then turned back to Lacey. "Okay, Red, pack your bags."

"For what?" Lacey said.

"We're going to Theopolis."

"Now? You're about six months early, you know."

"I figured you could use an extra holiday. And the offer still stands," Dr. Poole said, looking at Aeyrin with something much more than politeness in his expression. "You could join us."

Aeyrin looked away and focused too intently on the ugly bread dough in the mixing bowl. "I can't, though. Somebody's got to keep the house running."

"Jonas could stop being useless and make his own dinner," Lacey suggested.

Aeyrin shook her head. "I'm perfectly fine if you two have fun without me. Now, you really should pack."

Dr. Poole checked his watch. "Train leaves at nine."

"Oh." Lacey looked at the cuckoo clock hanging above the stove. She used to entertain herself on long winter nights by waiting for the cuckoo and trying to hit it with pelted kernels of corn. It now read 7:18.

A weight of finality settled on Lacey's shoulders. A strange knowing that this little home would soon grow distant, maybe disappear. It should have made her happy. Instead, her stomach twisted into knots as though she were back at the execution grounds.

"Is there any breakfast?" she asked.

"Of course." Aeyrin hitched up a smile and set a tray of small dry loaves on the scarred table. "I think there's still butter somewhere..."

Dr. Poole poked at one of the loaves cautiously. "I'm not saying you're a bad cook, love, but do you always make food that's so..." He picked up one loaf and dropped it. It clattered like metal against the tray.

"You try baking bread with the rations they give us," Aeyrin shot back.

"I wouldn't attempt baking even under the best of circumstances."

"Then shut it."

Lacey gamely bit into one of the rolls, crunching down to the softer guts. "S not so bad."

Dr. Poole sat at the table, holding up the loaf for further inspection. It was strange to see him here, no matter how many times he'd come before. His finely tailored suit and expensive wool coat stood in sharp relief to the grubby, old-fashioned kitchen. People from Theopolis seemed centuries ahead of the villagers Lacey had grown up with. In every way that mattered, they were.

Aeyrin swept past the table and flicked the back of Dr. Poole's head. "Eat it or put it back."

He winced as his teeth sunk into the hard loaf. "Good," he mumbled around a mouthful.

"It's a week old, at least," she said, sitting beside Lacey.

"So still fresh," Lacey finished off her loaf. She looked between her godfather and mother. Dr. Poole shot brief, guilty looks to Aeyrin, and Aeyrin pretended not to notice with the air of much practice doing just that.

Finally, his bread gone, Dr. Poole said, "Love, I stand corrected. That was delicious."

Aeyrin kicked him under the table, and they shared a swift, sweet smile. He reached for her like he meant to take her hand, but Aeyrin pulled away, rubbing her eyes.

"D'you want a coffee?" she said.

"I'll get it," Dr. Poole said, rising. "You two need some time together anyway." Before he left the table, he put a hand on Aeyrin's shoulder and squeezed. Lacey hid her own smile as her godfather went to the stove and started boiling water in the kettle.

"He's looking good, isn't he?" Lacey whispered. "Very...debonair."

Aeyrin gave her a look and took a bite of bread. "What about you? Sol tells me you and Saxon have gotten close."

"Hardly." Lacey scowled at her godfather's back. "We just happen to see each other when I visit. He's a prat, though. Honestly."

"A handsome prat?"

Lacey smiled. "Possibly." But her smile dipped the more she thought of him. Saxon *was* handsome—funny, charming, all that rot. But he was also rich, and a warlock. His family was Allied to the Elderon, and he was, therefore, far beyond her reach.

Dr. Poole returned, balancing three cups of coffee. Lacey dragged hers close, curling her cold hands around the hot ceramic. "So, why the sudden trip?"

It was Aeyrin who answered. "You deserve to see more of the world, Lace. You're not a child anymore. I hate that you're cooped up here."

"But so are you."

Aeyrin looked carefully into her mug. "I've had my adventures."

Lacey narrowed her eyes. "How long will I be gone?"

"Why not play it by ear?" Aeyrin waved her hand dismissively, but her eyes shone, and she blinked hard. "Jonas and I can handle things here. This'll be a long winter, I expect."

Lacey turned to her godfather. "What's really going on?"

He took a long swallow of coffee, wincing. "Your mother's right. You ought to see what else the world has to offer."

"Not a lot," Lacey said. "Least for someone like me."

"I wouldn't worry too much about it, Red," Dr. Poole said, and they fell into a strange, thick silence.

A while later, their coffee cups drained, Dr. Poole sighed. "Well, Lacey, it's a bit of a walk to the station."

Aeyrin looked suddenly ill.

"Okay," Lacey said. "Be right down."

She hurried upstairs. She had so few belongings to begin with that all her tattered clothes and moldy books would fit easily into her rucksack with room to spare. She opened her door to find the mess of candles and blanket still lumped together on the floor. She tossed the blanket aside, scooped the candles into her arms, and dumped them into a drawer along with her too-small clothes from years gone by. The Aññanym was smeared, chalk dusting across the floor in wide streaks. She quickly rubbed it away with her blanket.

It was a shame to see it go, but she knew it wouldn't have worked, either. Her even trying was the shame. Why disappoint herself? She knew she'd never manage to talk to her father again.

She donned her warmest trousers and a wool tunic for travel. The weather stirred chillingly, promising a dark, cold day. Already her window was clutched by fingers of ice, and gaps in the clouds carved a blackened smirk on the gray sky.

She started back downstairs but stopped halfway, stilled by her mother's harsh whisper. She inched down the stairs until she had a view of her mother and godfather standing by the sink, too absorbed in each other to notice her. Dr. Poole said something that made Aeyrin's cheeks color; when she spoke again, her voice had risen a notch.

"As if I, of all people, don't know it's his fault this happened."

"Aeyrin." Dr. Poole reached a hand out toward Aeyrin's face but stopped short; Aeyrin stepped back and looked down. Dr. Poole's hand fell.

"I don't care about Will. I just want you to promise me she'll be safe."

Dr. Poole's answer came a beat too late. "Of course. I'd never let anything happen."

"Fine," Aeyrin said. She turned to the stove and grabbed the pot, set it in the sink. "Just keep your friends on a leash."

"I promise you, they're not my friends," Dr. Poole said. He watched her scrub away encrusted stains.

Why were they talking about her father? What was his fault? Despite her curiosity, Lacey began to feel intrusive, watching someone watch someone. She walked down the stairs.

"Who aren't your friends?" Lacey said.

Dr. Poole looked up abruptly and half-smiled. "Nobody. I have no friends. You know that, Red." He chucked her under the chin and she tried to slap his hand away.

"We'd best be off," he said.

Aeyrin abandoned the pot and pulled Lacey into a long, tight hug.

"Take care of yourself, Lace."

"Don't worry, Mum, I always do," Lacey promised.

"I mean it, Lacey. *Be safe.* Nothing mental, all right?"

"Mum, honestly, I'll probably just go to the museum every day."

Aeyrin made a face. "You'd be surprised how life sneaks up on you."

Dr. Poole made a sound somewhere between amusement and pain; Aeyrin shot him a look.

"What?" he said.

"You know what," Aeyrin said.

Lacey looked at Dr. Poole; he shrugged.

"All right," Aeyrin said. Her eyes glittered, tears clinging to her lashes. "I'll let you go."

"Okay, Mum." Lacey hugged her mother again. "Love you. And I'll be back soon. I'll miss you too much to stay away long."

Aeyrin's arms tightened for a moment before releasing her. "Love you too, Lace."

Dr. Poole and Aeyrin looked at each other. "Er, bye, then," Dr. Poole said.

"Yeah. Bye." Aeyrin looked down. "You don't do anything mental either, all right?"

Dr. Poole's smile flashed, and he kissed her cheek. Before Aeyrin could respond, he walked out the door, waving as she blushed beneath a half-hearted glare.

4

THE POTION MASTER

-Hayven Hospital, Theopolis-

THE HOSPITAL CORRIDORS wound a dozen ways from the main lobby, but Saxon was only too familiar with the sprawling wing. He'd possibly spent more time here as a child than back home, happiest in his father's laboratory. Steaming potions and frothing beakers made sense, whereas his family, he was sure, did not.

He stepped into the research wing and bypassed the nurses' station, though not unnoticed. A petite woman not much older than Saxon stormed out from behind the desk. Her long nurse's gown fluttered around her legs as she hurried after him.

"Mr. St. Luke, where are you going?"

"I need to see my father."

The nurse caught up and stepped in the way of Saxon's stride, trying to draw him short. She walked backwards and held out her hands.

"Please, Mr. St. Luke, he's extremely busy," she said.

Saxon stepped around her. "Too busy for me? I'm wounded."

She matched his pace, despite his long gait. The comforting wood-paneled walls of the corridor whipped across his sight like a film reel, doors hiding much less homey sickrooms flashing in blurs.

"Saxon," she said. "You can't just bloody barge in on—"

"Celia, love," Saxon said, not trying to hide his laugh. "My name is on the bloody wing. I can go anywhere I want."

"Your *father's* name," she said. "The only thing your name is on are citations for public intoxication."

"Again," Saxon said, hand over his heart. "Wounded."

Celia gave him a withering look and started back the way they had come. "I'm calling the dean," she called over her shoulder.

"Tell him hi, from me." Saxon turned back to his mission. Every door was numbered and held behind it either an empty bed or a patient with some rare ailment the research scientists and potion masters found worth their time. Sebastian St. Luke maintained the research wing at Hayven—one of the illustrious duties of the Elderon's own potion master. He had an imposing office and a sprawling laboratory just beyond the many sickrooms, where he would no doubt be this morning. Saxon pushed through the oak double doors at the end of the corridor.

The laboratory was filled with doctors, nurses, and research students—Saxon's own classmates. The mix of Elonni and Allied mages might once have seemed representative, hopeful for Saxon's own kind. But he knew by now the Elderon were only interested in the Alliance for what it brought them—in this case, potions far advanced beyond Elonni medicine.

Saxon spied his father's clean-cut steel hair and broad frame across the room.

"Already on task?" Saxon said. He leaned against the lab table where his father was bent over a collection of beakers and a flask broiling with some dark green substance. Sebastian peered into a microscope and barely flinched at his son's presence.

"This isn't a good time, son," Sebastian said. He removed one slide from beneath his microscope and replaced it with another.

"Is it ever?" Saxon picked up a test tube of the green potion and peered at it. His father gingerly plucked it away with a gloved hand and set it back amongst its counterparts. "Question."

"Fire away," Sebastian said. He bent to prepare a new slide, carefully applying a dropper of potion on the narrow glass pane.

"Why is Lacey coming back already?"

Sebastian spared a short glance away from his microscope. "I thought you'd be pleased."

"Ecstatic. But you didn't answer my question."

"I imagine Absolom merely wishes to see his goddaughter again."

"So this isn't for her?" He tapped the flask.

Sebastian cinched his eyes, but didn't look up. "She isn't due for another six months."

"Then why brew a binding potion? Especially one this strong?"

Sebastian's lips formed what could generously be called a smile, but looked rather more like a twitch. "My God, have you actually been studying?"

Saxon cocked his head, waited.

"As I said, it's far too soon for Lacey's dose." Sebastian carefully lifted one of the tubes from its stand and held it up; the steamy light from the room's many lamps caught in the green liquid. "This particular batch is for Haylock. There are some powerful nocturne prisoners there who the guards can't control with iyrel chains alone. You're right that this is a more powerful dose. It won't simply lock their powers away temporarily; it'll cripple them for life."

Saxon took a careful step away from the brew.

"Yes, you might want to wear gloves if you plan to continue touching things."

Saxon nodded to the flask. "You're going to give that to the Elderon?"

"You object?"

"Dad—*we're* mages. What if Commander Lately decides he's got no choice but to use that on you?"

Sebastian returned to his microscope, focusing in on his slides. "I'll just have to make sure they never find cause to."

Saxon's jaw locked, his eyes on the potion. "But you don't mind if it's used on others."

Sebastian's eyes didn't stray from the microscope, but neither did they comprehend what they saw. "If you're so interested in moral quandaries, I might suggest you change your field of study to philosophy. Now if you don't mind, I'm rather busy."

Saxon clapped his father on the back. "Thanks, Dad. Always a pleasure." He pushed off from the table and didn't bother to glance back.

LACEY AND DR. POOLE arrived in the evening, just as the sun sunk toward the horizon, a bright yellow smear against pink sky. It was warmer in Theopolis than in the Northern Reaches, but still a layer of wet, crunchy snow covered the pavement and street outside the train station. A mix of autos, horse-drawn carriages, and pony traps clopped and rattled past, sending a salty, wet spray into the air. Pedestrians moved in packs: Women in sleek dresses and bulky fur coats, cloche hats capping smooth hair. Men in suits and fedoras, their coats unbuttoned despite the chill night.

A clunky black auto waited for them around the corner. Dr. Poole's driver stood by the door, bundled in a greatcoat and scarf. He stepped forward and collected Lacey's rucksack with care, as though it were a fine trunk rather than a ratty old bag.

"Here you are, Miss Falk." He opened the door to the backseat and offered a hand to help her in.

"Thanks, Piers. How's the family?"

"Lovely, miss, thank you. Professor." Piers nodded to Dr. Poole as he got in after Lacey.

Piers set Lacey's bag in the trunk and climbed behind the wheel, and they were off, headed towards the giant brick and marble buildings that peered out over the city.

As they wound through the cobbled streets of Theopolis, slowed by the mostly horse-drawn traffic, lamplighters darted by on the streets and set fire to the oil in the lamps that hung at intervals and cast a warm orange glow on the darkening street. Yet as they wound deeper into the rich heart of the city, the gas lamps gave way to a strange new magic, lampposts that glowed without fire, that flickered on at the command of a switch. Electricity hadn't yet reached the north, but in the last few years, Theopolis had begun glowing with it.

Lacey stared out the window, marveling at the city in wintertime. She'd only ever come in the summer, and despite the slush on the roads and the steaming breath of pedestrians, there was a joviality in the air, a sense of excitement and pleasure at the mere fact of being here, in the biggest city in all of Gryfel. More electric lights appeared in windows, dangling in strands like starlight, or wound around streetlights. The darkest days of the year were upon them, and even so, the people of Theopolis were surrounded by light.

But perhaps beauty belied something cruel.

"Are those..." Lacey pressed her face to the window to get a better look as they drove along Palace Circus, the sprawling Aetheli Palace and its signature white thorn tree on their left. Aside from the traffic, the circus bustled with workers tromping about: Most of them stood at least twenty feet tall and had skin the color of old gold. "They're giants," Lacey said.

"Good catch," Poole said dryly.

"I *mean*, what are they doing here?" Giants came from the country of Gyre, beyond the Crossing and the Godsfang Mountains. A small settlement existed in Gryfel, in the southern city of Geshun, but they never ventured north. As far as Lacey knew, they preferred to avoid the Elonni.

Poole bit the inside of his cheek. "The Elderon have...they've reworded their peace accords with the giants, I suppose you'd say. You'll be seeing them a lot more now."

The giants were dressed in thick furs and boots, their golden-brown faces peeking out through scarves and wool hats. The only Elonni in the square didn't seem to be working so much as commanding. One held a cat-o-nine-tails and swung it in an arc, bored. Many of the giants' clothes bore tears to match the weapon's prongs, and bloody gashes decked their flesh.

Lacey scowled. "This is part of a *peace accord*?"

"The ambassador to Geshun had convinced the Elderon the giants were planning an uprising against the realm."

"Is that true?"

"Depends on who you ask."

"I'm asking you."

"Then no, Red. It's not. The Elderon want power. They're good at getting it."

Lacey sat back in her seat. "That's disgusting."

"Couldn't have said it better myself."

"I thought the Elderon only went after nocturnes." Giants were mortal, like humans. They had no magic, no way of defending themselves against an Elonni's celestial abilities.

"They'll control whoever they can," Dr. Poole said, frowning.

The city, for all its beauty and innovation, left Lacey feeling vaguely ill. While she was here, she lived as someone of Dr. Poole's station would. She had beautiful clothes and multiple meals a day. She could bathe at her leisure or read without stopping. Yet there were so many here—without the benefit of Elonni blood to protect them—who suffered in the streets, impoverished, dying. Pretending she belonged in Theopolis, even for a moment, felt wrong.

They left the heart of the city, the great buildings falling behind, giving rise to neat lines of row houses down narrow, cobbled streets. Dr. Poole's home matched all the others, save for the worn brass number 960 on the front door.

Piers stopped the auto outside the door. Lacey didn't wait for him to open her door, but sprang out onto the street and ran toward the steps.

"Not that I'm not happy to be here," Lacey said as Dr. Poole joined her on the steps, fishing for his keys, "but you know I can't stay long."

"See how you feel after a while." He smiled, but didn't meet her eyes.

"I can't just leave my mom in that village. Besides..." She gazed down the neat, pretty street, its order unfamiliar despite the many times she'd been here before. "What kind of future do I have here?"

"You're Elonni."

"And human," she reminded him. "Mutts don't make it here."

Dr. Poole unlocked the door without comment. Piers tapped Lacey's shoulder and handed her the rucksack.

"Have a good stay, Miss Falk. See you tomorrow."

"Night, Piers."

She watched the driver go, climbing aboard his own little pony trap and riding off toward home. Piers was human. He seemed all right. Maybe she could drive people around the city. As long as she never let her wings out.

She followed Dr. Poole into the small, tidy foyer. He hung up their coats while Lacey wandered into the sitting room, its warm interior crowded with plushy blue furniture and lined with bookshelves. She dropped her bag on the floor and ran toward the tea table, where a crisp new book, bound in black leather, sat.

"Did you publish another book?"

"Oh. Yeah." Dr. Poole made for a cocktail cart parked between two bookshelves. "It was sort of rushed, but I'm at that stage in academia where I'm expected to have a brilliant new insight every year, and a book to go with it."

"*The Natural History of Magic.* What's that, then?"

He took a healthy swig of his drink. "Magic as a natural force, harnessed by magic users through their innate genetic makeup. No gods or blessings needed."

"Controversial, isn't it?" Lacey picked up the book and flipped through for first few pages, stopping at a dedication, small and solitary on the parchment.

Lacey grinned and turned to her godfather. "'For Aeyrin, as always'? Aw."

"Er, that's just—" Dr. Poole cleared his throat. "She—she doesn't need to know about that, all right? They *make* you do a dedication, I had to think of someone, and—"

"Sure, Dr. Poole, sure." She shut the book. "Can I read it?"

"Of course. Just, again—"

"Don't worry, I won't tell my mother you love her."

"You're impossible."

"I try." She tucked the book under her arm. "Well, I'll get to bed, then. Don't drink too much."

He glared over his cocktail. "Goodnight, Red."

She stopped in the corridor outside her bedroom and looked at the book in her hands. Dr. Poole was a naturalist, she supposed. He believed, as few did, that supernatural forces had an explanation outside of tradition, gods, and chapel sermons. And Lacey was inclined to believe he was right. She'd seen little of order and a lot of chaos.

But still...she had always hoped...

She tried to conjure something of her father to memory, but her mind was a faded tapestry. Her memories of him were really stories, things she couldn't have witnessed or would have been too young to remember.

Yet he felt so important. And she only wanted to talk.

Dr. Poole would say it was impossible. He ranked necromancy the lowest of magics. He'd have laughed at her stupid ritual that morning.

Maybe there wasn't room for hope. So why wouldn't it just go away?

5

AT WIT'S END

-The Eastern-

THE FULCAN LANDED on the roof of an old, spiky cathedral, shaking out its silken feathers from a long flight.

"We made good time," Isobel said, sliding from the beast's neck and dropping onto the roof. "Nathaniel?"

"I'm cold," he said bitterly. His thin trousers and shirt had done little to fight the icy gales of the high atmosphere, and his coat—a flimsy gray trench coat he'd taken off his last mark—was dotted with holes, each felt distinctly as the wind had pierced his skin.

"Stop whining." Isobel smiled. "You've got a job to do."

He scrambled off the great bird and joined her at the edge of the cathedral's roof, looking down over a grimy, neglected street. The people below wore tattered clothes, useless against even the milder winter temperature of the capital. They navigated around trash and waste, moving in huddled masses with everywhere and nowhere to go.

"So. Where's Ruark?"

Isobel shook her head. "We'll wait for the festival. He opens his freak show then."

"Killing him publicly seems...stupid. Sorry."

"He's impossible to nail down otherwise. Nobody knows where he goes." Her mouth slanted. "Even I can't track him."

"And the girl?"

"Her godfather left to collect her early this morning. It's possible they're in the city. More likely, he took her someplace far away."

"He knows?"

"Yes. And he's determined to keep her away from Elderon. And us." She looked up at him. "Work on finding the girl. You can have your shot at Ruark tomorrow."

He nodded. "I need a name."

She looked back at the street, her eyes on the glittering heart of Theopolis beyond. "Lacey Falk-Barker."

THE STREETS IN the Eastern were noticeably worse than those of Theopolis. The clumsily paved flagstone road turned to dirt, and chunks of broken brick littered the way. The air stank of rotted meat and smoking roasts from the market square, and the factory hovering over the line of shops and flats emitted a sulfurous stench. Nathy followed familiar roads to a place that had once been a home and hideaway both.

Madame San Clair's shop was nondescript, black brick and barred windows. The sign out front simply read, *Fortunes told here*. A bell jangled when he opened the door, and a familiar russet-skinned, black-haired man turned toward him.

"Nathy?"

"Sin." Nathy grinned. "Miss me?"

"No."

Nathy leaned on the long counter spanning the shop and tugged on a lock of Sinclair's hair. "Are you still mad about last summer?"

Sinclair slapped his hand away. "You left me. For a *mermaid*."

"Yeah, so I didn't think that one through all the way."

"You're a terrible person."

"I'll give you that one." He glanced around the shop. "Your mom around?"

"Downstairs."

"May I...?"

Sinclair rolled his eyes and stepped aside. Nathy vaulted over the counter and kissed him on the cheek.

"I really am sorry, y'know."

Sinclair blushed a deep red. "Fine."

It was probably all the forgiveness Nathy would get, or ever deserve. He took the door behind the counter, which led down to the basement of the shop. Sinclair caught the door before it shut and followed him down, grumbling. The place reminded Nathy of the old shop back in Denmoor, the one

Ruark burned away. A charge of vengeance spiked his blood. He would get Ruark for everything he'd done.

Madame San Clair sat in the flickering spill of light coming from a semicircle of candles lining the round table she used for readings. She had several tarot cards laid out before her, and she considered them, frowning. Nathy had never given back the Hanged Man; it sat in his pocket even now, a reminder—anyone could stab you in the back.

Madame San Clair looked up with a start. "Is that my *jana-kal?*"

"The one and only." Nathy dropped into the chair beside Madame and smiled. "Wondering if you could do something for me."

"What happened to a polite 'hello'?"

"Hi," Nathy said. "But I am in a hurry, so..."

Madame frowned. "What do you need?"

"A girl."

Sinclair snorted. "Figures."

Madame smiled faintly. "And?"

"Flynn wants her, actually. The one they're calling the Monarch."

"Hm." Madame looked at him solemnly. "I thought you'd parted ways with Flynn."

"I have. But times are tough. Sometimes working for a cult pays best. I have a name, if it helps."

"I don't need a name," Madame sniffed, as though offended. She held out her hand, and Nathy gave her his palm. She traced the lines there with her forefinger, following each one with a crease deepening in her brow.

"Anything?" Nathy said after a while.

Madame released his hand. She reached for the tarot cards, had him draw. He handed his choice back without looking. Her eyes roved across the image, growing sorrowful with the study.

"You will find her. And yet..."

Nathy waited.

"I think you ought to be wary of this girl, my *jana-kal.* She is something strange indeed."

She handed the card back to him, faceup. The drawing showed a woman in a flowing blue robe situated between two pillars; a turban and headpiece tilted on her red-gold hair. Shards of moonlight from her green eyes like tears.

"The High Priestess," Madame said, "reversed."

Sinclair leaned in for a look. "Uh-oh."

"I'm not following," Nathy said.

"I think it's best," Madame said, "that you put this girl from your mind."

Nathy gave her a tired smile. "Where do I find her?"

"She's coming to you." Madame sighed. "You won't have long to wait."

He quirked a brow. "Just like that?"

"This story has been told before," Madame said. "It's woven through time. You must see it to its end."

The bell on the shop door jangled above. Sinclair and Madame turned toward it.

"A customer," Madame said. "See what he wants, Sinclair."

Sinclair nodded and ascended the stairs. Madame began shuffling her tarot cards back in a pile; her fingers were thick and warped with arthritis, and she scraped uselessly at the table as she tried to gather every card. While she was distracted, Nathy slipped the High Priestess in his back pocket.

"Here," Nathy said. He took over gathering the cards and packed them into an even stack. "So. You two all right?"

Madame took his hand and kissed his fingers; her lips were papery and cold. "Of course. But what of you? Your aura is shadowed. Sad."

"Huh."

"Why not stay?" She patted his knuckles. "You've lost too many homes. But this one is always here for you, my *jana-kal*."

"I got some things to take care of." Nathy smiled. "Thanks, Madame."

"Of course." She looked up and smiled faintly. "Remember: Be wary."

"When am I not?"

THE NOCTURNES OF the Eastern weren't accustomed to autos on their streets. They barely had pony traps clopping by, and the public carriages were scarce.

The town was a wart on the smooth face of Theopolis, former Elonni land hard-won by a group of mages centuries past in a forgotten war. Once a sanctuary, the nocturne oasis had decayed into a slum and industrial hub, grimy and salt-stained by the coast, cast in the shadow of Haylock rising higher than the smokestacks of the factories.

So, Saxon's auto stood out plainly as he was driven deeper into the slums. He slid out of the back seat and pulled his collar up. He was obviously from the city; even his worst clothes were just so damn *nice*. Here among his own kind, the stench of betrayal clouded him. They knew; it was in their eyes, these poor mages and fey shuffling to the mineral factory by the coast: they would see his clean suit and wool jacket and know he had paid for it all in their blood and sweat. Wasn't that what the Alliance was really about? Keeping a few nocturnes happy to keep the Elonni in power.

He turned to his driver.

"Come back in two hours."

The driver nodded.

Saxon lit a cigarette and stalked down the pavement, face averted, but what good did it do? The St. Lukes were damningly recognizable, the face of magical medicine that could curse just as often as it cured. There hadn't been such a boom in industry since an Elonni physician had discovered that silver was just as good for killing werewolves as it was for fashioning dinnerware.

Some nocturnes scuttled away from Saxon. Others shouldered him with black looks. He kept his eyes averted and plunged on down the street. The Eastern was livelier at night, and crowds weren't ideal for him and what he had come here to do. But it would be harder to avoid the Watchmen's scrutiny in daylight, when much of the Eastern slept, and they were who he needed to worry about.

He was an idiot, a jackass, and he knew it. Admitting it felt good, every time, and provided the justification he needed. *I'm being stupid, but I know I'm being stupid. Admire my self-awareness.*

One last time—he'd stopped saying that years ago. He knew he was fucked by now.

WIT'S END COULD only be entered through a storm drain, via a portal the Watchmen had yet to discover and seal. Saxon finished off his second cigarette and slipped through the murky opening, barely large enough for his frame, and dropped through the air. But he didn't hit the swampy waste and concrete rushing up to meet him. He lurched suddenly to the left and landed on a street on the far side of town, close to the forest, right outside a nondescript door. He pushed his hair out of his eyes and glanced up. The door bore no establishment name, only a little paper sign affixed with a nail: *At your wit's end? Come on in.* Saxon got to his feet just as the door swung open. A pretty, plump girl with tapered ears and dark blue eyes glared at him from the threshold.

"Oh. It's just you," she said.

He grinned. "Hi, Gwen."

"Get in if you're coming in," she said, and he hustled inside, head down. She slammed the door behind him.

"He's at the corner table," she said, and glared at him. "And keep it down this time, all right? Patrons is money, and he scares my money away, y'know."

Saxon opened his wallet and offered her a handful of paper junes. She gave him the sort of once over that wasn't meant to be flattering.

"Piss off, Ally."

Saxon watched her go. She returned to her place behind the bar and leaned forward, smiling at a shaggy-haired man who had just slumped onto a stool. Saxon, too, found himself fixated on the man and his dark mass of black hair. Something about him shuffled Saxon's memories, flung him backward in time. That couldn't be—?

"Yo, Sax!"

Saxon winced.

"Neill," Saxon said, turning. The man smiling across the room at him was wire-thin and pale, with cropped white hair and blank, glassy irises like patches of moonlight. His delicate wings were tucked into an overlarge coat, and they poked from the hem, iridescent. Saxon crossed the room and sat across from him.

"Back again," the fairy said. "Figured your daddy could afford you some help. Ain't he a doctor or some shit?"

Saxon lit a cigarette. "Everyone needs a fault. I wasn't born with any, so here I am: Ruining my life for the sake of ruin."

Neill stared. "What's that, some philosophy shit?" The fairy sniffed loudly. "You got money?"

As if he needed to ask. Saxon doled out the usual fee—two hundred junes—and dropped it on the table.

The fairy's white eyes flickered from the cash to Saxon's face. "You kiddin' me? Supply and demand, brother. I'm the last dealer left in this shithole. I gotta up my game. It's hard, ain't it, gettin' in and out of the capital. Trips to Farynar ain't free, brother. And now I got the Watchmen five miles up my ass. And Fi? She's *ten* miles up my ass. I've raised prices accordingly."

Saxon smiled in a bored way. "How much do you want?"

"Five hundred."

"You're kidding me."

Neill leaned forward, his smile pearlescent. "*You* are a drug addict, brother. *I* am a drug dealer. Logic says you ain't gettin' any better, which means I'm just gettin' richer. If you think you can live without it, then fuck off. Otherwise, it's five hundred now. That's what they call a monopoly, ain't it?"

"You're an economist now. Your mum must be proud." Saxon detached a larger chunk of junes from his wallet and dropped it in the fairy's waiting hand.

"I adore you," Neill said. "Really. You're my favorite kind, brother, the rich and the reckless."

"Give it to me," Saxon said.

"Relax." Neill tossed a sealed parchment envelope across the table. Saxon snatched it too eagerly; the fairy grinned. "Here, I'll throw in a free pipe. Real glass, that is. Enjoy responsibly."

Saxon rose from the table without saying more. He wanted to get out of that hole, and the walk back would be long. His skin felt like it might jump from his bones—for days he'd gone without. He'd tried, because...

He shook his head. He'd just never tell her.

As he passed the bar, he looked up, and a pair of dark eyes flashed away from his. Saxon stared at the back of the man's head. Was that—couldn't be. He was almost sure Nathy Ferrickek wasn't stupid enough to return to Theopolis. He walked on.

Outside, he filled the pipe and lit the bane; his lungs burned and his skin stopped itching.

This would be his secret. Everybody needed one.

THE BAR WAS dim, flickering and loud, and the effect hit Nathy like a punch. Until Ruark's festival, all he could do was wait, too close to Theopolis for safety, but well-hidden in this secret dive. But being amongst the noisy and the ossified was the last thing he wanted at the moment. He was tired and sober and neither factor improved his mood.

"Drink?" the pretty bartender said, appearing behind the counter.

"Probably a good idea." He fished a couple junes out of his pocket. He needed to get paid soon. He'd cut the line a little close these past months.

He scanned the room, and his eyes landed on someone entirely out of place: amidst the low, grumbling nocturnes in ragged clothes there stood a tall man in a wool coat and three-piece suit. Prick. He was young and obviously handsome, though a shock of wavy chocolate hair obscured his profile just now. But Nathy would recognize his old friend anywhere.

Saxon walked to a corner table and sat across from a white-haired young man, fairy, by the looks of him, his wings just visible under his coat. Saxon's practiced air of *I-could-give-a-damn* suddenly evaporated, and he straightened up. "You're kidding me," he said over the din of the patrons. The fairy shrugged and apparently told Saxon to fuck off. Saxon sighed and fished from his wallet a very thick stack of junes. He counted out a large chunk of it and slapped it into the fairy's upturned hand.

So. Saxon had turned to bane. Figured.

Saxon left the table and looked up; Nathy turned away—maybe not in time, but if Saxon had recognized him, he didn't let on.

It figured—he returned to Theopolis, only to end up ten feet from the person he least needed to see.

"This place is an absolute dive."

He looked up at Isobel's voice. She considered the crowded pub, her nose wrinkled.

"Easiest place for a guy like me to hide, though."

"I suppose. Any progress?"

"You'll get your girl after I get Ruark."

Isobel's gaze narrowed. "You haven't looked for her at all, have you?"

"I'm going to find her." He thought of Madame San Clair's promise, her warning. How much trouble could one girl be? "Sit. Drink. You look like you could use one."

Isobel scoffed. "Some of us take our jobs seriously."

"You think I don't? The last two people you've sent after this girl have died, remember?"

She sat on the stool beside him, arms crossed. "About that."

"Yeah?"

"I worry," Isobel said carefully, "that you're too emotionally involved in this."

"Wasn't that the point?" Nathy looked over at her, his hair falling in his eyes, fracturing her image. "Nobody wants him dead more than me. You gotta figure I'll do a good job."

"*If* you can do a good job."

"Your confidence is stunning. Really." Nathy drained his drink and got up. "Well, night."

"Nathaniel."

He stopped, halfway to the stairs leading up to the rented rooms. "He killed the only people I had in the world. I won't mess this up."

She looked away from him. "Fifteen years is a plenty of time to harden your heart. But he's taken someone from you recently, too. So, tell me, how fresh is that wound?"

"I get by." Nathy walked on. "Night, Izzy."

IT STARTED TO rain. Nathy listened, half-aware; the murmur of the crowd downstairs mingled with the drumbeat of the storm.

He couldn't sleep, probably wouldn't until this was finished.

Artemis always came back to him like this, in pieces of life and death—reminders of what she'd been, and how she'd gone. A flutter of her laughter would run through his mind, followed by a flashing memory of marbled skin. The imagined sensation of her kiss chased by the knifing loss he'd first felt when he knew she was gone.

He couldn't pull Artemis out of the dirt, and even if he could...would he want to? The years both blurred her memory and clarified it. They were terrible for each other. But he couldn't remember why. He was all right with her being gone. But he wished she'd left a different way.

He figured you more easily got over things you let go; when something—someone—was ripped away, they stayed like a scar.

Ever since his mother and her sword, since Fryer's Grove and Flynn, his life had somehow revolved around the Monarch, on finishing what Artemis died for.

So, he'd finish it. And then...he didn't know.

He just wanted, finally, to be done.

6

THE ALLY

-Theopolis-

WATERY BEAMS OF early dawn light crept beneath the curtains when Lacey awoke, unsure why her bed was so soft, why her back didn't ache.

She pushed herself up, startled by the beauty of her room: an oak dresser and matching wardrobe, both carved with delicate rose-and-thorn reliefs along the trim; rich blue curtains containing the weak morning light; a canopied bed wider and longer than Lacey's whole bedroom back home.

Dr. Poole's house—she'd forgotten in the haze of good, deep sleep that she'd been shuttled here with little explanation.

Not that she much cared at the moment. This bed was so *soft*.

She'd nearly fallen back asleep when a bell chimed through the house, startling her up again. Right. She shook her head. *Doorbells*. And...

She turned to the lamp beside her bed and twisted a smooth dial. Without any fire or further prompting, light bloomed from the red shade. She clicked it off and on a few times, smiling the more times it worked.

"...are you doing here?"

Dr. Poole sounded less than pleased. Abandoning the joy of electric lighting, Lacey slid from bed and donned the plushy blue dressing gown she'd found in the wardrobe the night before. She crept to the door and opened it silently.

"I didn't think you'd stay the night," a voice said from the kitchen.

"That doesn't explain what you're doing here."

"I came to ask you," the familiar voice Lacey could nearly place said, then faded off. Dr. Poole's response came back strong.

"For the love of Elrosh. Go home."

Curiosity led Lacey forward. She tugged the door shut without sound and crept downstairs into the hall, arranging herself so she had an angle on the kitchen. The man standing with Dr. Poole was a few inches taller, at least two decades younger, and handsome in a way that seemed unfair to everybody else. Lacey's mouth dropped open.

"Saxon?"

The two men jolted at her voice. Saxon recovered first, grinning the full, shining smile that had first made Lacey's stomach feel detached and wobbly as a young girl.

"Lacey. It's good to—"

"Oh, God." Lacey looked down at herself. She wasn't dressed for company, not least of all handsome company. "I'll be back!"

She rushed back into the room and flung open the wardrobe. Her rucksack sat limp on the floor. She only had peasant's rags of her own, but the wardrobe was filled with summery dresses Dr. Poole had bought her over the years.

She shuffled through the clothes, their floral tones and light material ridiculous for winter, but better than a man's borrowed bathrobe or the hideous, limp rags in her own bag. She chose a slinky rose dress that hung just past her knees. It hung loose along her waist and hips. Modern fashions favored slim figures, but she'd lost even more weight since the lean winter rations diminished.

It must look ridiculous on her, but at least it didn't match a plowed field.

"Sorry," she said, returning to the hall. "I wasn't expecting anyone."

Saxon's eyes mercifully seemed to pass over her emaciated body and lingered on her face. "I sort of dropped in. It's good to see you again."

"Oh. You, too." She caught herself finger-combing her hair and winced. "What are you doing here?"

Saxon nudged Dr. Poole in the ribs. "I came to ask my favorite professor to change my grade in biology. He's not budging, though."

"Perhaps if you turned in assignments on time. Or at all."

"I'm just busy, professor."

Dr. Poole eyed Saxon warily. "Yes, well, sorry you can't stay for breakfast, given your busy schedule, so—"

"Actually, breakfast sounds lovely. Lacey? How about Koneli's? Have you ever been?"

Lacey opened her mouth, but Dr. Poole was already declining on her behalf.

"I don't think that's a good idea. We got in late last night."

"I'd like to go, actually," Lacey said.

"Perfect." Saxon said. "We'll go shopping, too. You'll need a dress for the festival."

If Saxon weren't sufficiently well-built, Lacey was sure her godfather would have knocked him over. He fumed quietly, eyes alight with the promise of murder.

"The festival? That's tonight?" Lacey looked at her godfather. "Is that what we're doing here?"

"Oh, gods, did I ruin the surprise?" Saxon grinned sheepishly at Dr. Poole. "Sorry, professor."

Dr. Poole pinched the bridge of his nose, seemingly concentrating all his efforts on not clobbering his student.

"Well, brilliant," Lacey said, trying to cheer him. "I've never been before. Is it fun?"

Dr. Poole shook off his annoyance with a shrug. "It's hosted by the Elderon, so there's that. Go for the propaganda, stay for the booze."

"But there's plenty to see," Saxon said. "Especially if you hardly get to be in the city."

Dr. Poole sighed. "Right. Well, don't take too long. I've got plans for this afternoon, and—"

"That reminds me," Saxon cut in, his eyes serious. "Do you know what's going on with the travel restrictions, professor?"

Dr. Poole narrowed his eyes. "Travel restrictions?"

"Yeah. The Watchmen are apparently at the harbor. They're shutting it down. And any trains leaving the city. Odd, isn't it?"

Something seemed to pass between the two of them, some deeper meaning Lacey couldn't quite follow. Finally, Dr. Poole picked up a mug he'd left on the kitchen table and drained the contents.

"I'll be right back." He left the kitchen, heading across the hall, and shut himself into his study.

"He doesn't seem to like you," Lacey said.

Saxon waved off her concern. "I'm his favorite student. He just doesn't know it yet."

"You still plan to be a physician, then?"

"Sad as it is, I'm better with natural medicine than potions. Or spells for that matter."

"Have you learned any new ones?"

"I think I've mastered a fairly decent stunning spell."

Lacey smirked. "Let's see it."

He laughed nervously. "Well, I can't use it on you."

"Because you know it won't work?"

"Lacey Falk-Barker, you've gotten meaner."

"One tends to become a cold, heartless wench out on the marshes."

Dr. Poole rushed back to the kitchen, his eyes bright, mouth pinched.

"Dr. Poole?"

"Hm? Um, Saxon. Here." He slapped a handful of junes into Saxon's hand, then turned to Lacey. "Sorry, Red, I've been called to a meeting."

"At the university?"

"No. With the Elder of Information." He turned to Saxon, reluctance and dislike simmering in his eyes. "Take care of her. Got it?"

"Sure, professor."

"I mean it."

Saxon nodded quickly. "Yes, sir. Um...I don't need this." He tried to hand the junes back. "I can—"

"Right. Terribly misogynistic of me." He took the money back and put it into Lacey's hand. "Buy whatever you fancy. In fact, buy two." He handed her another considerable stack of money.

Lacey's eyes widened on the crumpled bills piled in her palms. "Dr. Poole? Are you all right?"

"Course. I'll be back in a jiff." He glared at Saxon. "I'll meet you at the festival. All right? By the white thorn tree. Eight o' clock."

Saxon cleared his throat. "What if you're...late?"

Even Dr. Poole's smile managed to look withering. "I won't be. See you soon, Red."

She waited until the front door had shut to say, "Is there a reason everybody's acting so bloody odd around me?"

"How do you mean?"

"My mum acted like it was the last time she'd ever see me when she said goodbye. Dr. Poole's just handed me my stepfather's yearly earnings to do a bit of shopping. And yesterday he made it sound...like he didn't think I should go home." She shook her head. "I get the feeling people are hiding something from me."

"Well. I'd say a distraction is in order."

"See, that. That's precisely what I mean." She frowned. "Do you know something?"

"I know how to show a lady a good time." Saxon took her hand. "Let me give you the best Theopolis has to offer."

She cocked her head, eyebrows raised. "You say that every time I'm here."

"And you're never disappointed, are you?"

"You've gotten so much worse, you know."

He threaded her arm through his elbow. "I choose to take that as a compliment."

POOLE DROVE TOO quickly down the narrow, curved streets toward the university, braking frequently for the slow clod of carriages and hansom cabs. He appreciated the innovation of autos, but they were rendered a bit useless when the majority of Theopolines wouldn't, or couldn't, switch over.

He managed to pass a clog of traffic circling toward the shopping district and parked outside the university gates ten minutes later. The stone gargoyles on either end of the gate seemed to watch his movements as he jogged down the pavement toward the soaring stone library on the eastern end of campus. Its elegant façade rose up behind a line of dried, dead trees.

It was an old building, what used to be Theopolis's primary cathedral when the city first became more than a cluster of buildings behind a stone wall. The monarchs had asked for a house of worship more glorious than their own castle, and they'd gotten it—sweeping spires, windows woven with intricate metalwork, looming cloisters surrounding a delicate garden. But three hundred years ago, after a fire gutted it and the Elderon ordered a new cathedral built to match their palace, the university had bought the singed skeleton. Now it was a place where Poole could worship, a house of books and lost intelligence.

He paused at the steps, rounded and smooth from centuries of feet, first of the devout, and then of the curious. He relished the soft clack of his shoes against the ancient stone, the groan of the great double doors as he stepped into the foyer.

What used to be the nave of a church now served as a soaring room lined with shelves and dotted with tables, students crisscrossing the vast space laden with tomes. The winter holidays had officially begun, but still students could be found cramming for the next term. Westman-Samfrey had high standards, and no student, it seemed, felt safe to relax.

Poole scanned the busy room, and at last his eyes snagged on the wiry figure of Kimberly Law. The Elder of Information was here, officially, to review the newest printings of books for censorship. Poole wondered, distantly, if his own work would be allowed on university shelves.

Unofficially, Poole had told Law to meet him here, now, and explain. He crossed the nave and approached Law, who barely glanced up from the book in his hands. Poole tilted his head to catch the title. *Natural Magic.* Of course.

"Absolom." Law took his spectacles from his nose and tucked one stem into his shirt front. He flipped Poole's book back to the title page and stamped it—*restricted.*

"Really?" Poole said.

"I could ban it entirely." Law set the book on a nearby rack and finally met Poole's eyes. "We'll talk outside."

Law led him away from the nave, to a side door that let out onto the cloister. A neat square of garden with a fountain burbling at its center flashed between the thin stone pillars as they walked. Few students lingered outdoors thanks to the chilled air, and Law finally stopped when they were alone.

"There have been rumors of the Ruined Queen's heir," he said without preamble. He turned to Poole. "I expect you know about the execution that took place in Hollow's Edge?"

"It's why I got Lacey out of there. The..." Though nobody stood near enough to hear them, Poole lowered his voice. "Will's old mates were on to her."

"Yes, and the Elderon is very interested in why a member of the Nine would be searching a forgotten human village for the queen's heir."

"Goddammit." Poole ran a hand through his hair. "Do they know it's her?"

"Not that I've heard, no."

"I've got some time, then," Poole said, even as anxiety spiked his blood. He needed to find her now.

"I don't think you understand the severity of what's happening." Law plucked his glasses from his shirt front and pushed them back up his nose. "Absolom, they can easily see that you recently traveled from there. They'll investigate you. They'll arrest you if they think it'll help. I'm afraid Theopolis is the worst place you could have brought her."

"Do they know about Sebastian?"

"I wouldn't count anything out at this point." Law sighed. "My advice: Get in your auto, go get your goddaughter, and hope you can make it past a checkpoint." Sunlight caught in his glasses, blotting out his eyes. "But don't expect this to work out in your favor."

He walked past Poole, back toward the nave, and paused. "I am sorry, you know. I'd hoped this day would never come."

"It hasn't yet," Poole said, and turned away.

THE DRESS WAS too much in every way. Too extravagant, too expensive. Too revealing. She took a deep breath and turned toward the mirror hanging in the dressing room. The sleeves were mere strings, bleeding into a narrow neckline that would have been scandalous on a better endowed woman. The gown fell snugly along her hips, with the merest flair at her feet. The shimmery sapphire material seemed to gleam against her pale skin. She looked all right in it, despite her hair, tangled and lank down her back. She clawed her fingers and worked the knots from her hair.

"How's the dress?" Saxon called from the other side of the door.

"Fine? I think?" She ripped through a final snarl and shook her hair out. Despite the gown, she still looked like a poor farmer girl. People would assume she'd stolen the dress off a dead body.

Saxon opened the door without knocking. Lacey kicked a spiky heeled shoe at his head.

"Pervert," she said.

He rubbed his scalp where the shoe had made contact. "I assumed you were dressed. And so you are."

"Still." She grabbed the split ends of her hair and scowled. "This doesn't look right." Women were wearing their hair short in the city, or in elegant updos that seemed like masterworks of engineering.

"Here." Saxon took her by the shoulders and pushed her into the chair before the bureau. He scooped strands of her hair and began twisting them together into small, neat braids, which he then twirled into a loose bun at the nape of her neck.

"You do hair," Lacey observed as he worked.

She caught his smile above her in the mirror. "I help my sister with hers sometimes."

Lacey blushed. "Oh, right. I'd forgotten you had a sister."

He said nothing, and kept at her hair, which was becoming less a wild mess and more...beautiful.

"You hardly ever mention her," Lacey said.

"Sophie doesn't get out much." Saxon fixed the last braid into place with a pin and touched her shoulders. "There. You'll put everyone else to shame."

"I love your optimism." But she smiled. "Thanks."

"Course. Anything for you."

Lacey shifted awkwardly in the dress. "How much is this anyway?"

Saxon shrugged. "Who cares? I'll pay." He snatched an odd feathery length of fabric off the bureau and draped it across her shoulders. Lacey titled her head, startled by the effect. She looked like anybody else in Theopolis—just another young woman of wealth, going off to a party.

She looked away, feeling vaguely ill. "We ought to get back to Dr. Poole's."

"Or," Saxon said, smirking over her reflection. "We could walk on the bank. Go to lunch."

"Two meals a day? My, aren't we fancy."

Saxon leaned down, his breath lifting the fine strands of her hair from her temple. He kissed her there, soft and brief. Still, Lacey's heart lurched. "Since when do you say no to free food?"

Lacey twisted her lips, considering. Her stomach gave a happy rumble. "Fair point." She rose from the cushioned chair and took his offered hand.

"Should we stop at the house and see if Dr. Poole is back?" she asked.

Saxon shrugged. "He said he'd meet us at the festival. Besides..." He grinned. "I prefer we didn't have a chaperone."

Lacey rolled her eyes. "Scandalous."

"You don't know the half of it."

7

THE FESTIVAL

-Theopolis-

RAFFIC CLOTTED THE streets of Theopolis and nudged toward the heart of the city, autos and carriages and people thronging in every available space, closing in around the light and music of the festival. As they neared the city center, stalls appeared on the sidewalks, with merchants in drab winter garments holding hand-drawn signs, hocking scarves and wood carvings and fortunes for a coin. Posters called out from every available space of wall, and Saxon's auto moved so slowly against the traffic, Lacey could read every one. *Elixir of Life! The One-and-Only Genuine Article!* read one. And another: *Madame San Clair's Fortune Shop: Potions, crystals, and the future laid bare. Special half-off Festival Sale! Some restrictions apply.* And then...

"What's 'Roselyn Ruark and the Troubled Troupe's Fantastical Freak Show'?" she asked. The grinning, painted caricature of a man in a top hat with a trim handlebar mustache four times as wide as his body sneered at her. Maybe it was the man's pinpoint eyes, or the loud, curling words, but the poster struck her as tasteless at best, sinister at worst.

"Oh." Saxon frowned. He sat beside her with his arm slung across the back of the seat, nearly touching her shoulders. "He's just some travelling showman. He puts nocturnes on display. Ones with...problems. Disfigurements. Rarities, too. They say he's got a werewolf and a vampire."

"How'd he manage that?"

"He used to be a Huntsman, apparently. A big player in the War of Teeth. Figure he saved a few of his marks."

If the Elderon were to be believed, werewolf and vampire kinds had gone extinct after the war, obliterated in battle or executed after their surrender. The thought of a few solitary members of those depleted species out in the world, used merely as entertainment...

"Is that legal?" Lacey asked.

Saxon laughed shortly. "No. But the same blokes who would arrest him are the ones who watch his bloody shows."

"Have you ever thought— Does it occur to you how horrible everyone here is?"

Saxon stared ahead. "I think about it all the time."

THE LIGHTS AND noise of the crowd thrummed in Lacey's mind and blood like panic. She felt detached, clumsy, and all the while giddy, because Saxon held her hand as he guided her through the mob of festival-goers and stall-keepers. They faded into the crowded streets, anonymous in the center of everything.

"Having fun yet?"

"What?" Lacey yelled. Saxon grinned and tugged her along.

The bulk of the crowd thronged toward Aethali Palace, filling the courtyard and clogging the gateway. Festivalgoers circled around the white thorn tree growing through the flagstones, its skeleton fingers open as if to catch the stars should they fall. Lacey and Saxon hung back.

The palace sprawled for several city blocks, a pale stone structure rising in the heart of the city. It was newer and sleeker than the old castle resting to the east, but still it stood starkly against the other buildings, the heart of Theopolis's government, the home of the Elders.

Now, its huge front doors opened. A white head and flimsy body manifested, like a ghost from its tomb, and the audience crackled with applause. The man, as he appeared on the front steps, seemed somehow unreal, like dust kicked up by the wind and dropped just as suddenly. He waved away the sound of the crowd's admiration.

"That's Chancellor Crane?" Lacey asked, hopping to see over taller viewers.

"And company," Saxon said, nodding to the doors.

Four men stepped out behind the Chancellor in synchrony and stood staggered at either side, two by two. The Pontiff,

Father Priestly, took his place at the Chancellor's right. On the left, Justice Bromley, like a big black balloon in his judicial robes. Commander Lately stood just beyond the Pontiff, looking like a cat, tense and coiled to spring. Inspector Law, the Elderon's master of information, stood in the place of least regard, left of left. He smiled, bored and contemptuous.

"Don't they look dashing," Lacey said.

"Love his hat," Saxon said. The Pontiff wore a boxy gilt hat which seemed to throw Commander Lately into shadow. Lacey smiled and chanced a look at Saxon. He stared back, and the faint traces of a smile touched his face.

"We mark a glorious day," the Chancellor said, his voice amplified by a strange metal cube attached to the podium. "A day which, for our people, means freedom, justice, and righteousness."

There was generous applause at this. Saxon smirked.

"They act like it's so novel," he said against Lacey's ear. "But he says the same thing every year."

Lacey listed her head. "How is that box making his voice so loud?"

Saxon blinked. "You've...never seen a microphone?"

"We don't even have lights where I'm from, Saxon."

"Right. I— To be honest I don't know how they work."

Lacey wilted a little. "I wish we got some of these inventions back home."

He bumped her playfully. "All the more reason to stay, hm?"

She didn't look at him. The Chancellor's speech continued, a dull drone.

"Five hundred and eighteen years ago, our Elderon was formed. Our realm became a place of peace. Theopolis has never been more prosperous than it is today. We are safer, we are stronger—Elrosh has blessed us immeasurably."

Lacey stood on her toes to speak into Saxon's ear. "What's this festival about?"

"The founding of the Elderon," he said. "Today's the anniversary of when they overthrew the old monarchy. Don't you celebrate back in your village?"

She snorted. "Fat lot of good the Elderon's ever done for us. We're not about to celebrate them, are we?"

He seemed to fight back a laugh. "Fair enough."

The chancellor's crackling voice continued over the crowd: "Yet there are threats we cannot even understand in this world. The Lesser Gods have been hard at work, trying to undo many of our greatest accomplishments. The nocturne, the giants and dwarves, even humans—every year they step further from their rightful place."

Lacey's mood blackened like the sky, and all the lights of Theopolis couldn't chase the darkness away.

"He's boring." She turned from the palace and walked down the street, through the straggles of the crowd.

"Lacey?" Saxon called after her.

He caught up to her, matching her fierce stride down the pavement. "Something the matter?"

"It's a festival. So why are we standing around listening to some tosspot moan about the nocturne?"

"They do it every year," Saxon said. "Opening ceremonies, I suppose."

She stopped beneath a glaring electric streetlamp and looked up at him. "I know your family is protected, but...doesn't that bother you?"

"Sure. But... Look, I know it seems like they're just as awful as ever. But the Alliance at least—"

Lacey rolled her eyes. "The Alliance. How many nocturne families are actually in that?"

"Erm." Saxon rubbed the back of his neck. "A few dozen?"

"Right. And everybody else is treated like they always were."

"Well...the war didn't help."

"That wasn't the *nocturnes'* fault."

"Lacey. How about we not discuss politics? It's a festival."

She pushed off from the streetlight and headed farther down the street. She felt Saxon's presence behind, trailing her like a faithful dog, but she pretended he'd gone. A few other festivalgoers milled in a distant square around a bonfire, and Lacey moved toward it. But as she drew closer, the fire became a shape, humanoid and wilted by the curling flames. The people around jeered and tossed more sticks at the figure's feet.

"What's that, then?" Lacey asked the gathered Elonni, her eyes running up the effigy. It was made to look like a woman, wearing a fine dress, her red yarn hair smoking as the fire climbed higher. Two bright green buttons served as eyes, reflecting small puddles of flame back at Lacey. Her fingers twitched, wanting to go forward, absurdly itching to save the figure from the fire.

"What's that, she says," one of the men chuckled.

"I'm serious," she said flatly, pulling her eyes from the effigy.

Saxon came up beside her and took her hand. "It's the last queen of Gryfel. Come on."

"Last queen," a second man around the effigy said. "The *Ruined* Queen. Biggest tyrant Gryfel's ever known."

"Good riddance," the first man said, and spat into the flames.

"How d'you not know that?" A third man stepped around the flames, eyes narrowed.

"I'm not from here," Lacey said. "Where I'm from, we use fire to keep warm, not humiliate people who died centuries ago. Suppose we're rather less stupid."

"Lace." Saxon began to drag her away. Lacey made a rude gesture at the sneering men as Saxon pulled her down another street.

"What was that?" he said.

"They were being idiots," Lacey said.

"Do you pick fights with every idiot you meet?"

"If I've got the time," she said, and tugged her hand away. "So, let's see, this festival so far has burning effigies, supremist speeches, and apparently a humiliating freak show for nocturnes."

"Not having fun?"

"No, Saxon. No."

He smiled, but it looked more like a wince. "There's great food, though."

She sighed. She was stuck here until eight o' clock; might as well make the most of it.

The lines for the food stalls lining the streets were nearly nonexistent thanks to the Chancellor's speech, and the drifting scent of freshly fried meats greeted her like a friend. The many junes in her pocket became heavy with possibility.

74

She made for a cart advertising whole roast chicken when a hand descended on her shoulder.

"You're missing the Chancellor's speech, young lady."

She ducked away from the man's grip. He was probably in his late-fifties, his nose hooked like a beak. As he stared down at her he seemed like a vulture surveying a meaty corpse. His thinning dark hair ran in strands to his shoulders.

"Sorry, who are you?"

"Lacey." Saxon grabbed her elbow, tugging her back. She pulled out of his grip.

"What's *your* problem?"

The birdlike man smiled with his thin lips. "Ah, Master St. Luke. It's been too long. How's your sister?" His voice creaked, grainy and low.

Saxon's jaw locked, his back teeth grinding audibly. "Excuse us, ambassador. We were on our way out."

"What a shame. Chancellor Crane's speech is supposed to be most inspiring this year."

"Then I'd hate for you to miss it on our account."

The man bowed aside. "Have a good evening, Master St. Luke. Miss Barker."

Lacey whipped around to look at the man, but Saxon pulled her along by her hand, bypassing the food stalls and leaving the stranger behind them.

"Saxon, who was that?"

He looked as though he'd been wakened from a bad dream and was relieved to find her beside him. He smiled. "No one. Just a complete sod."

"How did he know my last name?"

He stopped, a haunted expression overtaking his eyes. "I don't know."

"Would Dr. Poole know him?"

"Know *of* him, yes. But they aren't friendly, I promise you."

"I take it we don't like this mysterious stranger?"

"He's the Elderon's ambassador to the western reaches. Eadred Kragen. Allied mage. Everything you find objectionable about this city, he relishes in."

"You seemed panicked to see him talking to me."

"I just—don't like him."

She sighed. "You lot never just say what you're thinking, do you?"

They wandered the street together, the silence between them stiff. Saxon's eyes hadn't recovered their light, and Lacey's stomach mourned the roasted chicken she hadn't gotten to buy.

"All right, we're getting dinner or I'm killing and eating the next thing I see."

Saxon smiled, finally. "There's a stall right over there."

"Kabobs! I love this city."

"You just said you hated it."

"All right," she said, rushing the stall. "I hate the snobbish people. But I love the food." She dug the money Dr. Poole had given her out of a small purse and bought herself two greasy, smoky kabobs.

They sat against an alley wall together, Lacey not giving a thought to the fine material of her dress as she dripped grease and sauce onto the skirt.

"Are nocturne allowed to practice magic in the city?"

"In the Eastern, yes. In the city proper, only Allies. And even we've got a list of approved spells and rituals and potions we're allowed to use."

"So." Lacey finished off her first kabob. "If I wanted to talk to a dead person..."

"*What?*"

"Who would I go to for that?"

"I—don't know anything about the Eastern," he said, yet a flush crept across his cheeks.

"Hm." She stood and walked out of the alley.

"Where are you going?"

"The Eastern."

"The... Wait!" He scrambled after her, pushing her hand down as she raised it to hail a passing carriage. "You can't be serious."

"Why?"

"It's dangerous, for one. And secondly, Dr. Poole asked me to keep an eye on you. And third, it's nearly seven and we're meant to meet him at eight, and if we're not there, I'm the one he's going to bury."

"We've got plenty of time for me to take a look."

"What did you mean, you want to talk to a dead person?"

"Just that."

"And why do we have to do this tonight? In the Eastern of all places?"

"Because you said that's the only place to find magic. Anyway, I've never been."

"That's a good reason not to go."

"Have a sense of adventure," Lacey said, hailing another passing carriage. It rattled to a halt a few feet away.

"Look, I don't want to be a prat," Saxon said, "but I need to insist you don't go."

"Wow, look at that," Lacey said, walking away, "I'm still doing it! Amazing!"

Saxon followed after her.

Lacey stopped beside the carriage driver and rummaged in her purse for the fare. Saxon flipped out his wallet and gave the driver several bills.

"The Eastern," he said.

The driver raised his eyebrows, then shrugged. "Get in, then."

"So you're coming now?" Lacey intoned. Saxon opened the carriage door and held out his hand to help her up.

"Never said I wasn't."

She smiled and took his offered hand. "You may be some fun after all, Saxon St. Luke."

8

THE PRICE OF FLESH

-*Middle Wood*-

CARRIAGES MEANDERED ALONG a wide path through the forest, carrying elite Elonni away from the festival and toward a shadier sort of fun. Nathy sat across from Isobel, fidgeting against the suit jacket she'd insisted he wear.

"Stop squirming," she said.

"How am I supposed to kill anyone in this?" He undid the bowtie circling his throat like an unforgiving fist.

"You think you've got it hard? Try wearing heels."

He looked at her small feet, crammed into strappy red heels that gave her another four inches of height. They matched her bloodred dress, formed to every curve in a way that must have made even the smallest movements a chore. Even so, she didn't seem bothered, sitting with one leg crossed over the other, her arms thrown back over the seat. A feathered headband rested above her forehead, a crimson gem glinting between her eyes. Her mask this evening was white, studded with rubies along one side.

"Just relax," she said. "You need to blend in if you hope to get close to Ruark. Security at his shows is intense."

Nathy grunted. "I'm surprised so many of the well-heeled turn up for this thing."

"They're the only ones who do. Ruark charges a small fortune in admission. He knows his audience."

"Assholes?"

She sighed. "You've such a way with words."

"We can't all be minstrels." He tied the discarded bowtie around his knuckles. Isobel scowled.

"For punching," Nathy clarified.

"Wear it properly, please."

He tossed it around his neck but didn't tie it.

The procession of carriages slowed and finally stopped in a clearing. Elonni dressed in their finest evening clothes poured from the many carriages. Nathy recognized a handful of them—top-ranking members of the Elderon, ambassadors and ministers. Watchmen. A large man in judicial robes lumbered out of an oversized carriage, accompanied by a girl in a tight black dress.

Justice Bromley? And coming out of the same carriage, a bulkily muscled man in a formal military regalia, followed by a tall, thin man with the look of a weary professor.

Commander Lately. And Inspector Law.

"Wait. The Elders are here?"

"Hm." Isobel shrugged. "I'm not surprised."

Nathy looked across the carriage at her. "I'm supposed to assassinate Ruark with the head of the military looking on?"

Her ruby smile seemed to shine. "That's why we hired the best assassin in the realm."

Nathy rolled his eyes. "Where does Ruark go before his shows?"

She waved for him to follow and they left the carriage behind, crossing the clearing and coming upon an overgrown forest path lined with covered cages. Small, muffled sounds came from beneath the cloths, drawing spectators to the promise of misery.

Nathy stopped at the nearest cage. "He's got nocturnes in these?"

"Don't concern yourself with it," Isobel said. "Once he's gone, there won't be a show anymore."

A gong sounded three times, and their attention turned to a giant farther up the path, wrists chained, beating the instrument and bellowing, "Come one, come all, to Roselyn Ruark and the Troubled Troupe's Fantastical Freak Show!"

The thick black covers over the cages suddenly lifted as though snatched by great invisible hands. Lost, wet eyes peered out at the crowds thronging around the cages. Nathy and Isobel stood nearest a young fairy girl with huge ram-like horns upon her head and weighty goat teeth. An Elonni man wearing a crisp suit and fedora picked up a rock from the ground and threw it at the girl. It struck her through the bars, and the man and his date laughed.

Nathy started toward the man but a small, firm grip stopped him. "You can't help her," Isobel said.

"No, but I can hurt *him*."

"You're sweet. Maybe that's your problem."

The fairy girl covered her cumbersome teeth and cowered against the bars. Tears ran over her scarred knuckles.

"Take care of Ruark," Isobel said quietly, "and you help all of them."

Nathy nodded, making note of the jackass in the fedora. Maybe he'd come back for that one later.

They passed more miserable nocturnes in cages. A group of Elonni watched as two boys pelted rotted apples at a cyclops chained between two trees, its great eye blinking tearfully. The sign by the creature read, *Top prize goes to the lucky lad who strikes the Eye thrice!*

Laughter, keening and pitched, carried through the air. Farther up the forest path a two-headed witch stood on a shabby plank stage—chained by the wrist to a stake in the ground. One of her heads told jokes while the other laughed with the growing audience around her.

"Ingrid."

Isobel stopped, her good eye twitching like a trapped bug. "Goddammit."

"*Ingrid?*" Nathy said.

"It's my first name."

"Isobel isn't a first name?"

"It's my second name."

"Then what's your last name?"

"Piss off," she snarled as the man who had called to her approached.

"Thought this sort of show was beneath you." Commander Ryder Lately stopped before them. He was Nathy's height but broader, corded with muscle that looked able to snap bones. His blond hair was cropped short, stark against the ruddy tinge to his pale face.

"There wasn't anything better to do tonight," Isobel said.

Ryder looked Nathy over, eyes narrowing. "Are you arresting this mage?"

Nathy opened his mouth, and Isobel, anticipating a stupid remark, elbowed him in the stomach. "He's an old friend," she said.

"I see." Ryder smiled, no warmth in his eyes. "Remind me, Ingrid, do I have you on an assignment?"

Nathy straightened. So, that's why Isobel was to tense. She was a Huntress, which made the Elder of War her boss.

"Nothing as of yet. Did you have anything in mind?"

"We'll see." The Commander lifted her hand to his lips and kissed her knuckles. "Enjoy your night."

Nathy waited until Ryder was well out of sight to say, "Sounded like a threat."

"It probably was." Isobel wiped her hand on her dress, banishing the Commander's kiss. "It's this way."

They left the many cages and makeshift stages behind. Ruark's black-and-white striped tent loomed nearer, in another clearing between the overgrown trees. A wash of color decorated one edge of the clearing. Heart sticking in his throat, Nathy realized it was the bright dresses of girls chained by their wrists to the trunks of trees. Each girl wore a sign around her neck with a scrawled price. They smiled without light and beckoned stray men forward with murmured words.

"What the hell?" Nathy looked at Isobel. "He's a pimp, too?"

"Don't get so worked up. You're here to kill him, after all."

The girls flinched against the chains as customers approached, their smiles drooping with fear.

Artemis had found Ruark. She'd fought him for Flynn's idiotic cause and died for it. But what if...

"Where is this piece of shit?"

"That's the spirit." Isobel nodded to the tent. "We'll wait for him to come on for his grand finale. One arrow to the heart should at least put him down until you can—"

"No. I need to talk to him."

Isobel blinked. "Excuse me?"

"He took my mother's sword. I want it back."

"Her— You're worried about that bloody *sword*? Nathaniel, who cares about some piece of metal? Ruark is one of the most dangerous threats to our cause."

"Your cause can wait."

"Don't forget it was your mother's cause, too. She died for this."

"No, she died because Ruark killed her. And he's going to answer a few of my questions. Then, if he's lucky, I'll shoot him in the heart."

"You aren't proving anything. Forget revenge. There are more important things. If we kill him now, without the bloody theatrics, we might stand a chance at getting the Monarch back."

"I'm surprised, Izzy. You never struck me as deluded."

"It's not a delusion. There are things you're simply too thick-headed to understand. The War of Teeth wasn't just some uprising of nocturnes. It was a revolution, and we can't chance failure again. The Elderon—"

He turned on her. "I still don't get why you care. You're Elonni. You're wealthy, safe. Why bother saving nocturnes?"

"I saved you, didn't I?"

He looked away. "Yeah, and look where that got us. I'll kill Ruark, Izzy. But this goes my way. Trust me. He dies tonight. But not until I have some answers."

"You *so* remind me of..." She clamped her lips, not looking at him.

"My father?" Nathy felt a dead, cold smile on his lips. "I'm sure I do. Let's go."

They bypassed the tent and walked toward the edge of the forest, where a wagon sat parked by the tree line. Its exterior was decorated with a caricature of Ruark's face, his thin, curling mustache twice as wide his giant head.

"Think he's still—" Nathy started, but a voice ripped across the clearing.

"Fekshti! Get over here!"

Isobel dragged Nathy out of sight, into the trees, where they could watch the wagon. A giant with a downward tilt in his great arched forehead lumbered toward the wagon.

"Yessir?"

The wagon door burst open, and a tall, thin man, clean-shaven save for a thin mustache waxed into curlicues, stepped out.

82

"Grab the freaks and get them to the tent. And bring Ambassador Marshall back here after my act. Goddamn vampire took a bite out of him and he's threatening litigation."

"Should I bring her in too, sir?"

"Forget her. She'll be crawling back once the cravings set in."

"Yessir."

"Don't give me that look, Fekshti. Goddamn mopey idiots, the lot of you. Hurry up! We're already late for the first act."

The giant solemnly sauntered off. Ruark fixed his hair beneath his top hat and righted the curls in his mustache. He crossed the clearing and ducked into the back of the tent.

"Perfect," Nathy said. "We'll wait for him inside."

Isobel pursed her lips. "This is an idiotic plan. He's strong, Nathaniel. I don't think you're ready for one-on-one combat."

"There's two of us."

"Even so."

"Izzy, he's a twig. I could break him in half even if I wasn't a mutt."

"Confidence *can* be idiotic, you know."

He waved her off and left the safety of the tree line for the wagon. In the center of the clearing, the crowd tapered toward the mouth of the tent, like water through a funnel. The show was just beginning. That gave them plenty of time.

Inside, the wagon was a mess—a bed in the corner with rumpled sheets, a cabinet overflowing with costumes and suits, a trunk spilling out props. The floor was littered with the overflow.

"Great. I get to look for my sword in this?"

Isobel eased the trunk open with the toe of her high-heeled shoe and bent to pick through its contents. "Is this what you're after?" She held out a short wooden sword, painted a flat gray.

Nathy took it and struck it against his palm. "No, but your sarcasm is noted."

"Great." She turned toward a cabinet standing against the thin wall and frowned. "What the..."

Nathy crossed the wagon. "What is it?"

"Blood." She opened the windowed door and plucked up a vial sitting on the middle shelf. "It's old, but...that's what it is."

83

Nathy took the vial and turned it upside down. A thick, black-red mass slunk toward the neck. "That's...peculiar." He checked the label. "It just says 'Malachi.'"

"What?" Isobel snatched it back. "Oh my God."

"What? Who's Malachi?"

"He was the king of vampires. Oldest in existence. Ruark was involved in the raid on their fortress in the war and took credit for killing him. This must be how he still has vampires in his show. He took Malachi's blood and uses it on humans."

"They don't have to be bitten?"

"No. It's the blood that carries the mutation. You do have to die after ingesting it, though."

"So, he doses humans, kills them, then waits for his newest showpiece to wake up?"

"Are you sure you don't fancy outright killing him?" she said, waggling the vial in his face.

"He'll get his." Nathy turned away to root through another section of the wagon.

"You don't honestly think it's here?"

"Probably not," Nathy said, opening a wardrobe and tossing identical black suits to the floor. "But if it's important enough to him, maybe he takes it on the road."

"Let me know if I can be of help."

They both spun. Ruark stood in the doorway, grinning.

"My oldest friends," he said.

"Ruark." Isobel smiled and slinked toward him. "We were hoping to catch you before the show."

"Oh?" He dipped into the wagon and stood inches from her. "Gods, you've gotten even more beautiful. Come to work for me? I guarantee it's more fun than being a Huntress."

Nathy stepped up beside her; he loomed above the showman, yet his presence had little effect. Ruark laughed.

"Aren't you just the spitting image of dear old daddy?" Ruark reached up to ruffle Nathy's hair. His eyes darted to Isobel. "Moved from one Fairborn to the next? Impressive."

Nathy pushed the showman back with one finger to his chest. "Where is it?"

"Use your words, kiddo."

"My mother's sword, asshole."

Ruark jerked his head to the wagon's door. "Come outside."

Nathy grabbed the front of Ruark's suit.

"I just need some fresh air, Charming." Ruark pulled away with ease, smoothing his lapel. "I don't do business where I sleep. Not this kind of business, anyway." He walked to the door and hopped out into the clearing. Nathy exchanged a look with Isobel; they followed.

"So." Ruark spun on his heel and faced them. "What's this sword you're after?"

Nathy curled his lip. "The sword my father took from me fifteen years ago? The sword you killed my mother to get?"

Ruark blinked. "Sword, sword... Oh, *that* sword. Gods, I'd forgotten all about it.... It's yours, mate. All yours. Really. I don't care what Mortimer Fairborn wanted. He's mental. You know how much help that bleeding sod's given me in all this time? None. He can die in a ditch for all I care."

"Really," Nathy said.

"Really. Just..." He reached behind him.

Nathy realized too late what the showman had behind his back, and the knife had already sunk into Isobel's stomach. She dropped to her knees, holding back a torrent of blood.

"What...the..." She screamed then, a cry like an animal sent for slaughter. Ruark stepped forward and ripped the blade from her stomach.

"It's new. You like it? The blade's demon-bone. Technically illegal, but hey, one of the perks of being a Huntsman, right?" He kicked Isobel onto her side and smiled at Nathy. "I went easy on her. You don't get the same luxury."

Nathy started toward Isobel, but she shook her head.

"I'm fine. Do your job," she ground out.

Nathy nodded, then faced Ruark. "*Hallas Elroi.*"

His black wings rippled down his spine, shadow and mass all at once. They spread out from his shoulder, the left one drooping and brushing the ground, dead weight. Ruark grinned.

"Mortimer meant it when he said he clipped your wings."

Nathy drew his wand. "Shut up." He launched a spell meant to stun the showman, but Ruark leapt nimbly out of the way.

"Nice try, kiddo." Ruark smirked, and his own wings materialized from his back, a foggy gray light coalescing into feathers and bone. "But you're not good enough for this fight."

Nathy launched another spell, a burst of rosy light spreading from the worn wand. Ruark batted it away with a flick of his fingers.

"I'll give you one more free shot," Ruark said.

"Okay." Nathy shoved the wand back into his jacket pocket. "*Sanat.*"

A burst of golden light tore at the air and headed straight toward Ruark, encompassing the showman in a glare like the sun. The light dissipated, revealing Ruark knocked to his side, grinning.

"That's more like it."

"Do you ever shut up?"

Ruark got to his feet with a flap of his dark gray wings. "You don't like to use your Elonni abilities. Why?"

Nathy responded by calling on the light again and sending it toward the showman. Ruark flew up into the air, landing safely out of the blast radius.

"You don't want to be like daddy?" Ruark continued. "Shame. He's strong. You could be, too, if you stopped licking your wounds like a dog."

Nathy curled his hand into a fist, focusing every shred of rage into the palm of his hand. "*Galvan.*"

A black, shadowy blade spread from his hand. Ruark laughed.

"Nice trick. It's your daddy's favorite, too."

Nathy charged, swinging the blade. Ruark took flight once more, landing behind Nathy ten feet away.

"You see the inherent disadvantage here, right?"

Nathy snarled, the shadow blade dissolving in his hand.

"A grounded angel," Ruark said. "You're worthless. Now the only question I have," he continued, "is what to do with you."

Nathy looked at Isobel. She lay on the forest floor, unconscious but breathing. Blood stained her hands, still guarding her stomach. He couldn't let her die here. It was his fault this assassination had become a one-on-one battle.

"Don't worry about her," Ruark said. "Cross my heart. I don't kill women; I have *some* standards."

"When did you decide that?"

Ruark blinked, then snapped his fingers. "*Right*. The last one Flynn sent was a girl. Little blond thing? Did I kill her? Right, I *did*. That was an accident. She was just so...mailable. Humans are like paper."

Nathy had had enough. His powers might not be enough, but he would at least get the visceral pleasure of knocking Ruark's teeth out. He threw a punch. Ruark drew his knife and swung up.

As Nathy's fist connected with Ruark's face, the knife sunk into his left shoulder. He tore the knife from his muscle and backed away, anticipating the same pain that had overtaken Isobel. But...

Nothing.

"Goddammit," Ruark said, rubbing his swelling jaw. "Guess it doesn't work on mutts."

"Yeah. And now you're fucked."

He flung the blade. It sunk into Ruark's abdomen.

"Work on your...aim." But the last word was strangled as Ruark fell to the ground, screaming through his teeth.

Nathy started forward, ready to retrieve the blade and saw Ruark's head off with it. But he was lifted off the ground mid-stride, huge corded arms circling his chest. The giant, Fekshti, tightened his grip.

"What seems to be the trouble?" Ryder Lately strode out from behind the giant and knelt by Ruark. "You all right?"

"Arrest...them."

"Obviously." The Commander rose and turned to Nathy, who struggled in the grip of the giant. "A Rakashi mage. I don't think I'll even bother to waste a cell on you. Giant."

"Fekshti, sir."

"Fekshti. Squeeze him to death."

"But...sir."

Nathy twisted, his broken wing slapping the giant's face. Fekshti dropped him, and Nathy landed like a cat.

"I'll gladly take you on next," he told the Commander.

Ryder laughed and drew a long iyrel sword. "And I'll gladly scrub a mutt from the face of the world."

Ruark struggled back to his feet, seething. "Leave him for me."

"No offense, Roz, but I think you've done enough."

"Have I?" He yanked up his trouser leg and drew what seemed to be another long knife. Its blade glowed orange, as though drawn from a forge.

"You wanted your sword," Ruark said, holding out the knife. It grew, shimmering and lengthening into a great blade. "Here it is."

Nathy shook out of his shock too late. Ruark took off on his gray wings, descending at a sharp angle and impaling Nathy's broken wing to the ground.

This was a pain like no other, a sharp, screaming thing buried somewhere in his chest, too horrible to be let out. He choked, blood staining his lips.

"Take Izzy away," Ruark told the Commander, turning back to Nathy. "I have plans for this one."

9

TEA WITH MADAME

THE COACH TRAVELLED east, toward the smoky coast, and the proud stone buildings of Theopolis waned. The noise of the festival became a murmur. Warm shopfronts lined with food and toys and dresses gave way to shabby row houses scrunched together. The smooth road cut abruptly into a clumsily laid flagstone lane lined with bent trees and crumbling stone buildings. A seedy shopping district sprawled before them, brick pubs emitting screams of laughter and drunken anger. Lacey peered out the window. The checkpoint lay just beyond.

"Lovely place," Saxon said, dropping the small dark curtain covering the windows.

"Never been this way?" Lacey said.

Saxon smiled lazily. "Who, me?"

The coach stopped hard. Watchmen stood outside, speaking with their driver.

"Papers, sir."

"Right here, there you go." The shuffling of parchment.

"How many passengers?"

"Two."

"They've got their papers?" A different Watchman, his voice coarse.

"Dunno, sir, reckon so. Ask them yourself."

A knock sounded at the carriage door. Saxon reached across and unlatched it. Two Watchmen, one a giant of a man with bulging eyes and a thick torso, the other a slimly muscled man not much shorter than Saxon, stood just outside.

"Papers," said the big man, thrusting out a hand.

Saxon flipped open his wallet and handed his papers over, an air of boredom in the movement. Lacey reached down the front of her dress for hers. Saxon raised an eyebrow.

89

"Well, I don't have a purse, do I?" she said, heat creeping along her cheeks.

"Sorry! No judgment."

"Well, stop looking."

Saxon, flustered, stared at the carriage ceiling. Lacey handed her papers off to the Watchmen.

"A warlock and a mutt?" The slim Watchman said. His eyes trailed over Lacey in a way that made her draw into herself.

"Warlock *Ally*, thank you very much," Saxon said with the flash of a smile. The big Watchman snorted and handed Saxon's papers back. The slim man still held Lacey's.

"Dangerous out there, you know," he said, dangling her papers out to her. "Roselyn Ruark's show's playing now." He turned to his companion. "I hear he wants a mutt for the Troubled Troupe."

Lacey snatched her papers back. "I'll be careful." She smiled. "Thanks *so* much."

The slim Watchman glared and slammed the carriage door. Moments later, the clopping of horse's hooves and the lurch of the carriage told them they were off again.

Saxon folded his papers and slipped them into his inner coat pocket. "Prick."

"He was just trying to get a rise." Lacey crossed her arms and glared out the window. "I'm not scared of some bloody showman."

"Hm." Saxon leaned back in his seat, hands behind his head, and shut his eyes, tension vibrating like ripples across his skin. His long mess of wavy chocolate hair fell over his face and gleamed with faint hints of gold when the moonlight touched it. His stubble was growing into a dark shadow. The smallest smile lifted the corner of his mouth.

"Are you staring at me?"

"Ass."

"Thought so."

"I'd say you should do a spell to shrink your massive head, but you're shit with magic."

He only laughed.

The carriage stopped ten minutes later. A melody of street-sounds bled through the carriage walls: the shuffling of feet, the roll of carts, distant yells filling the night with an eerie background noise. Lacey pushed open the carriage door and hopped out. The street was dirt here. All around people shuffled toward squat brick shops, above which dinky apartment windows glowed with feeble candlelight. A woman in a ragged dress, wrapped against the cold in no more than a headscarf, pushed Lacey aside to enter the shop behind her.

Saxon jumped from the carriage, his eyes darting up and down the street.

"Shit place," Saxon said.

Their driver didn't wait for a tip, but presently turned the carriage around, his horse clopping quickly, the carriage bouncing with speed.

"Do you know where we're going?" Saxon said, resigned.

"The poster I saw was for a Madame San Clair. But...no, I don't know where we're going." The many dark streets seemed suddenly longer, splintered with possibility.

"I might know the place," Saxon said, and jerked his head down a winding path. Lacey followed in his cautious footsteps.

People eyed them as they passed, murmuring. Saxon received more than suspicious looks—passersby watched his movements and hurried on after glancing at him. This dance of suspicion and fear went on until a tall, willowy man with pure white hair cropped close to his skull stepped out of a large group on the pavement, directly into Saxon's path. Saxon paled before folding his shocked expression into a frown.

"Back already?" the man said, grinning. He smoked a hand-rolled cigarette and took a long drag from it. "Needy little guy, aren't ya?"

"Do I know you?" Saxon said.

The man raised his eyebrows. "'Scuse me?"

Lacey took in the man's tapered ears, his white irises, the tips of iridescent wings glimmering beneath his long jacket. He caught her staring and, after taking another hard drag off the cigarette, blew the smoke in her face. She waved it away, glaring.

"Who's your girlfriend? She's cute. Kinda." He grinned at Saxon, sharp, perfectly white teeth flashing. "Maybe next time you can pay me in some alone time with her."

"Do I get a say in that?" Lacey asked.

"Depends." The fairy smiled and settled a tobacco-stained fingernail under her chin. "You'd go for a pretty penny in the forest, baby girl. You wanna help me make some extra cash? I split eighty-twenty."

"Generous," Lacey said, slapping his hand away.

The fairy blinked at her, cold rage in his flat white eyes. He grabbed her wrist and dragged her forward. "That wasn't very nice."

"Let me make it up to you, then." Lacey's blood warmed, her spine tingled. Saxon moved to get between them, but Lacey was faster. Her free hand locked onto the fairy's forearm and squeezed.

"Lacey!"

Saxon ripped her away, but not before the satisfying crunch of bone rippled along her palm. The fairy snarled, clutching his shattered forearm to his chest. Then, he smiled, slow and long.

"Elonni, huh?"

Lacey flexed her sore hand. "What gave me away?"

The fairy gave Saxon a derisive smile. "Screwing the oppressors, huh? Gutsy move."

Saxon scowled. "I said I don't know who you are. Now go."

"'Kay, pretty boy." The fairy slapped Saxon's cheek playfully and said, softly, "You'll regret it."

The fairy bumped Lacey with his shoulder as he went, his wings twitching beneath the jacket.

Lacey stared at Saxon, waiting. He ignored her glare, lighting a cigarette.

"You smoke?"

He grinned, the cigarette between his teeth. "Is that a deal-breaker?"

Lacey rolled her eyes. "How do you know that fairy?"

"I don't."

"Really? He sure seemed to know who you were."

"He probably does," Saxon said. "My name is mud around here. The St. Lukes are sort of traitorous scum."

"Well, warn me next time you see one of your friends coming," Lacey said.

"Warn me next time you're inclined to break someone's bones."

"I'm inclined to now."

He raised an eyebrow. "What did I do?"

She plucked the cigarette from his fingers, took a long drag, then tossed it to the pavement. "You shouldn't smoke."

"*You* shouldn't litter," Saxon said.

She turned and walked farther down the street. Saxon followed, keeping a closer proximity to her now.

The air was layered in smog, issuing from a spindly stone factory beyond the sprawl of shops, its smokestacks exhaling a pungent gray steam, a dying breath with no last request. Saxon led her down a narrow street where half the lamps were unlit, casting dark patches onto the pavement.

At last, they stopped at a tall, sloping building of dark brick. Stone steps, rounded from decades of use, led up to a narrow door. Barred windows glowed with the merest hint of candlelight. A hanging sign creaking in the breeze said, simply, *Fortunes told here.*

"Are you sure you want to do this?" Saxon said. Lacey mounted the steps and pushed the door open. A bell jingled overhead like sharp, otherworldly laughter.

Inside, a tall, wide counter spanned the shop from wall to wall. A few rickety wooden chairs were set up on the side of the entrance. One was occupied by a man with goat ears and a twitching tail. His eyes were bloodshot and puffy, and he nursed from a dented flask. He grunted at their presence.

"Wife's cheating," he said. "I just know it."

"Bad luck, mate," Saxon said. Lacey elbowed him.

"Don't be a prick."

The goat-eared man shrugged. "It's the tail."

They dropped into chairs of their own. On either side of the counter were two doors. Shelves packed with sealed scrolls, thick dusty books, and shards of crystal winking like animal eyes gave the place an overcrowded feeling. A little curio box in the shape of a pumpkin rattled around in a cage, jostling the items on the shelf beside it. One entire shelf held nothing but small glass jars and vials, all filled with a deep blue fire; they each bore a parchment label with a scrawled name. The air panted incense, thick as the jointure of intimate breaths.

Rain-patter footsteps sounded from above, and the door to their right behind the counter opened. A lanky boy with sleek black hair and a drawn, red-brown face shut the door behind him and stepped up to the counter. A Rakashi mage. Lacey let herself feel hope. The Rakashi specialized in divination magic, pulling whispers of the future from crystal, cards, stars, tea leaves. If anybody in this city could contact her father, experts in such magic had to be her best bet.

The boy looked to be about Saxon's age, but the way he gazed at them, like an animal in a trap, made him seem younger.

"Can I help you?" the boy said, and seemed to dread the answer.

"Yes," Lacey said, rising. "I wanted to see Madame San Clair."

"Oh," the boy said. He wore the expression of a man identifying a corpse. "Yeah, okay." He pushed a sheet of parchment and quill toward her. "Sign in. You're after Davik there."

Lacey scrawled her name on the parchment. As she wrote, the left door opened, seemingly on its own.

The Rakashi boy opened a partition in the counter and looked over at the goat-man. "Davik, go on down."

Davik rose with no enthusiasm and disappeared through the door.

Lacey set the quill aside. Before she could return to her seat, the Rakashi boy tapped her on the shoulder.

"Hang on."

"Er, yes?" Lacey froze, startled by the intensity in his black eyes.

"I didn't want to say in front of another customer, but...your aura is all over the place."

"I'm...sorry?"

He shook his head. "Gods, it's huge. Don't you feel that?" he asked Saxon.

Saxon shrugged. "Not my kind of magic, mate."

The Rakashi boy leaned forward, nearly crawling onto the counter now. "You're not... You *are*. Oh, gods, oh, gods, oh gods."

He opened the partition in the counter and waved them through. "Come this way. I'm Sinclair, by the way, Madame's son."

Saxon looked at him. "Your name's Sinclair San Clair?"

The boy looked at the ceiling. "Yes. Come on."

They followed him up the narrow staircase through the right door, into a crowded sitting room with scrolls and books on every available surface. Unfamiliar maps hung on the walls; paths across the strange lands were marked in red and purple ink, and pins pegged into certain destinations stood out against the stark parchment country. A woven rug with intricate geometrical patterns and the well-worn, sagging furniture upon it dizzied the room. A chandelier above tinkled as the wind blew and the house rocked with it.

"Have a seat," Sinclair said; he wrung his hands as though he'd like nothing more than to rip his fingers off. "Madame's just got to finish with Davik, should be up shortly." He paused, winced. "Can I, er...get anyone a tea?"

The two of them made noncommittal gestures and Sinclair vanished up another flight of stairs. Running water and the clinking of china made a melody above.

Lacey sat on a long sofa which sank with a noise like a sigh. In what she assumed was an act of defiance, Saxon sat beside her and slung his arm over the back of the couch. She caught the spicy bite of his cologne in her throat.

She scooted away from him.

"What have I done now?"

She gave him a withering look. "You're obviously lying about knowing that fairy."

"I told you, he probably recognized me because of my family. Most non-Allied nocturnes don't care for us, for obvious reasons."

"Seemed personal to me."

"I promise, it wasn't."

"Sure." She got up and dropped into a squashy armchair on the other side of the room.

Saxon seemed unfazed by the rejection. He sat there, ankle crossed over his knee, his arm still slung around the back of the couch, portrait-like. A piece of art, and something else at that.

Lacey couldn't say why she was so certain he was hiding something, only that his entire life—the wealth, the opportunity, the effortless way he moved in the world—made him too different. And she couldn't trust different. It wasn't his fault—his life was mapped out for him, a straight line with no stops. Hers felt chaotic, hungry. And incompatible with his.

Sinclair returned with a tea tray, his arms shaking, and set it on a low, chipped table. He poured a murky gray liquid from a cracked stone teapot. The cups came from different sets. Sinclair handed Lacey one with a badly painted hummingbird on its side. Saxon's was covered in garish pink flowers. He toasted it silently to Lacey.

"Madame would like you to drink your tea and let the leaves settle at the bottom," Sinclair said. "She's curious to know your destinies."

They drank their tea in silence, and Sinclair paced the room in tight, worried circles. The murky drink tasted the way it looked: swampy and stale. Lacey felt as though her tongue were coated in syrup when she had finished.

Saxon finished his tea and set the pink-flowered cup aside. He uncrossed his leg and leaned forward, hands steepled, and fixed Sinclair with an assessing gaze. "Will Madame be up soon?"

"Oh, she's coming. Never know how long she'll be with clients, you know. The visions..." He made a vague gesture and let his hand drop listlessly. He glanced at Lacey, flinched, and looked back at Saxon. In a quick, awkward bolt, he crossed the room and sat beside Saxon on the couch.

"She's dangerous," he told Saxon.

"I am *not*," Lacey said.

Saxon gave her a look. "You did just break someone's arm."

"He had it coming!"

"I need to make a call." Sinclair sprang from the couch and crossed to a wide, glass-fronted cabinet. From the top shelf he selected a murky crystal ball. It glowed faintly between his palms.

"Nathy?" he hissed into the crystal. "Nathy!"

Saxon straightened, his eyes widening.

"*Nathy!*" Sinclair shook his head. "No answer. Oh gods, gods." He put the crystal ball back on its shelf. "I, uh, I'll get

96

Madame." With that, he bolted down the stairs, calling back, "Don't touch anything!"

"What a strange person," Lacey said.

Saxon shrugged and looked at the chipped teacup on the table. Suddenly, his mouth flipped up into a smile.

"What?" Lacey asked.

"My tea leaves. They say I'm going to have an unforgettable night."

Lacey frowned. "*You* read tea leaves?"

"Only for fun."

"So, you're bad at that, too?"

"You're vicious tonight. I like it." He rose and walked to another end of the room, picked up the crystal ball, and shook it.

"He said not to touch anything," Lacey reminded him.

"I know." Saxon peered into the stormy glass. It didn't glow beneath his touch as it had done for Sinclair. "Hello? Anyone there?"

"Who d'you think is on the other end of that thing?"

"You never know."

Creaking, agonized footsteps groaned with the house as it bowed in the wind. The door swung open to emit a huddled woman with a bright, multi-colored scarf arranged around her crinkled red-brown face. Sinclair assisted her into the room, carrying more dread in his expression than before.

"Sorry to be late," the woman said. She hobbled to the couch and sunk into it with a satisfied groan. She eyed the teacup Saxon had left behind, peered into it, and looked up, alarmed.

"Whose is this teacup?"

"Uh, mine." Saxon set the crystal ball back on the shelf.

"My boy," she said, shaking her head, "before the dark sun sets on the next waning solstice, everyone you love will die."

Saxon blinked. Lacey snorted.

"So much for a night to remember."

"Don't joke about the whisperings of the gods, girl! It's worse luck than shattering a crystal under a birch on a blue-moon night." Madame shuddered.

"I'll try to remember that."

"Think you're funny?" The old woman leaned forward in her mass of shawls and snatched up Lacey's hummingbird cup. The medium cleared her throat and looked at Lacey with the withering clarity of a god with one foot outside of time. She looked into the cup and said:

"You will be torn asunder by your own self. You'll be made one at the cost of many. In you flows the blood of many gods, and in you lies the death of all humanity."

There was a long silence interrupted, at last, by Saxon's laughter.

"Death of all humanity? And I thought I had it bad."

Lacey sneered at him and turned to Madame. "Right, that's very ominous and all. But I didn't come here to have my fortune told."

"Ah, but you did. I've been expecting you, Miss Heartwood."

"It's Falk, actually," Lacey said. "Or Barker."

"No, no, you're she," Madame said. "I may be going blind, but the third eye sees just fine. You've got a dark spot on your soul."

Lacey stilled, suddenly afraid, and she couldn't say why. "I have a...never mind. Madame, I was wondering...I need to talk to someone."

"Your father."

"You knew?"

Madame leaned back against the couch, a tight look on her old face. "I'm afraid I can't help you."

"But you haven't even tried."

"Girl, I can feel the breath of every god ready to talk in my ear. But they only whisper the future. The dead are past."

"Look, I need you to please try. Everybody's keeping something from me, something to do with him."

"Lacey," Saxon said softly; his eyes met hers like some strange bright light calling her away from the rocks. "Maybe we should just go."

Lacey ignored him. "Madame, please, I—I need to know what's going on. Can you please try?"

Madame's thin lips curled in a tiny smirk. "I'm afraid not. You've got the wrong sort of witch, girl. I've done very little with the necromantic arts in my time. I read the stars, the cards, crystals, leaves, and the lines of your palm. But I cannot reach those who've passed beyond. You'd need a necromancer for that."

Lacey felt desperation clutch at her heart like a hook pulling her down. "Where do I find one of those?"

"You don't. Necromancy changes the soul, works away at a mage's very body." The old woman's smile sunk deep into her lined face. "You don't want to meet a practitioner of such arts."

"She's right, Lace," Saxon said. "Necromancers aren't like any mages you've met before."

Lacey sighed. "Then sorry to have wasted your time." She began to rise.

"Wait!" The old woman hobbled across the room and grasped Lacey's hands. Lacey flinched but didn't pull away as the woman examined her palm. Madame's face, its eyes and mouth nearly lost to the dune-and-desert skin, hovered very close to Lacey's.

"My, my," Madame said.

"What?" Lacey said.

Madame looked up; her small, pinched eyes were full of ancient sadness, a grief stretched across time. "Your life line stretches...into nine."

"So I'm a cat now?"

"Priestess," she said, almost to herself. "What you decide by book and sword will seal the fate of the realm. Seek the boy with a broken wing."

Lacey pulled her hands back uneasily. "All right, then."

Madame nodded, her little smile emerging from the folds of her face, and she sat back in her chair. She looked at her visitors in turn. "You may go now."

"One last thing, Madame," Saxon said. "What the hell was in that tea?"

Madame laughed, a strange sound like the caw of a large bird. "You ought to cherish her, boy." She inclined her head to Lacey. "While she's yours to cherish."

Lacey's face filled with color. Saxon looked at her, and then down.

Madame waved Lacey over and grabbed her elbow; with a sharp tug, she brought Lacey's face level with hers and whispered, "Say hello to Nathy for me."

Lacey raised an eyebrow. "*Who?*"

Madame released her. "You'll surely see."

"Brilliant," Lacey said; she drew her arm back delicately.

"Thank you, Madame," Saxon said. He grabbed Lacey's hands and pulled her close. "We should get back. I still say those tea leaves promised me an unforgettable night."

IO

CASTING STONES

-The Eastern-

THEY EXITED MADAME San Clair's shop, Lacey's shoulders slumping as they started down the pavement.

"I don't see any carriages," she said.

"Right," Saxon said. "The hired carriages don't usually come this way."

"Oh." It was the perfect punctuation to a ruined night. The festival had been a dull, depressing show of power; Madame San Clair was merely an eccentric hack; and she still couldn't get the feeling out of her gut that everybody was keeping something important from her.

"I can call for my driver," Saxon said, drawing his wand. He spoke unfamiliar words and aimed his wand skyward. Blue strands of light shot from the wand, travelling west, back toward the city.

"Neat trick," Lacey said.

"Don't sound so miserable," Saxon said, smiling. "The night's not over yet."

The words had hardly left his mouth when the many nocturnes crowding the street began moving as one in the opposite direction as Lacey and Saxon, battering them away. Saxon grabbed her hand, tugging her close to keep them together.

"What the hell?" he said.

"Look." Lacey pulled away from him, pushing against the surging crowd. Watchmen stood only ten feet away, grabbing nocturnes at random and shoving them to the ground. Their swords were drawn, sweeping across the crowd and herding them down the street. Houses along the street smoked, flames curling from their bases and rapidly crawling higher.

"Hey!" Lacey ran toward them, Saxon calling after her to stop. "What's going on?"

The Watchmen's eyes landed on her. The one nearest her grinned.

"Well. Looks like she found us."

Lacey stilled. "You were looking for me?"

"Lacey!" Saxon grabbed her around the waist and dragged her backwards. "We need to go."

"Stop them," the Watchman said calmly, and his men advanced.

Lacey and Saxon ran, darting down random streets as they appeared. The Watchmen's footsteps echoed close behind.

"Saxon," Lacey said between hard breaths, "we can't outrun Elonni."

"Right." Saxon drew his wand and grabbed her hand.

"Oh, no. You're not—"

He pointed the wand at his own chest. A dark vortex spread across the front of his shirt, rapidly engulfing his body. As it swirled around his hand, still grasping hers, a deep cold spread from Lacey's fingers throughout her whole body, until she, too, was drawn into the endless black.

There was a sensation of nonexistence, a cold unreality, and then, like breaking through the surface of a cold lake, Lacey woke on her back, air rushing her lungs. The gas lamps of the streets warped in her vision, bending into the sky and swirling together with the stars. She blinked hard.

"You idiot!" She sat up to find Saxon lying beside her, groaning and holding his stomach. "You can barely stun someone and you try a teleportation spell? You could have rearranged our organs!"

"I think I might have." He rolled to his side and vomited across the street.

Lacey checked her body over. Everything seemed to be in its correct place. Saxon sat up, pale but in one piece.

They had landed in a quiet, empty ally, amidst rubbish bins and stinking sacks of garbage. Saxon had actually done it. Wherever they were, there was no sign of a single Watchman. Only the pluming smoke roiling in the sky indicated they might be close to where they started.

Lacey got to her feet and loomed over Saxon, still panting on the ground. "Get up."

"Give me a minute."

"Why are the Watchmen after me?"

"How would I know?"

"I think you do."

He glanced up at her. "Don't give me so much credit."

"Don't treat *me* like I'm stupid. The second you saw them, you knew I needed to run. Why? What would they want with me?"

He struggled to his feet at last. A thin sheen of sweat still coated his skin, and his eyes were bright as though with fever. "Believe me, I don't know."

She stared at him, unblinking.

"But," he said, "I do know that Dr. Poole only brought you to the capital to escape. He meant to take you out of Gryfel entirely. But then the Elderon suspended travel. I guess we know why now."

"*I* don't know why."

"They're after you. And no matter the reason, you don't want to be captured. The Elderon aren't much interested in the truth."

"It doesn't make sense," she said, shaking her head. "I'm nobody."

"Evidentially not." Their eyes locked, blue on green, and Lacey had the brief and irrational desire to kiss him there, amidst the garbage piles, beneath the smoking sky.

"We should go," he said.

Lacey nodded and followed him down the narrow back alleys. He ducked down unmarked streets with ease, moving through the slums like he'd lived there all his life.

"You sure know your way around," Lacey said.

"I— It's easy to navigate. The city is a grid."

"It really isn't." She smirked. "You're hiding something."

"I told you what I know."

"I meant about yourself. What are you trying so hard to keep from me?"

"You're free to guess."

"Okay. Your favorite brothel is nearby?"

He grinned over his shoulder. "Do I look like I pay for sex?"

"Arrogant."

"Factual."

He held up a hand to stop her as a group of nocturnes ran past on an adjoining road; one of them smashed off the end of a beer bottle and brandished the jagged glass, checking up and down the street. Once their footsteps died, Saxon said, "Two more guesses."

"You sell your magic on the black market."

He paused and cocked his head. "Good one, but no."

"How about you just tell me?" She stood in front of him. "Secrets are annoying."

"Most people don't want to know bad things."

"I do. You know, if you don't tell me, I'm just going to assume you're the West Street Ripper."

He sighed. "Fine. That works for me." He stepped around her and walked on.

Lacey followed after, skirting a mysterious puddle of something thick and dark—blood?

"Looks like the Watchmen have been this way."

Saxon nodded but kept his eyes trained on the path ahead.

"If I'm the one they're after, why would they attack so many people?"

"Do you need to ask?" Saxon said, his voice defeated. "A lot of Elonni don't even think the Alliance should exist. Nocturnes outside of it...they're basically prey."

Lacey's power screamed beneath her skin. If there were only something she could do—if she wasn't one person, if she wasn't weakened by her human blood... She imagined snapping the Watchmen's bones, seeing *their* blood on the muddy streets.

"Bloody hell." Saxon held out a hand to stop her. Farther down the street, a company of Watchmen marched, seven of them. The Watchman at the front looked right at them. He waved his men forward.

"Run," Lacey said. "Come on, Saxon, what are you doing?" She tugged against his arm, but he wouldn't budge.

"You were right before; we can't outrun them." He took out his wand. "Get to the forest. Don't stop for anything."

"What are you—" But her words died beneath his lips. The kiss was light, brief, but sufficient to stun Lacey long enough for Saxon to aim his wand at her heart. The same black vortex that had dragged them into nothingness swallowed her body once more.

"S-Saxon!" What was he doing? He was being left behind, and she was—

She landed hard on her side and scrambled up, surprised she hadn't been disintegrated by another go through the vortex. She glanced around, finding herself in a cramped street, looming thatch-roofed buildings stretching above her.

One of the building's doors, blank but for a note pinned to its front—*At your wit's end? Come on in*—swung open, and a lank figure leaned in the open space. Lacey went cold.

"Hey there, baby girl," the white-haired fairy said.

Lacey turned and ran, but his footsteps were fast on hers. Lacey pushed herself as hard as she could. But it wasn't enough—she was disoriented, weak, sickness twisting in her stomach. The teleportation must have affected her the way it had Saxon.

But she couldn't let the fairy catch her. She didn't want to imagine what he would do.

"*Hallas Elroi.*"

Her wings burst from her back, light made solid, feathers fluttering like fallen stars. She caught the air, but it was too late. The fairy snatched her ankle, and the suddenness of the stop sent her pitching forward; her limbs screamed in protest as she twisted in his grip and fell facedown.

Her hands found something hot and sticky on the road: A puddle of blood, running like rivers through the cobblestones, bore a single, slippery handprint in its center. She shook as she stared at the deep ruby mess running down her wrist and wished insanely that it were her own.

The fairy pinned her, his knee digging into her spine. He leaned in close; his breath was vile, chemical and smoky, against her cheek. He snapped his jaws in her ear and she flinched.

He laughed loudly. "You scared, baby girl?" He shoved a cloth over her mouth, pressing hard, forcing her lips apart. The vile taste of the fabric coated her tongue, and something else, something acidic and dizzying.

She twisted against him, but her body seemed to drain. Her muscles stiffened, then stalled. Her eyes flickered.

"Don't fight it," the fairy said. "It's less painful that way."

Though frozen, she was still aware—terribly, terribly aware. Panic pulsed inside her but found no outlet. She could do nothing as the fairy wrapped a gag around her mouth and jerked her hands behind her back, binding them.

He turned her on her back and put his lips to her ear. "I'm Neill, by the way."

SAXON HIT THE ground hard. A boot made contact with his ribs. He clenched his teeth to hold back a gasp of pain, but it still hissed though. The Watchman who had thrown him kicked him again, this time flipping him on his back.

"Aw, look who it is. The warlock *Ally*."

Through pain-blurred vision Saxon made out the smarmy face of the Watchman from the checkpoint. His burly partner stood by. Five other Watchmen loomed behind them, chuckling.

"Seven to one," Saxon said. "Need a hand holding to beat up on one bloke?"

The Watchman punched him, barely missing Saxon's nose. The earth turned to mush beneath him.

"Good punch, lad." Saxon grinned, though he tasted metal and the stars danced above his head. In the sky the two moons split into four, then back to two.

"Get up, nocturne."

Saxon rose, trying to control his shaking limbs. "You seem to take particular issue with me. Did I sleep with your sister or something?"

The Watchman colored.

"I did, didn't I? Sorry, mate, it happens. Elonni girls, y'know?"

The burly Watchman put a hand on his partner's shoulder before he could lunge forward. The five others all had a hand on their weapons, ready to draw swords. Saxon leaned against the alley wall for support.

"Mind if I smoke?" He didn't wait for an answer. What he really wanted—what he needed—was a hit of bane. Mindless, multicolored ecstasy, a world both within and without, everything knifing through his defenses.

No. What he needed was to get to Lacey. He'd sent her tumbling to Wit's End—closest to escape, but closer still to danger. But how to get away...?

"Look. Gents. I know how this works." Saxon pinched the cigarette between his lips and dug out his wallet. He threw it to the burly Watchman, who scowled.

"You think this is about money, nocturne?" the slim Watchman said. "Things are changing for your kind. The Alliance won't last much longer. Pretty soon you won't be able to throw around your daddy's money. You're done."

Saxon exhaled smoke. "First I've heard of it."

"We don't have to listen to you anymore," the Watchman continued. "In fact, just to drive the point home..." He grinned at the other Watchmen. "Anyone else want to take a stab at Saxon St. Luke?"

The sound of steel—the Watchmen drew swords and knives. The burly one pocketed Saxon's wallet with a grin and cracked his knuckles.

"Right. Well—" Saxon reached into his coat pocket, but paused as the slim Watchman spoke again.

"Use that wand and the girl gets worse."

Saxon's hand clenched around the wand. "What?"

"We know where you sent her. Wit's End, right? Your favorite midnight haunt." The Watchman laughed. "We already have men going after her. But what condition she's in when she gets to Haylock depends on you."

Saxon's voice shook. "What do you want?"

"Nothing. There's nothing left to take from you." He twisted his knife in his hand. "Except that pretty face."

"You can't kill me," Saxon said.

"No. But nobody said we had to bring you back in one piece."

Saxon dropped the cigarette and ground it into the cobblestones. "Do what you want to me. But if you hurt Lacey—"

"You'll kill us?" The Watchman smirked.

Saxon met his eyes. "I can think of something better."

"Sounds good. Farus?"

The burly Watchman lumbered forward and grabbed Saxon by the hair, tossed him to the cobblestones. He felt the initial punches, the kicks to his ribs—cold steel and hot blood. They used the broad sides of their swords and beat him till tears lined his coat and cuts crisscrossed his skin. After a while, the pain seemed to fade, to become only an echo of the first injuries.

"That's enough."

The gang of Watchmen wobbled in dual image before Saxon's eyes. A new Elonni broke the group up with an impatient wave. A blunt, square face, warped like an old window, stared down at him. Saxon started to sit up, but the newcomer's hand on his upper arm brought him to his feet.

"C-Commander Lately." The slim Watchman coughed. "We—we—we—"

"Shut it," Commander Lately said. "I've had a long night." He tightened his grip on Saxon's arm. "You." He wrenched Saxon's face toward his. "You're Saxon St. Luke, yeah?"

Saxon wiped a thick clot of blood from his nose. "Can I help you?"

The Commander smirked. "You and your father have been up to some unsavory business, haven't you?"

Saxon grabbed his wand, but his hopes died when he found it broken in two, joined by mere splinters.

"No need, mate," the Commander said. "I'm only here to help."

"What do you want?"

The Commander's smile widened. "Tell me: Have you ever seen inside Haylock?"

Saxon's blood chilled. He shook his head, mute.

"Didn't think so." The Commander dragged him toward a carriage parked farther down the street. "But I think you'll find it rather educational."

II

THE ACCUSED

D R. POOLE CHECKED his pocket watch, scowling at the crawling minute hand that told him it was half past eight. He'd arrived at the palace early, hoping to find Lacey already there, ready to go. Her meager belongings waited in his auto. Piers was ready to take them away, anywhere they could go to escape.

He figured they'd drive south to Geshun, or north to Mondberg. They'd leave in a fishing vessel if they had to. They'd sail to the Ridge, or Iymar, or the fucking Endlands if it came to it.

He'd explain everything, finally, once they were safe. He'd promise to go back for Aeyrin, promise her life would be different, promise anything, as long as she was all right.

Whatever Will had done, Poole wouldn't betray his word. He would protect Lacey.

The festival wound down around him. Many of the elite had left in the carriages, probably to watch that despicable freak show out in the forest. Stragglers hung by the food stalls and silly games set up throughout the streets. Live music, all brashly patriotic songs, rose from Palace Circus and beyond. Smoke rose from the effigies dotted throughout the squares.

Poole checked his watch again. Another cursed minute had passed.

"Absolom Poole?"

He looked up. Three Watchmen stood before him, their crisp red uniforms like gashes against the pale city behind them.

"Can I help you?" he said.

"You need to come with us."

"Sorry, gents, I'm waiting for someone."

The Watchman who had spoken shook his head. "It wasn't a request."

"Tell Albion that whatever he's playing at, I haven't got the time for it." Poole turned to leave them behind, but the Watchman grabbed his elbow.

"I didn't want to have to say it," he said, "but you're under arrest, professor."

IT DIDN'T BODE well that the carriage rode north, then east, uphill, toward Gamault Castle. Once the home of the old royal family, it now served as the seat of judgment, imprisonment, and sometimes execution for criminals deemed too important to toss into Haylock. Its white turrets and fluttering banner loomed at the highest point above the city, visible to anyone who dared glance its way.

Poole held up his manacled wrists to the Watchman sitting across from him. "Is this really necessary?"

"Chancellor's orders."

"What am I meant to have done?" Poole smirked. "Was he offended by my latest book?"

"I wouldn't take this lightly if I were you."

The carriage stopped at the castle walls to allow the dark, spiked gate to rise for them. Those spikes had, over five hundred years ago, sported the heads of traitors and enemies to the realm, grinning at any who entered the royals' sacred space.

The Elderon had at least introduced some civility into punishments, if civility was keeping barbarism behind closed doors.

The carriage halted in the courtyard, and the Watchman guided Poole out. He hoped—really hoped—he wouldn't be taken straight to one of the castle's many imposing towers. Or Redlawn.

"Let's go." The Watchman dragged him forward through the courtyard. The place had a haunted feel, the castle's many old artefacts still lying out, rusted, rotted, forgotten. A wheelbarrow lay broken by the entrance to the great kitchens. Scattered tools remained where they had fallen, dropped by the hands of servants when the revolutionaries first broke through the castle walls. Poole couldn't help but think, as he crossed over the worn cobbles of the courtyard, of the many feet that had trod here once before. Not merely royals, but every person within the walls who had served them.

They'd all been annihilated when the Elderon took control.

The Watchmen pulled him through a door leading into the castle, up a grand flight of stairs, and at last into the great hall. Once the dining room of kings and queens, it now stood bare of its trappings. The many tapestries that would once have adorned its walls had been stripped and burned; its precious silverware smelted into weaponry for the new military.

The only thing that remained was a great wooden table in the center of the room. It gleamed with varnish and was lit by many spindly candles placed at intervals. The weak tremble of flame cast dark masks upon the faces of the four men around the table. Demonic, callous. Fitting.

"Gentlemen," Poole said. "What can I help you with?"

"Have a seat," Chancellor Crane said. He looked gaunt, thin. His wispy white hair fell across his forehead, drawing attention to the balding patch at the top of his head. He dismissed the Watchman with a wave. "So, Absolom. You have a lot to explain, I should think."

"If this is about my book," Poole said, "Inspector Law himself submitted it to the censors. Though he did restrict it."

Law, seated farthest from the Chancellor, met Poole's eyes briefly through the darkness. There might have been sorrow in the look, or maybe simple resignation. He looked down as the Chancellor continued.

"We know what you've been up to. You wanted to flee the realm entirely, is that correct?"

"No," Poole said. "I was planning an extended vacation."

"With your goddaughter."

Poole's head snapped up.

"Yes, we know about her. A simple farmgirl, it would seem, from Hollow's Edge. However did you come to be responsible for such a lowly child?"

Poole said nothing; they already knew, and now came the toying.

"Ah." Crane nodded solemnly. "I remember now. You were dear friends with her father."

With that, Justice Bromley pushed a thick folder down the table. It stopped inches from Poole's hand, clenched on the table.

"What's this?" he said.

"Open it."

Poole flipped the cover back. A photograph fluttered and then resettled on the pages. He picked it up.

Will's eyes were narrowed, his mouth locked in a sneer. They must have used a binding spell to hold him still for the photo. The strain in his eyes, the rage in his clenched jaw, brought the whole of Poole's old friend back to life, if only for a moment.

"William Barker," Justice Bromley said. "Know him, Absolom?"

"We went to university together." Poole tossed the photo down onto the table. "We were friends, once. We drifted apart."

"Then how did you come to be godfather to his only child?" Crane asked, tipping his head in mock confusion.

"The falling out came later. And I have a feeling you already know why."

"Forgive my pretense, Absolom. I just wanted to hear it from you. So, you were aware that William had joined the Cult of the Nine?"

"He told me himself."

"And your reaction to this was...?"

"I told him he was a fool. That he'd get his family killed if he didn't stop. I think he agreed. He left them. His wife and daughter were destitute. I helped them as much as I could, until his wife remarried."

"If she's since remarried," Father Priestley said in his high, floaty voice, "why are you still involved in their lives?"

"Aeyrin was my friend as much as Will was. Don't get the wrong idea, Father." Poole smirked.

"It's hardly a laughing matter, Absolom," Crane said, rising from the table. "You know the history of this place, yes?"

Poole scanned the great, sweeping room, its cold stone walls dense with age. "It's not in my wheelhouse, but sure, I know enough."

Crane nodded. "Our people fought a corrupt monarchy that would spread dangerous ideas across the land. Our powers, our very purity was at stake."

"Right." Poole shoved the parchment away. "Are we done here? So far you've only accused my dead friend of a crime. I don't see what I'm doing here."

"You're here," Bromley said, preening in his black robes, "because you knew."

"I knew *what?*"

Crane came around the table and loomed above Poole, though, frail and small as he was, the effect was more sorry-looking than anything.

"You knew her father possessed the royals' curse. You knew he was descended from the Ruined Queen. And you know that his daughter carries the same ability, hidden in her very blood."

Blood drained from Poole's face, leaving him cold. They couldn't know. He'd done everything. He'd gotten Lacey new papers, he'd hidden her far away, he'd had Sebastian—

Sebastian.

"Who told you this little story, hm?"

As if on cue, the great hall's doors flew open, and a woman dressed in a crisp red suit walked in. She was tall, beautiful, with a cruel smile twisting her ruby lips. Her honey-gold hair fell in a long braid over one shoulder.

"Well, Dr. Absolom Poole in the flesh! I'm so glad I could finally meet you. I've read all your books." She offered her hand, which he shook, unsure. "I'm so sorry if my husband's little confession had caused you trouble."

"So. You're Delilah."

"He told you about me? How sweet of him." She looked to Crane, her smile fixed, her eyes blinking. "Well? Are we ready?"

Crane nodded and retook his seat at the table. Justice Bromley rose now.

"Absolom Poole, you are hereby sentenced to house arrest, to serve this sentence until such a time as Lacey Barker can be proved innocent or guilty. Should we determine the girl is in fact of royal blood, you will be put to death as a traitor to the realm."

"House arrest?" It seemed too light, too easy. What made them think he couldn't just—

"Oh," Delilah said, catching his chin in her hand and turning his face to hers. "If you're thinking you might escape...that's what I'm here for."

She drew a slender white wand from the jacket of her suit and tapped it once against his forehead. Pain split his skull, crawling across every nerve until his entire body was a study in agony. He fell from the chair, clutching at his head, screams tearing free no matter how he tried to hold them down.

"Any time you leave your house," Delilah said cheerfully, "*that* happens. You should get home, Absolom. It's going to be a long ride."

12

THE ASSASSIN

-Middle Wood-

THE CAMPFIRE GLOWED like an earthbound star. Its deep orange was the exact color of an evening sun. Nathy sat in the hard, icy grass, sore, exhausted, bleeding, and chained to a tree.

Ruark's giant fumbled around, caging the freaks and girls; they regarded Nathy with something like fear. He winked halfheartedly, and the two-headed witch nodded one head. The other head looked away with a curl of her lip.

Other giants disassembled the tent. Ruark paced around like an animal and shouted orders between mumbled curses.

"Ruin *my* show."

"I said I was sorry," Nathy intoned.

Ruark kicked his face. "You're starting to piss me off."

"Then kill me."

Ruark aimed the sword—Nathy's sword—at his right eye. "You're looking a little asymmetrical, kiddo. How about a matching scar?"

"How's that?" Nathy eyed the bloody stain on Ruark's shirt where the demon-bone blade had pierced him. "A little achy? Feeling feverish?"

Ruark smirked. "Never better, mutt."

"Really? Because I was under the impression demon bone was poisonous to Elonni." Nathy leaned forward as far as his chains would allow him. "I think if I wasn't chained up, if I had a shot at you, you'd be too weak to defend yourself."

Ruark moved the tip of the sword to rest in the hollow of Nathy's throat. "Thing is, you are chained up."

"And mysteriously, still living."

"Don't think I'm doing you a favor, kiddo. I need something from you. Once I get it, I'll be dropping your body at Flynn's door. Just like your little girlfriend."

Nathy jerked against the chains, but it only made Ruark laugh. He moved the blade from Nathy's throat to his mangled wing.

"She cried when she lost. When I put the knife to her throat." He stuck the point of the blade into Nathy's wing, deeper with every word. "Course, you can't kill someone that pretty without having a little fun first."

The scorching pain in his wing was nothing, not even a whisper, to the agony in his heart.

"You know," Ruark said, "I almost think she liked that part." He ripped the blade out, sprinkling droplets of Nathy's blood on the grass.

"I'm going to tear you apart," Nathy said, his voice coarse with pain and rage.

"You keep saying that. But who's chained to a tree here?" He chucked Nathy under the chin. "I'll be back, kiddo. We've got a long journey ahead of us."

Nathy slumped against his chains and gritted his teeth. Despite the agony in his broken wing, he drew them in, letting them dissipate and absorbing the pain into his very core. It was a kind of torture, but he smiled.

Without his wings, the chains loosened against his arms.

SENSE BEGAN TO return to Lacey's limbs, but she didn't move. Her wings remained out, drooped with paralysis. She lay in a cart, staring at the moons. The gag in her mouth tasted sour, of other people's saliva and sweat and fear. A cacophony of chaos rumbled around her, stamping footsteps, clattering metal and wood. A man shouting again and again. The cart jerked to a stop, and Neill came around to stand above her. He smiled.

"Hey, baby girl. Got a surprise for you."

He wrested her from the cart and threw her on the ground. Her vision took a moment to focus, but when her eyes finally adjusted, she found herself staring up at a thin, dark-haired man with a curling mustache. She had only seen him in caricature, but still she recognized him. The remains of his show stood behind him: the collapsed tent, the huddled freaks, and six beautiful girls shoved together into a cage.

"Who the hell is this?" Roselyn Ruark said. He stared down at her with mild disgust.

"She's for you," Neill said. "For the right price, of course."

"Elrosh almighty," Ruark said. He rubbed his forehead, pinched the skin there. Blinked rapidly several times like he was hoping Lacey would vanish before his eyes. "Seriously?"

"Pretty, yeah?"

"For God's sake, you bloody idiot, you brought me an *Elonni*?"

"'Course, brother. Wing fetish, it's a whole market, trust me."

Lacey drew her wings into her back and glared.

"Yeah, well," Ruark said, "if you want to explain to the Elderon why I'm peddling an Elonni girl—"

"They'll never know."

"Yeah, sure. Bloody idiot, they know everything, don't they? Look, good for you and everything, but no. You keep this one for yourself."

"Come on, brother, I need the money." Neill gritted his teeth and took a deep breath, kept his voice level. "Look, you're really worried about the Elonni thing, cut her wings off. Sell her as a human or something."

Ruark snorted. "Gods, you're a prick."

"I just need enough to pay my way across the Fortress," Neill said. "One thousand junes and she's yours."

"One *thousand*? For that scrawny twit?"

Neill huffed. "Eight hundred."

"Five."

"Five? For her? Look at her! She'll make you that much in a week!"

Ruark rolled his eyes. "Seven. And you're sawing those wings off yourself. This is a new suit. You try getting blood out of silk."

"Whatever gets me home." Neill smiled and grabbed Lacey's arm. He dragged her forward, toward the wagon. Lacey fought against his grip, and he punched her in the stomach. Her body crumpled at the impact, and the fairy yanked her back up.

"Bad girl," he said.

"Hey," Ruark said. "Bruises don't sell. Mess her up too bad and I'm cutting two hundred off your price."

Chains rattled near the tree line, and Lacey glanced up, blinking against spots of pain. A black-haired man bound to a tree not far from the wagon shifted in his binds as Neill passed by with her. Ruark whipped around.

"Don't move."

"Where am I going?" the man asked, jerking his chin toward the chains.

"Who's that?" Neill asked.

"Some prick."

Lacey was hauled into the showman's wagon. It contained a single bed, a dresser, and a trunk overflowing with stage props. The rest of the space was filled with junk scattered here and there, and Ruark hunted through the mess until he found what he wanted. "Here, do the honors, then piss off." He tossed Neill a long, toothy knife, which the fairy barely caught.

"Now?"

"Yes, now. I've got to get away from here, haven't I?"

Neill looked down at Lacey and shrugged. "Sorry, baby girl."

She muttered through the gag. Neill bent down to pull it away. "What was that?"

"I said, get fucked, you bloody pervert."

"Will do." Neill tugged the gag back up. Lacey kicked at him. He dodged her foot just barely.

"Gods, Neill," Ruark said, "she's a kid, not a dragon."

"Sod off, I'm trying. Hold her down for me."

Ruark rolled his eyes and knelt beside Neill. He gripped Lacey's shoulders and held her fast. Neill swung the knife like a pendulum, a sickened twist to his face.

"All right," he said. "Wings out, baby girl."

Lacey gave him a look which she hoped communicated just how stupid his request was.

"Wings out," he said, holding the blade to her throat, "or I cut something you value more."

"*No scars*," Ruark said. "She's already ginger. Don't make it worse."

Lacey shoved her elbow back as far as it was go, into the showman's ribs. He grunted, but only held her tighter.

"Maybe one scar," Ruark said, pressing his fingernails into her skin. "Just to teach her."

Neill grabbed her face in one dirty hand and pulled her so close their noses touched; his chemical breath in her nostrils made her gag. The knife played at the edge of her throat. "Come on, Lacey. Be a good girl for once."

"Wait." Ruark dragged Lacey back, out of Neill's grip. "What did you call her?"

"Lacey. It's what her boyfriend was calling her, anyway."

Ruark grabbed her chin and twisted her to face him. He pulled the gag away. Lacey tried to bite his finger. "What's your last name, feisty?"

"Piss off," Lacey said.

"I've been getting that a lot lately," the showman said. "It's Barker, isn't it? Lacey Barker?"

Lacey's mouth opened, but no lie came to her rescue. How had he known? Who else was after her tonight?

Ruark laughed. "Elrosh Almighty. Neill. Drop the knife."

Neill instead clutched the hilt tighter. "Why? What, she important or something?"

Ruark rose and, with an impatient sigh, drew a small knife and sunk it into Neill's throat. He dragged the blade across his neck as easily as undoing the buttons of a coat. Blood spattered Lacey's neck and shoulders, each droplet like the point of a hot needle. She watched, open-mouthed, as Neill's body collapsed amongst the scattered junk.

"Sorry about him," Ruark said. He tossed the knife amongst the junk and leaned against a battered dresser. "Lucky he mentioned your name, really."

"Are you...letting me go?"

Ruark laughed once. "Oh no. No, no, no. You're going straight to Patriarch, lovely. Two in one night? Windfall, that."

"Who's Patriarch?"

Ruark shook his head, a cruel smile on his face. "That's not important, sweetheart. I knew your father, you know."

A loud humming overtook her ears, spread through her skull. She had to have misheard. He couldn't really—

"William Barker. Elonni. Looked like you a bit. Fought in the war."

She blinked. "How did you know him? Did you...fight with him?"

He snorted. "Oh, no, sweetheart. We were on opposite sides."

"That's not possible. My dad was Elonni. He fought—"

"With the nocturne. Yeah, he was a regular turncoat, your dad. Caused a bit of trouble." He stooped and tipped her chin up with his forefinger. "Want to know who finally killed him?"

She waited.

The showman grinned. "Me."

She jerked away from his touch. "Shut up."

"I'm not lying. Take it as a compliment. Your dad was so good they needed a Huntsman to do away with him. But once I found him... God, he bled like a stuck pig."

"You're on a roll tonight, Roz."

Ruark's head snapped up. Lacey whirled toward the new voice.

The man who'd been bound to the tree leaned in the doorway, broken chains dangling from his wrists.

"Shit," Ruark said. He grabbed the knife Neill had intended to use on Lacey and swung out. The man caught Ruark's wrist and jerked it. The crunch of bone echoed through the wagon.

"Stay down," the man said as Ruark dropped. The showman screamed through his teeth and clutched his wrist. Thin bone protruded from his flesh.

"I recommend icing that," the man said. He kicked Ruark beneath the chin, knocking him aside.

"Who are you?" Lacey asked wearily.

"Call me Nathy." He bent and retrieved the jagged knife.

Behind Nathy, Roselyn Ruark made to rise. Nathy kicked him back to the floor. "And who're you, kid?" he said.

Lacey looked into his black eyes; they were friendly, somehow. "Lacey. Untie me."

He kneeled beside her and took her bound hands in one of his own, holding her steady as he cut away at the rope. The cold blade nicked her skin and she flinched. "Steady, kid," he said. His breath warmed her neck, strangely pleasant. She stilled as he finished cutting, and at long last her arms fell to her sides. She rubbed the raw, red skin of one wrist. "Thanks."

"You're not all Elonni, are you?"

"What?"

"If you were, you'd have been able to tear right through those ropes."

"I typically *could*," she said. "He drugged me with something." Her eyes landed on Neill's corpse, the white eyes somehow paler without life in them.

"Well, looks like he got his." Nathy glared down at Ruark. "Now, for you."

"I know," Ruark said. "You want your mother's sword."

"Spot on."

"Looks like I've lost this one," the showman said. He reached into his suit pocket for a cigarette case. He lit up and took a long drag. "Fine." He dug through his pocket again and tossed to the floor what looked to be nothing more than a small pouch filled with some loose, powdery substance.

Nathy's eyes narrowed. "What is—"

Ruark tossed his cigarette. Its burning end made contact with the bag.

A sharp blast of sound cut the air, and a scream ripped from Lacey's throat. The showman took off on dark wings, knocking Nathy aside. There was smoke and the smell of gunpowder and, suddenly, fire. Fire spreading and eating the inside of the wagon.

The narrow space was quickly consumed. Lacey registered the heat, her body breaking out in sweat, but there was no pain. Nathy wasn't so lucky. His right trouser leg had caught fire and he fell backward, trying to bat out the flames.

"*Hallas Elroi!*" she shouted, and her wings burst out, throwing flame out around her. She took flight, catching Nathy around the waist, and together they broke through the wagon's thin wall. They landed in the grass, Lacey pinning him down.

"This has to be the best way to be rescued," Nathy said, smirking.

Lacey blushed and scrambled off him. "Come on."

"Stop them!" Ruark shrieked from somewhere behind. Giants lumbered from every corner of the clearing, circling in on them.

"You're Rakashi, right?" Lacey said. "Do magic or something."

"He took my wand." He poked her ruddy wing. "Fly us out of here."

"You're too heavy."

"Rude."

"Cover your ears."

He looked at her like her senses had abandoned her.

"Trust me."

He did as she said.

Lacey shut her eyes and tried to remember the stories Dr. Poole had told her, the prayers she could use if she ever needed her abilities. The Elonni didn't use magic, which was a part of nature, something outside its user. Their power was innate, unwieldy. She hardly ever practiced. She'd only ever really needed to summon her wings before. But now... She needed to remember.

She said a prayer, in a tongue not used in millennia, and as the word fell from her lips, her voice changed. It became sharp, echoed, a note too high and deadly for mortal senses. She had never known the translation of the prayer, and yet as she spoke the ancient word, she understood it, felt its intent in her heart and its power in her throat.

Achan.

Pain.

Nathy winced beside her, plugging his ears against the onslaught. The giants dropped to their knees, holding their heads, bass groans filling the clearing. The sensation of pain crawled from Lacey's voice and rippled in the minds of everyone nearby. It covered the clearing until its every inhabitant screamed.

Lacey opened her eyes. All but Ruark lay collapsed on the forest floor. Panting, clutching his chest, he met her eyes across the clearing.

"You're good," he said. "For a mutt."

She hauled Nathy back to a standing position. He swayed against her, but managed to stay on his feet.

"Thanks," she said, and spread her palm out before her. "*Sanat.*" A burst of energetic light issued from her palm and knocked him into the air. He landed farther off, not unconscious but struggling to rise.

"We need to go." She pulled Nathy along after her, into the thick of the trees. They didn't stop running until Lacey felt they were a safe distance away. All at once, her energy left her. She fell to her knees in the cool grass.

"Uh, kid?"

"I'm fine." Her breaths came out hard and pained. She'd never used so much of her power in one day. And what a day to need it. Aside from the physical tumults, her soul felt drained of everything—hope, happiness. It had all vanished the moment the Watchmen laid eyes on her.

"I'm scared." She was surprised to find she'd spoken aloud. "What...what happens now? Where do I go?" Her fingers dug into the grass, the dirt beneath. It was as though she was holding on to the very surface of the earth, afraid that, too, would vanish beneath her.

"I can get you home," Nathy said. "I might need a minute." He too dropped to the grass beside her and checked his leg. His trousers were burned, but the skin beneath was merely pink from heat, unharmed.

"Huh. I expected worse."

Lacey barely heard him. She shook her head. "I can't go back to Theopolis. The Watchmen are after me."

"You too, huh?" He raised an eyebrow. "Sorry, but you don't look the type to be in trouble with the law."

"I don't know why they want me." Angry tears lined her eyes. She ripped a fistful of grass from the ground. "I didn't *do* anything." She threw the mass of earth; it struck a tree and shattered into clumps.

"You got a name?" Nathy said after a moment.

"Lacey." She sighed. "Lacey Falk-Barker-Underhill."

Nathy stilled beside her. "What?"

"It's a joke," she said lamely. "I usually go by my mother's name, Falk. But my dad's last name was Barker. And my stepfather's is Underhill. So, I don't know."

"Lacey...Barker."

"Yes...?" She eyed him. This was the second time in not even ten minutes that somebody had reacted strangely to her name. He drew a thin piece of cardboard from his back pocket—a playing card, she thought, its back painted with red and green diamonds. He held the card up, looking from its face to her. After a moment, he pocketed it.

"Cute name," he said at last. She sighed, relieved.

"So, what's your story? Why did Ruark have you prisoner?"

"Oh, I'm an assassin. I was hired to kill him."

"Didn't work out?"

"Obviously." He shrugged. "Next time."

"Next time," she repeated. Somehow, the words struck her as absurd. Everything suddenly had the quality of a joke, the sky, the trees, this bloody, scarred man beside her. She laughed, and for the world couldn't stop.

"We need to get you somewhere safe," Nathy said, watching her cautiously. "You need to rest."

She caught her breath, sobering. "Safe. Is that even possible anymore?"

"Here." He got to his feet and offered her a hand up. "I've got an idea."

"I can't trust you," Lacey said. "I don't know you. And so, *so* many people have tried to kill me today."

"Well, I'm all you got. You can go off on your own. I won't stop you. But if you want help..." His hand still hovered, an offering, waiting for her trust.

"I'll probably regret this," she said.

She took his hand.

13

THE ONES YOU LOVE

-*The Eastern*-

THE CARRIAGE STOPPED abruptly, and Saxon, arms bound behind him, fell forward and smacked his head against the opposite seat. When the Commander opened the carriage door, it was to find Saxon groaning, crumpled on the floor.

"Don't be so dramatic," Ryder said. A pleased grin erupted on his face when Saxon sat up and rubbed a throbbing welt just below his hairline.

Saxon got uneasily to his feet. The world felt gelatinous beneath his feet as he stepped out of the carriage—likely an effect of the multiple head wounds the Watchmen had been eager to inflict.

"This way," the Commander said.

Saxon wished he knew where they were going; Ryder hadn't mentioned what this was all about, and he was beginning to suspect the worst. The streets were cluttered with trash and rubble. The air stunk and hit his lungs with a chemical punch, chased by a salty tang. They were in the Eastern, definitely, and near the sea. Which meant...

He'd never seen the building up close, but it was unmistakable. It looked more like a fortress than a prison, huge and towering and black. Turrets scraped the sky and blank, cracked windows stared across the dead lawn and courtyard. The place was enclosed by a thin metal fence rattling in the wind, topped with barbs.

Haylock. Saxon stepped back, but the Commander gripped his elbow, keeping him in place.

The guards at Haylock's doors opened them and gestured Saxon and the Commander into the weak light and heavy rabble. Saxon blinked and, as his eyes adjusted, the chaos took on a recognizable form: Dozens of nocturnes chained to benches, awaiting lockdown. Holding cells stuffed to capacity. The stink of shit and sweat clogged Saxon's nostrils as he was pushed further into the wide room.

"God, what is all this?" the Commander muttered. "Hey." He snapped his fingers at a passing Watchman. "What are all these nocturnes doing here?"

"You...ordered their arrest, sir."

"I also said you could kill anyone who resisted."

"Sorry, sir. It was rough out there. We were trying to control—"

Ryder waved him off. "Fix it. This place is a mess." He grabbed Saxon's arm and dragged him through the large receiving room, to a wide staircase leading up to higher floors. Barred cells lined the walls on the second and third floors, each one crowded with three or four nocturnes each.

"We haven't had high-profile prisoners since the war," Ryder said absently.

Saxon's blood chilled. "Who do you have now?"

Ryder mounted the steps to the fourth floor and threw a grin over his shoulder. "You'll see."

The cells on this floor were behind heavy metal doors, only a small barred window allowing a glimpse of the pathetic lives within. Screams echoed down the corridor; sorry mutterings bled through the doors. Haylock's most violent prisoners must live up here—the future victims, no doubt, of Sebastian's latest binding potion.

"Let's see," Ryder said, walking down the long corridor, smiling despite the heavy atmosphere. "I think it's...this one." He stopped at a door, no different than the rest, and nodded toward the window. Saxon walked forward cautiously and peered through the narrow bars.

A man with neatly cropped silver hair lay on his side, his fine suit at odds with the dirty floor, the sunken cot, and the waste bucket in the corner. He lifted his head at the sounds outside his door. Blue eyes, identical to Saxon's own, stared out from a pale, sweaty face.

"Dad?" Saxon scrabbled for a doorknob but found none. "Dad!" He whirled on Ryder. "Let him out. What the hell is this?"

"He'll serve a short sentence," Ryder said. "As long as he continues to cooperate."

"Cooperate with what?"

"Saxon!"

The voice carried an accent of the maternal, yet dragged with the husk of champagne-room whispers. He'd know it anywhere. Saxon turned toward his mother, like a ray of light through a magnifying glass: long, slender, and on course. Her murky blond curls were braided and knotted in a twist behind her head. She was dressed in a rose-colored suit, its skirt hugging at her hips. Her face, girlish in the smile but foxlike in the eyes, wore an expression of strangled kindness as she regarded her son.

She gasped delicately when her eyes landed on his bruised face, though her eyes gave away how little she really cared. "Darling, what happened?"

"Beat to shit by Watchmen," he said. "How're you?"

"Oh, fine, fine." With a flinch, she pulled him into a hug. She was tall herself, but she still had to pull him down for the embrace, and she clung to his neck like a millstone.

He detached himself indelicately. "Mum, what's going on? Why is Dad in there?"

"Oh, by the goddess, now look at your hair; when was the last time it was cut?"

"*Mum.* Honestly?"

"Sorry, no, this isn't the time." She grabbed his hands and looked up into his face; her eyes were the color of raw earth. "Dear, it's time to cooperate."

"What does that mean?"

"It means we need to go with Commander Lately and answer all his questions."

"And what about Dad? You're just going to let him rot in prison?"

She gave him a long, cruel look. "Saxon, someday you'll realize the whole world can be a prison." She brightened without missing a beat and turned to the Commander. "We're at your disposal."

"Great." He jerked his head toward the stairs. "We can do this in my office."

127

"Come along now, ducky." Delilah said, bustling down the corridor. Saxon hung back, staring into his father's cell. He looked so wrecked, so completely broken in that dank little space—a space perhaps once occupied by a nocturne whose mind Sebastian had helped destroy.

Irony was an utter bitch.

"Sweetheart?" His mother's voice like sugar and butter. Too much of a good thing.

He followed her up the stairs. Ryder let them into his office, an expansive stone room with a roaring fire and old news clippings from public executions framed on the walls. Some were—charmingly—illustrated. Saxon stared at an image of a warlock tied to a stake, burning.

"Tell me what this is about," Saxon said. "I've had a long day and I'd like to go home."

"Okay," Ryder said, flopping into the chair behind his expansive desk and kicking his feet up. "Along with your father, we've arrested your professor, Absolom Poole."

Saxon was grateful there were no chairs for guests. Otherwise, he would have collapsed into one, and the Commander, he figured, would have enjoyed that. "Why is that?" he said, forcing calm into his voice.

"I thought you might be able to tell me. Poole has been bringing his goddaughter to your father every year, right? And your father gave her a potion each time. Tell me about that."

"I don't know what you think I know."

Ryder grabbed something off his desk and tossed it to Saxon. "Tell me what that is."

Saxon looked down at the vial in his hand, the green liquid gleaming within. "A binding potion."

"And what does that do?"

Saxon sighed. "It inhibits a nocturne's magical ability for a period of time. Depending on the strength, its effects could last for over a year."

"Now, why would your father be dosing a sweet little country bumpkin with that?" Ryder shrugged. "See, I'm lost. I've checked Lacey Barker's papers over and over, and all I see is a human mother and an Elonni father. No magic blood."

"I don't know," Saxon said, wrapping his fingers around the vial. "They wouldn't tell me. I realized they were giving her the potion only the last time she was here."

"How'd you figure it out?"

Saxon rubbed his thumb along the murky glass of the vial, letting his focus drain into that single, pointless action. "There was another potion. For memory. I guess they didn't want her to remember taking the binding potion, so they'd wipe her memories of the last day or so. I...noticed she'd forgotten...things. After going to Hayven."

"You noticed she'd lost her memories?" Ryder smirked. "Of what?"

"That's really none of your business." Saxon tossed the vial back to the Commander.

"How cute. You and the mutt." Ryder grinned. "How was she?"

"Piss off." Saxon turned toward the door, but he'd forgotten about his mother. She stood in his way, arms crossed, her wand resting in her hand.

"The Commander isn't finished with his questions, dear."

"I don't particularly care, Mother."

Delilah St. Luke put on a good show of matronly decorum, but Saxon had been raised by the woman. That gilded sweetness covered every violent turn of mood until it didn't, and just now, she seemed about to crack.

"Saxon Raighne St. Luke, I am *not* in the mood for your antics."

"My antics?" Saxon coughed back a laugh.

She came so close to him that she had to crane her head back to look up at him, her small, thin mouth twitching. "Saxon, your father has nearly ruined this family with his stupidity. Everything we've worked so hard for, he threw away on that stupid girl and her foolish godfather. I will not let you do the same."

"You're the one who's sacrificed *this family* for your own selfish reasons," he said quietly.

She slapped him. Saxon flinched, not so much from the strike as from the shock of it. Delilah had resorted to cruelty before, but never publicly, where someone could see her unhinged.

She blinked and rearranged her expression into one of patient sympathy. "I know your feelings are all mixed up, dear. It's perfectly understandable. But this is serious. Don't think of the—of Lacey for a moment. Think of what's best for you." She took his hand in hers. "Don't give your heart away, sweetheart."

Saxon laughed, sharply, madly. His mother's smile was a spindly glasswork in the fingers of a careless child. One wrong move.

"What's so funny, dear?"

"That's rich. Give my bloody heart away..." He shook his head. "I'm going now. Bye, Mum."

She sighed. "I didn't want to do this." She tapped her wand once against his chest, right above his heart.

Icy pain seized him, stilling his heart. He fell to the stone floor, trying to suck in air, but his lungs, too, seemed to have stopped working. Delilah watched him squirm a moment, then flicked her wand. All at once, the agony left his body, leaving him empty and chilled.

Ryder let his legs down and leaned forward in his chair. "Let's wrap this up, shall we?"

Saxon struggled to his feet, glaring between his mother and the Commander. "I told you what I know."

"And now I'll tell you what we know," Ryder said. "Lacey is dangerous. Her godfather hid her from us. Her papers are forgeries. In fact, she was never registered when she was born."

"Why?" Saxon said, his throat still raw from the spell.

"Because this"—he slapped a folder on his desk—"was her father."

Saxon stepped forward and picked up the folder's top sheet. It listed the details of a William Barker. Elonni. Only thirty-two at his death. A veteran of the War of Teeth. And...

Defected to werewolf and vampire armies. Member: Cult of the Nine. Alias: Monarch.

"Seems fitting we'd uncover this all today," Ryder said. "I assume you know the story. Of the Ruined Queen and her cult."

Saxon nodded, his eyes still fixed on the parchment. Her father was a turncoat, a cult member. But Lacey couldn't know. What could she have to do with this?

"Some nocturnes," Ryder continued, "like to say that the queen's heir survived the revolution. That the child lived in secret and its descendants might still live today."

"Yeah," Saxon said, numb. "But it's just a story."

"No. It's not." Ryder nodded to the parchment in Saxon's hand. "William Barker is a descendant of the Ruined Queen. And so is his daughter."

"So? The monarchy fell ages ago. You can't really be scared of one descendant."

"But you must know the stories of the Ruined Queen's powers? What she did to earn that name?"

Saxon shook his head. "Impossible. It's just drivel."

"We happen to know it's not. William Barker proved that for us." Ryder met Saxon's eyes directly now. "Lacey's powers, if unleashed, could destroy the entire realm. It's an ability too great for one person. We need to bring her in. Contain her."

"Contain her? Isn't that what my father's potions were doing, then? Seems like he's done your job for you."

"This isn't something we can leave up to a mere potion. She's too dangerous." Ryder shrugged. "Problem is, she's most likely on nocturne land by now. She has rights to the protection of the Dark Guard. We can't bring her in without starting a war."

"Well, that's what you lot do best, isn't it? You want her in Haylock?" Saxon said, suddenly and strangely calm. "Do it yourselves."

"They don't want to hurt her, Saxon," Delilah said. "Isn't that right, Commander?"

He nodded. "We have a solution. In fact, it's your father's most recent iteration of his binding potion."

Saxon remembered the dark green liquid, the power within that single flask. It could do more than bind abilities—it could annihilate them.

"She'll get a chance to be normal," Ryder said. "We'll always have to observe her, of course. But she could live in the city as an Elonni. She could go to university, get a job. Get married." The Commander smirked.

"As of right now, however," he continued, "she's vulnerable to be used by the same people who got her father killed. The Cult of the Nine won't stop until they possess her.

They've been hunting her all these years. And they've found her."

Saxon's jaw clenched. "How do you know?"

"We've received a report from the Huntsman we had on her case. She was seen being taken into the forest by..." Ryder shuffled through a few sheets of parchment on his desk. "This man."

He pushed the parchment forward. A photograph of the sort taken upon entrance into Haylock rested on top. Saxon picked it up, his hands shaking.

"Nathy," he said.

"Ah. You know him."

"We used to be schoolmates," Saxon said. The smirking face in the photograph sent bolts of anger pulsing through Saxon's blood. The shaggy hair, the broken nose, that goddamn scar.

"She's with *him*?"

"As of our last report," Ryder said. "We have reason to believe this Nathy character was hired by the Nine to collect Lacey and bring her in. Of course, we don't know where he would have taken her."

"I do." Saxon curled his fist around the photo. "What do you need me to do?"

"Go get her, if you can. Convince her to leave nocturne territory. We can take it from there, once she's back safely. And if you need to hear it again, I'll say it: No harm will come to her."

"Great." He threw the crumpled photo onto the desk and turned.

"Where exactly are you going?" Delilah asked.

"Fryer's Grove," Saxon said. "It's the only place he'd take her."

SAXON DIDN'T STOP until he was outside the prison, in the cool reason of night once more. He was surrounded by the music of traffic and footfalls, of alarms singing a song of danger, of war: the staccato beat of panic and energy. Saxon glanced up, his gaze on the moons, like eyes watching the world, both locked behind clouds of ash and smoke.

Saxon leaned against the prison wall, breathing deep. Time passed, he didn't know how much. He felt the packet of bane inside of his coat like a nagging tap on the shoulder.

"Sweetheart...?" Delilah's voice was a siren song, a soft lie. She joined him on the pavement. "I know how hard this is for you, darling. But you're doing the right thing."

He lit up a cigarette. Delilah's sweetness melted.

"You're *smoking* again?"

He exhaled a gray breath. "That's hardly the worst thing I do."

14

SANCTUARY

-Middle Wood-

LACEY HARDLY SPOKE as Nathy led the way through the forest, shoving aside low-hanging branches and overstepping brambles. He looked back every now and then to ensure she still followed him. Shock, or maybe sorrow, had rendered her mute, and her silence was the last thing he needed. It gave too large a stage for the voices in his own head.

He'd failed, being the idiot that he was, and failing a job once meant it was a distinct possibility in the future. Maybe it was a fluke—but worst case, he was forming a habit. He'd let his rage ruin everything. Isobel was captured, Ruark had escaped. Surely the showman from here on out would only become more cautious.

Revenge is a boy's game.

He ought to let it go. Isobel might be right. But if revenge was a boy's game, complacency was a coward's excuse, forgiveness an idiot's last play. Artemis and his mother were dead—that meant Ruark had to die. He didn't want this merely for the thrill of spilling Ruark's blood. He wanted to recalibrate the world. Right now, it was unbalanced by Ruark's living breath. One arrow through the heart could tip the scales and set them right.

"That's it."

Nathy turned. He'd almost forgotten Lacey walked behind him. She stopped now, balancing against a tree, and undid the laces on her shoes—small, spiky heels that were now coated with dirt and leaves. She pulled them off and threw each in turn into the forest.

"You all right back there?" Nathy said.

"They were uncomfortable."

"Yeah, so's stepping on twigs and poisonous plants."

She ignored him, grabbing the skirts of her blue dress and tearing it at the knees.

Nathy blinked. "Uh...this is weird."

She threw the fabric aside. "Better."

He shook himself from a mild daze. "Well, if you're going to strip, you won't hear me complaining."

"Pervert."

"You're the one ripping your clothes off."

She rolled her eyes. "I could have left you to Ruark, you know."

"I could say the same thing, kid." He chucked her under the chin. "So let's just say we're even."

"Let's also not talk." She stalked past him, faster now without the hem of her dress dragging against the brambles.

"Hold up." He caught up and walked alongside her. "Do you know where you're going?"

"Didn't we agree on silence?"

"If you insist." He tapped his finger to her lips. She slapped it away, but when she opened her mouth to tell him off, no sound came out. She punched his arm, mouthing curses at him.

"Why, thank you," Nathy said, popping the collar of his suit jacket. "I do look killer in black."

She punched him again.

"All right, all right." He waved his hand, and with that, the spell released.

"How did you do that? Your wand is gone."

"Good warlocks don't need a wand." He shrugged. "Not for simple spells. But now that you mention it..." He eyed the trees above and snapped off a sizable twig from a high bough. He bent and tugged a small blade from a sheath at his ankle and began whittling at the wood.

"You can just make a new one?"

"The power comes from the wood itself. It's the earth that holds the power. It just lets us borrow it."

"My godfather says it's a natural force, like magnetism."

He made his face very still and serious. "Magnets are magic, too. Didn't anyone tell you?"

Lacey rolled her eyes. "I like you even less now."

"That's what they all say at first."

They trekked alongside each other in silence, Nathy carving the wand into a shape that felt right, inscribing small, careful symbols along the handle. It wouldn't be perfect until he could offer it in ritual, but he thought it would fire a few simple spells until then.

"You're not paying attention to where we're going," Lacey said after a while.

"I know where we're going."

"Is *Nature* guiding you?" she asked, and promptly tripped on a root sticking out of the ground.

"She is me." He offered a hand to her, but she pushed herself up on her own.

"I'm going to die out here," she said matter-of-factly. "I'm going to be eaten by wolves, and my bones won't be found for centuries. They'll put me in a museum. I wonder what they'll call the display...?"

"Lacey?"

"What?"

"There's a town right there."

She turned to where he pointed. The forest dissolved just beyond into a green park bordered ahead by a street. A little town of stone lay before them, shops and homes squished together in grey squalor. In the center of the town, above the brutish little buildings rose a church spire.

"Merciful Elrosh, thank you." She ran ahead of him, out of the trees. "Come on. I have an idea."

"Great..."

THEY WOUND THROUGH the narrow, cobbled streets of the town. Mercifully, there seemed to be peace here, no Watchmen out hunting, no nocturnes running for safety. The town slept; the houses sat quiet. Lacey envied the silence as her own life dissolved in turmoil.

"What town is this?" Lacey asked, keeping her sight always on the growing church spire.

"Mourdon, probably." He stuck close to her. "We're not far from Theopolis. Don't let your guard down."

"We won't have to worry about that long." The buildings fell away, leaving a wide square courtyard leading up to the chapel. Lacey ran across the flagstones, up steps buffed by the feet of many faithful masses. The chapel door was locked, so she banged upon it.

"Sanctuary! Sanctuary!"

"What the hell are you doing?" Nathy said, coming up behind her on the steps.

"They have to let us stay here," she said, and banged again. "*Sanctuary!*"

"Right. Some priest is just going to let us sleep in the nave, *not* alert the Watchmen, maybe give us a nice breakfast when we're in the mood?"

She whirled on him with a thin glare. "According to the law—"

"A very old law." Nathy shoved his hands in his pockets and checked the silent streets before turning back to her, his voice lowered. "The old monarchy let sanctuary slide, but the Elderon? I don't think Priestley wants criminals sleeping in his churches."

Lacey knew he was on to something, but she had to hope, to believe that these old buildings still meant safety for the lost. She needed the damn door to—

A groan that rocked the night sounded as the door peeled back against the stone landing. A thin, pale face peered out, that of a young man no older than Lacey. He held out a candle and pushed frameless spectacles up his nose.

"Can I...help you?" he said. He was dressed in a simple gray robe, belted with a rope. A monk.

Lacey beamed. "Yes, thank you. We'd like to invoke the sacred statute of sanctuary."

The monk blinked.

Nathy stepped up. "She means we'd like to sleep on your floor. And I wouldn't mind a drink."

"Are you criminals?" the monk asked.

"No," Lacey said.

"Well, yes," Nathy said.

Lacey shoved her elbow into his ribs. "I've been mistaken for a criminal. And *he's*—well." She cleared her throat. "Please, we've been through absolute hell—er, sorry. We've had an awful night."

"Well." The monk toyed with his spectacles again. "I suppose I can't turn you away, can I? Elrosh extends mercy to all."

"See, that's how to run a religion." Nathy clapped the monk on the shoulder and pushed in ahead of him. "Drinks by the altar, yeah?"

"Please don't!" The monk turned worried eyes to Lacey. "He's not serious?"

She bit her lip, wincing. "He...might be."

"WE CAN'T OFFER much," the monk said, leading them down the nave. The chapel wasn't as elaborate as the cathedrals in Theopolis, but it still contained that quiet, old beauty of an ancient place of worship. Lacey stared up at the sculpted stone saints watching from above the altar, their blank eyes holding neither judgment nor mercy. Above them bloomed a huge painting of Elrosh, sword in hand, conquering the Lesser Gods, who fell toward earth and scattered to their regions. The style was old, clumsy, like the millennia-old tapestries Lacey had seen in museums.

Thin, tapered windows let in moonlight across the rough stone floor, illuminating the bumps and cracks all along the nave. Only a few pews stood to either side.

The monk led them to the altar, where a wooden pulpit stood directly beneath the painting and the statues.

"I must first ask you confess your sins before Elrosh."

Nathy eyed the many statues lined up high above. "And...which one's he?"

The monk sighed. "The painting?"

"Ah. Got it."

"But you don't confess to an image." The monk set the candle aside on the pulpit and clasped his hands together. "Elrosh is everywhere, is everything. Prayer should be humble, fervent—"

"And then can we sleep?"

"Nathy," Lacey said between clenched teeth. She was starting to wish she'd left him to die in the wagon after all.

"You don't have faith. That's all right." The monk smiled. "Elrosh brought you here, though. He's obviously sought you out. Please. Kneel."

Lacey did, ready for sleep as much as Nathy but happier to jump through this last hoop. She was used to churches, though far humbler than this one. Nathy had yet to kneel; his eyes remained upon the painting, eyeing not Elrosh, but one of the gods beneath his sword.

"Nathy."

At the sound of her voice, he looked down, nodded, and kneeled beside her. The monk knelt with them and began a slow, quiet prayer of confession. They followed along, their voices amplified in the huge space. Only the steady guttering of the candle flame joined their halfhearted confessions.

"There." The monk nodded once the prayers were concluded. "I'll find you some blankets. You can sleep in the quire tonight."

As soon as he'd walked off, Lacey turned to Nathy. "Who were you looking at up there?"

He smirked. "That sword. Think he was trying to let everyone know the size of his—"

"You're disgusting."

"What?"

"We're in a chapel."

"You're religious?"

"No, but it's still...sacred, isn't it?"

"Only if you make it so."

Lacey narrowed her eyes. "He's been hospitable. At least try to show some respect."

Nathy's smirk faltered. He jerked his head toward the far end of the painting. "I was looking at her. Lye."

Lacey's eyes trailed to the edge of the painting, where a beautiful woman with black hair and brown skin lay with her hands thrown out, her face averted from the light exuding from the Elonni god.

"She's ours," Nathy said, rising from the stone floor. "And the painting's wrong. Nobody's defeated her yet."

Lacey opened her mouth, then shut it. Finally, she said, "I suppose it's not easy to see that."

"The Elonni can paint whatever makes them feel better," he said. "Doesn't make it true."

"Here we are." The monk returned, carrying two bundled blankets and limp pillows. "Quire's this way. Follow me."

They did, skirting around the pulpit, into a narrow open room lined on either side with tiered benches, each place marked by an unlit candle. The monk laid out the blankets and pillows, some distance apart, between the two rows of benches.

"I never got your name," Lacey said.

"Oh." The monk looked down. "I gave up my given name when I joined the order."

Lacey smiled, bemused. "Then what should I call you?"

"Um. Monk will suffice."

"I can't just call you *monk*."

A faint smile flashed before humbly disappearing. "I used to be Alastair."

"Alastair? That's a lovely name."

"Yes. Well. Sleep well. Um, please don't...get to close. Er, you're not...married, are you?"

"Oh, gods no," Lacey said.

Nathy had already laid down beneath his blanket and seemed to be fast asleep.

"He's rather too boorish," she said quietly.

"Heard that," Nathy said.

Lacey rolled her eyes, then smiled at Alastair. "Thank you for this. Really, you've saved us."

Alastair went a little pale at that. "I suppose you're welcome, then."

Lacey settled beneath her thin blankets, startling when Nathy scooted closer and stuck a flask beneath her nose.

Lacey's blood drained. "You stole the *sacrament*?" she hissed.

He took a swig. "Tastes like wine if you ask me."

"*What is wrong with you?*"

He took another hearty swallow of wine, shrugged.

She snatched the flask away. "I'm putting this back."

"I'll get it." He took out his newly carved wand and lifted the bottle, floating it across the quire and back to the altar. "Better?"

"Go back to your side of the floor."

"Don't you think we should cuddle for warmth?"

"*Move.*"

He did, but still his voice floated across the space. "You really don't know why the Watchmen came after you?"

"No." She lay down and turned away from him.

"Probably better if you don't, huh?"

She tugged the blanket farther up her shoulder and didn't respond. There was nothing to say.

15

RECKONING

-Mourdon-

THE CHAPEL WALLS filled with the echoing bass of the door's banging. Lacey awoke, a film of drool stuck to her cheek. She pawed at it, bleary eyed, the sharp stone outline of the chapel and the dark rows of rectory seats insensible to her mind. They blurred like an unfamiliar dreamscape. Wasn't she supposed to be at Dr. Poole's house? When had she...?

A hand clamped down on her shoulder. "This can't be good."

Nathy. And with the remembrance of him came the rushed memories of all that had gone wrong the night before.

"Maybe it's just other people...like us," she said around a choked yawn.

Nathy hauled her up without further reply.

"Yes?" Alastair's voice, though soft, travelled the length of the nave and slipped into the quire.

"Morning, Brother. We're looking for two criminals, might have come this way. We've reason to think they're travelling together."

A brief silence followed what could only have been the voice of a Watchman. Nathy jerked his head farther into the chapel, toward an elaborate altar.

Lacey shook her head, mouthed, "Alastair."

Nathy blinked.

"We can't just leave him," she said, she hoped too softly for the Watchmen to hear.

"We *could*."

"Yes, sir, they came by," Alastair said.

"Prick," Nathy muttered.

"They've sought sanctuary here, however. I'm afraid I can't allow you to take them."

142

The Watchmen—two of them, it seemed—laughed. "We can't convince you to make this simple?"

"They're allowed forty days to set their affairs in order. After that our local bishop will gladly take them before Father Priestley, but until—"

"Young man," the Watchman cut in. "Let me explain. You're harboring the two most dangerous criminals currently loose in the whole of Gryfel. We're not going without them."

Alastair turned at this, looked back. Lacey wasn't sure he could see her, but he jerked his head, subtly. *Run.*

He looked back at the Watchmen, still blocked from entry. "I first serve the laws of Elrosh, then those of the Chancellor. In rare cases when they are not aligned—"

"We don't have time for this."

And with that, the Watchman shoved Alastair aside. The monk toppled onto the hard nave floor with a surprised yelp. Five more Watchmen streamed in after the original two. The apparent leader pointed to Alastair.

"Detain the monk."

A Watchman grabbed Alastair by the hood of his robe, holding him like a cat by its scruff. Alastair scrabbled at the neck of his robe, his face twisting and going a shade paler.

"We can go through the catacombs," Nathy said.

Lacey ripped away from him. "Not without Alastair."

Nathy opened his mouth, eyes flashing. Lacey reached for his pocket and produced his wand.

"You're a warlock. Help me out and we can go."

"Unbelievable." But he didn't argue. As two Watchmen advanced behind the pulpit, crying, "They're here! Back here!" Nathy aimed his wand and spoke a few words that threw the Watchmen back. They crashed into the pulpit, which, with another word from Nathy, snapped in two. The top half gave with a groan and slid, landing at last upon the Watchmen.

Lacey stared, openmouthed. "I didn't say *kill them.*"

"Oops." Nathy ran toward the nave. The remaining five Watchmen converged, war in their eyes.

Lacey clasped her hands, whispered *"Hallas Elroi,"* and felt as the power deep in her core rushed out and around, lifting her, giving an ethereal air to her body and substance to the long ruddy wings forming like clouds at her back.

She flew forward.

The Watchmen were in flight, too, landing at intervals to launch attacks at Nathy. For his part he dodged, sweeping across the floor with an agility the Watchmen seemingly had not counted on. He caught sight of Lacey, and a small smile flashed before he spun and launched a spell at a Watchman, who took the blast full force. He collapsed to the floor of the nave, motionless.

Lacey flew between the Watchmen. She knew only a few prayers with any power behind them, but there was a simple one she had used in her youth to spur on stubborn goats.

"*Fasis*," she whispered.

A gust of air coiled down her arm and spiraled into the chest of a Watchman flying toward Nathy. He tumbled from his flight and crashed upon the floor. She only hoped his helmet spared his head.

The lead Watchman flew past Lacey, his wing knocking into her. She tumbled through the air, catching herself before she hit the ground. But she hadn't been his true target. While Nathy launched spells at the other Watchmen, the leader hovered in the air, brought his hands together.

"*Sannas capti avon!*"

Nathy swirled toward the Watchman, who twirled a golden strand of light like a length of rope. Anñanym danced around the cord, swirling and ephemeral, before the whip was spread to strike, snaking toward Nathy.

Nathy stowed his wand. "*Hallas Elroi!*"

Black wings bloomed like a sudden flight of birds from Nathy's back, as a dark light coursed around him, beating back the cord of light. It dissolved on the air, dissipating in a blast of sparks.

The leader of the Watchmen landed, his eyes glazed but steady as he regarded Nathy.

"So. You're Fairborn's kid."

Nathy's left wing twitched, struggling to stay up. Lacey flew close, landed beside him.

"You forgot to mention that," she said.

"Didn't seem relevant." His face twisted, either in concentration or pain, Lacey wasn't sure. Had he been injured? But—no. His left wing was utterly destroyed, feathers bent and mangled, the bone arched all wrong. A fresh wound still bled, shining on the black feathers like oil.

At once, Madame San Clair's voice echoed in Lacey's memory: *Seek the boy with the broken wing.*

She'd been meant to find him.

She glanced around at the fallen Watchmen. All but two remained standing, the leader, and the one holding Alastair, whose eyes darted from his leader to Nathy's black wingspan.

"You can't run forever," the lead Watchman said, even as he made further distance between himself and Nathy.

"It's worked so far. Let our friend go."

The Watchman holding Alastair didn't wait for orders from his leader, simply dropped Alastair to the ground and backed toward the door.

"Thanks." Nathy strode forward and pulled Alastair up by the hood of his robe.

"Excuse *me*," Alastair muttered.

The Watchman cast one final look toward Lacey. "She's all we want, you know. Why not hand her over and we'll leave you alone, mutt?"

"Door's behind you," Nathy said, and, with a flourish of his wand, sent the Watchman flying backward. The door slammed seemingly on its own.

A long silence stretched before Alastair turned to Lacey. "When you said you needed sanctuary, you—"

"I know," Lacey said. "But honestly, how were we supposed to explain that?"

Alastair shook his head. "Why are they after you?"

"I don't know. I really don't."

"And you?" He eyed Nathy.

"I'm always in someone's crosshairs. Why not the Elderon's?"

Alastair sighed, glancing around the chapel. His eyes popped at the row of statues beneath the painting. "You've broken the statue of St. Seralt!"

"He's fine." Nathy strolled across the nave, plucked up a dismembered stone head. "It'll balance up there nicely. Lacey?"

"Why don't *you* fly up there? You're an Elonni after all."

He stared at her, unblinking, and she realized—his wing was mangled to uselessness, a ruined length of feathers and skin merely holding him down.

She winced. "Right. Sorry."

Nathy let the stone head drop, eliciting a gasp from Alastair. "We should leave."

"Yes, you should," Alastair huffed.

"You too, monk. I don't leave witnesses."

Alastair snorted. "I'm not going anywhere with *you*."

Nathy pinched the bridge of his nose. "See, when I say, 'I don't leave witnesses,' that can go two ways. Get it?"

"Nathy!" Lacey said.

Alastair shook his head. "I can't leave my assignment. I'll be excommunicated. My family will...oh, Elrosh, they're going to disown me anyway, aren't they?"

"That's the spirit." Nathy cracked his knuckles and glanced around the chapel. He plucked a few lit candles, placed in vigil beside a portrait of Elrosh, and dripped their wax along the floor in a circle.

"Oh, no," Alastair said. "He's drawing unholy symbols. In my chapel."

"He also drank the sacrament," Lacey said. Alastair ran his hands down his face.

Nathy set the candles aside and unsheathed his small knife. "Gather round, kids."

Lacey and Alastair approached with considerable caution. Nathy dragged the knife across his palm, then clenched his fist around the blossoming blood.

"Once this portal opens, we've got about a minute to get through."

"You're making a portal," Lacey said.

"Yeah?" He held his bloody palm above the wax symbols. The wax seemed to drink the blood, growing dark with it. The floor groaned, then cracked, the stone floor crumbling away and leaving an endless, windy black in its place.

Lacey, at last, exploded. "*Why didn't you do this when we were in that goddamn forest?*"

"Because I've never done it before." He fixed Alastair with a twisted smile. "And I prefer to test it first."

146

He grabbed the monk by the front of his robes and tossed him into the swirling void. Alastair's scream cut out abruptly as soon as his head disappeared beneath the vortex.

Lacey looked from the twisting void to Nathy, who looked on in admiration. "You're a bloody lunatic!"

"Granted," Nathy said. "Well, I don't see any dismembered body parts." He hooked his arm around Lacey's waist. "So. Let's go."

He tilted backward into the portal, dragging Lacey in with him.

16

THE LION AND THE LAMB

-Hollows Edge-

JONAS ROSE BEFORE the sun, as always, and as always, Aeyrin pretended to sleep on. She listened for the thud of her husband's boots on the creaky floor, the slam of the door. When he was gone, she rose and walked to the window. Their small, pitiful farm lay before her, a bony territory stretching out below.

Aeyrin never wanted this. The farm. The stink of flesh and waste on the air. The white sky and dead ground.

She grew up here. The white thorn tree in the front yard was the first tree she ever climbed, the one she retreated to with her books and her imagination when her little sisters were playing too loud or crying about nothing. She would sit up there and pretend the thickest branch was the neck of a dragon, and she was riding across the sky.

It was where she went when her parents told her she would marry the boy down the lane. Where she was sitting when she decided to run away. She had collected change in a tin since she was a little girl—as if she always knew the day would come when she would need to pay her way out of Hollows Edge. She'd used that money to buy a train ticket to Theopolis. She was only fifteen—old enough, by law, to marry, but far too young to face the world alone.

She'd lived in the Eastern, and her odd jobs barely paid. Her tin of money began to seem a fortune. She never expected her life to change while she wiped down tables in a rowdy tavern.

"Hey gorgeous, come here often?"

Absolom. The bright spot, the riot. Always casting Will in shadow and, like a shadow, Will never left his side.

She remembered the first smile Will ever gave her, maybe because they would become so rare. His face was a study in agony, even then, even while ribbing his best friend. *"Ignore him. He hasn't yet learned the meaning of overcompensation."*

"At least I can spell it."

Absolom had, predictably, floated away to some other corner of the bar, to some other girl. But Will stayed. Even at their inception, in that first instant of their acquaintance, when the events of Aeyrin's life were still a pinpoint of unexpressed energy and circumstance about to explode, Will had needed her. He was reserved, damaged. Maybe that's what Aeyrin liked about him.

She hadn't known, then, of course. That the darkness was deeper than loneliness. She couldn't have known what he would become.

The sun began to rise, spilling blood across the snow and through the bedroom window. It cast a broken geometry of light on the floor. She pressed her forehead to the cool glass of the window and tried not to think of everyone she'd lost.

Even Lacey was gone now. She'd have a better life; Aeyrin had to believe that. But gods... Between Will and Absolom, she thought she'd known loss.

Nothing compared to saying goodbye to her daughter.

She left the window and dressed in trousers and a wool shirt; the day's work called, no matter how she wished to ignore it. Doing something would distract her, at least.

PINK DAYLIGHT FADED to purple night as Aeyrin marched back from the marshes, three bundles of firewood hung over her shoulder. The day had been blessedly dull, and she'd managed to avoid Jonas for most of it, too. Perhaps she could manage this life. She pictured Lacey, headed off across the sea, and smiled. She was safe. She might see the world. That was all that mattered.

She trudged through the heavy fall of snow, sinking up to her knees as she pressed her way across the lane and toward their property. She thought of summer, of Theopolis, how the city was humid and warm and the ocean scattered salt across the air.

She opened the gate, stepped into their yard and paused, informed by some imprecise extra sense that told her blood something was wrong. She crept through the yard, and the rising moon highlighted prints in the snow. The disturbed snow tracked toward the house. Her blood seemed to stop its reliable flow, reaching neither heart nor brain. The door was open, just a sliver.

She plunged through the heavy snow and stopped just before the door, letting the firewood drop. She pushed it farther open and let the twilight fall on the kitchen floor.

Dressed in his work clothes, with his shotgun by his crumpled body, lay Jonas, dead in his still-pooling blood, working its way through a hole in his chest like oil from the ground.

Aeyrin dropped to his side and shook him uselessly, not knowing what she hoped to accomplish. A detached, clinical corner of her mind noted he had died recently: The blood was fresh and death hadn't sucked the malleability from his muscle; his body was soft with life only recently vacated. Aeyrin scrambled back and nearly fell, the soles of her boots slick.

She ran to the barn and stopped in the doorway, struck by the pungency of manure and blood mingling. Their five cows all lay dead in their cubbies, their throats and stomachs slit. The absence of clucking chickens from the coop next door hinted that the birds, too, were slaughtered.

She turned, panic twisting her vision and making her world unsure. She ran into the yard.

"There you are."

Arms encircled her waist and lifted her off the ground. Her scream scattered across the acres of untended land, never to be heard by anyone but this monster now pinning her to the snow.

He wore the red uniform of a Watchman, and even now, with his hands gripping her throat and his cold eyes staring down, she couldn't believe he would hurt her.

"Sorry, ma'am," he said, a smile on his lips.

Aeyrin kicked out, landing a blow to his groin. He jerked off her just enough that she managed to scramble up and break into a run. Behind her, the Watchman struggled against the heavy snow, his shiny boots slipping.

Aeyrin turned her eyes back to where she was going—as though driven by some childish instinct, she was on course for the white thorn tree, her old escape. But what she saw drew her short.

The shade of a man leaned against the tree. She felt his eyes locked on her body—but he didn't come toward her. The Watchman drew closer; Aeyrin leaped suddenly to the side, skidding into the snow. The Watchman spun to face her.

"This is just pathetic," he said. "You can't outrun me. Please, let's just make this easy, hm?"

Aeyrin watched in silence as the shadow detached itself from the tree and moved toward the Watchman, its steps unhurried, yet purposeful. The sound of metal carved the night, and the rising moon glinted off a drawn blade.

The dying light caught the shadow, revealing neat gray hair, a tall, lean build. The man stepped up behind the Watchman and drew his blade across his neck.

Red speckled the snow, then drenched it. The Watchman's head tilted back, farther, farther, and then *off*. It hit the snow with a muffled thump.

"I can't stand men like that," the stranger said. "There's no call to treat a lady in such a ghastly manner."

Aeyrin stared at the severed head. She swore its eyes still blinked.

"Ma'am?" The stranger held out a hand; Aeyrin took it habitually, numb to everything except the new feeling of unreality throwing the yard into violent twists and jerks. She wobbled on her feet.

"Steady." The stranger put his hands on her arms, holding her up. "I'm sorry about your husband. I wasn't in time to save him."

"I didn't like him," she said, and couldn't believe she had. How cold it seemed. And yet in the face of such incredible distress, the truth seemed to pour out. Shock perhaps was stronger than the finest wine.

"Nonetheless, it must have startled you to see him so."

"What's happening?" Aeyrin said. "Why...that Watchman...why would he...?"

They must have realized. After all these years of quiet and safety, they must have figured out who Aeyrin was. Rather, who her husband was.

The stranger squeezed her arms, bringing her back to the moment. "I'm afraid you're no longer safe here. Go to Theopolis. Find Absolom."

She shook her head, fully waking from her shock now. "*What?* How do you know Absolom?"

"And give him this," the stranger said, pressing a small, parchment-wrapped box into her hand.

"I can't...I can't go to Theopolis. They'll know who I am; they'll arrest me."

"Here." He handed her a coin purse, heavy with fare for her passage. "Don't concern yourself with being recognized, Aeyrin. I'll see to it you arrive safely."

"You know who I am?"

He merely nodded.

"Then who are *you*?" She stared up at him. He was older, probably in his sixties, with a pleasant yet unremarkable face. Still, she felt she knew him from somewhere. It was his eyes, their deep intensity, that teased her memory.

"That's not for you to know," the stranger said.

She shoved the coin purse back into his hand. "Then I can't trust you."

"You seem to have little other choice. I'm a friend. That's all you need to know." He stepped back, giving her space. "Leave before the sun rises. The Elderon will soon realize you're still alive."

With that, he crossed the yard and stepped beyond the gate. Too soon he slipped out of the moonlight and vanished down the path into town.

Aeyrin walked with detached calm to the house and shut the door behind her. Her heart beat a rhythm of distress as she rummaged through drawers for a candle and match.

When the small fire snapped to life, she shone the candle around the room. She couldn't look at Jonas. He was a brute and an idiot, but he'd never harmed her. He didn't deserve this, to be shot by his own bullets.

Her eyes were forcibly drawn to him nonetheless, to what she hadn't noticed before: Words inscribed with his blood, writ large across the floor.

To end the Ruin.

She dropped the candle and it was snuffed out.

17

FRYER'S GROVE

HE PORTAL LET them out into a cold, wet world. Nathy's throat filled with the burn of rushing water, his lungs pressed tight in an airless ache. He flailed about a moment and then kicked, propelling himself and Lacey to the faint blue light above. They broke the surface into the bony winter air. Lacey gagged on a mouthful of the stale, leaf-strewn water.

It was warmer here, though a chill soaked into Nathy's skin as he pulled himself and then Lacey over the mouth of a well, into an overgrown garden.

Trees rose up around them, heavy with moss under the bright white glow of the moons, terrible with secrets. A faint misting rain fell, as it almost always did, and beneath the gentle sound grumbled distant waves hitting the cliffs just beyond a withered apple grove.

They stood in a small, ruined garden, choked with weeds and dead vegetable plants. The well's water rippled, calming after its disturbance. An old voice, as if spoken only in memory, whispered on the wind.

You're back.

Chilled, Nathy stepped away from the well.

"What have you done? Where am I?"

Nathy looked down. The monk sat curled against the side of the well, pale and shaking.

"Oh, good, you made it."

The monk looked up and said, miserably, "Why did you bring me here?"

"I needed to test the portal."

Lacey squeezed water from her long hair. "Where is *here*, anyway?"

"Fryer's Grove," Nathy said.

"Which is where?" Alastair demanded.

"Nearest town is Bishop's Hole."

Lacey and Alastair exchanged startled looks. "That's on the other side of the realm!" Lacey said.

"Look who knows her geography."

"What was the point of bringing us here?" she demanded. "I need to get back. Dr. Poole will be looking for me."

"Yes," Alastair said, rising. "And I need to get back to Mourdon."

"In time. It's the middle of the night." Nathy feigned a yawn. "I need sleep."

Lacey stared at him. "You're a crazy person, aren't you?"

He didn't answer, but looked back at the tilting black-brick house leaning slightly toward the groves. The windows were dark but for one on the fifth floor. A candle burned at the latticed window as though in welcome.

A face appeared in the window, and after a moment a girl threw the latch up and leaned out.

"*Nathy?!*"

"Hi," he said wearily.

The girl crawled out, grasped the growth of ivy by her window, and descended like a spider down the side of the house, landing catlike in the garden. Her pale blue eyes were overlarge in her pinched, slowly prettying face. She'd grown a foot since last he saw her. She must be—he added the years he'd been gone—gods, thirteen now.

She ran across the garden and trapped him in a hug. Her head didn't even come up to his shoulder and rested warmly on the center of his chest. He patted her head. "Um, hi, Alice."

She broke away. "Where have you been?" she said. "It's been years."

"I got a job."

She scowled. "What kind of job?"

"Don't worry about it."

"Who's *she*?" Alice's smile glanced like light off a knife.

"This is Lacey." Nathy reached for Lacey's cold little hand and pulled her closer. She was drenched, hair tangled in her face.

Alice was shorter than Lacey by half a head, but she managed to loom over the newcomer. "Oh, hi," she said.

155

"Hello?" Lacey said.

"What's with the monk?" Alice turned her glare now on the shivering man by the well.

"He threw me through a portal," Alastair said. "I had absolutely no say in—"

"Yeah, yeah, I'll send you back later." Nathy waved him off.

"Wait," Lacey said, lowering her voice so that only Nathy could hear. "What if he tells someone where we've gone?"

"Even if he does," Nathy said, "we're on protected nocturne land. Watchmen show up, the Dark Guard kill them." Nathy smirked over his shoulder at Alastair. "He's the one who needs to worry. Second he gets back, the Watchmen are gonna want to know why he helped us escape."

Alastair paused from ringing out his damp robes and scowled. "I didn't *help* you."

"You did."

"I would never—"

"*Ahem.*" Alice stared at Lacey like a spider to a fly. She dragged her glare away to look up at Nathy. "Are you going to tell me why you've brought these two idiots here?"

"I'm not an *idiot*," Lacey said.

"Shush," Nathy said, then turned back to Alice. "Wake Flynn for me, would you?"

"Okay..." Alice threw Lacey another distrusting look.

"Thanks, Alice." Again Nathy patted her head, and her expression darkened. She turned back to the house and ascended the climbing ivy into her bedroom.

"Who is Flynn?" Lacey asked.

Nathy rubbed at a forming headache, turning back toward the well. Sleep, he just needed sleep and then he'd...

He froze, eyes fixed on the well. A girl with pale, damp hair stood there, her face white, gasping. Blood ran from her neck and chest in long, steady streams. She reached out toward him, mouth peeled wide. Though she made no noise, he knew she was screaming.

He blinked and she was gone, and his eyes went to Lacey. She was staring, too.

"Did you just see that?" she said.

He shook away a shiver and started toward the house. "See what?"

NATHY, REALIZING HE was more hungry than tired, meandered through lightless corridors to the kitchen. He helped himself to a slice of stale bread sitting out on the kitchen table and snuck a bottle of wine from the loose floorboard Flynn hid them beneath. He went down the hall to the parlor, a cozy room with red-papered walls and old furniture. Lacey was half-asleep on the couch and rolled over with an annoyed grunt when he sat by her feet. Candlelight cast her fair coloring into even starker whiteness. He chewed the bread and washed it's stale pulp down with generous swigs of wine.

Lacey stirred and sat up on her elbows. "Give it."

He handed her the bottle. She drank several healthy gulps.

"How about you, monk?" Nathy said. "A little sacrament to calm the nerves?"

Alastair sat by the cold fireplace. He didn't look up or say anything.

Lacey handed back the bottle and rubbed down goosebumps on her arms. Nathy grabbed a blanket off the floor and threw it over her. "You looked cold."

She tugged the blanket up to her shoulders. "For an assassin, you're quite the gentleman."

"You definitely spoke too soon."

She almost smiled. "You'll take us back in the morning. Won't you?"

"Sure," he said, and set the wine bottle on the floor.

Lacey lay back on the couch, the blanket tight around her shoulders. "You'd better."

She seemed to sleep. Nathy sat there, ignoring the twisting in his gut. The familiar atmosphere of Fryer's Grove weighed on him, sickening in its hominess, wrong for its comfort. After the past night, nothing should seem so simple. Isobel was captured. Artemis and his mother were unavenged. And this girl, Lacey...she had no idea...

The silence made every feeling sharper. He looked to Alastair.

"So. You're a monk."

Alastair grunted.

"How's that?"

"It's *fine*."

"Uh-huh. What made you, ah, want to do that?"

"Let's not talk, please."

"Gotcha."

He grabbed the wine again.

"I wondered when you'd be back."

Nathy started at the new voice. Flynn stood in the doorway, smiling. The man was mid-forties, handsome, and striking in coloring: his hair was an unattended disaster, coppery blond transitioning into white, his skin a sun-baked bronze. His eyes were like orange, dancing fires, wide with the look of a mad scientist on the verge of a breakthrough.

Flynn stepped into the room and stopped short. "Oops, didn't realize you were, ah, entertaining."

"I'm not," Nathy said. "They're quite unentertained, in fact."

Lacey, not sleeping after all, kicked him beneath her blanket.

"Ow. Why?" he said.

She curled deeper beneath the blanket.

Alastair rose. "Sir, please, are you in charge here? This madman has kidnapped me."

"Hm." Flynn aimed a hand in Alastair's direction. Fire streamed from his palm, crossing the room in a twisting inferno. Alastair yelped, but the fire missed him, filling the fireplace instead.

"That's better," Flynn said.

"So you're *all* crazy," Alastair said, his voice small.

Flynn shoved his hands into his trouser pockets and turned to Nathy. "I'm surprised you've come back."

"You know why I'm here." Nathy leaned back, unsmiling. "I'll be leaving as soon as I get paid."

"Isobel got you to agree?" Flynn tilted his head, puppylike in his curiosity.

"I wouldn't be here otherwise."

Flynn squeezed onto the couch next to Nathy, blinking swollen, black-bagged eyes. He patted at his pockets,

158

frowning, and extracted from one a miniscule object, which he stared at closely, then offered to Nathy. "Peanut?"

"Er, no."

Flynn held the peanut out to Alastair.

"I'm all right," he said.

Flynn threw the peanut into the fire where it vanished into the flames.

"See you're as stable as ever," Nathy muttered.

"Did you get Ruark?" Flynn asked; his eyes flicked to the fire, to the past.

"No." Nathy looked at the fire and tried to blind his memories with its pure-white after image. "I messed up."

"Where is Isobel?"

"Either Haylock or dead."

Flynn buried his head in his hands, ruffling his hair. "*Nathy.*"

"You're the one who thought to pay me in revenge. Speaking of—where are you going?"

Flynn was already at the door. He turned back. "It's nearly midnight."

"Observant."

"Back in a jiff." He disappeared down the corridor.

"He seems..." Alastair stared at the fire, burning too close. "Strange."

"He was dropped as a child," Nathy said.

Lacey shot up suddenly. "Will you all stop talking? I can't sleep like this."

"Cranky," Nathy said.

Her eyes darkened. "I've truly had just about enough of you."

"I'll be out of your hair soon." Nathy checked the empty doorway. He needed Flynn to get back, so this could be over, so he could find a way to get back to Ruark, to maybe forget this. This, and everything else.

Flynn finally reentered the room, his fiery eyes landing immediately on Lacey. He blinked rapidly, his flame-colored eyes like lights flickering on and off. "Who...how..."

Nathy looked up at him and grinned. "Like I said, pay up."

Flynn's mouth dropped open.

159

Nathy rose, dragging Lacey up with him. "I brought you your Monarch."

LACEY STARED UP at the man leading her down the corridor. Flynn—he was striking with his sun-darkened brown skin, unkempt golden hair with strands of aged ash blond, and his eyes: a strange color, pale orange, like a newly born fire.

Lacey had never seen a Ferno, the fire elementals from Sumri. She wondered why he was here, so far from home, in mage territory.

Flynn turned his head to look back at her, his eyes wide. "Gods, you know, you look just like—tea?"

"I look like tea?"

"Ah, yes, would you like one?"

"Might help keep me awake," Lacey muttered. She looked at Nathy, who walked beside her. "What's going on, exactly? Who is this?"

"Antenor Flynn," Nathy said.

"I don't care about his name. What's he want with me?"

Nathy only shrugged.

"Come in," Flynn said, opening a door at the end of the hallway.

They followed him into a study. Books lay scattered on the floor, apparently fallen from the desk. The curtains covering the windows didn't match, and a sickly green chair bearing a horrible floral pattern sat behind the desk. The two side walls of his office were dominated by bookshelves, packed with heavy tomes and scrolls and jars full of strange things Lacey couldn't identify. Another large jar sat on his windowsill, and inside swam what at first glance appeared to be a regular goldfish. On second glance, Lacey saw it bore great fangs and looked at Flynn with a rather intelligent and suspicious gaze.

Flynn hurried to his desk and started shuffling papers out of the way. "I'll make that tea, or coffee, or..." He took the lid off a teapot sitting on his cluttered desk and peeked inside. "Or essence of Wrycok. It's wonderful for curing headaches. And for killing small rodents. I use it for the former, of course.

Mostly. Anyway," he said without pause, "please sit down...on whatever you find. I seem to have lost my other chair." He looked accusingly at the fish. "And it was a lovely paisley, too."

"That's...too bad," Lacey said.

Flynn turned his attention back to his desk. "Aha! Biscuit?" He held a stale and vaguely green biscuit out to Lacey, who politely declined. Flynn tossed it into the fish's bowl, where it was promptly devoured.

Flynn settled behind his desk in the green floral chair. Lacey found a stack of books to sit on. Nathy leaned against one of the bookshelves, eyeing the room with boredom.

"It's wonderful to finally meet you," Flynn said. "Your father always told me stories, of course. I feel as though I've known you since you were young."

Surprise didn't come, as perhaps it should have. Rather, Lacey sank lower on the stack of books, deflated. "You knew my father, too?"

"Well, yes... Has Nathy not explained...?"

"I was hired to find her, not give her a primer," Nathy said.

"You were also hired to kill Ruark."

"I'm not done with him," Nathy said, his voice unrecognizable in anger. His dry sarcastic tones had been replaced with a deep, low conviction.

Flynn snapped his fingers. "Blast. I forgot the tea."

"Oh, fuck the tea," Lacey said, throwing up her hands. "Just tell me what the hell is going on!"

"Er, right." Flynn cleared his throat. "Lacey Barker. We are the Nine."

She leaned her face into her hand, staring at him. "Okay."

"We're acolytes of the old royal family, and to the Ruined Queen."

"You're a load of nutty monarchists, then?"

Nathy snorted. Lacey hadn't the energy to respond to him.

"Well, no." Flynn listed his head. "I mean, yes. Okay. Let me explain. You've heard the story of the Ruined Queen?"

Lacey thought back to the festival, to the burning effigies. She didn't know much of Theopolis's history. It had never seemed to matter much. She'd only heard snippets of stories, told and retold, becoming less real as time wore them down.

"I dunno. Is she that one that went mad and used dark magic to slaughter her entire court?"

"That's the story you would have heard," Flynn said. "What really happened was this: The last queen of Gryfel, together with eight representatives of the nocturne kinds, acquired a power beyond imagining. She used that power to liberate nocturnes. But the Elonni resistance overcame her. She was killed."

"All right..."

"But she had a child. An heir not only to the throne, but to her power. The child was hidden away and raised by an Elonni family. We've always known one day her descendant would arrive, and we could at last put an end to the Elderon's cruelty."

"And I'm that heir."

Flynn blinked. "Well, yes. Very good."

Lacey rose and brushed down her ruined dress. "You're mental. Bye."

She turned to the door, but Nathy grabbed her by her shoulder. "You're not going anywhere."

"Why, so you can get paid?" She shoved his hand off her. "Try and stop me."

"You don't want to go down that road."

"Please," Flynn said. "Lacey, if you'll allow me to explain—"

"How about *I* explain?" Lacey said, advancing on his desk. "He just grabbed me and brought me here. He's got no idea who I am, and I doubt you do, either. You've got no proof I'm some bloody descendant of some mad queen. I'm nobody. And I'd rather be that than whatever the hell you want me to be."

"Are you sure?" Flynn asked. He put his elbows on his desk and leaned toward her. "Your father always wanted to be something more. I thought you'd have that same fire."

"Stop talking about my father. You don't know a bloody thing about him."

"We were friends, actually," Flynn said. "During the war. We fought alongside one another."

Lacey thought back to what Ruark had told her: Her father had rebelled, had fought with the nocturne kinds. He, too, might have been a liar. But she didn't like the coincidence.

"I'm afraid I ought to confess," Flynn said, ruffling his hair. "I'm the one who told your father who he was—what he was capable of doing."

"Yes, and apparently got him killed."

Flynn's gaze fractured. "Lacey—please, just listen."

She marched to the door, shoving Nathy aside. "Get out of my way."

He didn't try to stop her this time.

18

THE DARK GUARD

-Fryer's Grove-

LACEY RUSHED FROM the office only to be drawn up short by a figure standing in the hallway. A frail-looking man consumed by a large, rain-drenched duster stood before her, smiling placidly. He wore a fedora, shimmering rainbow-black hair like an oil spill spilling from the brim. His face was typical in every respect, handsome, even, but for the fact that it was a raw, ashen color, his veins black and clearly visible beneath his skin, twisting in strange patterns.

"'Ello, there."

"Please, I don't want to meet any more people today," Lacey said. "They've all been awful."

"Don't look so nervous, love," the man said. "I ain't 'ere but to 'elp." He grinned, and Lacey felt the coolness in her blood fade. He seemed...well, less horrible than anyone else she'd encountered that day.

"Name's 'Arry Ryken," the gray-faced man said. He took her hand and kissed it, and Lacey flinched.

"Er, hi. I'm—"

"Lacey Barker. I know. You're already bloody famous, love." He shucked off his duster. He wore a tattered black suit beneath it, and Lacey thought of the undertaker in Hollows Edge. His suit had always been slightly grubby with graveyard dirt, and when he passed by in the village square, he carried the scent of incense and dirt and something sicker, sweeter. Of course, Harry Ryken looked more like the sort of thing going *into* a grave, not the person filling them.

"So," Ryken said. "You're interested in my legal services." He reached into his jacket pocket and produced a much-abused business card. Lacey took it and read: *Harry Ryken, Dark Guard. 1 Undermine Road, You-Know-Where; Bishop's Hole.*

Lacey looked up. "I...don't... Who are you?"

"Member of the Dark Guard. 'S my job to make sure you don't end up back in Elonni custody."

"Oh, no. No. I want to go back. I promise you, they're much less mental than this lot. No offense."

"Ah. See, there's a problem with that." Ryken smiled sympathetically. "If you go back, right now...well, bit complicated, really, but, ah..." He sat scratched at his gray face. "Er, let's say you'll be staying 'ere a while, actually."

"Why...?"

"See, it's like...the Elders—gave 'em a call, awful people, Bromley's a regular cunt, ain't 'e?—and Master Justice 'imself says they've got some funny idea 'bout a potion, like maybe you been takin' somethin'd seal up your 'powers,' their words."

Lacey blinked. "They think...I've got powers."

Ryken nodded.

"Other than my Elonni abilities?"

"Seems so, love."

"What potion are they talking about?"

"Seems your godfather's been takin' you to the Potion Master hisself. Dr. St. Luke's been dosin' you with a binding potion every year since you's a baby." Ryken's eyes were deep black pits, yet Lacey could see sorrow in them as he delivered his next news. "'E's been arrested. Your godfather. And the doctor."

Dr. Poole...he was in the Elderon's hands. He was in danger. He might be... Lacey sank against the wall, sickness clawing at her stomach.

"Suffice it to say," Ryken continued, "if you so much as step foot on Elonni territory, you'll be arrested within an hour. And that's only if they's behind and taking their bloody time."

Lacey felt her mouth hanging open but couldn't seem to close it. "So I really can't go home?"

"Love, you're only safe as long as you's with me. Out 'ere, in nocturne territory."

"Please move."

Ryken stepped aside, allowing her to plow past him down the corridor.

She couldn't—she wouldn't—believe any of this. It was too much, it was impossible. A life couldn't change so drastically in only one night. And if it could—if this was happening...

She could not do this.

LACEY STARED OUT over the grounds of Fryer's Grove, at the gate holding back a mass of thick, close trees, their branches dripping with pine needles. A patch of stony sky held the shadow of the newly risen sun. It was dawn, and she hadn't slept but for that moment on the couch.

The air held the weight of water, and the ground was spongey, as if it rained all night. The trees cried drops of water which gathered in murky black puddles across the pine-strewn ground.

The house itself was barely visible through the thick of greenery. A small, slouching shed stood at the end of the grounds, close by the gate where Lacey stood.

She gripped the bars. Escape. But that had proved impossible. Despite her innate strength, she hadn't managed to break the winding chains keeping the gate shut tight.

Footsteps whispered from the forest, and she looked up. Nathy stood behind her. When she said nothing, he rocked back and forth on his heels, whistling tunelessly. The surrounding woods picked up the rhythm, insects and birds humming along, patternless yet musical.

"Has he paid you?" Lacey asked, mostly to stop him whistling.

"Yeah."

"Congratulations."

He came up beside her. "Look, ultimately, it's still your choice. He can't force you to do anything, let alone believe this crazy story."

"You think it's bollocks, too?"

"If there were heroes to save us, they've been auspiciously absent so far. I'm not about to count on one." He looked at her. "Ask Flynn what, and *who*, he's had to sacrifice just to find you, and you'll see my point."

Lacey's head jerked up. "Have people actually died looking for me?"

"Two that I know of. The last one was executed in your village from what I've heard."

"Oh my God. I was there." She looked across the endless green, cold to her soul. "I witnessed that..."

His blood had stained the snow. He'd been so young. He'd cried out—gods, what had he said? *Long may she live?* Did he mean her? She wanted to sink into the mossy grass, to vanish into the very earth.

"Why would someone die for me?"

"Because they believed Flynn when he told them they would build a better world." Nathy finally looked at her. "But you probably know already you can't change anything."

"Of course I can't. If I had some bloody mythical powers, wouldn't they have shown up by now?"

"You'd think." He shook his head. "I guess there's a ritual?"

"Isn't there always," Lacey muttered. She paused, took a breath. "Who was the other person? The one who...died trying to find me."

"Artemis."

The way he said the name—the pain and loss in those brief syllables—made her heart clench in sympathy. "You knew her?"

His laugh came out dry, broken. "Yeah. You could say that." He shook his head. "Don't feel too bad. She never got around to looking for you. She went straight after Ruark."

"Oh..."

"Yeah. He killed her. Mutilated her. Then left her body on the doorstep." Nathy pointed back toward the house. "Right over there. Her left arm was nearly detached."

"I didn't need to know *that*."

"Yes, you did. Because the same's gonna happen to you if you're stupid enough to join up with Flynn."

"May I remind you, you're the one who brought me here?"

"Right. And I've been paid, so you can plan your escape accordingly." He patted her head. "Good luck, your majesty."

"Don't call me that. And don't pretend you're not responsible for this."

"Yeah. I'll try to find a way to carry on through the guilt."

"You're awful, you know that?"

He shrugged and walked off, waving. "Have a nice life."

"Sod off."

He'd barely made it onto the path back to the house when the gate rattled. Lacey spun toward the sound. A figure hunched against the bars, defeated but rattling at the gate incessantly. Nathy turned and stalked toward the gate before Lacey could move.

"Hey," he said, kicking the bars. "Private property. Move along."

The hunched figure pushed against buckling knees and gripped the bars with shaking hands. *"Nathy."*

Nathy stepped back, less afraid than surprised. "Saxon?"

Lacey ran toward the gate, shoving Nathy aside when she arrived. "S-Saxon? Oh my—how did you—what the hell *happened?*"

He met her eyes with a grin, even as blood flowed from his mouth. "Lace. Long story..."

And then he collapsed.

"TRANSPORTATION SPELLS ARE hard magic," Nathy said.

They stood in a small room within the house used as an infirmary. Several small beds lined one wall. Another consisted of many drawers stacked one on top of the other, each wide enough for a supine body. Lacey tried not to look at those. She picked up Saxon's hand and checked for a pulse at his wrist for the dozenth time.

Nathy, uselessly by Lacey's standards, poked Saxon's forehead a few times. "The longer the distance, the more strain it puts on a body."

"Your portal worked just fine," Lacey said.

"Yeah. That was a *portal*. They link two places and allow you to cross. He's too shit at magic to make one—I'm *assuming*—and so he used a transportation spell. On himself. Like an idiot."

"Oh, shut up." Lacey squeezed Saxon's chilled hand in hers. "Will he be all right?"

"I mean, sure, as long as he reformed properly and his liver isn't where his brain used to be."

"Have I said I hate you?"

Nathy propped his elbows on the bed and smirked at her. "You have, which means my plan is working: Leave 'em wanting more."

"If it turns out I do have amazing powers, the first thing I'm doing is killing you."

"Just how I like it."

"Gods, just stop saying things!" She dropped Saxon's hand. "You're so...*annoying.*"

He opened his mouth. Lacey picked up a scalpel from a nearby medical cart and brandished it.

"*No.*"

"Well, excuse me, princess."

"*I'm not a bloody princess!*"

He raised his hands, defeated. "All right, all right. I'll shut up."

"You can leave while you're at it." She tossed the scalpel back onto the cart. "You've been paid, haven't you? Why are you still here?"

"Interesting turn of events."

Lacey considered him. "How do you know Saxon?"

"Who says I do?"

"You said his name. He said yours. I imagine, therefore, you know each other."

"Ask him, then. If he wakes up, that is." Nathy pushed off the hospital bed. "It's his secret to keep, anyway."

"Where are you going?" she said as he retreated to the door.

"You told me to leave. So long, princess."

Lacey shook her head, rage making her grip unsteady as it held Saxon's cooling hand. The multiple transportation spells may have led to his current state, but he'd been through more than that the past night: His face was purple with bruises, his lower lip swollen, an eye blackened. The Watchmen had evidentially found him and punished him for aiding her.

"Wake up," she told him softly, "and...I'll let you buy me dinner? And I promise I won't laugh at how bad you are with magic anymore." She squeezed his fingers. "You actually saved me last night, so...thank you."

His shoulders twitched a little; his eyelids flickered and squinted as though a nightmare played out behind them.

"Saxon?"

His mouth opened, burbling blood and spit. His chest sank with a hard breath, and in the next second, he was choking on the mess he'd coughed up.

"Saxon! I..." She glanced around the infirmary, at rows of potions and herbs she didn't recognize. She had no idea what do to—she couldn't save him. He'd...

She hit his chest, trying to expel the mess caught in his throat. "Help!" she shouted toward the door. "Nathy! Flynn. Somebody, dammit, he's dying!"

Nathy leaned into the room. "You called?"

"Shut up and help me!"

Flynn pushed past Nathy in the next moment and grabbed a potion without breaking his stride toward the bed. "Prop him up."

Lacey tried, but Saxon's limp body was too heavy. "*Nathy.*"

He sighed, but relieved her of the burden. Flynn pried Saxon's lower jaw down and dumped the contents of the vial down his throat.

"But—he's choking," Lacey said. "How is putting something else down there—"

Saxon sucked in a hard, long breath, then proceeded to vomit across the hospital bed.

"It dissolves organic matter without harming the body," Flynn said, setting aside the empty vial. "Perfect for cases such as these."

Saxon's breathing came hard and scratchy, but he was alive. He glanced at Flynn, his eyes registering mild surprise.

"Who are you?"

"Don't mind me." Flynn patted Saxon on the head. "Our Monarch wanted you alive, so I did as her majesty deems."

"Your...?" He looked, at last, to Lacey. "Oh, thank gods." He tried to rise from bed, but Flynn grabbed his shoulder.

"You'll want to rest. If I understand it, you're an inexperienced warlock who used multiple transportation spells in a single night? Yes, your organs are probably in failure. But—" He clapped his hands together. "I've got just the thing. Sit tight." Flynn went to a cabinet beside the door and rummaged through it, vials and jars clinking in a strange music. He selected a few ingredients and set them aside on a nearby table, humming while he worked.

"Lacey," Saxon said, strained. "Where is—"

"Hi," Nathy said.

Saxon spun in bed to face him. "You."

"Been awhile."

Saxon again tried to scramble from bed, but Nathy easily pushed him back down.

"Save it. It's not a fair fight when you're like this."

Saxon turned back to Lacey, his face tight with anger. "Did he hurt you?"

"No. I mean, he did sort of kidnap me."

"For a good cause," Nathy said.

Lacey shook her head. "It's been a mental day. I'll explain when you're better, all right?"

Fever made Saxon's eyes bright and glittering, his gaze on her more frantic. "No, Lacey, we need to go. These people are dangerous."

"Here we are!" Flynn returned with a mortar and pestle, grinding down some noxious-smelling herbs. "Chew this, then wash it down with a nice cup of elven blood."

Saxon stared at him, unblinking.

"It's sustainably sourced from donors," Flynn said.

Saxon cautiously took the mortar and scooped out its contents. "Are you sure I have to drink the blood?"

"Yes. Let me get it. I know I've got a dram or two somewhere." He hurried back to the cabinet. Saxon, his face screwed up in disgust, pushed the mushy herbs into his mouth and chewed, clearly fighting the urge to gag.

"Missing modern medicine yet?" Nathy said.

Saxon mumbled an obscenity around the mouthful.

"Drink," Flynn said, returning with a decanter of thick green liquid. "You'll need to rest for the day."

Saxon winced, but powered through a few gulps from the decanter. "Okay, that'll do."

Flynn nodded. "Finish off the rest before you go to sleep."

"Sure." Saxon wiped his mouth and set the decanter on a side table. "Can I have a moment with Lacey?"

Flynn leaned in close, his eyes level with Saxon's. "Are you one of us? Ready to see the Elderon fall to rubble and ash, and the rightful queen arise to her throne in glory?"

Saxon stalled, his mouth working. Nathy came around to the other side of the bed and pulled Flynn back.

"Let them be. He's not going to hurt your precious Monarch."

"But...well, all right." Flynn stopped in the doorway and looked back at Lacey. "Please, when you're through here... I need to speak with you."

"We'll see," Lacey said, though some part of her knew she would go. Some part of her had begun to wonder.

When they had gone, Saxon took Lacey's hand. "I've got to get you out of here."

"About that," she said. "How did you know where I was?"

"Commander Lately showed me a photograph of the person who'd taken you. It was Nathy."

"And you know Nathy, how?"

"Well..." He cleared his throat. "You know how Allied nocturnes aren't allowed to use their full powers in Theopolis? My mother wasn't too happy that I'd grow up not knowing any magic. She's a brilliant witch herself, and she didn't want me to be so...well, weak. She sent me away for a few years. To a school in nocturne territory."

Lacey nodded for him to go on.

"The school was in the town just beyond the forest, Bishop's Hole. And...that's where I met Nathy."

"You were schoolmates?" This hadn't been the terrible, dark revelation she'd expected. "That's all?"

"I didn't last long at the school. The other kids didn't much like me, seeing as how I was an Ally, and I wasn't improving much anyway. But Nathy was—I guess he was all right back then. He kept some of the bullies away from me. He was a couple years older and just...sort of looked out for me."

"Then why do you hate him? You nearly attacked him just now."

"I learned what he does for a living. Lace, he's an assassin."

"Oh, I know. He mentioned."

He ran a hand down his face. "You don't sound properly concerned about that."

"He did save me from Ruark."

"You met *Ruark*?"

Lacey narrowed her eyes, the previous night's horrors unfolding anew. "Yes, about that. Your fairy friend brought me to him. He dosed me and tried to sell me to Ruark. They were going to cut my bloody wings off and whore me out."

Saxon paled, his eyes going distant, not truly seeing her anymore. "I...am so sorry."

She took a deep breath. "You knew him after all, I take it?"

"Yes, but—look, I wasn't ready to explain. I'm still not ready."

"Well, take your time, I suppose." She reached across his bed and snatched up the decanter. "And stop being a pansy and drink the rest of this." She shoved it into his hands and spun away from him.

"*Lace.*"

"I'll talk when you're ready to." She shut the infirmary door behind her.

19

THE LIFT

NATHY DRAGGED HIS hands through his hair, noting he needed a shower sooner than later. He stank of blood and dirt and his hair was caked with grease. He stalked the corridor, exhausted and shaken. He hadn't expected, of all people, Saxon St. Luke to slither back into his life.

For a poor farmgirl from Hollows Edge, Lacey sure kept fancy company.

"Ex—excuse me!"

Nathy halted in the corridor and tipped his head back, glaring at gods he wasn't sure were above. "I thought you'd gone home."

"I'd like to," Alastair said. "But you've yet to take me back."

"There are trains in town." He started back down the corridor.

"I haven't any money."

"Monastery doesn't pay good?"

"They don't pay at all! It's a service to God, not a job."

"Sounds like Elrosh is a stingy bastard." He stopped at the lift at the end of the corridor and finally looked at the monk. Alastair still wore his damp robes, and the smell of soaked wool wafted from him. His sleek mousy hair had come loose from its neat tie and hung around his face in a stringy mess.

"I need sleep," Nathy said. "I'll take you back when I'm feeling up to conjuring another portal, okay?"

Alastair sighed. His glasses slipped down his nose and he didn't bother to right them. "Is there...maybe...somewhere I could lie down, too?"

"Sure. Everyone's welcome. This is a very diverse cult."

"This is a cult's house?" He grabbed a fistful of hair, breathing hard. "Oh, God."

Nathy unlatched the lift gate and drew it back. "Don't panic. They're just monarchists."

"That's still horrible."

Nathy shrugged and gestured into the lift. "Get in if you're getting in."

Alastair complied, and Nathy closed them in. For a moment, nothing happened. Alastair looked around, concerned. "How does the lift, ah, go?"

"Brownies."

"Of course." Alastair lowered his voice. "What are they waiting on?"

"The tithe. You can't ride for free."

"What, every time you've got to pay them?"

"Mostly in crumbs and whatever you got in your pockets, but yes. Cheapskates take the stairs." Nathy rummaged in his pockets and produced a slightly bent thumbtack. "I'll cop you this one, but this shit don't grow on trees."

Nathy set the thumbtack in the middle of the lift floor and stepped back. "Third floor, please, Jack."

"Yussir," came a faint, rubbery voice from above. The lift clattered and jerked up. Alastair stumbled, grabbing the wall for support.

"So," Nathy said, leaning against the wall. "What made you want to be a monk?"

"I wanted to serve Elrosh with my life," Alastair said.

"Yeah, sure. You're, what, twenty? Aren't you a little young to give up on life?"

"I haven't given up on life. This is my chosen path."

"You're full of it, aren't you?" The lift clanged to a stop and they exited. "Come on, tell me. I promise I don't run with your crowd. It won't get back to them."

Alastair huffed out a breath. "It was my father's idea, originally. But I've come to see he was right to send me to the monastery."

"Your own dad sent you to live with monks?" Nathy snorted. "What'd you do to piss him off?"

"I—" Alastair blushed and looked away. "Why are you asking so many questions? You can't really care that much."

The monk was right—Nathy didn't care. He didn't think he did, anyway, but there was something about this skinny, pathetic kid in heavy wool robes that made him sad. Some imperceptible tic that drew his attention.

"What made you want to be an assassin?" Alastair said at last.

"It's nice to hurt people who deserve it for once." They stopped in the center of the corridor. "Most of the rooms on this floor are empty. Take your pick. Washroom's the last door on the left."

One of the doors along the corridor opened then, and a pale, wire-thin boy about Alastair's age stepped out. Black hair streaked with bleached locks hung in his dark, kohl-lined eyes, and two silver piercings jutted from his lower lip.

"Nathy?" The boy blinked. "You came back?"

"Poe." Nathy smiled. "How's it been? This is Alastair." He shoved the monk forward.

Alastair stared at Poe in silence, though whether in shock at his strange appearance or something else, it was hard to say. Poe caught one of his piercings with his upper teeth and nibbled it.

"Oh, hi."

"Er. Hello." Alastair nodded. "I'm not staying, of course. Ah, he, well..." He gestured to Nathy with a vague wave. "He kidnapped me."

"I used *you* as a test for my portal," Nathy said. "I kidnapped Lacey."

Poe smiled tentatively. "Nice outfit."

Alastair fiddled with his glasses, straightening them several ways. "I'm a monk."

"Ooh. I didn't think there were any handsome monks."

Alastair turned a deep red and hurried away, farther down the corridor. "I—washroom. Nice to meet you!"

"I can show you the way," Poe offered.

"No, no! Goodbye!" Alastair bolted into the last door on the right and didn't come out.

"Does he know that's the broom closet?" Poe said.

Nathy smirked. "He's probably figured it out."

"Oh." Poe smiled ruefully. "Did I scare him?"

"Think that poor guy is more scared of himself."

Poe's pale cheeks turned slightly pink. He looked up at Nathy. "What brought you back?"

176

"I just dropped off the Monarch."

"You found her?" Poe breathed in, shut his eyes. A moment passed, and he smiled. "Hm. Latrice is nervous."

Nathy looked around, but saw no flicker of the ghost Poe claimed to hear. "She said that, huh?"

Poe shook his head, his fine hair dusting his cheeks with each pass. "I can feel it. The whole house is sorry right now. The walls...the floor...they're screaming."

"Okay. Good talk."

Poe's eyes fluttered open. "She says you should stay."

Nathy paused his retreat. "That's not gonna work, Poe. I'm done with all this."

There was a long silence between them, tense with potential, of unsaid things they both knew and couldn't express. Finally, Poe said, "I try, you know...to find Artemis out there. She never answers."

Nathy was glad he'd turned away; his eyes stung in a dangerous way. "I don't need to talk to her. I know what she'd say."

"Oh?"

"Yeah. She'd tell me to forget her and move on. That's what I'm doing. Seeya, Poe."

He closed himself into what had once been his room. His eyes skipped over the bed and dresser that remained as they were, paused as though years had not passed since their last use, ready to resume their duties. His chest ached above his heart, a pain that for once didn't come from a wound of the flesh. Artemis's face came back to him then, clear and perfect despite how he'd tried to forget it. The past night had torn the past wide open and everything rushed against his senses, her laugh, her smile, her lips.

He made a fist and struck the pain above his chest. It replaced it with a physical ache that was somehow easier to bear.

LACEY WOKE CURLED on the parlor couch, her body aching from the cramped space. She stretched, her spine popping in musical rhythm. She still wore the ruined dress from the previous night, its fabric heavy against her legs with grime. She sat up and stared into the dead fireplace.

Ryken had told her it wasn't safe to leave. But Saxon was here now. Maybe he had a way to get her safely into Theopolis. She needed to find a way to help Dr. Poole, a way to get back to her mother. They could leave the realm together, all of them. There had to be a way.

"Thank gods I've found you," Alastair said. He slid into the parlor and shut the door. "Everybody here is mental."

"What'd you get up to, then?" Lacey said.

"Nathy took me upstairs to find a room. And there was this boy, a warlock, I think, and he told me I was handsome—"

"Was *he* handsome?"

"How—how would I know?"

Lacey pressed her lips together, shrugging. "I—never mind. How are you holding up?"

He sat beside her on the couch. He'd changed out of his robes into a simple tunic and trousers that were too big for his frame. "I just want to go home. I shouldn't be here."

"You really like your monastery."

"It's better than this place." He twisted his fingers together, staring down at them as though mesmerized. "Nathy said he'd take me home after he'd had a rest, but that was hours ago."

"Well, let's go find him." She rose and offered a hand up. "Come on. You shouldn't have to stay here if you don't want to."

He let her pull him to standing. "Will you leave, too?"

Lacey bit her lip. "It's complicated. I've got to figure some things out. But never mind that. Where's Nathy?"

Alastair led her out of the parlor and down a long corridor toward a gilt lift gate at the intersection of two hallways. They entered it, and Alastair felt in his pockets, a look of dismay on his face. "You don't happen to have any useless junk in your pockets, do you? The lift is run by brownies—apparently, they demand a tithe."

Lacey held out the hem of her torn dress. "No pockets. But, um..." She tore another strip of fabric from above her knees. Alastair cleared his throat and looked away. "You really are a monk," she muttered, then held out the length of cloth. "Will this do?"

"Quite nicely," said a disembodied voice from somewhere above the lift. Lacey jumped.

"Bloody hell. Who said that?"

"Jack," said the voice. "Now come on, you're not the only ones in need of the lift, you know."

Lacey set the fabric on the floor and the lift jerked upwards. "Where to?" the brownie asked.

"Wherever Nathy is," she said.

The brownie let off a burbled laugh. "Of course."

"What's that supposed to mean?"

The brownie only laughed again. The lift stopped on the fourth floor, and they disembarked. Alastair led her left, to a doorway at the far end of the hall. "I think he went in here." He knocked. Nobody answered.

"Should we...?" Alastair looked at her.

Lacey shrugged and pushed the door open.

Inside, Nathy sat on a large bed, legs crossed, wearing only trousers. Damp hair hung across his ruined eye as he twisted to get a view of his outstretched wing.

"Dammit," he muttered.

Lacey stared. His chest was carved with scars, the most notable—and most deliberate—being a strange symbol like an eye cut clumsily above his heart. Lying over the scars was a network of tattoos crawling down his arms and ribs. On his right inner forearm crawled an inked snake with eerily intelligent eyes. Nestled above the waistband of his jeans, on his left side, was a blue-inked pentacle filled with networking runes. And then there were the words—all along the skin of his left arm he'd inked snatches of poetry and prose in a few different languages.

"I know." He flipped his fringe away, revealing tired and teasing eyes. "I'm stunning to behold."

She plunged into the room. Alastair hung nervously in the doorway, blushing.

"What are you trying to do?" Lacey said. Nathy held a cloth in his right hand, laced with some chemically scented liquid.

"This." Nathy flicked his eyes toward the wound on his left wing; even now it dribbled blood, which dotted the bedspread. "I'd keep them in, but it makes my entire body hurt."

"Give me that." She took the cloth from his hand and pressed it to the wound. He winced, but made no noise of complaint.

"Did you hit your head and forget who I was?" He pushed her hand away. "You don't have to be nice."

"You helped Saxon. A little. Consider us even after this." She returned pressure to the wound. She glanced up to find Nathy's eyes on her face.

"What?" she said.

"Nothing. Thanks. I guess."

She gave him a small smile. "You're welcome. I suppose."

Alastair cleared his throat. "Should I...go?"

Lacey's hand slipped, drawing her thumb across the open wound. Nathy made a sound like he'd been struck in the gut. "S-sorry," she said.

His russet skin went a shade paler. "'S fine." Wincing, he said, "So, how's St. Luke?"

"He'll live," she said.

"Are you and him...?"

"No." She almost laughed, but found her chest ached too much for the effort. "I can't imagine that's even possible."

Nathy shrugged. His eyes flicked to meet hers. "Did he tell you?"

"He mentioned you were schoolmates. And that you protected him from the other children. Don't see why that was such a big secret."

He looked down. "Just...seemed like he should be the one to tell you. I dunno."

She drew the cloth away to find it soaked in blood, and still the wound bled. "What did Ruark use on you?"

"An old sword he stole from me. It's special, somehow. I don't know anything about it. But he killed my mother for it, so..."

"He killed your mother *and* Artemis?" She set the cloth aside and sat beside him on the bed. "I see why you hate him." She turned to him. "Did you love her?"

"Yes, princess, I loved my mother."

"*Artemis.*"

He rolled his eyes. "Look, if we're gonna talk, you ought to know, I don't talk about her. So don't bring it up."

"You're the one who told me about her."

"Yeah. To warn you what can happen when you're with Flynn." He uncrossed his legs and hopped off the bed. "Speaking of which, he wants to see everyone. Even you, monk." He drew his wings in till they vanished in a haze of black light. He winced as though their merging with his body caused him pain as he slid his arms into a shirt.

Alastair slumped against the doorframe. "What happened to sending me home?"

"You might want to delay a return trip," Nathy said. "Come on."

Lacey and Alastair looked up at him with mirrored expressions of distrust.

"I'll see what I can do," Nathy said. "After the meeting."

"You don't even seem to like Flynn," Lacey said. "Why do anything he says?"

Nathy frowned. "I'm curious, that's all."

"How do you even know him?"

"Drop it, princess." He left the room without another word. Alastair looked over at Lacey.

"Now what?"

She sighed. "We see what Flynn wants, I guess." She slipped off the bed and followed after Nathy.

20

LATRICE

NATHY LED THEM to the second-floor study, a dark, sturdy room in a far corner of the house. Several wingback chairs sat gathered around a fireplace. Flames crackled before a great red rug like a blood spill on the glossy wood floor. On the side of the room opposite the fireplace stood a large desk with bookends holding up a collection of huge, dusty tomes. A chandelier hung above the room and scattered firelight along the walls. A wide window let in the weak glow of day permitted by the rain and clouds, its deep red curtains held back by claw-like hooks.

A younger girl, maybe thirteen years old, waited for them in the center of the room. It took Lacey a moment to remember she was the odd girl from the night before. Alice. She bunched up the overlong sleeves of her sweater to cover her hands and hugged herself like a nervous child.

The girl had an unhealthy pallor about her, and her black hair hung lank around her face. She had clearly been a cute child, and would grow to be a pretty girl, but currently her face looked pinched, her body awkwardly stuck between youth and womanhood. Her pale blue eyes met Lacey's, and she frowned.

"Is she really the Monarch?" she asked Nathy.

He flopped into a large wingback chair, legs tossed over the arm. "Dunno. Flynn will figure it out."

Alice's knifelike smile appeared. "You don't look like a princess."

"I'm *not* a princess." Lacey looked at her torn dress, wishing she'd thought to ask for a change of clothes. Her fingers, gripping the ruined folds of fabric, were dirty, the nails stubby and caked with grime. Her bare feet could have belonged to a hobgoblin in their current state.

"I knew it," Alice said, plopping down onto the floor, cross-legged. "Nathy just grabbed the first girl he saw." She looked his way. "Flynn will make you give the money back."

"Why would he do that?" said a voice behind Lacey. She turned to find a boy, strikingly similar in appearance to Alice: the same lank black hair, the same icy skin, the same pale eyes. Alastair stiffened beside Lacey and went to find a seat deeper into the study.

"Are you the Monarch?" the boy said in soft, musical tones. He held out his delicate hand. "Ptolemy Sharpe. But everyone calls me Poe." He smiled. "I hope my sister isn't bullying you."

"Look at her," Alice said. "She can't be the Monarch."

Poe scrunched his mouth to one side, staring deeply into Lacey's eyes. She blinked back, uncomfortable. "You're the one the house is screaming about."

"Oh. I'm sorry." She cleared her throat. "What do you mean, the house is screaming?"

"The souls," Poe said. "The bits of long-ago people trapped in the bricks and wood and air."

Lacey looked cautiously around the room, half-expecting to see spirits peeling themselves from the walls even now. "I see... Are you...a necromancer, then?"

He nodded once. "I'm best at clairvoyance. Alice is the true master. She can summon the dead with a snap of her fingers."

Lacey looked over her shoulder at the grinning girl. Alice snapped her fingers; Lacey flinched.

"Are you scared of the dead?" Alice said.

"No," Lacey said, though she was beginning to fear Alice a little. She extracted herself from the siblings' curious gazes and went to sit beside Alastair by the fire. Its warmth welcomed her. Though Fryer's Grove was warmer than Theopolis, and certainly Hollows Edge, it was damper, grayer. She tucked her legs under herself and rested her chin in her hand.

"What d'you think?" Lacey said to Alastair, who huddled in the chair beside her.

"About what?"

"About which of them seems the most mental."

183

He almost smiled. "Alice."

"She beats Nathy, does she? Sadly, I have to agree."

A moment passed in which only the crackle of the fire filled the silence. Then, with a bracing sigh, Alastair spoke.

"You don't seem...all that bad."

Lacey cocked her head. "Did you think I was?"

"Not when I first met you. But I suppose I thought, if the Watchmen were after you, well, there had to be *some* reason." He looked at his fingers, twisted anxiously together. "But you seem all right."

Lacey stared into the billowing arms of the fire, the golden afterimage following her as she shut her eyes. "Whatever they think I've done...or what I am...I don't know anything about it."

"What do you mean, what you are?"

The slamming study door interrupted them, and they both glanced up. Flynn stood by the door, his eyes casting about at the many empty corners of the room. Harry Ryken stood just behind him, checking over a sheet of parchment in his hands.

"Oh, hell," Flynn said. "I call a meeting and hardly anybody shows."

"Jade says she's busy tonight," Alice said.

"And Landon's still not back from Mondberg," Poe added.

"You could get Saxon," Nathy said.

"He needs rest," Lacey started to protest, but Flynn's clapping hands cut her off.

"Excellent idea! We could use him anyway. I'll let the brownies know."

He dipped out of the room. Once the door shut with a click, Lacey turned to Nathy.

"This is it? He runs a cult with only five bloody members in it?"

"There *were* six."

"Seven," Poe said. "Where's Isobel?"

Nathy said nothing.

"Still," Lacey said. "I thought this was a proper operation."

Nathy blinked. "I hope *I* didn't give you that idea."

Lacey grabbed the ends of her long hair and tangled her fingers through it, an aggravated sound roaring in her throat. Alastair patted her shoulder awkwardly.

"There, there."

The door banged on its hinges once more, emitting Flynn and a bleary, limping Saxon. "Here we are. Have a seat anywhere."

Saxon limped over to the cluster of chairs around the fire and took the seat nearest Lacey. "Any idea what's going on?"

"I'm realizing this lot is less threatening than hopeless," she said. "Feeling better?"

"Loads." His bruises had faded a bit, but still stained his ivory skin blue along his jaw and cheekbones, now coated with light stubble. A hazy distance hung in his eyes. "Thought you weren't talking to me."

"I'm...not. Oh, fuck it." She took his hand.

Alastair leaned forward in his chair, eyes wide. "Is that Saxon St. Luke?"

"You know him?" Lacey said.

"I know *of* him." Alastair sat up primly.

Saxon spared the monk a short glance. "And you are?"

"Alastair...Marshall." His surname he said in a murmur.

"Wait, Marshall?" Saxon looked more fully at Alastair now. "Any relation to Julius Marshall?"

"Well..."

"Yeah, you are. Oh, my gods. I'm mates with your brother Hayden."

"That's nice." Alastair's shoulders hunched up around his ears as though he might manage to disappear.

"Who are you talking about?" Lacey asked, looking between the two.

"The Marshalls," Saxon said. "They're an Old Name, really big in Theopolis. His father is ambassador to the northern reaches. His brother goes to Westman-Samfrey with me." Saxon raised an eyebrow. "But I thought Hayden was the youngest."

"I'm not frequently brought up," Alastair said in a tone that ended the conversation.

"All right, everyone," Flynn said. He shooed Alice and Poe toward the cluster of chairs and stood before the fire. The flames jumped at his presence as though excited. He gently reached down and patted the tongues of fire, calming them back into a dull glow.

"Good boy," he said.

"He's talking to the fire," Lacey muttered.

Saxon rubbed his eyes, blinking away exhaustion. "I'm sorry, sir. You're...Ferno, are you?"

"I am." Flynn scooped a swirling bit of fire into his palm and held it out toward Saxon. "Fire is the most beautiful force of nature, isn't it? Powerful yet delicate, dangerous yet necessary, the harbinger of modern society as we know it, and the destroyer of that which we hold dear."

"Er, yes." Saxon cleared his throat. "I hope you don't find this rude, but... I didn't think any Fernos lived in Gryfel."

Flynn bounced the flame between his hands, smiling absently. "You're nearly right. My family were brought here by the previous owner of this house. He kidnapped them, forced them to serve the household. My family never had the means to return to our island." He tossed the flame back into the fireplace with a wistful look. "I've never seen Sumri."

"Oh. Sorry." Saxon slouched in his seat, withering in the silence that followed.

"You're an Ally," Flynn said. "Nathy told me. Serendipitous that you're here, really. Perhaps you can help me convince Lacey that what I've told her is true."

Lacey sat up straighter. In the hours since Flynn's bizarre introduction, so much had happened that she'd nearly forgotten what Flynn had told her—about her godfather, and the potion that had sealed her supposed powers.

"You might have guessed," Flynn said, glancing from Lacey to Saxon, "that it was his father who brewed the potion that has kept you tame all these years."

Lacey turned her head slowly toward Saxon. He stared down at his hands, clenched together between his knees.

"You *knew*?"

"No. Well, yes, but only recently."

"What was the bloody potion for, then?" She shot up from her seat. "Is he right? Do I have some power I don't know about?"

Saxon sighed. "I truly don't know. I promise. All I know... This past summer, when you visited, Dr. Poole took you to my father's laboratory at Hayven. You always went when you visited, but I thought it was just, you know, a checkup. But when I saw you later that afternoon..."

"Yes?"

"Well, your memories were gone. Only from the night before. But who uses a short-term memory potion like that?"

"Perverts," Alice chimed in from the floor.

"I—that's—*no*." Saxon shook his head. "I checked my father's lab. And I found your records."

"That's rather personal," Alastair said.

"Bit creepy," Poe agreed.

Alice propped her elbows on the arm of Saxon's chair and squinted at him. "Are you *sure* you're not a pervert?"

"Oh, piss off." Saxon inched away from the girl, keeping a wary eye on her. "The point," he said now to Lacey, "is that I discovered my father had been giving you a binding potion, every year since you were three. The doses kept going up. The memory potion, I assume, was so you wouldn't remember being treated."

"Fix it."

He blinked. "Sorry?"

"You're good with potions," Lacey said, quietly but severely. "So make a different one that fixes it. And I want my memories back too."

"I can't. Lace, my father is the Elderon's own potion master. His potions are too strong. Even if I could reverse it—"

"Nathy could do it." Alice turned to Nathy, who had endured the proceedings silently thus far. "He's the best warlock we've got."

"I don't do potions," Nathy said. "That stuff's for mages who can't figure out how wands work."

Saxon bristled. "At least it's respectable magic."

"Yeah, stealing a girl's memories and locking her powers away without her knowledge is how I tend to define *respectable*."

Saxon rose, looming above Nathy. "Don't act righteous with me."

"Oh, are we finally doing this?" Nathy hopped up. The two were equal in height, and though Saxon looked physically stronger, Lacey didn't think he truly stood a chance against someone with Elonni blood.

"Okay," Nathy said. "Hit me. First shot's free."

"I only need one."

Nathy spread his hands. "Whenever you're ready, gorgeous."

"Stop it, both of you," Lacey said. "This is honestly pathetic."

"This is the best meeting we've ever had," Poe said.

Saxon balled his fist, planted his feet. "Don't move."

Nathy winked.

Saxon moved forward, but backpedaled at the last moment as a fireball shot between the two men. Nathy pinched out a small flame crawling up his fringe.

"Some warning, Flynn?"

Flynn snuffed out the fire crawling along his hand with the flick of his wrist. "Sit down and behave. Both of you."

Nathy and Saxon returned to their seats. Lacey shoved her chair closer to Alastair's, giving Saxon a wide berth.

"Perfect." Flynn nodded, then turned to Alastair. "You. Little monk-person."

A small sound squeezed from Alastair's throat. "Y-yes?"

"Mr. Ryken has some news for you." Flynn beckoned to Ryken, who removed himself from his post by the door and stopped in front of Alastair. Alastair, trying, it seemed, to be brave, stared into Ryken's ruined face, but shook all the while.

"Take it y'know what I am," Ryken said.

"The—the—D-Dark Guard. Sir. Sorry."

"Ah, come off it. I wouldn' 'urt ya, even if you was a typical Old Name. As it is, y' seem all right. So I'm sorry I's got t' be the one t' tell ya, but the Watchmen've named you as an accomplice in Miss Barker's escape."

"But I didn't..." Alastair's words died, his eyes flickering with memory. "Oh. I did."

"Yeah, felt it best t' warn you. You go back, well, little bloke like you wouldn' last long in 'Aylock, would ya?"

"But my father—he's an ambassador. He can get me out of this."

"Eh...he *could*. If 'e weren't the same one who named you as the monk on duty at that chapel, that is."

Alastair's expression faded into stark, pale shock. "My own father...gave me away."

Lacey reached out, only just brushing his shoulder when he suddenly stood.

"I need to go." He hurried from the study, his footsteps harried and uneven along the corridor. Poe rose from his seat.

"I'll check on him. Carry on without us."

"Well." Flynn beamed at those remaining. "Quite a dramatic afternoon."

"Come on, Flynn," Nathy said. "Get to the point of this."

Flynn nodded. "Right. Lacey. Let me tell you the story. If you don't believe me after I'm done, I won't try to stop you leaving."

"Perfect. Let's have it, then."

"I grew up on the stories of the Ruined Queen," Flynn began. "But to the nocturne kinds, she is not a tyrant, but a hero. Under her rule, the mortal, celestial, and nocturne kinds lived in harmony. But of course, this didn't appeal to the Elonni nobility who once had every being across the realm under their heels.

"Legends of the queen suggest she had a power beyond imagining—a power that put even the purest Elonni bloodlines to shame. Fearing her power, the Old Names of the realm rebelled. Though the queen was killed, stories tell of her only daughter escaping death thanks to her most trusted advisor.

"These have been dismissed for centuries as hopeful stories, nocturne lullabies. I thought so, too. Until I heard the haunted story of this house."

Lacey, despite herself, leaned forward in her chair, rapt to his every word. "What's the story?"

"The man who owned this house was called Donoveir Fryer. Once the Elderon's ambassador to the western reaches, he had since retired to the very land he'd once overseen. In his growing age, he sought a new bride.

"The girl he chose was young, and from a family with no noble connections. Latrice Heartwood almost certainly didn't love the old ambassador, but she accepted his hand. She had two children by him. She lived life as a dutiful wife for years.

"And then, unexpectedly, he slaughtered his entire family."

Lacey shuddered, and warmth only returned to her blood when Saxon came to kneel beside her. Her took her hand, rubbing her knuckles.

"It's just a story, Lace."

"I don't know that it is," she said.

Flynn continued: "He stabbed Latrice over and over with a knife. When the Dark Guard finally arrived to investigate, she was in pieces."

"That's enough," Saxon said, but Flynn went on as though he hadn't heard.

"He took his two sons through the groves, following the sound of the rushing sea. He first took his youngest son, a mere baby, and tossed him over the cliffs. The eldest boy soon followed. The youngest, sadly, was dashed upon the rocks."

Lacey covered her mouth with her free hand. Her other remained trapped in Saxon's intense grip, shaking with his rage.

"Thankfully," Flynn said, "the older boy—William— survived." He looked at last at his stunned audience, his flame-colored eyes fixed on Lacey. "Donoveir Fryer accepted arrest. He left the house ranting that his wife was a demon, that his children were therefore demons. He told the Guard he had to do it."

Ryken nodded along at this. "All on record, by the way, case anyone's interested."

"My dad lived here?" Lacey said. "And his own father...tried to kill him?"

Flynn nodded; behind him, the fire lowered its flames, bowed as though by sorrow.

"And all that," Lacey said, "that's why you believe I'm the Ruined Queen's descendant? Because my...my grandmother"—the word felt strange, wrong to belong to a woman she had never known—"Because Latrice was murdered by her husband?"

"It made me curious," Flynn said. "I acquired this house decades ago to research the matter. Since then, I've found compelling evidence for my case. Not least of all when Latrice's own son returned home."

Lacey stared at him. "My father came here on his own?"

"He wanted to face his past. After surviving his father's cruelty, he was raised by Latrice's brother. They moved to Theopolis and lived under a different surname. Will's uncle told him of his mother's fate. Will came to Fryer's Grove after

I'd been living here some time. I shared with him what I knew. And I'll tell you now, if you're ready."

"I think we've all had enough," Saxon said, rising, not letting go of Lacey's hand. "I don't mean to be rude, but you're mental. The lot of you."

"I want to hear it," Lacey said, her voice dead in her ears. But she meant it—and that was perhaps more terrifying than the story itself. She had come to see these figures—the ghosts of a family she had never known—as real.

Flynn might be a madman. But if he wasn't...

"Just tell me," Lacey said.

"I found a book among Latrice's old possessions. A spell book with missing pages."

"So?"

"So. In the old legends, the source of the Ruined Queen's power was a spell book, whose powers could only be awoken if eight rituals were completed. One for each of the nocturne kinds. The pages containing these rituals are gone, hidden among a representative of each kind. An heir, if you will."

"So...the nocturnes were the source of her power?"

"In the original ceremony, it's believed one of every kind sacrificed a measure of their power to create a spell which would allow the queen to become stronger. The resulting spell book was called the Book of the Nine." Flynn stepped closer, his hands raised as though he meant to take her hands. "And Latrice—your grandmother—had the book. It was here, in the house, thrown amongst her things like rubbish. But I knew what it was."

"I still can't... How do I know she was really my grandmother? My father might have been tricked for all I know."

Flynn smiled and offered her a slim, bronze hand. "Let me show you, then."

21

THE PORTRAIT

-Fryer's Grove-

FLYNN LED THEM to the lift. He pulled back the ornate gate and placed a hard candy, fuzzy from its time in his pocket, on the lift floor.

"Thank you, Mr. Flynn," the brownie squeaked from above.

"Of course, Jack. Come on, all in."

Lacey stepped inside. Both Nathy and Saxon attempted to follow after her, their shoulders ramming together.

"Excuse me," Saxon said.

"I will, if you move."

Lacey rolled her eyes. While the two men glared in their impasse, Alice hopped onto Nathy's back and crawled over his shoulder, dropping into the lift with catlike grace. It startled Nathy enough that Saxon was able to shoulder in and stand beside Lacey. Nathy sulked in after.

The lift rattled to a stop at the fifth floor. Flynn guided them down a corridor lined with candles set along the floor, their wax collecting on tarnished plates.

"Who puts lit candles on the floor?" Saxon muttered.

"*I* do," Alice said. "They're a pathway for the spirits."

"They're a fire hazard."

"Oh, come off it," Lacey said. "They're probably bewitched." She passed her hand over a line of green and white candles and felt only a faint, warm breeze. "See? Harmless?"

Saxon bent and pressed his palm over the flames, and immediately jerked it back. "Shit. Harmless?"

Alice smiled in the darkness. "I guess the spirits don't like you."

They walked down the hall in silence. The dark paneled corridors reminded Lacey of nightmares, of wandering aimlessly in the dark, doors rising up on all sides, holding secrets or monsters.

At last, Flynn stopped at the end of the corridor. A long, ornate mirror carved with a repeating motif of snakes coiled in on each other hung on the wall. Flynn stepped aside, gesturing Lacey closer. "If you please."

Lacey stepped up to the mirror. She flinched at her reflection, the dirt on her cheeks and arms, the twigs poking from her hair. The dusky hall was reflected around her face, a blur of dark reds and deep brown and shadow. Something pale and flashing lit across the mirror, but whatever it had been, it was too fast for Lacey to name.

"What am I supposed to be doing here?" Lacey asked. She plucked a twig from her hair.

"Waiting," Flynn said. "The house must accept you."

Lacey turned back to the mirror, glaring at her dirty visage. After a moment, the glass rippled, her reflection melting away, falling like water over rock. A pair of narrow, dark stairs lay on the other side of the frame.

"You may pass," Flynn said.

"Lovely." Lacey stepped forward. The stairs led to a narrow landing and then twisted back, going farther up. She climbed carefully, the old steps groaning. A narrow door greeted her at the end of the stairs. Flynn squeezed by her on the landing and produced an old, rusty key.

"When I came to the house all those years ago, everything from the Fryers remained." He shoved the door wide. Inside, a clutter of old trunks and loose household items spread across the floor. Lacey stepped across the piles of junk, her feet slipping on old newspapers, her hands brushing broken furniture. Flynn guided her to the back of the attic and stopped beside a large rectangular object covered by a blanket.

"This is your proof," he said as everyone gathered round. He tore the blanket away and backed off with a short bow.

The object was a painting of a young woman, her long red hair twisted into an elaborate braided bun, her green eyes downcast. She wore a white dress run through with strands of gold twisting into floral patterns along the skirt. A large, raw emerald hung on a delicate chain around her neck.

The girl was, unmistakably, Lacey. Except, Lacey had never sat for a portrait, had never worn a wedding dress or worn chunks of precious stones around her throat.

"Your grandmother," Flynn said. "Latrice Heartwood, on her wedding day." He gestured to a dress standing farther away, dangling from a headless, limbless mannequin. The same dress from the painting, but yellowed with age and bruised with wear. Lacey walked numbly toward the old gown. It looked as though it were her own size, as though it had been tailored for her own wedding day.

"You weren't lying," Lacey said, her voice distant to her own ears. "She is my grandmother."

"Lace." Saxon came to her side, drawing her away from the ruined dress. "This doesn't prove anything. They...they could have had the painting commissioned to look just like you."

"Why would they do that?" She pushed his hands away. "Why would they want me unless it's true?" She turned now to Flynn. "You knew who my father was. Why did it take you so long to find me?"

"Your godfather hid you well. I suspect he had your papers forged. And, of course, we didn't know who your mother was—Will was careful to leave you both out of everything. But we had a connection within the Elderon—a brilliant huntress who discovered Will's old friend, Absolom Poole. A scientist and university professor. It didn't seem a promising lead, until she looked at his published works. Everything he wrote, he dedicated to a woman named Aeyrin. A human, it turns out, from Hollows Edge. We'd never have thought to look there."

Lacey wilted. Dr. Poole would never forgive himself if he knew his sentiment had led to this. He'd wanted to keep her not just from the Elderon, she realized, but from Flynn and his followers, too.

"You were destined for this, Lacey," Flynn said. "You were always meant to find us."

"The way my father was meant to find you? And my grandmother?" She waved her hand at the portrait. "She was killed because of what she was. And my father—he died fighting your war. You think I'm prepared to do that? That I'm *destined* to?"

"Things are different now," Flynn said. "Your grandmother was alone in this, with only the Book to guide her. And your father..." He looked down. "I admit, we were ill prepared. But we've had time since then to plan."

"What, you and five other people are going to stop the Elderon? At least last time there was a war on. You don't have anything."

"We have you."

"No, you don't." She flung her arm to indicate the portrait, the dress. "She died. You just told me her husband thought she was a demon, that he slaughtered her. And my father? Whatever he believed, he still died for this! He left my mother behind. She had to marry some horrible man she never loved because he left us with nothing."

Flynn reached out for her; she stepped away, and his hand fell limp to his side. "He wanted to make a better world, Lacey. For you."

"Well, he didn't. I grew up with a stepfather who hates me, a godfather I see once a year. No friends. And my mother is miserable. I see it every day. Our lives are so much worse because he's dead. But he cared more about this power than he did about us. And you expect me to be proud of him? To want to do what he did?"

"Everyone has to make sacrifices," Flynn said. Nathy, leaning against the attic wall and watching the conversation thus far with disinterest, narrowed his eyes.

"Let us know when you make one, okay, Flynn?"

Flynn flinched at the words. "I have, son."

Nathy snorted. "Oh, yeah. I forgot about that time you buried the remaining pieces of your girlfriend in the forest. Oh, wait, that was me."

Flynn spun on him, fire cascading down his arms. "Artemis believed in this cause."

"And she's dead, too. Sure are racking up an impressive kill count, aren't you?"

"Nathy."

"I'm just saying what your precious Monarch is saying. Maybe you should listen to her." He pushed off the wall and easily swerved around the piles of junk littering the attic. The door slammed a moment later.

Alice looked from Flynn to Lacey, her pale eyes big and mournful. "You really won't help us?"

"Ugh." Lacey followed Nathy's path through the junk, though less gracefully. She stumbled over a box of ornate shelving, only missing the floor when Saxon caught her around the waist.

She pushed him off her. "I need to be alone."

"Lace—"

"Please. Just—everyone piss off for the next few hours, all right?"

"You can't run away from this," Flynn said.

Lacey gripped the doorknob, her fingers clenching around it. Small dents formed on the tarnished metal. "I have an idea."

Everybody remained silent. Lacey turned back to them and pointed at the portrait of her grandmother.

"If you can get *her* to tell me it was worth it, maybe I'll reconsider."

She rushed back down the attic steps, blind in her rage and sorrow. The stairs slipped from under her feet, her hip bruising against the banister as she caught herself against the wall. She pounded her fist into the paneling, satisfied when she felt it break against her knuckles. A wet, trailing warmth on her face told her she was crying, and that was somehow the most depressing bit of all—they'd gotten to her. She believed them, and it hurt.

Thinking her dad had died in a pointless war was bad enough. Knowing he'd abandoned her to come here and train with Flynn—that he'd chosen some idealistic revenge over his family...

A fire stirred in her heart, a feeling she got when she looked at the averted faces of the villagers, when her stepfather screamed at her for some assumed failure. Hate. In that moment, she hated her father.

And if felt sickeningly right.

22

DUSK BLEEDS OUT THE DAWN

POOLE'S EYES DRIFTED to the window looking out of his study, across the city he knew so well. A steady rain fell, humming across the pavement, tapping at his window. A purple haze pushed the sunset lower toward the horizon.

A drastic peace hung over the streets, at odds with the truth of what went on to the east. Elonni walked along the flagstone streets beneath umbrellas, bustling home from work, stopping at shop windows, aware and yet, it seemed, so oblivious. Only a night ago, the Watchmen had raided the Eastern. The death toll contrasted terribly with their supposed purpose: Hunting a single, dangerous criminal.

Lacey.

Kimberly Law had conducted his newsmen flawlessly, it seemed. The day's paper claimed the Watchmen had apprehended their man without incident, putting a few additional deserving nocturnes into Haylock while they hunted. The resultant calm of pleased Elonni going about their days played out as Poole might all along have expected. In the wake of unpleasant realities, false comforts won the day.

Poole reached for his flask. He'd had enough long ago, but he never managed to get sufficiently drunk to forget.

In the faded gloaming, Poole tried with every honest effort to go back to work—Inspector Law had sent him a brief note entreating him to stay out of matters he couldn't control: *Just keep your head down for now. There's nothing to be done until we know what Crane and Bromley are planning. I'm doing what I can, but I'm sure you appreciate the position I'm in. Do me a favor and burn this note when you've read it. Best, K.*

But Poole's mind couldn't focus on anatomical drawings and slides of blood. Pointless, wasn't it, to try and solve the great riddles of modern biology when every agony of his life was converging at once.

He pushed the parchment and sample jars to one side of the desk and spread the day's newspaper out before him.

While the citizens of Theopolis enjoyed a successful Festival, our Watchmen worked tirelessly into the night, hunting and eventually apprehending a dangerous criminal who has for months now terrorized the Eastern. The suspect, a dark fairy going by the name Neill Sonyi, is suspected of having run the largest bane den in the district. He was killed last night after resisting arrest, and our city is safer for it.

Poole couldn't know if the fairy had indeed died, or even existed, but if he had, he was hardly the Watchmen's true target. He had to believe Lacey had escaped, that she wasn't now in custody while he remained under house arrest, useless.

He reached for his flask, only to find it empty. He sighed and rose from his desk, emerging into the too-bright light of the sitting room. He stumbled toward the liquor cart and reached for the strongest thing on offer.

A knock on the door unsteadied his hand. He dropped the bottle and winced as it shattered on the floor. The liquid splashed up, drenching the cuffs of his trousers.

"Well, shit," he muttered, and lurched toward the door.

Aeyrin's pale, hair-matted face warped convexly through the peephole, big perfect eyes tiny in the mutated geometry. He opened the door without consideration for the mid-life crisis waiting to be unveiled: *Here it is, my cry for help.*

"Aeyrin? How did you get here?"

She scanned him with raised eyebrows. "That's a good look for you."

He looked down at his open shirt and liquor-stained trousers. "Ah...sorry. You caught me at a bad time."

"You don't say."

She was beautiful, and he almost said so. The cool look in her eyes stopped him. She was dressed for farm work, in trousers and heavy flannel, soaked from the storm. Her hair was matted by the rain, stuck to her neck and face, a pretty mess. He stared at her wordlessly until she cleared her throat.

"Er, come in." He stepped aside, and she brushed past him, her eyes landing on the shattered bottle of rye.

"You've got to be kidding me."

Poole pushed his hair back like she might forgive him if he at least acted embarrassed. He very nearly was. "Right, er, I know this doesn't put me in the best light..."

Aeyrin whirled on him. "Where is Lacey? And why haven't you left the realm?"

"We were...delayed. And...she's...not...here."

Her jaw locked, her eyes going dark with anger. "Absolom."

"I've got it under control."

"Oh, do you?" She took a long, shaky breath and fixed him with a look. "Absolom, all I care about right now is Lacey. And you owe me an explanation. A real one. None of this smoke and mirrors, top-secret, closed-doors political bull—will you button your shirt?"

"Oh, right." He worked the buttons into place, glancing at her beneath his eyelashes; her eyes flickered to his chest and down to the floor, and he felt the faintest flicker of hope. Maybe she...

Not the time.

"Right." He slapped his cheeks, trying to clear his head. "So. Seems we've been betrayed. Sebastian, you know, the potion master—"

"I know who he is. Get on with it."

"Right, well, he's a bloody turncoat. He let the Elderon know...well, about Lacey. And the potion."

"I *told* you I wasn't comfortable trusting someone from the Elderon! Goddammit, Sol. You..." She grabbed fistfuls of her hair and bunched them at her skull, pacing in tight circles before him. "Where is she? I swear to God if they've got her—"

"I—well—look. This is sort of good news, bad news."

She stopped pacing, eyes boring into his.

"See...if the Elderon had her, I would know. And therefore know where she is. But...I don't. Know where she is. That is."

"*You lost her?*"

"I—"

"*How d'you know she isn't dead?*"

"Aeyrin, please, stop yelling."

"Stop yelling? You lost my daughter, you pompous, overbearing, self-indulgent prat!" Her anger dissolved suddenly into a whimper, her grief morphing seamlessly. "She's dead, isn't she?"

"No. Aeyrin, just give me a moment to explain." He reached out cautiously to place his hand on her narrow shoulder. "Sit down, all right? D'you want a drink?"

"No."

"Mind if I drink?"

She just stopped herself rolling her eyes. "Go on."

He started toward the cart, but the cold knife of her accusation twisted in his back and he turned. At the meeting of their eyes, her rage resurfaced.

"You're unbelievable, you know? My daughter is lost, gods know where, the Elderon are looking for her—yet here you are, doing nothing to help her. Getting drunk, or, let me guess, you're already drunk, probably have been since the sun was up."

He pinched the bridge of his nose, as if that could stop the onset of a headache, as if it could keep his descending sobriety away. His voice was tight and off-tune as he said, "Aeyrin— for God's sake—"

"Don't you dare—"

"What?" he said. "What is it? What the hell do you want from me?"

She paled, but only briefly. Her face filled, red with anger and hurt and everything he'd done to her. This was it. Every crack in the dam accumulates to a break, and, as every relationship was a feat of engineering too intricate and deliberate for a fool of Poole's caliber to maintain, he figured he could expect to get his feet wet.

"What happened to you?" she said, relentless now. "I swear you used to care about someone other than yourself. You used to be a good person. I thought you were, anyway, maybe my perception was off."

He leaned against the liquor cart. "Good people don't get far in Theopolis, love. Don't get me wrong, I'm not denying it: I'm a terrible person. But since you insisted I keep my life here, y'know, I couldn't really afford to be the man you used to know."

She shut her eyes tight. When she opened them, she looked...worse than disappointed. Something else. Like she knew he would say that and couldn't muster the surprise necessary for disgust. Poole looked away.

"I get that, Sol, I do. And whatever you get up to here, I really don't care. But my daughter, the girl you brought to this place, is being hunted by the Elderon, and you're too busy getting drunk on scotch—"

"It's rye."

"Oh, lovely, *that* makes all the difference!" She flushed with the release of anger and subsequent embarrassment. "You—you're so—I don't even know why I came here, you obviously don't care. I'm sorry I interrupted your evening."

He wanted to be angry—maybe he was. It was hard to know, because what he felt wasn't any one thing. His eyes stung, a threat of tears, so he shut them. When moments passed and he didn't hear her leave, when she stayed right where she was, looking at him, he glanced up, at her eyes— those goddamn eyes the color of old photographs. He was relieved that she was crying, too. He went to her without thinking about it. She flinched away from him.

"I'm doing everything I can, Aeyrin. But what I can do is limited. I'm under house arrest for concealing her in the first place. If I step outside—well, here, why don't I just show you?"

He started toward the door, aware of her eyes on his back as he stepped out onto the porch. The cool night touched his skin, and in the next instant, his heart seized, ripping, it seemed, against its anchors in his chest. Before he could buckle from the pain, before it made his vision go black, a hand grabbed the back of his shirt and dragged him back inside.

"I get it," Aeyrin said, slamming the door.

He leaned against the foyer wall, catching his breath, letting his rattled heart still. "Then you see that there's nothing I can do?"

She glanced away from him, her eyes hard and her jaw locked, keeping whatever she wanted to say at bay. He took her chin and turned her face toward his. "What do you *want* me to do? Because I'll do anything, anything you want, to make you to stop blaming me for what happened. Then and now."

She stood unmoving, glaring. And then, suddenly, she wound her arms around his waist and buried her face in his chest. She was soaked and cold, shivering in his arms, twitching with silent sobs. He held her, afraid she'd pull away, and he couldn't lose this rare moment of her actually needing him.

"Aeyrin."

She looked up and pushed him back. Only the tear tracks on her face, like footprints in the snow of someone long gone, told him she'd been, for that brief moment, the same woman who'd once needed him.

"D'you want a tea?" he said. She looked at him like he was mental, then shrugged. She sat on the couch and curled her legs up to her chest.

A moment later, he brought out two mugs of tea and held one out to her. "Dash of milk and a godless amount of sugar."

She almost smiled as she took the mug. "You remembered."

He sat beside her. "D'you...I can lend you some clothes."

"I'm fine." She suppressed a shudder and took a sip of tea. "I'm only here to find out what's happening to my daughter."

And then you're leaving. She hadn't been in his home, sat beside him on this couch, in fifteen years. And it was all she could do not to run for the door.

"We'll figure this out. I promise."

The mug shook in her hands. A trickle of tea splashed down her wrist. She seemed not to notice. Poole watched her: skin white and lips blue from the cold, like any moment she might snap in a shatter of ice chips.

No. Aeyrin didn't shatter. She didn't even crack. Of the two of them, she'd managed their fates with far more dignity.

"You promised she'd be safe," she said at last.

Poole didn't expound on what he'd already done to ensure Lacey's safety—the forged papers, the risky potion, the exhaustive coverup that it was to hide a person in the Elderon's watchful world. Because none of that mattered if one thing went wrong, which it had. So, he'd failed. He knew that.

"Did I tell you," he said cautiously, "what Will said to me before he died?"

She sighed, her eyes misty as the steam rising from her tea. "Probably. I can't remember."

"He said, 'Take care of them, you lucky bastard.' I told him he was an idiot. Now...I see how much he probably regretted everything. Suppose he thought it was too late."

Anger flashed in Aeyrin's eyes like heat lightning, an echo of storm trapped in the clouds. "There are times... Sol, I hate Will so much sometimes it scares me. There are days I think I love him still, when I almost miss him. But what he did to us...I swear to God if he wasn't dead, I'd have killed him myself."

"He was a selfish bastard." Poole shook his head. "He was broken, too. But it shouldn't have fallen to you to fix him."

"He couldn't *be* fixed."

"Fair point." He inched closer to her. "As if I've got room to talk, though, hm?"

She shrugged. "You have your faults. But you also didn't leave your family behind to join a cult and murder droves of innocent civilians."

"Oh, is *that* why you left him?"

She honored his terrible joke with a wry smile. "You're more insufferable, however."

"Handsomer, though."

"Bit of a prat."

"A charming prat?"

She considered him, then smirked. "No. Just a prat."

"How you wound me."

She put a hand to her lips, but her laughter slipped through. "God, I can't believe I find anything funny right now. Sol, what are we supposed to do?"

"Kimberly Law is helping me."

"Oh, the Elder of Information? I feel much better, thanks."

"He's on our side."

"So was Dr. St. Luke."

"I concede that I haven't always picked the most...reliable friends. But in this world, it's the most I can do."

"You keep saying that," she muttered, and set her tea aside. She didn't rise to go, as he feared she would, but rested her head on his shoulder and let his arm wind around her waist. "I suppose I can sympathize. I've had my fair share of choosing horrible friends."

"I hope you don't mean me."

Her silent laughter rumbled against his side. He tightened his hold around her, unwilling to let the moment pass.

"I forgot to tell you," she said.

"What's that?"

"A Watchman came after me."

He pulled away just far enough to look into her face. "What? When? Where was this?"

"Back home. Last night. I came back from getting firewood... Jonas was—is—dead. Just lying on the floor in a pool of blood. The Watchman came after me when I ran from the house."

"How did you escape?"

She took a breath to tell him, but he found himself not waiting for the answer. He tipped her face toward his and kissed her, startling a gasp from her. He fully expected to be punched for this but gods, he'd missed her. He might have lost her. Waiting any longer was a bargain he'd never take.

He broke away when the ache of breathlessness became too much. She blinked.

"Sol."

"I know. I'm sorry."

She looked down at her hands, biting her lip. Their eyes met.

Aeyrin grabbed the front of his shirt, pulling him toward her.

23

NECROMANCY

NIGHT HAD FALLEN, and darkness filled the first-floor parlor before Lacey stopped reading. She shut her book and stretched, letting the weighty tome fall to her lap. She rose to start a fire in the grate and continue reading when a voice startled her.

"I can help you."

"Bloody hell!" Lacey spun, and her bleary eyes focused on Alice. The girl sat on the floor, engulfed in an overlarge sweater, her scrawny legs clad in black tights. Her blue eyes glowed like will-o'-th'-wisps in the dark room.

"Gods, you scared me," Lacey said. "How long have you been sitting there?"

"Three hours."

Lacey, startled by her own lack of perception, looked at the girl warily. "Why?"

"Because I can help you."

"With what?"

"Latrice."

Lacey blinked. "How?"

"*I* am a child of Necropola, goddess of the undead."

"Wouldn't that make you a vampire?"

Alice fixed her with a look. "Necropola isn't *only* for the damned. Some Mages worship her. Necromancers."

"Right." Lacey eyed the door hopefully. "Anyway, that's nice, but I ought to..."

Alice brought her hands together, steepled for prayer, her eyes glinting. "Do you fear death, mortal?"

"Why are you talking that way?"

Alice wilted in her big sweater. "Look, do you want to know more about Latrice or not?"

"Er, sure. But—I mean, is it a good idea? Is it safe?"

Alice rolled her eyes. "I do it all the time. We'll be fine."

Lacey smiled despite herself. "All right, then. Show me what you can do."

"Just one thing."

"Yeah?"

Alice stepped far too close, her pale eyes filling Lacey's vision. "Cast aside all you thought you knew of life after death, and prepare for the horrors of what lies beyond."

"I'm...not really religious anyway, so..."

Alice rolled her eyes. "You're honestly no fun. Come on then." She turned and headed out of the study, and Lacey followed her, feeling her way through the dark room.

MIST CRAWLED ACROSS the forest floor like a foamy wave licking the shore—like a hand, reaching and finding no purchase. As Alice walked ahead in the garden, cutting through the rotted autumn harvest toward a spindly fence ahead, Lacey thought perhaps she could believe in ghosts. This cloudy, damp world was primal, behind the rest of time, and she wouldn't find it so hard to believe these groves contained secrets and souls more ancient than anything she knew.

Alice stopped outside the fence. Beyond lay clustered, crumbling headstones, half-hidden by drooping trees and overgrown weeds. Alice looked up at Lacey expectantly.

"Did you bring the sacrifice?"

"Wait. You never mentioned *that*."

"Only joking." Alice tugged against the old, bent gate and gestured inside. "After you, my queen."

"Please don't call me that." Lacey marched ahead, scrubby weeds scratching at her ankles. Alice skipped on ahead, cutting a diagonal line through the uneven headstones toward the far end of the graveyard, tucked into the groves.

"I get the best results over here."

Lacey caught up to Alice and found one large, imposing grave with three other, smaller headstones to its left. The large stone bore the name Donoveir Fryer.

Alice's smile glowed, white against the darkness. "The family. Donoveir, Latrice, and their sons."

"But..." Lacey knelt in the grass by one of the small graves. William Fryer.

She knew her father wasn't there. He was in Hollows Edge. Still, a chill shuddered down her spine, cold sorrow filled her soul. It seemed she was mourning him once again, even as her new anger towards him seemed to rot her very blood. She turned away from the headstone.

The other tiny grave... Lacey had never known she'd had an uncle. Though he'd died young—the grave markings put him at little more than a year old—it felt perverse, knowing he was trapped down there, his potential wasted by a single man's cruel act.

"I don't want any of this to be true," Lacey said finally.

"You saw the painting," Alice said. "You look just like her."

"I know, but..." She ran her thumb across her father's name, black with mold, faded by time. "It doesn't make sense. He seemed so ordinary."

"So do you. But hey, isn't it better to be special?"

"I don't know."

Alice sat cross-legged on the ground beside Donoveir Fryer's grave and patted the spot before her. "Come on. Maybe Latrice can answer some of your questions."

Lacey knelt in the wet grass, her skin breaking out in goosebumps. Alice grabbed her hands and shut her eyes. Lacey followed suit, though she peeked every time she heard a rustle in the forest, the hoof-beat of an unseen creature. After several minutes of silence, Alice spoke.

"Latrice Heartwood-Fryer, by the wishes of Necropola, I ask you, come to me. Bring yourself before us, the faithful and the faithless."

Lacey rolled her eyes. She was grateful Dr. Poole couldn't see her just now; he'd be in stitches already.

"Latrice, we want to help you. Let those who have life bear your sorrow in death. Come to us and share your—ah!" Alice dropped Lacey's hand and pitched forward. Lacey stared, unsure what to do as the younger girl shook before her. Alice put a hand to her throat; her eyes watered.

"Something's—wrong." She sounded as though she was choking. Lacey wondered for a moment if it was all part of the show, when suddenly Alice retched and vomited in the grass between them. Lacey scrambled to her feet. For a moment Alice sat there, head hanging, breathing slowly—and then, whip-fast, she looked up and grinned, a string of yellow saliva running from the corner of her mouth, her eyes focused and full of lust.

"There's my dear girl," Alice said. It was her own voice, but the tenor had changed, and her smile flashed like a knife blade.

"Alice...?" Lacey said. She stepped back as Alice rose and walked toward her.

"What are you hiding, my pet?" Alice reached out a hand and brushed Lacey's cheek. In that moment, Lacey felt pain course through her entire body. A sharp, sudden terror gripped her. A scream rattled in her head—her own, or another's? She fell to the ground, hands over her ears, trying to drown out the sound, but it continued, louder, louder. Hands crawled across her body, but she was frozen—she couldn't fight him off. She couldn't stop him.

"Get back in your grave, Donoveir!"

With those words, it was over. Lacey opened her eyes with a sharp inhale. She was on her knees in the graveyard, unharmed. Poe stood before her, holding a shard of glass between him and his sister. Alice snarled, spit clinging to her dry lips.

"Leave that vessel." Poe's soft, lilting voice was strong now, certain in a way that made him sound years older. Alice stumbled, her back striking the grave, and at last, she collapsed.

"Alice!" Lacey rushed forward and turned the girl on her back. She felt for a pulse and found only the slightest, slowest murmur.

Poe joined her in the grass and lifted his sister's head onto his lap. Another figure moved between the graves and stopped beside them.

"You've been here one night," Nathy said, "and you're already causing trouble."

Lacey shook her head. "I didn't—we were trying to talk to Latrice."

Nathy scooped Alice into his arms; she hung like a rag doll, her thin limbs and wispy hair reaching back for the damp earth. "She isn't experienced enough in her craft to control it. When she tries to summon, anyone can jump in."

"I didn't know..."

Poe placed his moonlight-pale hand over hers. "It's all right. My sister claims to be better practiced than she truly is."

"Will she be all right?" Lacey asked, but Nathy was already walking back through the graveyard. Poe rose and offered Lacey a hand, which she accepted.

"I saw you two headed out here from my window. I'm sorry if I've caused you trouble, but...Alice has hurt herself before, trying to do this sort of thing."

"No," Lacey said. "*I'm* sorry. I should have known... She's only a child, after all."

They began walking back toward the house, a huge black mass looming above the trees, darker than the night bleeding out around it.

"Spirits are attracted to those they can best manipulate," Poe said as they walked along the path. "Alice has a sorrow in her that brings crueler spirits to her. They feed on her pain. It's like...a weak spot they can penetrate."

"Necromancy sounds...dreadful."

"It can be beautiful. I've never had a knack for summoning myself, but I'm clairvoyant. I can hear spirits whispering all around."

"Doesn't that get a bit maddening?"

He shook his head, his pierced smile glinting moonlight. "It's like a song, always playing in the background. And if I want to listen, they're always there." They stopped at the front door, and Poe touched his fingers to Lacey's cheek. "Latrice knew it the moment you arrived. Her voice never comes clearly... It's always a little broken... but..." He dropped his hand, his head listing to the side as though trying to hear something in the distance. "I feel her love. Her pain. A longing. She has something she wishes she could say."

Lacey shuddered, though not, as she would have liked to pretend, because of the damp chill on the air. "Why can't she say it?"

"I feel…" Poe's hand drifted up, resting at the hollow of his neck. "A hand around my throat. Her throat. Someone doesn't want her talking." He shook himself, as though waking from a trance, and smiled. "Let's see how Alice is doing, hm?"

Lacey nodded, her own throat suddenly tight, barring the words she was too scared to say.

THEY ENTERED THE infirmary to find Alice sitting up on the cot next to Saxon's, gulping at a flask of brownish liquid. She downed the contents and handed the empty flask back to Nathy, who stood beside her bed.

"More, please."

"Do *not* give her more," Saxon said.

"I know." Nathy set the empty flask on a high shelf, sparing Lacey a brief glance. "Oh, hey, killer."

"Shut it." She looked to Alice. "How are you?"

"Great. Your handsome friend here fixed me a potion and I feel *amazing*." She bounced in her bed, giggling madly. "I bet I could fly!"

"Is she drunk?"

Saxon smiled. "It was a strong revival potion. The main ingredient is Yashan's mushroom. It produces a slightly euphoric effect."

"Slightly?"

"Let's do that again, Lacey." Alice tried to slide out of bed, but her legs tangled in the sheets, trapping her. "I want to talk to *every* ghost in the graveyard. And you can bring the handsome one, and if I faint, he can revive me all he wants."

"Oh, my," Poe said.

Lacey rubbed her forehead, trying to push back the start of a headache. "Let's…not for now, okay?"

"Oh, but I had an idea." Alice worked at the knot of sheets around her legs, chattering all the while. "If you want to get close to Latrice, I know just the thing, and nobody has to faint or anything!"

"Perfect. What's that?"

"Stay in her bedroom, of course! Ta-da!" Alice hopped out of bed, finally free of the sheets.

"Her...bedroom? You mean her bedroom is still here?"

"Where else? They don't exactly walk off."

"But...are her things still there?" It seemed somehow perverse to think of a dead woman's belongings, standing lonely and rotting through time.

"Yeah, everything's as she left it. The brownies tidy up now and then. He can stay with you if you're scared." Alice pointed to Saxon, grinning. "He'd love that."

Saxon rose from his cot, still unsteady, but better than he'd been that morning. He came to Lacey's side and took her by the hand. "Actually, we can't stay. Sorry."

"And how are you leaving?" Nathy said. "One more transportation spell and you'll be shitting out your mouth."

"We'll take the train."

"Right. And the moment she crosses into Elonni territory, she'll be arrested, tried, *and* killed, all in one afternoon. You're a deadly romantic, Saxon."

"He's right," Lacey said before Saxon could retort. "Ryken told me what's happening in Theopolis."

"Lace." Saxon sighed. "Ryken is one of them. He'd tell you anything to make you stay. Nobody wants to hurt you. I'll tell you everything, but the point is, you're safer away from here."

Alice broke into the space between them, standing on her toes to get a better look at Saxon. "You are so *romantic!*"

"Thanks..." He gingerly pushed her aside. "Lace, please. We have to leave this place."

She crossed her arms around herself as though she could hold down the welling anxiety in her stomach. Nothing made sense. She'd believed Ryken—but why? The Dark Guard worked to protect nocturnes, and she certainly wasn't one of them. And yet...she didn't trust Saxon, either. And that, she certainly couldn't explain.

"I'm going to sleep. I need time to think about— everything." She turned to Alice. "Where is Latrice's room?"

Alice hopped on her heels and clapped her hands. "Follow me, my queen."

"I'm not—oh, bloody hell. Whatever."

24

THE PARCEL

-Theopolis-

THE WINDOWS STILL showed the glittering darkness of a city night when Poole awoke to a distant ringing. Aeyrin lay curled against his side, her head resting on his chest and her fingers fixed around the fabric of his shirt.

If anything should have been a dream, it was this. But somehow, she was real. She was here.

The doorbell rang a second time, but he couldn't muster the urgency to rise, given there were few people in the world he cared to see just now. Aeyrin shifted beside him, her eyes squinted against the sound.

"Who is it?" she mumbled.

The thought occurred that it couldn't be anyone good.

"Go to my room. I'll let you know when it's safe."

"Sol?" She sat up, sleep leaving her eyes in an instant. "What if—could it be Lacey?"

He couldn't believe it himself, and he hated to give her any hope that would only crush her. "I don't see how she could have gotten back into the city. I'll be right back, okay?"

She nodded and left the couch, disappearing down the hall toward his bedroom. Poole approached the door just as a third ring reverberated through the walls. He checked through the peephole and sighed, opening the door fractionally.

"What?"

Sebastian St. Luke managed an apologetic visage, but barely. The bastard held the unfortunate position of being married to a sharp-witted woman who had likely run through and subsequently disposed of her husband's many unconvincing facades, leaving him bare and honest to no one's benefit.

"I wanted to...explain."

"Why you turned Lacey in, you mean? Or why I shouldn't shove you down those steps and watch you bleed on the pavement?"

Sebastian looked over his shoulder. "Of course, a fall of this magnitude wouldn't exactly guarantee my death, would it?"

"Always a literalist." Poole held the door wider and admitted the doctor, conscious of Aeyrin only a room away. "Make it quick, whatever you've come to say."

"I'm sorry, of course," Sebastian said. "But when the Elderon threatens your entire way of life—"

"Believe me, I know all about it."

Sebastian smiled. "So, explanations aren't in order?"

"No, but begging for my mercy may very well be."

Sebastian looked around the room, eyed the couch, and sat. Poole sat across from him in an armchair and waited.

"I prefer," Sebastian started, "to go about things...diplomatically." He cleared his throat. "What I'm saying is—"

"You like to play both sides."

"Yes." He seemed relieved at being understood, if not sympathized with. "I believe your goddaughter has as much right to exist as anybody. But I value my family's security above all else. I won't put her before myself, or my own son."

Poole said nothing.

"Come on," Sebastian said. "You're a naturalist, Absolom, you know how this goes."

"You're copping out with survival of the fittest?"

"In this city, sometimes it's survival of the cruelest." He sighed. "That said, I can empathize with your predicament. So, I thought, as a last gesture, I would tell you what I know."

"Well, don't keep me waiting."

"My son has been sent to bring her back to the city. They've convinced him she'll be spared any...drastic punishments."

"Is he an idiot?" Poole asked slowly. "No offense."

"Of course." Sebastian smirked. "She's gone to a place called Fryer's Grove, in the western reaches."

"Fryer's Grove..." Poole shut his eyes. Shit. It was the same place Will had gone. Where all of this began.

She'd escaped the Elderon only to fall into the hands of the Nine.

"You know the place?" Sebastian said.

"It's where her father met those lunatic revolutionaries." Poole leaned forward. "Can you get in contact with Saxon? He can't bring her back here, but she can't stay there, either. If he could get her away..."

"My wife is tracking his every movement," Sebastian said. "If he brought her anywhere but here, she'd know, and she'd find him."

"So you're all useless, then."

Sebastian rose, straightening the lapels of his jacket. "I truly am sorry, Absolom. Perhaps you ought to contact that Dark Guard."

"Hold it."

Both men turned. Aeyrin stood at the mouth of the hall, something indefinable in her eyes. Something new and fierce and hungry.

"You're the one who turned Lacey over?"

Sebastian had the decency to attempt a flicker of shame. "I take it you're the mother?"

"You're goddamned right, I'm the mother. And if you had an ounce of self-respect—"

"Then indeed I'd do well to tell you that you're not safe within the confines of this city, Ms. Falk."

"Because the Elderon are after me? I figured as much when a Watchman tried to murder me in my own home."

"A Watchman...tried to *murder* you?" Sebastian shook his head. "I'm sorry, that just doesn't make sense."

She looked at Poole. "Is he serious?"

"I think you'd better go," Poole said, taking Sebastian by the shoulder and guiding him back to the door.

"Absolom—think about it. A Watchman attacking a human, on human territory? It's a war crime."

"The Elderon seem fond of those." He opened the door and pushed Sebastian back onto the stoop.

"You're not hearing what I'm trying to say. If the Commander truly sent a Watchman to *kill* her—he was acting without the Chancellor's knowledge."

"You want me to think the Elderon are so above destroying innocent lives?"

"If Crane were that bad, why wouldn't he just storm the western reaches and slaughter Lacey where she stood? They're still following the laws at the moment. What she just told me—a cold-blooded murder—the Elderon didn't do that."

"She was Will's wife," Poole said, "I'm sure they were only too happy to arrest her."

"Arrest her, yes. When have you truly known Crane to order a murder? Without trial? He couldn't do that, nor would he."

"Your loyalty is charming, Sebastian. Now get the hell off my stoop." He slammed the door on the doctor's protests.

He joined Aeyrin on the couch where she sat, her face in her hands, staring at nothing. "What's on your mind?"

"I—nothing. It's just, last night was so odd, and...I almost wonder if your friend was on to something."

"He's just trying to make himself feel better. Trying to shove the guilt onto someone else."

"I meant to tell you, before we...well." Aeyrin reached for her coat, discarded on the floor, and fished something from one of its pockets: A small package wrapped in parchment. "When the Watchman attacked, someone rescued me. The town preacher..." Her eyes narrowed. "But not the old one. He was Elonni. I'd only seen him once or twice in town. He told me to come here. He specifically told me to find you."

Poole took the package with numb fingers. "He wanted you...to find me."

"Yeah. One of your friends, maybe?"

Poole shook his head. "Sebastian and Kimberly are the only people I've told."

She eyed the package. "Well? Should you open it?"

The scientist in him was curious to find out what was inside, while the Theopoline reminded him that one should never open an unmarked package. His better half won out and he slipped the string, ripped the paper away, and lifted the lid of the box.

His blood left him in a cold rush.

Inside was a vial, its glass murky with age, its label peeling but legible: *Cericide.* A used syringe lay at the bottom of the box, along with a note, folded into a triangle. Poole unfolded it, though he knew. He was so sure what it would say. The words blared from their blank surroundings, as familiar as his own name, scrawled in expert mimicry of an unsure hand, though there was no true hesitation in the hard-pressed letters and the ink blotches like bullet holes.

Only the guilty run from God.

POOLE ROSE FROM the couch, the box shaking between his hands. "What did he look like?"

"The preacher?"

"Yes. Everything you remember, Aeyrin, I need to know now."

"Okay, okay. God. Um...he was tall, your height, I'd say. Older. Gray hair, maybe a little black in it. I dunno, he looked like a posh old gentleman."

"*How* old?"

"I don't know, it was dark. He looked sixty, maybe?" She eyed the box. "What is that? What's got you so worked up?"

"Nothing," he said, and walked calmly toward the kitchen. He tossed the package into the rubbish bin and poured himself a fresh cup of tea. Aeyrin appeared in the doorway, her umber eyes watching him cautiously.

"Sol? Who was that man?"

"I can't be sure. Not yet. But...he's dangerous. Insane."

"And...he's looking for you."

"No. He's found me."

They stayed silent, as though the mysterious man might be listening even then. For all Poole knew, he was. Why had he saved Aeyrin? Why had he wanted her here? Poole looked over at her. She wasn't safe. A dark new reality grew near for them. He needed answers.

He needed his father's old book.

25

THE HAUNTING

-Fryer's Grove-

LACEY COULDN'T SLEEP. The bed was comfortable enough, but the house emitted strange sounds in the night: wind hissing through the cracks, floorboards groaning unexpectedly, animals howling and hooting from the groves.

The single-window room was brought to light only by a weak stream of moonlight fighting through the clouds and a solitary candelabra set upon a bureau, angling the shadows to form dark corners. The deep maroon wallpaper brought Flynn's story back, this time in gruesome color.

She was in pieces.

Lacey threw back the dusty covers and stepped onto the chilled wood floor. If she couldn't get any rest, she'd at least get clean—her tattered dress smelled of the forest, her skin like dirt and blood. She abandoned her grandmother's old room and maneuvered her way down the darkened corridor to a small washroom, equipped with a clawfoot tub. A narrow cabinet stood in one corner, offering a bright collection of soaps and a neat stack of towels.

Lacey ran the water as hot as it would go and let the warmth tug at her jangled nerves and coat her aching body in ease. The prickly scent of lemongrass lifted off the water and she let herself be submerged.

"...still here."

Lacey poked her head out of the water. "Hello?"

Only the dripping of the faucet answered.

She'd been underwater; she couldn't have heard a voice, even if someone had been there.

She scrubbed herself clean with a newfound haste and stepped out of the tub. The water danced in her wake, brown and grainy. She drained it with a grimace and wrapped herself

217

in a towel. The ruined dress would go straight in the rubbish bin; she'd happily never look at it again.

"He's still here."

Her head snapped around to the voice, so close to her ear and yet...nobody stood with her in the tiny space.

She hurried from the washroom, her wet feet slopping on the carpet runner as she bolted down the corridor. Lacey shut herself into her grandmother's old bedroom and crawled back into bed, wearing only the towel.

"Okay," she said to the dim room. "What do you want? Have you...got something to tell me?"

Silence stretched the seconds into minutes. Lacey sighed and pushed out of bed, walking to the candelabra resting atop the bureau. She blew out each candle and turned to go to sleep.

A woman sat on her bed, head down, hands held over her stomach. A knife stuck at an angle, up into her ribs. Blood pooled from wounds all along her chest and arms and neck, dripping to puddles in the woman's lap. She lifted her head slowly, meeting Lacey's eyes with her own—big, green, and running with blood.

"He's still here," she said, blood trickling from the corners of her mouth. She lifted a gore-smeared hand to her heart, and blood pumped between her fingers, running in rivulets down her wrist. "Still here."

Lacey clutched herself around the waist, trying to control her shaking. "G-Grandmother?"

The woman blinked, blood clinging to her lashes. She looked at Lacey, her eyes focusing through the cloud of death slowly coming over them.

"You."

A scream ripped from her throat, curdled and low against the surging blood. Lacey stumbled, trying to make what distance she could between her and the agonized spirit. Her foot slipped against the sleek floor and she fell back, her head smacking against the bureau. And then, she only knew darkness.

IT WAS THE cold that finally woke her. Lacey found herself shivering atop the bath towel, her damp hair splayed across the floor. She rose and went to the wardrobe, relieved to find a dusty line of old dresses within. She ripped the nearest one from its hanger and dressed quickly. It was obviously old—High-necked with a dangerously tight waist and a ridiculously flowing skirt. The sort of thing to be worn with a corset and petticoats. It must have been her grandmother's.

Latrice. All at once the image of the tortured, bloody woman came back to her, the scream echoing in her aching head. She cast her eyes around the room, her stomach tight with nerves. But the woman had gone. Only one thing had changed about the room that Lacey could see—a tiny, glinting circle of metal on the floor, not far from where Lacey had fallen.

She bent to pick up the object. It was a bronze ring, thick as though designed for a man's finger. Symbols representing a language Lacey didn't know wound around the band. Inside, somebody had carelessly carved a new inscription: *For L, my Love.*

Lacey slipped the ring onto her thickest finger, but still it hung loose. She shoved it onto her thumb, where it sat comfortably above her knuckle.

She left the haunted room behind and made for the lift. The gate resisted her pull, and a moment later the soft snores of Jack drifted down through the metalwork. She stepped back and scanned the darkened corridor until the shadows peeled away from a narrow door just beside the lift. Behind it lay a steep, dirty flight of stairs winding up and down. She hurried downstairs, counting the floors and departing on the second. Flynn's office was just around the corner.

Somehow, she knew he would be awake, even in the middle of the night, and wasn't surprised when her knock was answered by the sound of overturned books and a hard banging. A moment later, he called from within, "Come in."

She pushed the door open and found Flynn holding the side of his head, his orange eyes fixed accusingly on the fanged fish swimming in its bowl. He looked up at the sound of her footsteps.

He paled, his mouth working. "Latrice."

"Flynn?" At the sound of her voice, he seemed to wake.

"Lacey! What's wrong? You look troubled."

"You might say that. I take it you've seen her, too."

He blinked. "From time to time." He shook himself, and a crooked smile brightened his face. "Can't sleep? I can whip up a sleeping draught that promises pleasant dreams."

She glanced around the cluttered office. Many of the shelves were jammed full with bottles, thick with strange liquids. "Do you make many potions?"

"Oh, loads."

"But... How? You're not part-mage, are you?"

"Oh, no." He smiled. "But we Fernos have our own methods. Sumri is brimming with herbs and plants that cure many ails. The fabled elixir of life is purported to flow through a river that cuts through the island." He stared at a cluttered row of jars above him, his eyes distant. "I learned the art...from my father," he said, rushing the last words. "Before he was brought here, he was rather adept."

Lacey frowned. "What were you about to say?"

"Just that."

She was too tired to argue. "I saw Latrice. Well. Her ghost, I suppose."

Flynn sank down into his floral chair, his hand going back to his temple, gripping absently at his hair. "Did you now."

"She was..." Lacey shook away the memory, the blood and screams and the staring eyes.

"She wouldn't hurt you," Flynn said after a moment, his eyes unfocused, like flames forgotten in an old grate.

"I think she wanted to tell me something. But all she could say was, 'He's still here.'"

"Strange."

"I thought so."

Flynn shuddered and rose, the movement electric and quick. "I'll give you that sleeping draught." He came around the desk, chose a few jars from the shelf. "I understand that you don't trust me entirely, but I hope you'll— Where'd you get that?"

He was staring now at her hands, clenched awkwardly above her stomach. She broke them apart and stared at her fingers, only now remembering the thick gold band around her thumb. "Oh. It was in my—Latrice's—room. After her ghost left. It was just lying on the floor."

He nodded along, mouth pinched to one side. "Stranger still." He brought a handful of jars to his desk and let them scatter among the books and the teapot, and plucked one up, seemingly at random. He dumped the contents of the jars into the teapot, humming, and at last lidded it and shook it.

Lacey winced. She didn't really want to drink anything he made here, in this dirty little space. "You mentioned something," she said. "That the Ruined Queen needed nocturne representatives to get her powers?"

"Indeed," he said between vigorous shakes of the teapot. "They are the heirs to the pages of the Book of the Nine. Guardians of her power, if you will."

"Did my dad...find any?"

"Several." He set the teapot down and peeled the lid back to check inside. "He was nearly fully realized until— Draught's done."

Until he died, Lacey finished for him. "Where are the heirs now?"

"Many were killed in the war." He beamed at her over the raised teapot. "But I'm here!"

"Right. You're the Ferno heir." It only made sense. "Any others?"

"Landon Woods, the werewolf. He's...in the process of convincing his pack to go along with this."

"And the Book?"

"It disappeared with your father."

"Well. It sounds like you've got no Book, almost no heirs, and a Monarch who doesn't want to help you."

"I've faced greater odds."

Lacey couldn't stop her smile in time. He grinned back.

"You know, I find your skepticism quite refreshing, actually," Flynn said. "Shows you've got a brain. You think things through."

"That doesn't make me the best candidate for your cult."

"But it makes you a fine queen."

Lacey narrowed her eyes. "I'm not a queen. I don't want to be, either. I know the Elderon is awful, but how's a monarchy any better?"

"Maybe it isn't. The point isn't to bring back the old ways. It's to carve a new path forward."

She broke their matched gazes. "Bit late for a political discussion."

"Of course. Help yourself." He deposited the teapot into her hands and backed away with a bow. "Goodnight, my— Goodnight, Lacey."

"Night." She turned for the door, but stopped, her eyes snagged on a photo resting on the bookshelf nearest the door.

The photo showed Flynn, seemingly as he was now, in a rumpled suit, his white-gold hair unkempt and stark in the colorless photo. He had his arm around the shoulders of a skinny, black-haired boy of eleven or twelve, with a long, jagged scar running down from his left eye.

"Nathy?" she said, stepping closer to the photo. "How long have you known each other?"

Flynn joined her, taking the picture into his hands and staring down into the past with sorrow in his eyes. "A while now. We used to be close."

The sorrow morphed easily into tension, and Lacey knew not to pry anymore. "Well. Goodnight, then."

She left the office with the teapot. Back in her room, she pulled the lid back and drank a small amount, setting the teapot aside on her dresser. She didn't expect it to work, but at least...

MORNING LIGHT CUT through the thick curtains, pale from the filter of cloud cover beyond the window. Lacey blinked in surprise at the teapot by her bed. Flynn might be mad, but he was good at potions after all.

She'd fallen asleep in Latrice's dress, and changing seemed pointless at the moment. She made her way to the lift and plucked a bit of lint from her hem. She set the little lump on the lift floor.

"Think lint is a tithe," a voice muttered above her. "Oh, I see, it's only a *brownie*."

"Can I have the second floor?"

"*Second* floor? For a bit of *lint?*"

"Please. It's all I've got."

"Fine." The lift rattled downward. Lacey stepped out, with apologies to the brownie, and made her way down the corridor. She found the study they'd all met in last night. The fireplace stood cold, burnt logs crumbled in its grate. The curtains stood open, letting in the milky light of day.

The door opened behind her and she turned. Saxon smiled at her from across the room. His long chocolate hair was rumpled and damp, his blue eyes sleepy, his bruises faded. He had dressed down, in trousers and a simple shirt which outlined his broad shoulders and tapering waist fittingly. Lacey stood very still, just looking at him—staring, possibly. How did he manage to look so bloody wonderful all the time?

He crossed the room and, taking her hands, drew her close.

"How'd you know I was here?" she asked.

He smiled. "Brownies told me."

"Gossipy little gits, aren't they?" She put her hands on his chest, intending to push him away, but instead her fingers lingered there, not wanting to move. Faint creases of muscle were just visible through his shirt. She felt him breathe in, unsteady, and she forced her hands back to her sides.

"I'm not leaving," she said.

He sighed. "Why?"

"Because there's something going on here. I want to know what."

"Lacey, you aren't safe here."

"I'm not safe anywhere, Saxon. At least here I might get some answers." She walked away, toward the desk, and pretended to take interest in one of the many tomes stacked on its surface. She flipped open the cover. The title page was written in Annanym. She thought back to that morning in Hollows Edge, when she'd tried hopelessly to contact her father. Maybe Latrice wasn't who she needed to talk to.

The thought that Alice or Poe might be able to bring her father back from the grave, if only for a moment... Her throat closed against the desire to cry. She needed more than ever to see him again.

"Lace." Saxon turned her toward him, his fingers soft against her shoulders. "I know it's hard. And I know you probably hate me right now. But I promise I'm just trying to protect you."

"I'd rather have answers than your protection, thanks." She broke away from him. "You never mentioned how you knew my memories had gone."

"O-oh. Right."

She narrowed her eyes. "Tell me."

"Well, see... We, um..."

"Oh, my gods." She punched his arm. "No, we didn't!"

"It wasn't that! I promise, Lace, that's not what happened. We just kissed. A bit."

"You kissed me?"

"Yeah."

She crossed her arms, unable to look him in the eye. Her skin flamed, not entirely with embarrassment. "And was I happy about it?"

"I got that impression, yes."

"Well. Fine, then." She looked at him. "Do it again."

"What? Now?"

"I deserve to know what it was like, don't I?"

"I—just—we're in the middle of an argument, and it's not quite the same..."

"Fine. But you've got to tell me, Saxon—right now—if there's anything else you're keeping from me."

He looked off to the side, his face tight. "There isn't. I know this situation hasn't put me in the best light. But I'd really never do anything to hurt you."

"On purpose, anyway."

"Right." He smiled. "So. Am I forgiven?"

"For now." She let herself smile back.

"Brilliant." He took her chin in his hand and leaned in. His mouth met hers with a sudden warmth, his stubble sharp on her lips. Gently, his hands cupped her neck, and the kiss deepened, melting what little anger Lacey had held on to. She gripped the front of his shirt, sure she would lose balance as her body titled toward his. Moments turned to pure feeling the longer they stayed like this, bound together in a soft heat.

"Is that what it was like?" she said against his lips.

"I think this was better, actually."

"What did we do then?"

"More of the same."

"Oh. Good."

He pulled her back in, and they stayed lost until a chill swept across Lacey's back, like fingers trailing across her ribs. She broke away from Saxon and checked behind her. A flicker of red hair vanished beyond the study door.

"What's wrong?" Saxon said.

Lacey shook her head. "Nothing." She didn't think it wise to tell Saxon about Latrice's ghost—he'd only want her to leave all the more.

"Let's explore the house," she said at last. "See what's around."

He captured her hand in his and entwined their fingers. "All right. We'll pick this up later, then?"

She considered him, then shrugged. "If you behave."

He grinned. "I'll see what I can do."

26

THE SWORDSMAN

-Fryer's Grove-

NATHY'S OLD ROOM was bare but for a rumpled bed and an old wardrobe standing against one wall. It had always been this way, sparse, a haunted sense of semi-habitation clinging to the undecorated walls and surfaces. He had never really intended to stay, never much believed he could, even as those first unsure months became a steady stream of years when he might have reasonably thought he belonged.

When he decided to leave—abruptly, struck senseless by grief—he just did. No packing, no sentiment. He left everything, and the room felt the same, because what little he owned stayed tucked away.

With how little there was to go through, it was easy to see something was missing.

"Dammit."

The false bottom to the imposing black wardrobe lay empty, dust collecting in the corners. He replaced the floor piece and stood, his back cracking with the motion. He still ached everywhere, thanks to the bleeding wing infecting his body.

"Looking for something?"

Nathy turned. Flynn stood in the doorway, his golden hair falling into his eyes.

"I take it you moved my weapons stash?"

Flynn blinked innocently. "Oh, that. Yes. Alice was getting into it."

"I'd rather not leave unarmed." Nathy turned back to the meager collection of clothes hanging in the wardrobe. A streak of olive green caught his eye.

"Hey. I forgot about this thing." He pulled out the duster and threw it on. The hem fell halfway down his shin, the rumpled fabric billowing from the waist. He pressed the collar to his nose. The fabric still smelled of fire, dirt...and a girl's perfume. Roses.

He winced. Artemis. She'd always find ways to invade his memories.

"They're locked away in my office," Flynn said.

"Huh?" Nathy had forgotten his old guardian standing there.

"Your weapons? I can collect them for you. Of course..." He looked down. "I'd rather you didn't leave."

"I've got things to do."

"I understand, you know... I blame myself, too."

Nathy shook his head. "She was human, Flynn. You knew she'd die if she faced Ruark, and you let her go anyway."

"I didn't know that. She was a warrior. You taught her well." Flynn pushed his hair back, his hand shuddering. "I had full confidence in her abilities. I still believe she put up a fight."

"Whatever gets you to sleep at night." Nathy slammed the wardrobe shut. "I'll take my weapons now."

"We need you here, Nathy."

"You got your Monarch." He shoved his hands into the duster's pockets, considering Flynn through narrowed eyes. "And I think I've lost enough for your cause."

"We've all lost someone to this." Flynn's hand clenched in his hair, pain flashing in his fiery eyes. "It's the cost of war."

"Right. Remind me who you've lost?"

"You, for one."

"That's not the war's fault." He brushed past him. "I'll be outside. Bring the weapons when you get a chance."

He hurried through the corridors, as though he could outrun the flashes of memory. He almost saw himself, younger, flitting out of doorways, hanging back in the lift, curled in the alcove of a deep window. He saw Artemis, too, flashes of blond hair whipping around corners, never fully visible, but so obviously her.

He shook his head. Fryer's Grove had ghosts, but she had never come back. Only her memory hung around, clinging to every thought, haunting him in a different way.

And what good were memories like that?

Lacey and Saxon walked along the corridors, their hands entwined. Every so often Lacey tested a door to see what lay beyond, but most rooms were musty old testaments to the house's former inhabitants, crowded with covered furniture and cobwebs.

"Flynn hasn't taken great care of this place, has he?" Lacey said. They approached ornate double doors and Lacey pushed them open, expecting to find another moldering room.

Instead, she found a library. Every wall in the long room was lined with bookshelves that reached to a loft above, packed with even more texts of its own. There were dozens of desks and writing tables set throughout the room haphazardly, and they, too, overflowed with tomes and scrolls that would not fit on the shelves. One shelf, nestled in the far right corner of the room, was filled with scrolls sealed behind glass.

One of the writing tables was occupied. Alastair sat slumped over a text, his glasses slipping down his narrow nose.

"Alastair." Lacey approached the desk. "How are you? I didn't see you after you left last night."

"I'm well, thank you." He barely looked up from his book.

"What are you reading?" she asked.

"The Amerand."

Saxon leaned over the table, tilting his head to read the book. "Is it any good?"

"It's the foundational text of my religion," Alastair said tersely.

"So, yeah?"

Lacey kicked Saxon's ankles. "Why don't you go find yourself a book on spellcasting for young warlocks? Since that's the level you're at."

He smirked. "I love how cruel you are." He kissed her cheek and sauntered off to the other end of the library.

"Sorry," Lacey said. "He thinks he's charming. Not that it's any excuse."

"I can see how he's mates with my brother." Alastair stuck a torn piece of parchment between the Amerand's pages and shut the book.

Lacey sat in the chair beside him. "How are you doing with all this?"

He shook his head. "I—just can't believe it. I'm trapped here. And my father..." He propped his elbows on the table and held his head. "I just want to go home."

"I know. But...would it really be better? I mean, your father sounds awful."

Alastair sighed. "He is. That's why I didn't make a fuss when he sent me to the monastery. And there, life was just simple. I thought I'd finally found my place. I thought I had a purpose."

"I get it. It's hard when you don't have someplace to really belong. But I think you'll find it someday." She shrugged. "It might not be so bad here."

"They're a cult. I'd rather not *belong* here."

"They're not so bad. Most of them."

"Suppose Poe is..." Alastair shook his head. "Never mind."

Lacey bit her lip. "Can I ask—and tell me to piss off if it's personal—why did your father send you to a monastery?"

"Because...I didn't want to get married."

Lacey raised her eyebrows. He couldn't be any older than she was—old enough to marry, perhaps, but too young for it to be a real issue. "Were you supposed to?"

"Most Old Name families arrange engagements between their children. Keep the bloodlines 'strong', you know. I wasn't any different."

"And you...didn't like her?"

"I'd...been seeing someone else." He checked over his shoulder to make sure Saxon was still far from them, then lowered his voice. "A bloke. Henry."

"*That's* why your father shipped you off to a monastery? What a prick."

"He was right to do it."

"He really wasn't."

"According to this, he was." He pulled the Amerand closer; he stared down at the holy book with a mixture of reverence and sorrow. "But I couldn't— I mean I *tried*. Everything. But prayer, ritual—*nothing* worked. When my father couldn't stand it anymore, he sent me away. Thought being a monk would fix it."

"Well, he's a wanker." Lacey nudged him gently. "And you seem like a lovely person. You deserve better."

Alastair nearly smiled. "Thanks."

"Lace. Look!" Saxon returned, bearing a huge pile of old books. "Flynn's got dozens of books on potion making. Maybe I can find some way to make that unbinding potion." He dropped the books on Alastair's table, right on top of the Amerand. Alastair paled.

"You—can't—on top of the—"

"Oh, sorry, mate." Saxon moved the books aside, knocking the Amerand to the floor in the process. Lacey thought Alastair might faint in his chair.

Saxon stooped to retrieve the book. "Sorry."

Alastair swiped the Amerand from him and held it to his chest. "It's *fine.*"

"So," Lacey said, nodding to the pile. "Potions?"

"Yeah. I mean, they're Ferno potions, which is different than what I usually do. But I'm sure I can find something in one of these that'll help."

Lacey nodded, though she hardly dared to hope. She wasn't even sure she wanted whatever power was locked away inside her. But still... She ran her finger down the many spines of the books.

"Get to reading, then."

Saxon picked the first book off the pile and flipped it open. His face fell. "It's written in Sumrian."

Lacey held her forehead; she felt a headache coming. "What did you expect?"

"I'll...see if Flynn will translate."

"You do that."

The library doors opened then, and Alice and Poe rushed in. "Hey, Monarch." Alice vaulted onto the desk and sat cross-legged on top of it. "You know that spirit that attacked us last night?"

"I seem to remember, yes."

"The grave..." She paused, her smile growing with anticipation, "is open."

Lacey shook her head. "What?"

"It's true," Poe said. "The ground just crumbled away... The house is quaking... It's sorrow bleeds into the air... Oh. Hi, Alastair." He waved quickly and dropped his hand.

"Hello." Alastair squeezed the Amerand tighter to his chest.

"How does a grave just open?" Lacey asked.

Alice shrugged. "Dunno. But obviously it's calling to you. So, let's go see what it wants."

"Not you," Poe said, placing a hand on his sister's head. "The spirit injured you last night. It knows you're susceptible."

"I'm not *susceptible*."

"Poe's right," Lacey said, remembering his warning from the night before. "I'll go see what you're talking about."

"The ground probably just caved in around the coffin," Saxon said. "Old grave like that, it probably wasn't filled in properly."

"Oh, really, Mister Science?" Alice crossed her arms over her chest. "Since when are you an expert on improperly sealed graves?"

He glared at her. "I liked you better when you were high."

Poe giggled, then cast his eyes on Alastair. "You can stay here with me and Alice, if you want. I can show you all the best books."

Alastair cleared his throat. "Actually, I think I'd better go with Lacey. Just in case she needs...moral support."

Lacey looked between the two boys, Poe's eyes shy and downcast, Alastair's averted, his face filling with color. As she, Saxon, and Alastair left the library, she whispered, "What's that all about?"

"N-nothing. I don't *like* him. I mean, he's fine. But... God, I shouldn't have told you."

"I'm not going to say anything. I promise. That's up to you."

He smiled in a painful way. "Are all humans so...blasé about this sort of thing?"

"Not all of them. More so than the Elonni, I expect. But for the most part—"

"What are you two whispering about, then?" Saxon said, falling back.

"Nothing!" Alastair said, and stormed off ahead of them.

"Sorry, mate!" Saxon called after him. He looked down at Lacey. "What's with Marshall?"

231

She only shrugged.

THE SWORD ARCED through the air, splitting a tree branch clean from its trunk. Sap eked like blood from a wound. Nathy stepped aside and swung at another, another. He hacked and cut until his arms ached, until a voice interrupted the meditative release of exertion.

"What did the tree ever do to you?"

Lacey stood a few feet away, Saxon by her side. Alastair stood farther back, eyeing the pile of weapons across the grass.

"It looked at me funny." Nathy stuck the sword into the ground and rested his hand on the pommel. "What do you want?"

"I heard chopping." Lacey shrugged. "Thought you might be killing someone."

"That's always a possibility."

"Hey," Saxon said.

"Oh, calm down, Saxophone. I would never hurt her royal majesty." Nathy yanked the sword from the ground and swung it in a careless arc. Saxon flinched back.

Nathy's eyes drifted to Lacey. She was dressed like a grandmother in an old, high-necked dress, and yet there was nothing ladylike about the way she eyed the pile of weapons, as though fascinated by the dull glint of metal. "You ever handle a sword, princess?"

She tore her eyes away from the stash. "No. But I'm handy with a shotgun."

"This takes a little more skill." He held the sword out. Lacey grabbed the hilt, her warm fingers beneath his. When Nathy let go, she stumbled forward, the weight of the sword pulling her off kilter.

"That's called a claymore. Come to think of it, it might be heavier than you."

She gripped it with two hands and found her balance. "I think I can manage."

"Just don't aim it at Saxon. The blade's made of iyrel."

Saxon stepped slowly backward.

"What's wrong?" Lacey asked.

"Iyrel is toxic to the nocturne kinds," Nathy said.

"Hm." She smiled, her green eyes sharp. "So, what would happen if I hit you with it?"

"You'd never get the chance."

She touched her fingers to the broad side of the sword, then ripped them away when a sharp, stinging burn coursed through her nerves. She hissed and dropped the blade.

Saxon was at her side the next moment. "Did you cut yourself?"

"No," she said, sticking her aching fingers into her mouth. "It burned me."

Nathy raised his eyebrows. He and Saxon exchanged a glance, which Saxon ended.

"Strange," Saxon said.

"You part witch or something?" Nathy asked.

Lacey shook out her fingers. "No. Just Elonni-human."

Nathy looked at her for a long moment, then finally shrugged. "Whatever. Here." He walked to the pile of weapons and picked out a smaller, thinner longsword. "Try something you won't kill yourself with."

Lacey took the one-handed sword. She swung it, sending Alastair and Saxon skittering.

"Watch when you're aiming it, huh?" Nathy said. "Good news is that's ordinary steel, so you don't have to worry about fatally poisoning your boyfriend. Or yourself, apparently."

She looked down at her fingers. The skin was gray and puckered where she had touched the claymore.

"Does this have to do with the binding potion?" Lacey asked Saxon, waggling her poisoned fingers at him.

"No," he said. Then, "I don't know. I told you they weren't letting me in on anything. Iyrel probably burns you because of that bloody curse."

"It's not a curse." Lacey planted the blade in the ground and leaned on it with one hand. "It's actually sort of nice, if you think about it."

"Nice?"

"Sure. I have unstoppable powers. That's something, isn't it?"

Saxon threw up his hands and said no more.

233

Alastair wandered toward the pile of weapons and turned to Nathy. "Why do you have all these?" he asked. Still lying in the grass was what might be considered an excessive collection—five swords of varying sizes and metals, a halberd with a significant crack in it, an old mace, and a battered shield.

"Overcompensation?" Saxon suggested.

"You'd know all about that," Nathy said. He looked back at Alastair. "My father gave them to me. Call it my inheritance."

Lacey perked up. "Was he a Watchman?"

"Huntsman."

Alastair and Lacey stared at him, wide-eyed.

"What?" Nathy said.

"Well," Alastair said. "It's just...you're mixed, aren't you? And Huntsmen work for the Elderon."

"*Oh.*" Nathy smiled darkly. "You're wondering why an upstanding Elonni would go in for a Rakashi witch?"

Alastair flushed. "I—no. Sorry. I'm sorry."

"Don't be." Nathy shrugged. "They didn't last very long."

"Who *is* your father?" Alastair said. "If you don't mind me asking."

Nathy sighed. "Mortimer Fairborn."

"Are you *joking*?"

Lacey looked over at the monk. "What? Is that bad?"

"You"—Alastair pointed at Nathy—"are a *Fairborn*?"

"Call me that again and they'll never find your body."

Alastair winced. "Well, you don't have to be rude about it."

"So..." Lacey swung the sword like a pendulum, a bored look on her face. "Anyone interested in explaining to the provincial why his last name is so interesting?"

"The Fairborns are one of the oldest of the Old Names," Saxon said. "They were nobles in the old monarchy, and they were integral in helping the Elderon take power. They can trace their bloodline back over a thousand years."

"And I'm the stunning result of all that inbreeding," Nathy said. "Well. Have fun, kids."

"Wait." Lacey followed after him as he started to leave. "Do you want to help us investigate the open grave?"

He turned back. "What now?"

"The grave Alice and I disturbed last night? It opened up."

"Fascinating."

"And," Lacey said, "We're all going down there. So, I thought maybe you'd come."

"And why would I do that?"

"For...a sense of adventure? A touch of derring-do?"

"Dear goddesses." He ran a hand through his hair, sighed. "Okay. Fine." He slung the shield over his back and grabbed the claymore. He turned toward the graveyard without another word.

Lacey smiled and bounded ahead to catch up. She held the sword out before her. "So, how does this work? I just hold it like this and poke at people, right?"

"Now you're just trying to annoy me."

"Maybe."

She thought she saw his smile, more fleeting than a passing ghost.

27

THE CRYPT

-Fallor Wood-

DIRT CRUMBLED AWAY, hitting worn stone steps below. Lacey sheathed her new sword and stepped close to the gaping maw of the grave. "It's a secret tunnel."

Nathy peered over her shoulder. "No kidding."

Lacey threw him a withering look and stepped forward onto the narrow stairwell.

"Er." Alastair tapped her shoulder. "Don't you think we should tell Flynn about this? And not go down there, as well?"

"You don't have to come."

She took the steps carefully, brushing the dirt wall with her fingers to guide her as darkness swelled, the gray daylight shuddering away with each step.

Heavy footsteps thundered after her. "Lacey," Saxon said. "This is mental. Come back up."

"On your left." Nathy shouldered his way past Saxon on the narrow stairs. Saxon caught his balance against the wall, glaring down.

"Come on," Lacey said. "I just want to see what's at the bottom."

"Probably a dead body," Saxon said. "As it's a grave."

"It's okay, Saxophone." Nathy slung his arm across Lacey's shoulders, dragging her more quickly down the steps. "You stay up top with the monk. I'll just poke around in a dark, underground vault with your girlfriend. Don't worry about a thing."

Saxon shut his eyes and a took a long, deep breath through his nose. "Wait up."

Lacey smiled, shoving Nathy's arm off her shoulders. "Nicely done."

"I'm coming, too!" Alastair's small voice echoed in the narrow space, farther up the steps.

"Now it's a party," Nathy said.

The stairs ended in a dark room; only a bare puddle of daylight made it down the stairs, pooling at their feet. Lacey felt along the walls until her hand struck metal. She snapped her fingers, lighting a torch along the wall.

She turned to find the three men staring at her. "What?"

"How did you do that?" Saxon said; his face was inscrutable in the shadows.

"Friction," Lacey said. "I thought all Elonni could do that."

"Nope," Nathy said.

Alastair shrugged. "I can't."

Lacey looked down at her hands. She'd always been able to light candles with the flick of her fingers. "Suppose it's one of my powers."

The light of the first torch glinted off the metal of several more along the wall, and she lit them in turn until the room glowed a deep orange, the light of the flames reaching to a huge sarcophagus in the center of the room, an elaborate stone figure atop its lid.

The carved clothing would have better suited the memory of an old king that an ambassador to a forgotten reach of the realm. The stony robe detailed repeating motifs of conjoined eyes, one shut, the other open and spilling rays of light like tears. The hands were shaped together in prayer, tilted horizontal to the chest, aimed at the proud chin and serious mouth of Donoveir Fryer. His carved eyes regarded the roof of his tomb without expression, the flat stone making him seem cruel.

Lacey bent to read the inscription, but it was written in Annanym, the old Elonni writing system of millennia past.

"The dead are not dead, whom His blood hath chosen, for they rise again," Alastair said.

Lacey raised her eyebrows. "You can read that?"

"It's required to join the church. We're only permitted to study the Amerand in its original language."

"I take it Donoveir was the religious sort, then."

"I don't know." Alastair ran his fingers across the inscription, frowning. "That's not a passage from the Amerand."

"Look at this."

Lacey and Alastair joined Nathy, who stared up at a tapestry hung along the back wall. It depicted a man seated upon a glowing throne, his hand outstretched to a kneeling figure before him. The first image bled into a second, of the kneeling man now seated upon his own throne, a glowing crown upon his head. The final image showed the man casting his crown aside, where another, humbler figure stooped above it, fingers outstretched, head bowed to the retreating king.

But someone had taken a torch to the final image; the corner was burned away, partly obscuring the figure of the humble man reaching for the crown.

"Oh." Alastair ran his fingers along the frayed edge of the tapestry. "It's the succession of power." He pointed to the heavenly figure upon his throne in the first panel. "Elrosh choosing the first king of Akhratan—the Trueborn Son. And here, the Trueborn's bloodline ruling peacefully. And finally..." He placed his hand over the burnt spot on the tapestry. "Legend says the Trueborn sons abandoned the throne to mortals, to let them rule their own affairs. The Trueborns left peacefully, and the new monarchy ruled until..."

"The Ruined Queen," Lacey said. "Why isn't she on this?"

"It's far too old," Alastair said. "This tapestry...it's got to be a thousand years old. Long before Elonni settled in Gryfel."

"Yeah, *settled*," Nathy muttered. Alastair shot him a thin glare.

"When you say Trueborns..." Lacey let the sentence drift away, her eyes roving back to the scorched panel. Whoever had done that hadn't been pleased about the supposed transfer of power from Elrosh's chosen ruler to a new monarch.

"The Trueborns... Well, they're just a legend." Alastair pointed to the woven image of Elrosh. "But in the stories, it's said they were the very blood of Elrosh. Gods upon the earth. In the old monarchy, the Trueborns ruled over the Elonni.

They were Elonni themselves, by all appearance, but...better. Invincible. And immortal."

"Is that in the Amerand?" Nathy asked dryly.

"No. There are old writings, stone carvings, that sort of thing. But nothing in the sacred texts."

"Good. The world has enough gods as it is." Nathy frowned, his eyes falling on something below the tapestry. Another Annanym, clumsily carved into the wall like a bit of ancient graffiti.

Lacey squinted at it. "What's that one—oh, my God, *what are you doing*?"

Nathy had pulled a knife from his boot and was dragging it across his palm. He pressed the bloody stream to the stone wall.

"It says 'blood,'" he told her.

"So, you decided to give it some?"

He stood, wiping his palm on his trousers, and waited. A faint rumble came from somewhere behind the wall. He held out his arm, ushering Lacey and Alastair back. Saxon hurried over from another corner of the tomb and clutched Lacey's hand.

"We ought to go," he said.

Lacey nearly agreed. And then, the section of wall where the Annanym had been crumbled away, leaving a tunnel just tall enough to crawl through.

"All right," she said. "Who's coming with me?"

THE TUNNEL WENT on seemingly forever. Nathy led the way, using his elbows and knees to propel himself through the cramped space. Lacey trailed behind, her palms wet with mud, her dress tearing against small stones in the dirt.

"Can we slow down?" Alastair panted from the back of their procession.

Lacey hoped they wouldn't slow. Grueling as the trek was, the ache in her arms was nothing compared to the pressure on her chest, the nearness of the tunnel's walls making her stomach seize. Visions of the tunnel leading to a dead end flashed across her mind. What would they do? The space was too narrow to turn in, they'd be trapped, oh God, they'd rot here...

"I see light," Nathy said.

"Oh, thank Elrosh." Lacey pushed herself faster across the ground.

A ladder jutted from the wall ahead of them, planks of wood crudely hammered into the dirt. Nathy gripped a low rung and hauled himself up; Lacey followed close behind. Daylight trickled in thick cracks along the walls, drifting through a wooden plank above them. Nathy shoved it up and aside and hauled himself out, reaching down to take Lacey's hand. He dragged her out of the tunnel in an easy motion, and she stumbled against her sudden footing and fell into him.

"Well, hey there." He grabbed her shoulders and pushed her back. "Fair warning, Saxon is the jealous type."

"I didn't mean to..." Lacey blushed and marched away as Saxon pushed out of the tunnel, Alastair scrambling behind him.

"It's just more forest," Saxon said, glancing around. The thick, rain-weeping trees rose around them like a stoic army. The distant roar of the sea was gone, so they must have travelled east quite a way. Each direction looked the same—impenetrable, dark, winding. Even the daylight, which had given Lacey hope in the tunnel, faded as gray clouds moved above the tree tops, the whisper of rain on the air.

"Why would the tunnel lead here?" Lacey asked. It wasn't even a clearing, just another claustrophobic corner of forest. What significance could such a place hold?

"River," Nathy said.

"Where?" Lacey swept her eyes across the brown-and-green world.

"Half a mile...that way." Nathy pointed with his claymore and started walking north.

"I don't hear a river," Saxon said.

"Neither do I," Nathy said. "I feel it. You could, too, if you got in touch with the Sisters from time to time."

Saxon sneered at the back of Nathy's head. Lacey walked beside him, taking his hand and giving it a squeeze. "Who are the Sisters?"

"Lye and Lilith. Mage goddesses."

"They're spirits," Nathy corrected. "Lye is the soul of the moon, Lilith, the woods. They guide travelers. Well, travelers they like, anyway."

Alastair lagged behind, sighing. "We're being guided by pagan spirits?"

"No," Nathy said. "*I'm* being guided by pagan spirits. You're following me, unless you want to end up lost in the woods."

They followed him in silence after that. Saxon's grip on Lacey's hand tightened the farther they walked. Occasionally, he brushed his fingers across his trouser pocket, as though checking something was still there. Lacey studied him beneath her lashes as they walked; his skin glowed with sweat, yet he was paler than usual. He swiped irritably at his forehead.

"Are you feeling sick again?" Lacey said quietly.

"Just tired."

"You don't look well."

"I said I'm fine, Lace."

She pulled her hand free of his and walked ahead. "All right, then."

He didn't say anything, or try to stop her, and the small triumph of leaving him behind her died by his apathy. She caught up to Nathy and walked beside him, wordless.

After a long moment, Nathy spoke. "He's an idiot. But he cares."

"How would you know?"

"I don't. Just trying to be nice."

"I like you better when you're being an ass."

"Noted, princess." He smiled down at her, then jerked his head to the right. "We're almost there."

They broke through the line of trees. Lacey, relieved to see the sky, stepped toward the sudden sound of a rushing river. Nathy caught the collar of her dress just as her feet missed the ground and she pitched forward.

The forest floor sloped sharply down, rolling into a valley. A crumbling brick house sat nestled below, tucked between trees and bordered by the river.

Nathy pulled her back onto the ridge. "Wonder who lives there."

Lacey stared down at the house. Even from this distance, discarded bricks and rotted planks of wood stood out on the overgrown lawn, weeds drawing everything back into the earth.

"Nobody," Lacey said.

"You hope."

Saxon and Alastair emerged from the tree line, joining them along the ridge.

"Fascinating," Alastair said. "A house. Suppose your forest spirit can take us home now?"

Nathy exchanged a look with Lacey; they smiled. Lacey pressed her palms together and her wings curled from her back, red light spreading and solidifying into wings. She jumped from the ridge and caught the air, twisting back to hover before the others.

"Well?"

Alastair made a low sound of distress, but pressed his own palms together. His wings emerged, mousy brown like his hair. He joined Lacey in the air.

"I can't fly," Saxon said. His eyes darted between each of them, unfocused, restless. Nathy clapped him on the shoulder.

"Why don't you stay here, Saxophone? If we're not back in an hour, sound the alarm."

"I'm not staying here while you—"

Nathy tightened his grip on Saxon's shoulder. "I insist. You don't look so good anyway. Maybe there's something in your pocket that will make you feel better."

Saxon's darting eyes focused, narrowing on Nathy's. His lip curled, his fist clenched.

"One hour." Nathy chucked Saxon under the chin. "Use it to your leisure."

"Wait," Lacey said. "You can't fly, either."

"I don't need to." He drew his shield and set it on the ridge, the pointed end jutting across the empty air. He hopped onto the shield and pushed off. The shield scraped down the valley wall like a sled, and Nathy guided it around the rocks and branches jutting from the grass.

"He's insane," Alastair said.

Lacey turned back to Saxon. "We won't be long. One hour, all right?"

"Okay, okay. Just—be careful."

Lacey and Alastair flew down to the ruined yard and landed outside the ramshackle house. Nathy ground his shield to a halt beside them seconds later.

An unmoving waterwheel sat in the river beside the house. A small shed, its door hanging open, spilled tools across the ground. There was no front door to the main building, only the gaping maw of the entrance. Lacey crept warily toward it and, as she did, stepped on something hard, which broke underfoot. She looked down on the shattered face of a porcelain doll, its marble eyes locked on hers in accusation.

"All right, that's creepy," Nathy said.

Lacey nodded, mute, and started once more to the doorway. Inside was a sitting room in states of decay: a moldering couch bleeding its stuffing; a piano missing several keys; a chair with broken legs strewn aside; and, strangest and somehow worst of all, the tattered remains of a dress, fifty years out of date, hanging over the back of a writing desk.

"We shouldn't be here," Lacey said.

"Probably not," Nathy agreed.

Alastair breathed out in relief. "Oh, thank Elrosh, you've come to your senses."

Lacey looked over at Nathy. "Want to go inside?"

He smiled. "I like you, princess."

Alastair slumped. "Oh, hell."

"Did the monk just say *hell?*" Nathy said. "Alert the deacons."

Alastair's cheeks colored. "Ass."

"Well, you're definitely sacked now." Nathy stepped into the sitting room. Lacey grabbed Alastair by the arm and pulled him along, a strange sense of elation overcoming her.

They moved further into the house, through a moaning door, and into a dark corridor. The remaining patches of wallpaper peeled like scabs, revealing the raw skin of the house beneath. A staircase yawned at the end of the hall, leading up and down. Nathy held a hand up.

"Hear that?"

"No," Lacey and Alastair said together.

He looked down at them. "Stay close."

They tried the first door along the hall. It creaked back to reveal a damp, musty study. Lacey walked ahead. The books lining the shelves were ancient, older and huger than any she'd seen before. Many bore no titles. She pulled one tome from a low shelf—it was heavy with age and importance, its bulk somehow delicate. She set it on the floor and kneeled to read the first page.

"It's Anñanym again," she said.

Nathy and Alastair kneeled on either side of her as she ran her fingers across the ancient words. The pages were like moths' wings, thin and translucent. Three words were printed in large text across the first page, heading a smaller sentence below.

"*Hkanakim, lyshim, reyim,*" Alastair read.

Nathy stared down at the words, then said softly, "Might, sight, and wisdom."

Alastair's head shot up. "How did you know that?"

"I've...heard it somewhere before." He pointed to the longer sentence beneath the three words. "That next part says: 'With these devices, we will halt the very motion of the sun.' Doesn't it?"

"Ah...yes." Alastair shook his head. "I can't believe you know any Old Akhratian."

"He knew that Anñanym in the tomb said 'blood,'" Lacey said.

"Right." Alastair frowned. "How do you know what this says?"

"How the hell should I know?" Nathy said. "Maybe it's a popular book."

"A popular book," Alastair said, "in a dead language, in a writing system that hasn't been used in a thousand years?"

"I don't remember, okay?" Nathy pulled the book from Lacey's lap and rose, tucking it under his arm. "I'm keeping this."

"What if somebody notices it's gone?" Lacey looked around; she suddenly felt watched.

"Who's gonna notice?" He gave her a hand up, smiling, but his confidence only left Lacey more afraid. Someone, certainly, claimed possession of these ruins. She didn't know why she believed it, but now...

"I hear it, too," she said, and Nathy looked at her. "Chanting."

He listened and whispered, "That's what I heard before."

Below the floorboards, in the belly of the house, a solitary voice repeated the same few muffled words again and again.

"We should go," Alastair said.

"Why?" Lacey said, and then realized. "What are they saying?"

Alastair listened to the chanted words, in a tongue Lacey couldn't give name to. His breath shook as he recited, "'Arise, arise, your king has come. Arise, arise, the enemy is nigh.'"

"All right," Lacey said, her voice faint. "You're right let's...g-go."

The chanting shifted then to a single word, spoken louder each time. *Mulrot. Mulrot. Mulrot.*

"Ruined," Alastair translated.

Lacey held her forehead, suddenly hot with fever. "I'm not...ruined."

"Lacey?" Alastair reached out and gripped her arms. "Lacey."

You were born ruined, something said in her ear. She whipped around, and the room fractured. Ice rushed her blood; darkness worked along the edge of her vision, cloudy and then thick, black. She sank, but didn't feel herself hit the floor.

28

THE MARK OF ISCARIOT

POOLE HAD THOUSANDS of books in his house, but only one he was ashamed of. He knew enough to consider the opinion of his enemies, even of fools. But there was one text, at least, which perhaps should have been burned, should never even have been written. And it was under the floorboards in his bedroom.

He pried the loose board up and there it was—the *Malus Vylarus*, a copy kept intact for nearly a thousand years, passed down father-to-son through his family. Until stolen by him, the seventh son, the destined traitor. It would have been Arctan's, but Arctan was dead—all Poole's brothers were dead but him.

Unless...the package...the vial and the used needle. He hadn't wanted to believe, because it was too horrible.

Poole pulled the *Malus* from its hiding place and gingerly lifted the cobwebby cover. The book fell open to a page which, in its time, must have been frequently perused. Poole knew the Annanym better than the alphabet he wrote in every day. The complex symbols held a strange sense, each tick and bend of the thin, swirling markings meaningful where they should have been arcane.

For we are the chosen Sons of Elrosh, his very blood is ours. Our inheritance is the Earth, our dominion the sky above mortal men.

There was an annotation cramped in the margins, in a hand Poole recognized as his father's: *God has surrendered his throne.*

"Sod off, Dad." Poole flipped the pages.

For one who uses magic, or associates with the wicked, let his flesh be parted from his bone and his blood drained into a pool of blessed water, that it may be diluted and purified and removed from the earth. And their form shall be placed upon a stake and burned, that they may be cleansed in the Sacred Fire. Know there is no Salvation for such a Being, but do these things only that their Blemish may not infect the Earth and bring the Wrath of God.

Nearer the end of the book, Poole found the passage he remembered, the one he had sought. He felt cold anger as he read the ancient, deadly words.

Let the Son who betrays his Blood be Marked, but do not spill of his Blood, for it is the Blood of Elrosh. Rather banish him, and cut his wings, and let the Mark upon him be punishment all his days.

Cut his wings. Well, Poole had gotten off easy, then. He tugged up his left sleeve and stared at his inner forearm. A pale, risen scar crawled along his skin: Seven slashes, crossing over one another and looking something like a dagger. The scar was now stretched and taut, withered from time. But he always felt it.

The Mark of Iscariot. He'd only been sixteen when his father had held him down and carved the hated symbol. His father had done what the book said, the only thing he *could* do: He banished Poole. And Poole had found a new name and an anonymous place in the city.

He shut the book. With a feeling like he carried something infected, something poisoned, he left the room, went downstairs, and stored the book in his briefcase.

Sebastian's warning came back to him now—Albion Crane was not the enemy. The Chancellor might not know. Poole hadn't known—he couldn't have believed, until he saw the contents of that package.

He would show the *Malus* to Crane, he would explain, and the old bastard wouldn't do a goddamn thing. But there was a difference between denying the truth and merely being ignorant of it. He would take away the Chancellor's only possible excuse.

It was undeniable now. The cult which had dominated Poole's early years, which had taken his mother, was thought to have faded away centuries ago. But he had the evidence here in his briefcase. On his skin.

Sannus Eyreh were back.

Perhaps they'd never left. Poole had thought his father's death had crippled the shrinking league of Elonni supremacists. There were so few Elonni who could truly claim to be Trueborn anymore.

But someone had sent him that package—that threat.

The front door opened softly, startling Poole. He kicked his briefcase under his desk before Aeyrin moved out of the foyer.

"How'd it go?" he said, meeting her by the couch.

She shook her head, melted snow sticking to the collar of her coat, dripping to the floor. "I went where you said to go, but Law wasn't there. I waited nearly an hour. But...there were Watchmen, and I..."

"You did the right thing." He pulled her into his chest. He'd hated letting her be a part of this, hated it more knowing Law had blown her off. He'd risked her going out into the city for nothing.

She pulled herself back enough to look up at him. "But—Sol, listen. His office wasn't locked. The door opened when I tried it. It looked ordinary, nothing out of place, but...I got the feeling he hadn't been there in a while."

"Why do you say that?"

She shook her head. "Just a feeling."

Law was the last person in Theopolis Poole had trusted. If he'd scarpered off, or worse, Poole had no allies left. He would have to do this all alone.

"Right. Then I'll write to the Chancellor myself."

"What makes you think the Chancellor is going to believe you?"

"He's not an Old Name. Neither was Law. The other three, though, they'll be a part of this if I'm right."

"And you're still thinking the Old Names...are in a cult."

"That's the gist of it, yes."

"But the Chancellor isn't."

"Right."

"But he's the one going after Lacey."

Poole looked off in the distance, considering. "I don't think Albion knows what he's doing. I think he's on strings, and I think he's terrified. He's a pawn afraid of the player."

"So, they're using him?"

"The Chancellor can't appear too fanatic, not these days. But the people standing behind him...they can be as mental as they want. Sannus Eyreh made sure a moderate Chancellor was selected—a man of the people. It lets them work in secret."

Aeyrin wrinkled her nose. "I wouldn't call Albion Crane *moderate.*"

"For the Elonni he is."

"You called them Sannus Eyreh? What's that mean?"

"It's Old Akhratian...for Sons of God."

"Ah. Not too bold a claim, is it?"

"Cults are rarely humble."

She blew out a breath, stirring stray hairs along her cheeks. "Can I ask you something? And if I do, will you promise to tell me the truth?"

Poole stiffened. "Okay."

"How do you know so much about this?"

"I...might have known some members when I was growing up."

"How might you have known them?"

He gripped the edge of his left sleeve and rolled it back, baring the Mark. She'd seen it, of course, in their stolen days together. When she asked all those years ago, he'd grinned, lied: *Bar fight.* They were too busy with other things for an old story to matter much.

She ran her fingers across the warped skin. "Your scar? What about it?"

"It's not just a scar. It's the Mark of Iscariot. My father did it to me when I was sixteen." Poole tugged his sleeve back down. "He was a bit overzealous, and I never was a model son. He thought he might brand me as a traitor for...well. We didn't get along."

"Your father... He was in this cult?"

"He was more than it in," Poole said. "He lived it. Everything he did, he did in their name."

Aeyrin sank onto the couch. "God. Why did you never mention it?"

"Bit embarrassing, I suppose." He smiled. "Especially me being me."

She laughed. "Right. But...no. That doesn't make sense. You're not an Old Name."

"Well. There are always acolytes. Hangers-on."

"And they just let him join?"

Poole didn't answer. He sat beside her on the couch, taking her hand and twisting their fingers together. "Certain things are too much to say. Even now," he told her, meeting her sad gaze. "I hated every moment in that house. He made our lives hell. Especially for my mother. She...she never bought it. Paid for it, though."

Poole remembered the estate's hardwood floors—the floors his mother polished every night, on hands and knees, wiping away her own tears and sweat and blood. *Penance,* his father had said. *A woman must know her place.* And a single vial of Cericide—an occasional spoonful for depression. Mum had handed Poole a syringe: *I'm too afraid, I can't do it myself. Please.*

Poole shut his eyes until the memory faded. "She told me the worst place to be was in a cage. That she could bear any torment, even death. But she hated her cage."

"She was strong," Aeyrin said, tilting his face toward hers. "And I know she was lucky to have you."

He kissed her, and kept kissing her, until they were tangled on the couch, Poole's hands seeking her waist. She ducked away from him only briefly.

"Any other family secrets?"

Her umber eyes were wary. He looked away.

"Not at the moment." He brought his lips back to hers, burying the truth like a knife in his chest.

29

SCARS

L ACEY LAY ON a cot, unmoving but for the flicker of her eyelids. Nothing seemed truly wrong, except perhaps a bad dream. Yet she hadn't awoken, and it had been hours since Nathy had carried her from the ruined house.

"I can't believe you let this happen." Saxon paced the length of the infirmary, his eyes still glowing with fever, his skin sticky with sweat. His fingers tapped against his trouser pocket, striking a papery rhythm from something within. So, he hadn't taken Nathy's hint. Or had, and chose to ignore it.

"I'm trying to read." Nathy sat up on the cot beside Lacey's, his legs crossed, the ancient book from the house open on one knee. He focused on a single page, a web that looked almost like a family tree, but instead of branching from an ancestor, the names splintered from a symbol—two conjoined eyes, one shut and weeping, the other wide, rays like sunlight branching from its pupil.

His fingers went instinctively to his heart, pressing the raised skin beneath his shirt. A memory sliced through his mind—his father, the sword, blood and metal and words: *An eye to see the truth, another to shut out darkness.*

Saxon's voice dragged him back. "Read somewhere else, then."

"I'm keeping an eye on the princess. Maybe make yourself useful and fetch me a coffee."

"I'm not your butler," Saxon said through his teeth.

"You're also not good at hiding your little problem." Nathy glanced through his fringe. "When's the last time you burned?"

Saxon grabbed the front of Nathy's shirt, his knuckles cracked and white. "How did you know about that?"

251

"I saw you buying from Neill the other day." Nathy detached Saxon's grip with a lazy pull. "Also, you're shaking, sweating, paler than a corpse, and your pupils are so dilated I can't tell what color your eyes are."

"Okay. Fine." Saxon breathed in through his nose. "I'm trying to quit."

"Then why"—Nathy reached into Saxon's pocket and held the captured parchment packet between two fingers—"are you carrying it with you?" He flicked his wrist, sending the packet soaring into Saxon's waiting hand. "Do us all a favor and take a hit."

"No." Saxon crumpled the packet in his fist. "I can't keep doing this."

"The question is why you started in the first place." Nathy shut the book and smiled. "I don't remember sweet little Saxophone having an addictive personality."

"Sod off."

"Things that bad at home?"

"Don't you dare."

"Ooh. Now we're getting somewhere." Nathy leaned back on the cot, arms behind his head. "So, tell me: Did your little problem solve itself?"

"*Little* problem?" Saxon advanced on him, but stopped as Lacey turned in her cot, eyes shut in a grimace. "We're not doing this here."

Nathy yawned. "Look, if you want your money back..."

"It's not about the money." Saxon shook his head. "It's about the job I asked you to do."

"You still wish I'd killed him, huh?"

"Every day." Saxon sank down onto Lacey's cot, digging his knuckles into his eyes. "You can't imagine what it's like."

"I think I can." Nathy sat up, drawing his legs to his chest. "Look, I didn't skip out on the job to be an ass. I never meant to just take your money and run."

"And yet, you did."

"Because I didn't want to ruin your life. Saxon, killing someone—you don't come back from that."

"Which is why I hired you to do it."

"Okay. But the blood would still be on your hands. Think you can live with that?" Nathy swung his legs over the cot, facing Saxon directly. Saxon kept his gaze averted, locked on a spot on the floor. "You know it won't bring your sister back."

Saxon's hands clenched on the stiff white sheet of the cot. "Will killing Ruark bring Artemis back? Why is your revenge so special?"

"It's not. But at least it's mine. You want Kragen dead? Do it yourself."

Saxon snorted. "You're an assassin. Isn't that a bit hypocritical?"

"You weren't a customer, Saxon. You were my friend. And if this means as much to you as you say it does, I want you to be the one holding the knife. That's the only way you'll know if it's worth it." He grabbed the old book and rose. "Let me know when she wakes up."

SAXON TWISTED THE parchment packet between his fingers. His pulse jumped at the idea of relief, at the possibility this twisted agony might stop. It wasn't pain, it wasn't an ache—it was need. His blood beat like the cadence of an alarm: *You need it. You need it.*

He needed it.

"Saxon?"

He shoved the packet into his pocket and turned. Lacey sat up in bed, rubbing one eye with the heel of her hand. "How did I get here?"

"You fainted. Nathy carried you out of the house." He hated the petulance in his voice, the childish annoyance that he recognized as pitiful but felt keenly nonetheless.

"I fainted? From what?"

"He said you just dropped. I don't know."

"What's got you so worked up?"

Nathy was right; if Saxon carried on like this, trapped in withdrawal and snapping at Lacey for every little thing, he'd ruin what tentative trust she'd given him. He stalked toward the potion cabinet and pretended to rummage, half-hoping he might find a potion strong enough to sink him into blissful darkness.

"I need a minute alone, okay?" he said at last.

"Okay, crazy." She slipped out of the cot. "I'm going to find Nathy. Join us when you're done with...whatever...okay?"

"Yeah."

Her hand rested briefly on his arm, then fell away as she moved toward the door, away from him.

As soon as the door thumped shut, Saxon reached into his pocket.

LACEY MOVED ALONG the fourth-floor corridor, trying to remember which of the many identical doors was Nathy's. This house was so dark, so lifeless and grim from its mahogany floors to its damask wallpaper. She snapped her fingers, creating a tiny light, but without a wick to hold onto, it fluttered and died against her skin. She envied Flynn's ability to tame fire. To never feel lost in darkness.

A bend in the corridor struck Lacey, at last, as familiar. She knocked on a door, relieved to hear movement inside. Nathy leaned out, his visible eye wide.

"Huh. She lives."

"Saxon tells me I fainted?"

He opened the door wider and let her pass into his room. The clutter had somehow redoubled since her last visit: He'd strung a clothesline from one wall to the other, and sheets of parchment hung like shirts drying in the sun. Each page contained an Annanym, crudely drawn but recognizable.

"Are those from that book?"

"Yeah."

"Why are you so interested?"

He flopped onto his bed, hauling the strange old book from the ruined house across his stomach. "Weren't we talking about your fainting spell?"

She touched one of the newly inked pages, its symbol striking her memory: Two eyes, blending into one another, one open, one shut.

"Yeah," she said, distracted. "What happened?"

"There was someone in the house, chanting. And then you fainted."

"Not much of a story." She plucked the page from the clothesline. "You have this on your chest."

He sighed. "I knew you were staring."

She sat on the end of his bed, holding the drawing up. "What does it mean?"

"I don't know."

"Then why is it on you?"

He sat up, casting the book aside on the bed. "My father did that to me. I didn't exactly get to pick what pattern he sliced in."

Lacey's hand dropped, the page fluttering away. "Oh. God, Nathy, I'm—"

"For the love of Lye, don't start. I don't care. It was a long time ago. I barely remember it. I'm just curious to see if it means something." He rose and picked up the page she'd dropped. "One eye to see truth, the other to shut out darkness."

"Sounds...cultish." She watched him hang the page back on the clothesline. He truly seemed unbothered. But she remembered how he'd looked, his chest and arms lined with scars, some faint against his coppery skin, others raised and red. And the tattoos, placed along his body as though to hide the destruction marring his skin. She'd thought they were battle wounds, the collateral for being an assassin.

She found herself moving toward him without consciously choosing to. He watched her approach, his good eye levelled on her face as her hand rose slowly to his face. It felt like reaching out to a wounded animal, the measured movements a pitiful promise to do no harm. She pushed his fringe aside. The scar on his face had sunk into his left eye, squinting its vision, and ran like a gorge past the corner of his mouth, to the ridge of his sharp jaw.

He flinched when her fingers brushed against the raised, ruined skin. She began to pull away, only to find he'd closed his hand around hers.

"He did that one too," he said, and let her hand drop.

She almost said sorry, but caught the pitiful condolence in her throat. "He must have been horrible."

"Sometimes." He turned away. "Anyway. You should see Jade tomorrow."

"Jade?"

"Another of Flynn's acolytes. She can probably tell you why you fainted."

"Oh. I mean, I feel fine."

"But you might not be. Can't hurt to be safe."

"Right. Sure."

He nodded, still not looking at her. "Good. Well..."

"Oh, right." She twisted a strand of hair around her finger. "I'm in your room."

"Night, princess."

"Okay. Goodnight."

She hurried from the room, her stomach dense with nerves. What had she been thinking? He must be angry, of course he'd be angry, she pried into his life, touched his bloody face. God, she was an idiot.

She took the lift to the fifth floor and hurried into Latrice's room.

NATHY FOUND THE monk in the second-floor study, nervously examining the spines of the many books gathered there. He whistled, startling Alastair from his perusal.

"Is Lacey okay?" the monk asked.

"Don't know. You're coming with me."

Alastair scurried across the study, his eyes landing on the book under Nathy's arm. "Where are we going?"

Nathy led him along the corridor at a quick pace, the doors blurring as they passed. "Have you ever heard those words before? Might, sight, wisdom?"

"Well, I mean, yes, obviously. But not...together like that. Not as a phrase."

"What about the other part? The thing about blotting out the sun?"

"N-no. It's not from the Amerand, if that's what you mean."

"Okay." He halted suddenly, causing Alastair to collide with him. "And what about this?"

He opened the book to the page after *might, sight, wisdom*. On it was scrawled the web of names, each written in its original Anñanym. He recognized one—his own. Fairborn. "Any of these look familiar?"

"They're the Old Names," Alastair said. He pointed to one. "There's mine there. And Bromley, Lately, Ellicott...Fryer."

"I get it." He resumed his hurried stride. "What's with the order they were in?"

"If I had to guess...rank? My family's name was fairly low, which is fair, I'd say, but Priestley and Lately are toward the middle, and...well, yours...is up higher."

"Interesting." He stopped at the door he wanted and threw it open without knocking. Flynn looked up from his teacup, his golden hair sticking up like he'd only just risen from bed.

"Nathy! You're still here."

"What would you know about an abandoned house sitting out in the forest? About two miles north of here, right along the river."

"Well..." Flynn sipped his tea. "Nothing. I don't take much air these days, the weather is so dreadful. I miss the sun. Once this is over, you know, I've got to get to Sumri, I just—"

"Flynn." Nathy dropped the heavy book onto Flynn's desk, displacing papers and broken tea cups and empty vials. "Focus. Have you ever seen a book like this before?"

Flynn peeled back the cover, his eyes glazing over at the Annñanym. "I don't read anything Elonni. It's all so depressing, isn't it?"

"It says, 'might, sight, wisdom.' Ever hear that before?"

Flynn sighed. "I'm afraid I don't know what you're getting at."

Nathy placed his palms on the desk, leaning over Flynn. "What do you know about my father?"

Flynn set his tea aside, focused at last. "What do you want to know?"

"Anything. I..." He looked away from Flynn's steady gaze. "I know what he did. I just don't know why. But this book— my family name is in it. All the Old Names are. What if they were organized? Fryer, the Elders, my father...this guy." He jerked his thumb at Alastair.

Alastair blustered a moment. "I-I'm not in some *secret society*."

"But maybe your family is." He turned back to Flynn. "And my dad...maybe the reason why he did all those things—"

"Nathy," Flynn cut in, "he was a monster. Monsters don't need a reason to hurt anyone."

Nathy ran a hand through his hair. He should have known Flynn wouldn't understand. But his suspicion felt like so much more than that—he had discovered something with this book. Something that promised answers. "Either way, you got your wish. I'm staying."

"That's—that's wonderful."

"Not for you," Nathy said. "I'm going to figure out what this book means." He glanced back at Alastair. "You're translating. Let's go."

"I'd really rather..." He met Nathy's glare. "I mean, sure, yes."

"Good. Let's get to work, then."

30

UNDERMINE ROAD

-Bishop's Hole-

FOG CRAWLED ACROSS the worn cobbled streets in Bishop's Hole's main square. The town was a haphazard sprawl, and Lacey was already impossibly turned around. A twisting network of modest dirt roads converged at the busy, jostling center. The many shops exuded strange scents: incense from the fortune teller's booth and the strange chemical sting of brewing potions from the apothecary. A nearby bakery's freshly steaming loaves competed hopelessly with the overpowering smells. Another familiar tang hung on the air, coating Lacey's tongue—iron. Blood.

Lacey turned toward the source—a slanting wooden butcher's shop, its proprietor standing between hanging hanks of meat, a scarred table set up before him. A fat, squirming pig lay on the table, twitching in the congealing blood of whatever beast had come before.

Lacey halted, trapped by the pig's eyes darting around in its squashed face. Nathy grabbed her shoulder, but not soon enough.

The butcher's cleaver spat fresh blood as it slipped through the pig's neck. Lacey shut her eyes and saw the thick snow of Hollow's Edge, the red spill, the dimming eyes of the executed man. The preacher, his knowing smile, his words: *Gets no easier to see death.*

He came to find me.

"Lace?" Saxon took her hand. "Come on."

Lacey shuddered, suddenly cold. The air was damp with the promise of rainfall, and only a moment later, the sky rumbled and opened to a storm. The rain washed the spilled blood away from the pavement before the butcher's shop, and it flowed through the streets, watery red.

She let Saxon guide her away from the butcher. Nathy, walking ahead, peered over his shoulder at her.

"What, you don't eat meat?"

"No, I do... Nathy? That man who came looking for me in Hollows Edge—"

"Don't go down that road, princess." He spoke casually, yet his muscles had stiffened, his posture suddenly tense. "As far as you're concerned, he was a brave little soldier and he died on the battlefield."

"I don't think you're helping," Saxon said.

"Speak for yourself, Saxophone."

They devolved into a boyish back-and-forth; Lacey tuned them out. Artemis had died and left Nathy behind. Maybe the mysterious man in Hollows Edge had loved someone, too. Perhaps somewhere, in this very town, a brokenhearted person mourned a death that had merely been a grim part of Lacey's day. An entire life was destroyed, and she'd gone on home to milk the cows. And meanwhile, somewhere far away from her, someone else had died a little, too.

"His wife was murdered."

Lacey lifted her head at the sound of Nathy's voice. "What?"

"The man looking for you." He turned to look her in the eye. "His wife was murdered in the Eastern by a rouge Watchman. That's why he joined Flynn. Nobody misses him. So stop blaming yourself."

She swallowed, nodded. But what little comfort his words offered burned out like an ember in the rain. A man had still died. For *her*.

They wandered out of the bustle of the main square, down a narrow alley overlooked by towering chimneys and sagging roofs. It was deserted but for a huddled, hooded figure dozing by a storm drain a few yards away. Nathy walked right towards it, and it held out a waiting hand. Nathy dropped a few coins in its pale gray palm.

Saxon paused at the mouth of the alley. "Is Nathy actually giving money to a transient?"

Lacey shrugged and started forward, but Saxon caught her hand.

"Lace. Hold on. I—I wish you wouldn't trust him so easily."

"I...don't." She tugged her hand out of his grip. "Why do you hate him so much? Honestly? I know he's an assassin, but it's not like he's slaughtering innocent people. You've got another reason you don't like him."

Saxon shook his head. "It's not important."

Her shoulders slumped; she'd thought they'd gotten past this. "You're still keeping things from me."

"If I am, it's for your own good."

"*That*—that has got to be the most arrogant thing you've ever said to me."

"Believe it or not," Nathy said, coming up behind Lacey and steering her down the alley by her shoulders, "you can walk and talk at the same time. Maybe not Saxophone. It's a skill only possessed by the mostly evolved."

Saxon rolled his eyes and followed them to the huddled figure. Lacey forced her eyes away from him—from the pain so clear in his eyes. She focused instead on the strange person at the drain, eying them beneath his hood.

"Extra fee for non-regulars," the figure croaked.

Nathy's eyes narrowed. "You're killing me, Charlie."

Lacey raised her eyebrows. Somehow, the crumpled man beneath those dirty robes didn't strike her as a *Charlie*.

"Say for argument's sake they're not guests," Nathy said, "so much as marketable goods. Ginger here was clearly made for the pole, and this guy has every single valuable organ a healthy mage adult could want."

"Where in Elrosh's name are you taking us?" Lacey said.

Charlie shrugged. "Fine." He shuffled to his feet and lifted the grille blocking the storm drain. Rain gurgled in the cavernous space below. Though the water channeling through the cobblestones ran clear, Lacey saw blood in her memory.

"Don't talk to anybody down here, all right?" Nathy said. "And watch your back."

He dropped himself into the drain, down into the bowels of the town. He landed after a much longer pause than Lacey would have liked.

"Don't worry," Nathy called up, "I'll catch you."

"I can fly," Lacey said.

"I was talking to Saxon."

261

Saxon dragged his hands down his face. Lacey rolled her eyes, then pressed her hands together. *"Hallas Elroi."* Saxon ducked out of the way of her unfolding wings.

"I'll spare you Nathy's chivalry."

"What does that mean?"

Lacey kicked his legs out from under him and caught him as though he were a swooning maid in an old story. She hopped down the drain, straining against his weight but managing it. She dropped him a few feet above the dank sewer floor and landed beside him.

"Honestly?" Saxon said. "That was probably more embarrassing for me."

Lacey withdrew her wings and stalked off down the sewer. "Chauvinist."

Nathy led them into seemingly endless darkness beyond. Pipework echoed all around, carrying water and sewage, and the walls were damp, the ceiling dripping. In the oppressive dark, Lacey could barely see the floor below. At the end of the tunnel, a door with a tiny sealed window waited. Nathy knocked twice, and the window screen drew back. A pair of glinting eyes hovered beyond it.

"Name and business?" a gruff voice asked.

"Ferrickek. And mind your own business."

The eyes narrowed and the window snapped shut. To Lacey's surprise, the door opened, and a tall, spindly man with tapered ears and waist-length green hair gestured them inside. His skin was the mottled color and texture of tree bark.

"Didn't mean to offend, Mr. Ferrickek."

Nathy grinned and clapped the elf on the shoulder. "Take it easy, Griff."

"They with you?" Griff's eyes hovered on Lacey, something like concern in his emerald eyes.

"Yeah, they're friends. Jade won't mind."

The elf's mouth turned down. "Keep an eye on your girl there. The Sonyi clan expanded their business since you been away."

Saxon's head snapped up. "Sonyi?"

Griff's eyes narrowed. "What about it?"

"Nothing. Funny name, is all."

Nathy muttered something indistinct and shuttled Lacey and Saxon deeper into the tunnel. "Good looking out, Griff."

Griff grunted behind them, slamming the door and resuming his post.

"One more rule," Nathy said, his eyes on Saxon. "Don't buy anything down here. Also." He turned his gaze on Lacey. "If anyone grabs you, don't hold back. Down here, it's kill, be killed, or have someone do your killing for you."

"Oh. Lovely."

Gas lights fluttered further down the dank underground, pooling light along the flagstone road. Stalls began to appear, at first sparse, but gathered in greater numbers the longer they walked. Other tunnels shot off the main one, each filled with stalls and shopkeepers and buyers. A few stalls promoted seemingly innocuous items—bolts of dark fabric, crumbling books, chipped dinnerware. Others displayed more sinister wares: A hooded man kept a stall with nothing but a cage of diamond-headed snakes slithering over one another. Another stood over a set of vials, each filled with what looked like human blood. Many stalls displayed bottles of strange liquids and caught fire—will o' th' wisps, bobbing listlessly.

Nathy cut the crowd, people jumping back or flinching away as he neared them. He received dark looks from the sellers, especially those he waved to.

Saxon walked along Nathy's other side. "You sure seem to have a reputation down here."

"Why, thank you."

"I take it they...know what you do?" Lacey said, keeping a careful eye on a man selling what appeared to be finger bones. He held one up, waggling it as Lacey stared—the finger wore a large ruby ring. Nathy cleared his throat, and the stall-keeper set the finger bone down, scowled, and turned away.

"I don't think that's what bothers them," Nathy said. "Plenty of assassins—but most aren't half-Elonni. Play along, all right, princess?"

"Uh, sure, what—"

He took her by the wrist and tugged her along behind him. They stopped beside a stall run by a stout, thick little man whose head only came up to Lacey's shoulder. He wore a long, rust-colored beard and kept his hair back in a ponytail. His small black eyes twitched, but he pretended not to notice them.

His stall looked like a rummage sale, every item different from the last and all chipped, cracked, dented, or broken. The few buyers hovering by his stall looked up at Nathy and scattered. Left with no choice, the dwarf sighed and looked up at his latest clients.

"This is why I hate when you come by," the dwarf rumbled. His eyes narrowed on Lacey. "Where'd you get her from? She for sale?" The dwarf opened a small metal box on his cart; it was filled with rumpled junes. "I'd give you top dollar, of course."

Lacey's eye twitched. "What's *that* supposed to mean?"

"She's an associate," Nathy said.

"Hm." The dwarf eyed Saxon now, hovering uneasily behind Nathy. "*He* for sale? I got a couple blokes interested in that. He's pretty enough."

"Really," Nathy said, looking back at Saxon with an assessing gaze. Lacey subtly stepped on his foot, and he snapped out of it. "Not today, no. He's my blood type. I keep him around in case I need a new liver. So. Shiv."

The dwarf sighed. "I know, I know. You'll get your money, Ferrickek."

"Make it sooner rather than later and I'll give you a discount."

Shiv glared but, after a moment, nodded. He rummaged in his metal box and produced a handful of junes. "How much've a discount?"

"Make it an even thousand, just 'cause I'm so nice."

Shiv nodded once and counted out the money. "You got proof Danic's gone?"

Nathy reached into his duster pocket and dropped something thick and fleshy onto the cart. Lacey leaned around him for a look and instantly regretted it: A withered hand lay curled like a dead spider, the long fingernails clotted with dirt and blood.

"Was that in your pocket this whole time?" she demanded.

Nathy grinned. She inched away from him.

Shiv, for his part, picked up the hand with a quiet reverence. "Good, good." He rummaged through his junk until he found a weathered cardboard box. He placed the hand inside and shut it, patting the lid. "Well. Here you go, then."

He handed over the junes; Nathy shoved the crumpled money into his back pocket.

"I'll give you three thousand if you can get Tomlin Sonyi," Shiv said.

"I'll get back to you. Schedule's full at the moment." He turned away from the dwarf, keeping a hand on Lacey's shoulder as they turned back into the crowds of nocturnes shuffling between the booths.

"Where did Saxon go?" Lacey asked. She hadn't noticed his departure, but now, he was nowhere in sight. The crowds were too thick and roiling for her eyes to focus on anyone for long.

"That idiot," Nathy said.

Lacey looked up at him. "You know where he is."

"Yeah. Come on."

They wove between the shoppers, their footsteps smacking on the water running the length of the tunnel. Nathy stopped at a turnoff that seemed ghostly compared to the bustle of the main artery: Only a few people stood about, all lethargic and watery-eyed, posted lazily against the tunnel wall or curled in the shallow water, apparently sleeping.

A fairy dressed in a black trench-coat and high boots stalked out from the shadows. His long white hair fell around his face like a curtain, swaying with his even steps. Lacey grabbed Nathy's wrist, her fingers shaking. He had the same white eyes, the same lean, hungry face, as the fairy who'd taken her to Ruark.

"Nathy Ferrickek," the fairy said with a smile. "I thought you were long gone."

"Hey, Tomlin. Have you seen an idiot recently? We lost ours. Tall, strong, handsome. Stupid."

Tomlin's lips twitched. "Who's this?" He reached a finger out to stroke Lacey's cheek, but she grabbed his hand before he could make contact.

"Don't touch me."

The fairy smiled. "Elonni. How sweet, Nathy. You found another one."

"Right. About our incredibly stupid friend..."

"I don't disclose information on my buyers. You know that. Now, if you're not going to share"—he flashed Lacey a smile, sharp teeth creasing his lower lip—"then please go away."

Nathy turned away from the fairy, Lacey jogging to match his frenzied pace back down the tunnel.

"Who are the Sonyis?" Lacey asked.

"Fairies," Nathy said.

"I gathered as much. What do they...do?" Her question faded as she caught sight of Saxon ducking between shoppers, making his way toward them.

"There you are!"

Nathy grabbed the front of Saxon's shirt and dragged him closer. "Remember when I said don't buy anything?"

Saxon shoved Nathy, breaking free of his grip. "What would *I* buy in a place like this?"

"Huh. I dunno, Saxophone. What would you buy down here? Hmm... What's it called...rhymes with—" He whipped his arm out and caught Saxon's wrist before he could swing a punch. He smirked. "Pain."

Lacey looked down the tunnel, then back at Saxon. "You burn *bane*?"

"Oops," Nathy said.

Saxon ripped himself free of Nathy's grip. "No! I— Lace, let me explain."

"That fairy," she said slowly, finally understanding. Neill and Tomlin Sonyi—they looked nearly identical because they were related, in more ways than blood. They shared a business. "Neill...he was your bane dealer."

"Well—yes, okay, but—"

"He went after me because of you! All over some stupid fairy drugs? Are you insane?"

"This is why I didn't want you to know," he said quietly.

"Go back to the house," Lacey said.

"What? No. I—I'm coming with you."

"I don't want you to," she said, her voice weary. "Please just go."

He laughed shortly. "All this, just because I burn once in a while?"

She shook her head. "No, Saxon. It's because I have no idea who you are. And now I don't think I want to."

266

Nathy clapped Saxon on the shoulder. "Bad luck, handsome. Princess?"

"Lacey, *please.*"

She brushed past Saxon, fighting pain as her heart seemed to constrict into nothing.

31

JADE

-Bishop's Hole-

THEY CONTINUED ON without Saxon. Nathy led Lacey down a narrow bend in the tunnel, its floor bathed in pale light. The staccato splatter of rainfall hinted they were nearing aboveground, and at last they came out onto a narrow flagstone road overlooked by leaning, tightly spaced shops and flats. Nathy stopped at the door to a bright pink row house.

Nathy opened the door and led them into a small foyer, which opened onto a homey sitting room crowded with squashy furniture and shelves of various divination tools—crystals and cards and an assortment of tea sets. Burning incense gave the house a thick, sweet atmosphere that pinged every nerve in Lacey's skull. She wanted to turn back outside to the fresh air, but someone had risen from one of the many armchairs and started toward them.

The woman was pretty, with high, bladed cheekbones and round brown eyes. She was dressed in baggy olive-green trousers and a tight black sleeveless shirt which emphasized her nearly flat chest. A loose, floppy cap covered her unkempt chin-length black hair, complimenting her coppery skin. She had more tattoos than Nathy, each arm covered from shoulder to wrist in sharp, stark markings like runes. Her willowy figure cut through the clutter and she stopped before Nathy, one hand on her narrow hip.

"Wings," she said.

"Hey, Jade."

A small, sharp smile flicked across her lips and she pounced on him with a hug. "I knew you'd come back."

He slipped out of her fierce grip and patted her on the head. "Yeah, well, you're psychic, so it's not that impressive."

"Have you been eating well? Staying out of trouble? You haven't been back to prison, right?"

"Leave off, woman. I'm fine."

Jade twisted her lips to one side, then went at Nathy's fringe with deft fingers and sharp nails. "When is the last time you brushed your hair? Look at you!"

Lacey watched the exchange with wide eyes. "Um. Are you two...together?"

Nathy's eye twitched. "She's my cousin."

"Yeah," Jade said, smoothing down Nathy's fringe. "Only Elonni marry their cousins. But I do try to take care of this filthy little ragamuffin."

"Please stop," Nathy said.

"Flynn told me you were finally helping." Jade cast her eyes from Lacey to Nathy, frowning. "Where's Izzy?"

Nathy opened his mouth, shut it. Jade's narrow shoulders drooped.

"I see."

"I tried to save her, Jade."

Jade nodded, her lower lip twitching a little. "She's not dead. I'll find her. Anyway. Who've you brought for me?"

"The Monarch." Nathy gave Lacey a gentle push forward. "She's already attracted the attention of an evil spirit. Figure she could use your help."

Jade cocked her head, giving Lacey a casual once-over. "Mm-hm. Yeah. There's definitely a presence attached to you."

Lacey blinked. "You mean, right now?"

"Yep." She placed her hand over Lacey's heart and shut her eyes. "Strong one. Hateful. Yeah. You're being haunted." She pulled her hand away and shook it as though she'd been burned. "I'll give you some sage, do a cleansing of your vessel."

"Thanks. But... I thought only necromancers could, y'know, deal with spirits."

"I *am* a necromancer. And a diviner. My mother is Rakashi, but my father's Lyvian. Actually, he's in the same death cult as Poe and Alice's parents."

"*Death cult?*"

"Morturi Nox. Tiny one. No big deal." Jade turned now to Nathy. "You."

"Yeah?"

She placed her hand over his heart. Nathy tried to back away, but his feet stalled, as though she'd frozen him in place. Her eyes squinted and her fingers tensed. Nathy, too, shut his eyes, but in pain, it seemed. His jaw locked and, as Jade's hand remained over his heart, he began to shake. A tear dropped from his ruined eye down his cheek.

"Jade," he ground out.

She backed away, holding her hand away from herself. "Nathy...your heart is so tangled up."

He held his hand against the center of his chest, his breathing ragged. "That's considered an asset in my line of work."

Jade shook her head. "You can't go on like that."

"I didn't ask you." He slumped into a weathered green armchair, breathing like he'd sprinted a mile. Lacey crept closer with the feeling that she approached a wounded animal.

"Nathy?"

He shook his head. "Go get your vessel cleansed. I'm fine."

She didn't move.

"I promise," he said a little softer. "Go."

Lacey nodded and joined Jade on the other side of the parlor. With a last worried glance at her cousin, Jade turned to the cabinet and withdrew a bundle of sage and a few sticks of incense. She lit one end of the sage and brought it over to Lacey, moving the bundle like a wand. The smoke and soft scent crawled over Lacey's skin like a curious, friendly spirit.

"Hold this." She handed the bundle to Lacey and then placed an incense stick behind each of Lacey's ears.

"Is this the cleansing?" Lacey asked.

"Mm-hm. Hold still. Close your eyes. Clear your mind. Breathe in..." Jade waited.

"Oh, right now?"

"Yes, now."

Lacey took a slow, deep breath, and released it when Jade said to. She kept up the slow breathing while Jade sprinkled what felt like soot over her head and chanted in an unfamiliar language.

After a while, Jade tsked. "Is your mind clear?"

"I don't really know what that means."

Jade shook her head. "Elonni. It means emptying your mind of distractions, of thought itself. When a thought visits, you thank it for its concerns and dismiss it."

"Okay?"

Jade sighed. "I could try to sever the connection manually. What's drawing the spirit to you?"

"Oh, well. It's the ghost of, um, my dead grandfather? And he murdered my grandmother because she was, y'know, whatever I am."

Jade blinked. "Donoveir Fryer is haunting you?"

"I think it's him, yes."

"Oh, boy." She sighed. "I need more sage. I'll give you some to take with you, too." She plucked the incense sticks from behind Lacey's ears and dipped their burning ends in a shallow saucer of water. "You have to keep it burning while you sleep, okay?" She began piling jars and boxes from the cabinets into Lacey's arms. "Salt your windows and door." She plucked a large onyx stone from the shelf. "Put this under your pillow. And bathe in blessed waters tonight." She hauled up a ceramic jar and set it by Lacey's feet.

Lacey looked at the mess of objects in her arms, blinking.

Jade smiled. "No charge."

"Thank you," Lacey said dully.

"Oh, sorry, let me get you a bag." She fluttered off to a set of drawers and extracted a silky purple sack. Lacey dumped the items into it with relief.

"Do you like dressing like that?" Jade asked, frowning at Lacey's dress. It was a sickly maroon color, another item from Latrice's wardrobe.

"I'm not attached to the style, no."

Jade turned and yanked open a drawer. She tossed a few pairs of loose trousers and tunic-like shirts into the bag as well. "There. Dressing like Donoveir's dead wife probably isn't endearing you to him."

A relieved smile crossed Lacey's lips. "Thanks. Really."

"If it doesn't stop after tonight, call me on this." She added a chunk of purplish crystal to the bag. "Nathy can work it."

Lacey caught the glimmer of several lumps of gem stones in varying sizes and color lined atop the dresser. "Do you deal with many hauntings?"

"A few. But my clients come to me for all sorts of things. Speaking of." Jade turned back to Nathy. "Did you get Ruark?"

"No." The word came out hard and short. "Is there any way you can look for him?"

"You know he's impossible to track."

Lacey raised her eyebrows. "You can track people?"

Jade smiled. "Divination isn't only good for readings. I use it for information." She pulled an opaque crystal ball from the cabinet. "I can see a lot. Track people, find missing pets, spy on the Elderon—"

"How?"

"All I need is something that carries a person's aura. People put so much of themselves into certain objects and actions. It's how ghosts are formed, actually, but it works on this side of life, too."

"Why couldn't you find me?"

"I didn't have anything that belonged to you. We tried tracking you with some of Will's old things, but...I couldn't get a connection. Sometimes, good, old-fashioned groundwork is the best way. That's what Izzy was best at." Her face fell as she gazed into the crystal ball, her eyes as inscrutable as its murky glass.

"You said actions?" Nathy said, breaking the solemn silence.

"Mm-hm. That's a lot harder, because I have to go to a place someone did something significant, which means knowing about it beforehand. But it's doable. It's how I spy on Justice Bromley. I happen to know of a brothel he's a particular fan of."

Nathy leaned forward in his seat. "What about a stab wound?"

Jade wrinkled her nose. "What about one?"

"Could you track someone who stabbed me if they did so with enough...gusto?"

"I *think* I could."

"Good." Nathy stood, crossed the room, and let his wingspan unfold, darkness molding into feathers and bone. The wound on his left wing still glowed red, sticky with old blood.

"Nathy!" Jade set the crystal ball back on its shelf. "How long have you had that?"

"Few days."

"You're letting me patch that up."

"After you read it for a trace of Ruark."

"Fine. But go to the washroom. If you get blood on my new carpets..."

"I'm going." He left the parlor and disappeared up a narrow set of stairs.

Jade turned back to Lacey. "Are you in love with him?"

Lacey shook her head adamantly.

"Well, still, try to look after him. He's a bit of a mess." She picked up her crystal ball and a few broken bits of chalk. "You all right to wait here while I read him?"

"Sure. But...can I ask you something first?"

"Yeah. What is it?"

"I've just been wondering... If Nathy hates the Nine so much, why was he ever even involved?"

Jade blinked. "Well, Flynn raised him. He didn't tell you?"

"No." She'd realized on some level that Nathy and Flynn must have been close, but she hadn't imagined their relationship went to that extent. Then she remembered the photo Flynn had—of himself and a younger Nathy, seemingly happy together. The memory made her suddenly sad. "He doesn't have much to say, usually. How did he come to be at Fryer's Grove?"

Jade checked over her shoulder, then lowered her voice. "One night, fifteen years ago, Nathy's mother stole his father's special sword. She entrusted it to Nathy and told him to find William—well, your dad. Isobel was there to help him. But his father and Ruark found them trying to leave Denmoor. They took the sword back and..." She drew a slim finger down the left side of her face. "I went looking for him when he never showed up. Found him in the streets of Denmoor with half a face."

"How long had he been like that?"

She shrugged. "Days. It was too late to heal the cut, or even stitch it. He...wouldn't let me anywhere near him, besides. He walked ten steps behind me the whole way to the train station, so he could run away any time he needed to."

"And you brought him to Flynn? Why didn't he come to live with you?"

"My mom and I lived at Fryer's Grove, too. Nathy and his mom were supposed to join us there. Y'know, after it went to shit with his father."

"So, Nathy's mother was involved with the Nine."

Jade nodded sadly. "He blames the Nine for her death. And Artemis's. He's certainly lost more than most people his age. But I wish he hadn't tangled his heart up so much. He was such a sweet kid."

"That's...so strange."

She tried to picture Nathy as a boy, sword in hand, fleeing the city. And a man, cruel enough to hold a child down and carve such a gruesome wound into his face.

"Can I tell you something?" Jade said. "I know Nathy probably acts obnoxious and rude. You've probably wanted to punch his face a time or two..."

Lacey nodded.

"But after all he's been through... I think it's just easier for him to make everyone hate him."

"When you say his heart is tangled..."

"It's his aura. His soul. It's shattered, and all the pieces ended up in the wrong places."

Lacey bit her lip, her eyes intent on the bag of cleansing materials Jade had given her. "How does somebody fix a broken soul?"

"If I knew, I'd tell you. Just know he's not rotten all the way through." She patted Lacey on the head. "Watch out for my little cousin, okay?"

"I'll try, I suppose. But I don't know what I can really do."

"Maybe he only needs a friend. He won't admit it. But you seem resilient enough to deal with him. And it doesn't hurt that you're cute."

Lacey began to protest, but Jade had already turned away.

"I'm gonna deal with his wound. Don't forget: Salt the windows."

31

MORTIMER

ISOBEL AWOKE TO the slamming of a door. She pushed against the dirt floor until she sat on her knees. Even such a simple act drained her. Her stomach ached with a steady, sharp pain. The wound Ruark gave her hadn't healed; every stray movement broke the scabbing skin and let it bleed afresh.

"Dinner time."

She lifted her face to the bars. Ryder stood beyond, in one hand holding a plate of steaming meat and a tender potato wafting a buttery smell. The other hand held a dead rat. Two Watchmen stood behind him, motionless and silent.

Ryder held the plate closer to her bars. "You can have the good stuff if you talk."

"I'll take the rat, then."

He tossed the tiny corpse through the bars. Isobel kicked it away to where the others rotted in the corner of her cell.

"Come on, darling, you're smarter than this." Ryder picked up the hank of meat and took a large bite, speaking around the mouthful. "Is it really worth dying over?"

"Close your mouth when you chew, Ryder."

He tossed the plate behind him. It shattered, its savory contents splattering against the far wall. The Watchmen looked at each other briefly but said nothing. "We're going to get the Monarch either way. I'm trying to offer you mercy. You could still change your mind."

She rose and slinked to the bars. "No."

Ryder leaned against the bars of her cell and smirked. "Come on, Ingrid. I'd still take you, even with that face."

"But, see, I *wouldn't* take you, especially with yours."

Ryder's smirk fell, only a fraction, but Isobel caught the sudden falter of his confidence. "Then I guess you can rot here.

Course, I can't go back to Patriarch and tell him I didn't at least try to convince you."

"*Oh*," Isobel said. "Torture—how sweet. But I didn't get you anything." She smirked. "Go ahead, Commander."

He turned to the Watchmen behind him. "Leave us."

"Sir?" The Watchman to his right cleared his throat. "Are you sure? She's—she's labelled as highly dangerous."

"Leave." Ryder drew his sword and swung it out. The Watchmen scrambled to the door without another protest.

Isobel stepped away from the bars. "Oh, are you going to do it *yourself*? My, this is a treat. The Elder of War taking time out of his busy schedule just for me? I'm blushing."

"Up against the wall, Ingrid."

"Since you asked nicely." Isobel walked to the other end of the cell and leaned against the dirty brick wall, arms crossed. Ryder opened her cell just enough to fit his bulky frame through, then slid it shut. Locked it. Isobel's fist involuntarily clenched, but she splayed her fingers, stretching out the nerves, before he noticed. A Huntress might expect torture, might play strong through it—that didn't mean she didn't dread it. Ryder crossed the cell with a strange, feral smile that sucked the humanity from his eyes. He put a hand on her stomach, digging his fingers into the broken skin. Breath hissed through her teeth; pain sang through every nerve.

"Get on the floor."

"What?"

Ryder pulled a knife from his jacket, and Isobel's anticipatory dread shifted into something harsher, a primal terror that demanded she flee; but she couldn't.

"Where did you get that?" she said. The demon-bone blade was a deeper shadow in the dark cell, its blade inscribed with symbols Isobel recognized from her work with cursed objects and the grimoires of Death Cults. A language spoken by monsters made of dark dreams and shifting shadows.

Ryder murmured the inscription on the blade and it flared as though it were coated in flames. He peeled away Isobel's mask and dropped it to the ground. He ran the blade down her cheek, experimentally. She screamed. There were reactions you couldn't control, flinches and gritted teeth, but she'd always thought screaming was optional, a weak response.

The last time she'd screamed, she'd been fifteen, pinned beneath Roselyn Ruark in the streets of Denmoor, sure he would kill her or worse. She'd taught herself to stay quiet after that. She learned that men like Roz liked it when you screamed, that you could lessen the blow if you just took it.

Even when Mortimer had poured the acid down her face, scorching her vision and warping her skin, she'd kept her jaw locked tight.

But at the touch of the demon-bone blade, her body was overtaken by a pain so profound and acute that she would have done anything to make it stop.

"Do what I say, Ingrid." He pressed the blade flat to her cheek. Even that hurt, not nearly as badly as the feel of the sharp end on her open flesh, but still it burned and burned.

"Demonic weapons are illegal," Isobel said. "You're suddenly above your own laws?"

"I didn't write the laws," Ryder said. "If it were up to me, me and my Watchmen would have complete access to any weapon known to god, man, or devil. Anything to break you monsters down."

"I'm Elonni, Commander. I have a right to fair charges and a trial by the Elderon."

"The Elderon isn't doing anything to you. I am." He poised the blade just below the hollow of her neck and dug the tip of the blade into her flesh. And she screamed, even as she told herself it would only satisfy him. Her voice just now was controlled by something more powerful than reason, something animal and afraid.

He pulled her away from the wall and threw her onto the floor of the cell. "Now hold still."

"Ryder."

The Commander dropped the knife. It clattered beside Isobel's head, ringing a tune of pain.

"Lord Fairborn." Ryder bowed at the waist, but his eyes showed no submission; they glinted with cold hate.

Isobel turned her head against the dirty stone floor. A tall figure dressed in a black coat and dark trousers approached the bars. Mortimer Fairborn regarded the Commander with a bored look. "What are you doing, Ryder?"

"Questioning the prisoner. I'm sure Patriarch wanted—"

Mortimer gripped one bar in either hand and peeled them apart, stepping through the gap he'd made. He flicked his wrist, and Ryder flew across the room. The Commander's skull hit the stone wall with a satisfying crunch. Isobel propped herself up on her elbows, her eyes fixed on Mortimer as he crossed the cell.

"I don't particularly care what Patriarch wants," Mortimer said. "I thought you knew: Izzy is mine."

Ryder scrambled back to his feet, his chest heaving. "How *dare* you. I am your commanding officer."

"Hardly." Mortimer offered a hand to Isobel. She gritted her teeth, but took it, and he hauled her to her feet. "What have you done to the poor girl?"

Isobel tore her hand away from him. "You're one to talk."

"It's bad form to criticize the man saving you, my dear."

She glared up at him. He looked so much like Nathy, though pale, his yellow hair smoothed back with pomade and shining in the low light of the prison. Even the disinterested way he cast his eyes on Ryder evoked memories of his son's tired contempt.

"Stay away from Miss Isobel in the future, boy. Or you'll answer to me."

"I'm not afraid of you," Ryder said through his teeth. "You're not Patriarch."

"Right." Mortimer spread his hand, palm facing Ryder; the Commander flew backward, denting the stone wall and collapsing in a pile of rubble. "I'm far worse." He smiled at Isobel. "Come along, my dear. We have things to discuss."

THEY EXITED HAYLOCK onto the streets of the Eastern, and Isobel stumbled into a nearby alley. There she fell against the wall and clutched the wound below her throat, teeth gritted against the unending pain.

"Demon bone?" Mortimer asked.

Isobel swallowed, tasting blood. "Why help me escape? I thought you of all people would be helping the Elderon."

"This is no longer about the Elderon," Mortimer said. "But, to answer your question, I remain fond of you, no matter how you've disappointed me in the past. You were my most promising apprentice."

She snorted. "Please tell me you still smoke."

He slipped a cigarette case from his coat and tossed it to her. He lit a match and held it to the tip of the cigarette she placed between trembling lips. The scent of a rich, burning tobacco chased away some of the clamor of Isobel's mind. She tapped ash to the alley floor and exhaled. The pain was receding. The nicotine shot through her blood and made the world a little softer.

"I take it you want something," Isobel said after a moment.

He didn't respond, just watched her with blue eyes lighter than the sky and more formless than muted daylight.

"What are you doing here?" she tried again. "How——" She faltered, and rather than choke in front of Mortimer Fairborn, rather than watch satisfaction fill those empty eyes, she turned away. "Fine. Well, thanks for the smoke and the jailbreak." She got to her feet, stubbing the cigarette out on the alley wall.

He sighed. "How's Nathy?"

Her nails dug into her palm. "You care, do you?"

"Roselyn told me everything." He chuckled. "Is it wrong to say I'm proud?"

Isobel turned with her own cool smile; she could always match Mortimer's demeanor, even if she didn't mean it, even if she hurt in every possible way when she looked at him. "Tell Nathy that. If you're not too much of a coward to face him."

Mortimer stepped closer; Isobel shrank back. Her animal instincts still ruled her, and, like prey from a predator, she retreated at his presence.

"I have plans for my son. He's powerful. And now, he's angry. He could be useful."

"Has anyone mentioned you're a perfect bastard, Mort?"

"And you...you're still so delightful, my dear." He reached out like he might caress her cheek, but his eyes landed on her face, still uncovered, and his hand dropped. Her wounds were a handiwork even he could not admire. "You and my son share similar wounds. Have you ever wondered why?"

"Because the same sadistic bastard mutilated us, perhaps?"

"I'm guided by a higher reason than mere sadism, dear girl. When I punished you and my son, I did so in the name of Elrosh, in service to the blood that we all share with him."

"You never struck me as the religious type."

"You know of what I speak. You're an Ellicott, try as you might to bury your past."

She shook her head. "You've lost me, Mort."

He placed his hand on her cheek, his thumb caressing the warped skin of her face. "One eye to see the truth, the other to shut out darkness. You lacked Sight. So I gave it to you."

Her lips parted, a question she dared not ask on her tongue.

"You remember," he said, letting his hand fall away. "I had hoped you would. Your grandfather tried so hard to teach you the way."

"That club..." He would leave her alone some nights, dressed in a dark coat, and in the morning, he'd come back smelling of iron and sweat. Some nights, the cloaked men came to their manor house. Grandfather, playing the perfect host, would serve brandy and a meal cooked up by Isobel's small hands. He'd let her watch from the stairs until the men became drunk, bawdy.

Some things, you are not ready to know, child.

She'd always assumed the screams were her own nightmares. That the sounds coming from downstairs were conjured by her tired imagination, her swelling fear.

Grandfather and his peculiarities hadn't crossed her mind since she'd run away to become a Huntress. But Mortimer's words—they were her grandfather's, too. He'd been full of cruel, cryptic phrases. *You lack sight, little girl. Don't make me give it to you.*

"Sannus Eyreh," Isobel said. She met Mortimer's waiting gaze. "Who are you people?"

"That's beyond your concern. For now, just do me a favor, my dear. Protect my son. I'm afraid my acquaintances don't appreciate what he is."

"And you do? You mutilated him, *tortured* him, for what he was. I had to drag your son out of a fire that you and Ruark started. Jade had to explain to a little boy why his father would cut his face open. And now—"

"He's just like me."

Isobel shrank back. "No."

"That's what you were thinking. And you're wrong. I never meant to kill him. I made him stronger. He'll be useful to me soon."

"I will protect Nathy," Isobel said. "From you."

Mortimer bent, his breath tickling the fresh cut on her neck, and kissed her cheek. "Please do, love. I'm begging you."

32

THE MALUS VYLARUS

ALASTAIR SLUMPED OVER the old book, drawing a candle closer to its pages. Silence hummed through the library. He felt for a moment that he was at his room at the monastery; the same feeling of reverence and peace exuded from these many books.

The same could not be said for the book before him. It used the language of religion and suggested a reverence for Elrosh, but there was something wrong—something twisted and cruel in its old, cramped Anñanym. He'd gleaned the title from the faded, stamped words along the spine: *Malus Vylarus*— terrible truth.

He was bent intently over the text when a dark figure suddenly dropped into the seat beside him. When he looked up, his stomach flipped and his heart beat faster, symptoms he tried to ignore but couldn't, not when Poe smiled at him like that. His big black eyes were shielded by a fringe of silky hair, but they flickered to meet his.

"Hi there."

Alastair swallowed and returned to his book.

"Hey, um... I'm sorry," Poe said.

"W-why?" Alastair looked up, startled by the words. "You haven't done anything."

"I keep bothering you."

"You're not bothering me," Alastair said, meaning it. "I like when you're around."

Poe bit his pierced lower lip. Alastair stared. He wasn't handsome in the way someone like Saxon was. He was skinny and moonlight-pale, his eyes too big, accentuated by kohl. He was like a painting made by someone beautiful and sad.

Alastair's stomach rushed with fire. He quickly looked back at the book.

Poe scooted his chair closer to Alastair's. "So, what are you reading?" He leaned in close; he smelled like smoke and soap. "What are the weird symbols?"

"Oh. Um. Do you really want to know? It's a bit dull if you're not, you know, a monk or something."

"I'm interested 'cause you're interested." Poe smiled.

Alastair tried to suppress the sudden flaring happiness that crashed in around him. "The symbols are called Anñanym. They made the primary Elonni writing system first invented a few millennia ago. Old books, especially religious ones like the Amerand, were first written in Anñanym. Those of us in the Church still read the original texts. It makes for the most accurate interpretation."

"So...this is the Amerand?"

"No. It's one I haven't encountered before. We found it in that old house, when we went into the grave."

Poe brightened. "Wicked. So, it's some secret text, huh?"

"I think it is. The ideas put forth—they don't square with Church teachings. In fact, the closest thing I could relate any of this to is the old legend of the first earthly king."

"Like, Lacey's ancestors?"

"No. Before the monarchy as we know it, some old legends say that Elrosh flowed his own blood into a single chosen Elonni. That man became king, but eventually abdicated the throne to let mortal men rule once more."

"So...the king was immortal?"

Alastair nodded. "It would have been the closest thing to God being upon the throne. An undying incarnation of Elrosh himself."

"And what's the book got to do with that?"

"It talks a lot about having the blood of Elrosh, about being *Sannus Eyreh*—literally, sons of God."

"Aren't all Elonni sons of God?"

"Spiritually, yes. But the word here, *Sannus*, that's only ever used when talking about blood relations—not a metaphorical relationship."

"Okay." Poe nibbled his lip. "And you found this book on the property?"

"Nearby, yes."

"Gotcha. So, maybe Donoveir is the Son of God. Or, one of them."

"Well...it's just a legend."

"Legends don't write books." Poe stretched out his hand, his delicate fingers hovering over the book's pages. "May I?"

"Um...sure."

Poe's fingers brushed the pages; his palm settled upon the ancient words. He closed his eyes and clenched his jaw as though suddenly overtaken by some unpleasant sensation.

"Donoveir," he said. "It belonged to him."

"You can tell?"

"He's still attached to it. He...still wants to obey it. And...no. He's proud. Demanding. But he's reverent, too. There's someone he fears. Someone he...worships."

"Poe...you can come back now. You shouldn't—"

"It's a name. He's saying a name. Solomon." Poe flinched. His teeth gritted and his fingers twitched across the page. "Stone."

"Stone?" Alastair looked down at the book.

And suddenly, he understood.

He pulled Poe's hand away, severing the connection. Poe gasped and tilted out of the chair. Alastair barely caught him before he hit the floor.

"You saw Solomon Stone?" Alastair said, righting Poe in his chair.

"I heard the name. It was ringing in my head. Why? Do you recognize it?"

Alastair nodded. "The Stones were the greatest Old Name that ever lived. They were the purest line of Elonni ever recorded."

"*Were?*"

"They all died off. But...if Donoveir was saying that name...maybe Solomon Stone was a sort of leader." He flipped back to the second page of the book, the strange branching hierarchy of names. Fairborn was second to the top, but the one above it...

Stone.

"It's not just a hierarchy of the purest names," Alastair said. "It's a line of ascension. This symbol, the two eyes—I think it

284

symbolizes the group. And here...Stone, then Fairborn, then Sanso, Rose, Ellicott...it all fits. It makes sense."

"You've lost me," Poe said.

"The Old Names—they're not just obsessed with their nobility. They think they literally carry the blood of Elrosh. And some of them are in this group—"

"Cult," Poe corrected.

"Right. But you see, the names are ordered by purity. They want to follow a leader who has the strongest connection to Elrosh."

"But if all the Stones are dead..." Poe flicked the symbol for Fairborn. "Nathy's father is next in line."

Alastair took in a hard breath. "We need to talk to Nathy. Now."

NATHY HAD BEEN silent on the journey back to Fryer's Grove, and the moment they walked through the front gate, he broke away from Lacey, heading toward the graveyard. She waited on the mossy flagstones of the courtyard, holding her bag of cleansing materials, watching his figure grow distant through the trees.

"Oh, bloody hell," she said, following him. He walked into the graveyard and meandered between the headstones, coming at last to a stop before a bare patch of grass. He sat, unmoving, and Lacey waited beyond the gate. It felt wrong to bother him, to disturb whatever peace he sought. She could guess who he'd come to visit.

At last, she summoned a tenuous courage and peeled back the groaning gate. He didn't look up or in any way acknowledge her approach, even as she sat beside him on the damp grass. "I sort of know what you're feeling."

He stared ahead. "Do you."

"I don't mean I've been through anything like you have. But I know how it feels when everything just...hurts."

He threw his head back and groaned. "Are you trying to bond with me?"

"As a matter of fact, yes."

"And now you're going to tell me your tragic story, yeah?"

"If you insist." She took a deep breath, sure he would laugh at her, but maybe Jade was right. Maybe it was worth trying for Nathy. "I've never been accepted in my village. They think I'm a freak, or dangerous, because I'm part Elonni. I've never had a friend other than Saxon. Even my own cousins wouldn't play with me. And my stepfather—he wishes I didn't exist. He wanted to marry my mother, to get her land, but...I know he wishes he had his own children, and not me."

"That's rough, princess."

"So I know how much easier it is to just harden your heart and keep anything else from hurting it. Which I think is what Jade meant about you."

"Yeah, maybe."

"You do see that you're doing it right now."

He laid back on the grass, hands behind his head, eyes shut. "I know. But what good does it do to give a shit? Really?"

"I don't know that it does do any good. Except...maybe you can only really bear pain with other people to help you carry it."

"People *are* pain."

"Maybe just try it? You never talk about anything real, do you? Tell me one real thing and see if you feel better."

"No."

"Fine. I'll tell you one, then. My stepfather never actually hurt me; he knew he wouldn't get away with it, not with my mom. So, he'd find me when I was doing chores away from the house, and he'd threaten me. He'd tell me if I didn't behave, he knew the perfect spot of forest where I could disappear, and even my mother would assume I'd just gotten lost and died on the marshes."

"Why didn't you tell anyone?"

"I was scared. Telling on him was misbehaving. I thought he meant it. Maybe he did. I think now he was just trying to scare me, but...when you're little, you believe that stuff."

Nathy was silent a moment, his eyes on the moons dancing in orbit above. "It was supposed to be me who faced Ruark. Not Artemis."

"Oh."

"I was the best fighter. I was the strongest. Maybe I wasn't ready, but if we were gonna send anyone, it had to be me. But the day before I was set to leave, Flynn called it off. He told me it was too dangerous, that I was too important to risk. I thought that meant no one would go. Me and Artemis fell asleep that night in my room...when I woke up, she was gone."

"She...she didn't tell you."

"Not even a letter." He turned his head away. "It was supposed to be me. But Flynn didn't want to lose me. Course he *did*, after that."

A heavy silence hung between them, Lacey considering the bare ground before them. If Artemis was buried here, there was no stone marking her place. She wasn't about to ask. Instead she said, "What was she like?"

"Seriously?"

"Yeah. Don't always focus on the end. You were happy with her once."

He grunted; it didn't seem like the worst response, all things considered.

"How did you meet?" Lacey asked.

"You're really not letting up? Fine. She came here when she was twelve. She was human from March Grange, and her parents had been killed by Watchmen for harboring a warlock they were after. She was put in an orphanage in her village. But she escaped and pickpocketed enough money to take a train west. She ended up in Bishop's Hole. End of the northern railway. The farthest she could get from her past."

He took a steadying breath. "I found her one night when I was walking home from school. She was rooting through a heap of trash in a back alley, looking for food. So I told her about Fryer's Grove. Flynn took her in without even thinking about it."

He continued now without prompting, the story rushing like a stream cleared of debris. "We were always good friends. Not that she had many options for friends, it was just me and Jade at the time. But even after Poe and Alice came, it felt like just the two of us. She wanted to learn to fight, in case the Watchmen ever messed with her again. I taught her everything I knew." He seemed to catch himself, to realize how much he'd said. "And...y'know. The end."

"She sounds amazing."

"She...was." He squeezed his eyes shut, but not quick enough to hide the sheen of tears. "Call me obsessive, but..." A cruel twist came over his lips. "I'm going to kill Ruark one day. I don't care how long it takes or what it does to me. He's going to pay."

"You still love her."

"You never stop loving people who die on you." He flicked his gaze to her briefly. "She tried to do this, too, y'know. She couldn't stop asking questions, but I didn't want to tell her why I was here."

"It obviously worked out for her."

He surprised her by laughing. "You want me to fall in love with you, too, princess?"

"I...no! What? I didn't mean... I... I didn't..." Lacey cleared her throat. "I think we'd best stay friends."

"We're friends now?"

"We could be. On one condition."

"Shoot."

"Stop calling me princess."

He considered it for a moment. "Okay, kid."

She found herself smiling at a little flutter in her stomach. "We'll workshop the new nickname a while."

Footsteps thudded on the grass behind them. Nathy propped himself up on his elbows and turned his head.

"Monk."

Alastair stopped behind them, panting. Poe followed behind, casting his eyes warily between the graves.

"Nathy...your dad...is..." Alastair heaved a deep breath. "A cult leader."

"How auspicious."

Alastair and Poe exchanged a worried glance. "You're taking this rather well," Alastair said.

"I'm screaming on the inside," he deadpanned.

Alastair shook his head. "Just—come with us. I have to show you what I found."

34

THE LETTER

ALASTAIR LED THEM to the library. The book they'd found in the crumbling house sat open on a writing desk, turned to a page of scattered Aññanym, all branching from the symbol of the eye Lacey had recognized from Nathy's scars.

Alastair pointed to the Aññanym directly beneath the eye. "It says Stone."

Nathy shrugged. "So?"

"So, all the Stones are dead. The Old Names still talk about it. Solomon Stone had seven sons, and he murdered every one of them before slitting his own throat." Alastair dragged his finger to the next Aññanym, the one branching off from Stone. "Next is Fairborn."

"I see that," Nathy said.

"Nathy." Alastair tossed his hands. "I think you were right. The Old Names were organized. They were in a cult. And they followed the command of the purest Elonni in their ranks. That used to be Solomon Stone. Now..."

"It would be my dad." Nathy blew out a breath. "Well. That's something."

Lacey peered down at the book, her fingers hovering over the pages, yet not daring to touch them. They felt dangerous, dark, like the words might somehow infect her. "What else does the book say?"

"Horrible stuff," Alastair said quietly. "All sorts of rituals for punishing nocturnes, half-breeds. Disobedient women. Men who, ah, lie with men."

Nathy's eyes darted to each of them. "So, us."

Alastair sighed. "The point is, the people in this cult—they really believe that old legend, the one I mentioned in the tomb. They think they're actually descended from Elrosh."

"Which in their minds makes them gods," Nathy said.

"Right. And they think they're entitled to the throne of Gryfel. It's all over the book, some nonsense about reconquering the land." Alastair pressed his hands onto the desk, staring down at the book. "And I think they finally did."

Lacey blinked. "Oh, my God. The Ruined Queen. They killed her. They orchestrated the revolution?"

"And built the Elderon to replace the monarchy," Alastair said.

"That doesn't make sense," Lacey said. "Not everyone in the Elderon is an Old Name."

"Three of the five Elders are," Alastair said. "And a lot of the senators and ambassadors. They can't make it too obvious, I expect, or else average Elonni might revolt themselves. They're being smart. Waiting."

"Waiting for what?" Lacey asked.

"Until they're unopposed." Nathy looked at her. "You have claim to the throne. And, potentially, world-ending power."

"But nobody's going to just make *me* queen," Lacey said.

"You never know," Poe said, pushing his fringe out of his eyes. "The Ruined Queen wasn't unpopular. A lot of people liked living in harmony with nocturnes. It was only the Old Names who really opposed. They riled up support out of fear, not any real loyalty."

"Yeah," Nathy said. "Not to mention most Elonni are mixed. They might not advertise it, but nearly all of them have human blood somewhere down the line."

"But...not this lot?"

Alastair shook his head. "They call themselves Trueborn. There are even directions in here for how to intermarry and ensure the bloodline continues *unblemished*. Their word."

"And how long have they been around? As a cult, anyway?"

"Given the age of this book?" Alastair sighed. "At least a thousand years. Since the Elonni conquered Gryfel, at least."

"I don't understand, though," Lacey said. "They want to reconquer the throne, but wasn't it the first of these Trueborns who gave up the throne? Shouldn't they respect that?"

"They think it was a mistake. That the first Son of God was wrong to trust mortals, and now it's his descendants' duty to reclaim the throne."

"And even though they have it," Lacey said, "they're still determined to eliminate the competition. Me."

"It's why Donoveir killed Latrice," Nathy said. "He found out what she was and got rid of her."

"And my dad... The Elderon realized what he was when the Nine started fighting in the war." She swallowed. "And now, they know about me. And they're going to kill me."

Nathy, for once, looked truly bothered, his face twisted in a grimace. "That's heavy, kid."

"I need my powers." She stepped away from the desk. "Right. I should just go to Flynn and tell him I want to do this whole—Rite thing. And then I'll...kill your dad, I guess?"

"I'm fine with that last part," Nathy said. "But you're forgetting. You can't do any Rites until you have the Book of the Nine. And your father died without telling anyone where it was. Not to mention the only heirs we know about are Flynn and Landon, and he's all the way off in Mondberg at the moment."

"Right." She sank into a chair. "I'm just going to die, then."

"No, you're not." Nathy pushed himself up onto the desk and looked down at her. "Kid, these Old Names—they're nothing. I'm one of them, and I don't have any amazing powers. And look at this guy." He hooked a thumb at Alastair. "He's not exactly a heavenly warrior, is he?"

"I know you're just trying to make a point," Alastair said, "but you don't have to be rude."

Nathy ignored him. "These people think they're special because their god made them special. But they're not."

Lacey buried her face in her hands. "They've killed the last two generations of my family, Nathy."

"Yeah, but they didn't have me there. You do have me."

Poe covered his mouth with both hands. "Aww."

"Stop," Nathy said.

"Sorry." Poe smirked. "We'll leave you alone, anyhow." He took Alastair by the hand and tugged him from the library. Lacey only glanced up when she heard the door shut.

"You—you don't have to help me, you know."

"Hey, if being on your side means I get to fight a cult, I can't think of anything I'd rather be doing."

She smiled. "Thanks, then." She rose. "I wish I could talk to my father. Do you think maybe Jade could...?"

Nathy shook his head. "She tried contacting his spirit years ago, when we were first trying to find you. There's no reason why it shouldn't have worked. She had a lot of stuff that had belonged to him. She even tried summoning him in the house, in the bedroom he used. She couldn't get him."

"Does that mean... Do some people just not become ghosts?"

"Most don't, I think. People who die violently, or too young, they're more likely to." He shrugged. "It would make sense if he were a ghost. But sometimes, it doesn't happen. Artemis isn't around anymore, either."

Lacey hadn't even thought of that, but of course he would have tried to find Artemis. And maybe not finding her, not even having the cold comfort of her spirit, had broken him all the more.

But Artemis hadn't died at Fryer's Grove. Neither had Will.

"Where was my father when he died?" she said at last.

"I don't know exactly," Nathy said. "Flynn said he'd gone off to the Northern Reaches. I can ask."

Lacey nodded along absently. "Maybe he's out there somewhere."

Nathy didn't look like he believed that; maybe he couldn't. Picturing Artemis's spirit, wandering lonely through some distant corner of the realm... Lacey looked away.

"Get some rest," Nathy said after a moment. "We'll figure something out in the morning."

"All right." She rose with the bag Jade had given her and left him sitting on the desk, the book open beside him.

LACEY WALKED SLOWLY back to Latrice's bedroom, her pulse quickening as she drew nearer. The heavy old door loomed at the end of the corridor, like the lid of a tomb containing forgotten remains. Her hand trembled as she wrapped her fingers around the doorknob and twisted.

The doorknob caught. She tugged against it, but the door only rattled in its hinges.

She hadn't locked the door. But perhaps Latrice had.

She set the bag of cleansing materials by the door. Just as she turned away, thinking she'd find Alice and sleep in the other girl's room tonight, the next door down the corridor creaked open, a groaning invitation.

It was clearly a bad idea to go into this new room. She had no idea what lay beyond the door, or what sort of creature might be waiting on the other side. Yet she found herself moving slowly toward it, her hand brushing the door wider, her feet moving across the threshold.

The door slammed shut behind her.

Panic was quickly overridden with curiosity. She stood in a large, cozy study, a little library unto itself, so crowded was it with books and scrolls. A huge blue marble globe hung in a spinner, the world's eleven continents raised in green glass. The desk at the center of the room was large and dark, and a deep green rug spanned the center of the room. A bronze-plated phonograph sat on a spindly table in the far corner.

It must have been beautiful once, but the room seemed not to have been entered for fifty years or more. Dust coated everything; the stench of mold and rot choked the air. The window overlooking the courtyard and forest beyond had been left open a crack, leaving decades of rain and mist to dampen the carpet. The pages of books curled under their covers, yellowed and mildewed.

Lacey stepped forward and, when nothing horrible happened, she walked around, examining the various objects upon the shelves and the desk. An hour glass, a marble paperweight.

There were photo frames, but not a single picture to occupy them. Many of the frames were smashed, their contents presumably taken. Yet here they sat in their old places, collecting dust and offering no memories.

All of the books were historical, but not the sort of history books one found in an Elonni library. The spines bore titles in languages that belonged to nocturnes—Rakashi, Lyvian, Wynish, even Draconian. Their accounts, Lacey had thought, had been burned up. Destroyed to make room for tales more comfortable to Elonni ears. Lacey passed her fingers over the spines. They felt dangerous with possibility.

293

The phonograph suddenly sprung to life, scraping a rusty tune in a warbled yet soothing voice. Lacey backed away from the device and her back hit the corner of the desk. Her eyes watered in pain.

And I told you once
But sure I'll tell you twice
Cause darlin' you're so nice

If ever there was
Another girl by me
I ain't the man I oughta be.

Cause it's you, yeah it's you
Oh, you're the girl I love.

Lacey sat in the desk chair. Her heart had only just calmed from the shock when the desk drawer by her right elbow shot open with force. She stifled a scream and peered to it.

Inside was a mess of papers: old receipts, bank statements, memos. Lacey rifled through the papers until her hand came upon something solid and heavy, and she lifted it out.

A book with a cracked brown leather cover, its parchment pages yellow and stiff from elemental exposure. She flipped through the pages quickly and found them blank. She set the unused diary on the desk.

Suddenly, the pages gusted, fluttering and falling until the book lay open to a page near the end of the diary. Lacey leaned forward, heart beating in her throat, to find a short note in hurried, slanting handwriting.

I have hidden the Book. It is gone. And now I will die for what I am. My dear teacher—my love—you will not understand. But I cannot be your weapon. Let your fire be enough, and forget me.
Latrice Heartwood-Fryer

The lock on the door clicked. Lacey looked up.

"Can...can I go?" she asked. She didn't expect a response, and she wasn't given one. She pushed back from the desk, diary tucked under her arm.

Cold crept from the air into her bones. She turned back to the desk, half-knowing what—who—she would find.

The ghost that had visited her last night—her grandmother—sat behind the desk, her green eyes translucent, yet unmistakably fixed on Lacey.

"He's still here."

"D-Donoveir? I know...Grandmother." She stumbled over the unfamiliar word.

"He's still here."

"Are you trapped?" Lacey took a careful step closer.

The ghost tilted its head to the side. Its eyes glassed over, going white in its pale face. "Still...still..."

"Grandmother?"

A ruby bulb of blood formed in the corner of Latrice's mouth, slithered down her chin. "Run. Run. *Run.*"

Lacey did as the ghost asked.

SHE JUMPED DOWN the stairs, too impatient to take them, and ran down the fourth-floor corridor. She threw open Saxon's door without knocking.

"Lace?" He sat up in bed, his eyes hazy and hooded. The room smelled of cigarette smoke and something sharp and clinical. Bane.

"I'm still furious with you. But move over."

He moved aside in his bed and she hopped up beside him, holding her knees to her chest. The diary dangled from her fingers, and she tossed it to the floor. She needed a moment away from ghosts and tragedy.

"I...should tell you...I'm very high," Saxon said.

"Really," she said dryly. "You hide it so well." She found a limp pack of cigarettes on his nightstand and fished one out. She snapped her fingers to light the end.

"You shouldn't smoke," Saxon said.

She looked at him with a glare that could cut metal. He shrank back.

"One won't kill you."

She touched the cigarette to her lips and inhaled, wincing at the taste. "This is awful." But a moment later, pleasure shocked her blood and rushed her head.

"Lacey."

He said her name with such gravity, such a stark longing, that she faced him. He looked into her eyes, his blue gaze swimming, his mouth turned in a soft smile.

"What is it?" she asked, her own voice small.

His hand brushed her long hair from her face and tucked it carefully behind her ear. He leaned closer, his breath warm on her neck. "I need to tell you...finally..."

She shuddered. "Yes?"

"You have five eyes. And every one is *beautiful*."

She shoved him back. "How much did you burn?"

"Loads," he said, falling onto his side. He began to snore a moment later.

She glared at his limp body, but a twitch of sympathy ached in her chest. His wavy chocolate hair fell over his eyes, and single strands caught in the stubble growing along his jaw. She slipped off the bed and tugged the rumpled blankets over him.

"Night," she said, and blew out the candle on the nightstand. Then she left the dark room.

She followed the bends in the corridors without really admitting to herself where she was going. She knocked on the door, telling herself he wouldn't answer. But when he opened the door, bleary-eyed and shirtless and beautiful, her heart jumped around her ribcage like a startled animal. She swallowed.

"Can I stay with you?"

His eyes widened.

"There's a ghost in my room," she clarified.

"So this isn't a...social call," he said. She thought she must be imagining the slight strain in his voice.

"Is that what the kids are calling it these days?" she said in a flat tone that didn't at all match the gallop of her heart. She was trying, honestly, not to imagine what the light lines of his muscles would feel like against her skin. She truly was. But.

"This is weird," he said. "Okay." He held the door open for her.

She glanced up at him as she passed into his room and—
no, she wasn't imagining it. He was blushing, too.

35

THEN FALL

THE CHANCELLOR'S PRIVATE study would have been comforting had he not set out to deliberately remove any sense of hominess from it. While the carpet was a lush scarlet and the handsome rows of books behind an imposing black-wood desk helped the place feel like a small, safe library, the oil portraits of chill-eyed former Chancellors cooled the room. Albion Crane hated that his own face stared down at him every day, hated that he hung in the shadow of old Filbard Grenning. Grenning's portrait was framed in black; a few others were as well, and it signaled that they had died in office. Assassinated, usually.

Filbard had met his end during the War of Teeth, and the hurried appointment of Crane had been one of concession and necessity. He knew nobody was pleased with him, and the fifteen years of his ineffectual rule had only further division to show for it. Post-war years were hard on great men, and he was no great man.

He could admit it. He was ill-equipped to fuse the fractures between magical, celestial, and mortal beings. Mortals were poorer than ever; the nocturnes, further removed; and the Elonni, tense. Those in power were never content to hold it; they needed to know they could keep it. It was the tragedy of Crane's everyday life.

Nobody wanted a man who tried to walk the middle of the road. Those of a more progressive mindset, who looked back on the war shaking their heads, thought him an insensitive bastard, ignoring the plight of nocturnes languishing at the edge of the city.

The old guard of Theopolis wished he'd take a harder stance. They wanted someone like Ryder Lately at the head of the Long Table, cleansing the Eastern not of its plight, but its citizens.

In short, he had no idea what to do—whom to please—and, as it was, his realm was unhappy on every front.

A knock came at his study door, and his handmaid stepped inside, bearing a parchment envelope laid flat on her palm.

"Letter for you, sir," the young human girl said.

He'd gotten more letters in the past few days than at any other time in his career, excluding those fractious months after the war, of course. The people's sleeping sense of safety had been wakened violently by the raid on the Eastern. Nobody was happy. On the one hand: *Injustice! Murder!* On the other: *Not nearly enough, sir! Lock them all up!* Indeed.

He took the envelope from the servant girl with a brief nod and found his letter opener on his desk. Inside was a short note, scrawled, it seemed, on the nearest bit of scrap paper available to the penman. The harried script stuck him, initially, as a note from a madman. And then, he saw the signature.

Absolom Poole.

He looked carefully over the note now, curiosity driving him more than any real desire to engage with the ramblings of the malcontent professor. His eyes narrowed at the cramped words, then popped wide.

Albion— I understand you're unlikely to listen to a thing I've got to say, but please hear me out. I need your help. A mad, murderous cult has infiltrated the Elderon and you're in as much danger as anybody. I'm afraid to say more here. I need to speak with you in person. Burn this note.

He had always believed Poole an eccentric, but brilliant. Sadly, it seemed the professor was just as cracked as the patients languishing in the city asylum.

His handmaid returned, meekly tapping the doorframe. "I'm sorry, Your Excellence. But there's...a visitor?"

Crane pocketed the note. "Send him in."

He half-expected a harried Poole to shuffle in. Instead, as the handmaid stepped aside, the door flung wide, and Ingrid Isobel Ellicott stood before him. She wore a standard prison jumper, torn in places and crusted with blood along the rips. The mask she was always known to wear was gone, baring the ruination of her lovely face. The skin was rippled, pink, as though it had been burned away. Her sightless eye hovered like a moon over a barren landscape. She caught his stare and pulled her long hair over her face.

"Madame Huntress," Crane said, bowing instinctively.

"Chancellor. I'm glad you could see me on such short notice." She stepped forward, crossing her arms over her chest. "I'll get straight to the point. A cult has infiltrated the ranks of the Elderon, and you're in terrible danger, sir."

His mouth opened and shut, words failing him. He plucked Absolom's note from his pocket. "I—I— Are you and Absolom Poole in on this together?"

"No, sir." The Huntress raised an eyebrow. "Has he said something?"

Crane blinked at the note, the hurried words scattered like needles across the rumpled page. "Perhaps I ought to go see him."

"Very good, sir. I'll explain on the way. But first." She smiled down at her ruined clothes. "Might I use your washroom?"

POOLE HADN'T EXPECTED a response, but that didn't stop him pacing his sitting room, waiting for a knock at the door, the ring of the telephone. Aeyrin sat on the couch, watching his frantic motions with growing concern.

"Let me go talk to him," she said. "I'll wear a disguise. I'll use a false name."

"It's too dangerous," Poole muttered.

"It's better than waiting around here. He's not going to come to you. He hates you, remember?"

"He could recognize you. Anyone could."

"I didn't do anything wrong."

"But you were married to Will. They'd love to have you behind bars, too, believe me."

"Sol, every moment we waste here is a moment we could be looking for Lacey."

Poole slumped against the wall. "I'm trapped here."

"I'm not." She sighed. "I know you don't like the idea, but I could make it to the Western Reaches. I could go to her."

"And the Nine'll just, what, hand her over?"

She shook her head. "You're impossible."

"I'd just...rather you not wander into a cult that helped orchestrate the last epic war, all right?"

She pursed her lips, thinking. "How many of them are there?"

"Their numbers will have depleted since the war. The vampires and werewolves were their greatest allies, and with them gone, they'll be smaller. But still, they were a force. I imagine a lot of mages are still loyal."

"I'd still rather risk it with them than with the Elderon. They may be violent, but they wouldn't hurt me. Will was their leader, wasn't he?"

"He was a weapon. Nothing more." A knock stirred Poole from his slump, and he jolted to answer the door.

A beautiful blond-haired woman stood on his stoop, an opera mask concealing the left half of her face. She was dressed in a sharp black suit and heels, and a sword was slung across her back.

"Who are you?" Poole asked.

"Ingrid Isobel Ellicott," the woman said, placing a hand on his chest and pushing him back into the house. "I brought the Chancellor for you."

He looked up. Sure enough, Albion Crane stood on his stoop, looking at his shoes. "Hello, Absolom."

"You...you actually came?"

"I was prepared to dismiss your note as the product of a tired mind. But Ms. Ellicott seems to share your concerns."

"Ellicott." Poole looked at the woman. "You're Octavian's...what, granddaughter?"

"Oh, you knew him, too. Good." She stepped forward and grabbed Poole's right arm. His sleeves were rolled up, clearly displaying the Mark. "I never would have suspected."

"You...know who I am?" He cast his eyes briefly to Aeyrin. Isobel caught him, smiled. She dropped a quick wink.

"I was the one who found Lacey for the Nine," she said, stepping into the sitting room. She caught sight of Aeyrin standing by the couch and smiled. "Hello. You must be Aeyrin."

Poole shook his head. "I'm sorry, but why are you in my house?"

"I'm a Huntress." Her ruby smile curved. "And before you ask, I betrayed the Elderon fifteen years ago. I'm only here to help."

"Help?" Aeyrin echoed. "You turned my daughter over to a cult."

"They're less a cult, more a...badly organized but well-meaning group of revolutionaries."

"How did you find Lacey?" Poole said; he had to know. The Elderon had come to know about her through his own stupidity; he'd been sure, though, that Lacey was a secret to Will's old gang.

"You should be more careful with your dedications, professor," Isobel said. "Will talked about you sometimes. I looked into you—you seemed so *solitary*, so without human connection." She smirked. "Your published works say otherwise."

Aeyrin turned her gaze on him. "Sol?"

He winced. "I might have dedicated all of my books to you."

She blinked. "You're an idiot."

He tossed his hands. "I didn't know they'd recruited an Elonni! Nocturnes aren't allowed in Theopolis. I thought—oh, never mind. It was stupid."

"But sweet," Isobel said. "Anyway. Enough about me. I've brought the Chancellor to you. Tell him what you know, professor."

Crane stood awkwardly in the foyer, looking around at the many bookshelves in Poole's sitting room. He now stepped forward, eyeing the available seating. He sat on the edge of an armchair without removing his coat.

"Get on with it," Crane said. "I'm busy."

"Of course you are." Poole sat with Aeyrin on the couch. The Huntress stayed standing, arms crossed, her eyes moving between the two men.

"Right," Poole began. "So. There's this cult. Sannus Eyreh, or Sons of God. It's a loose collection of Old Names who fancy themselves descendants of Elrosh himself."

"That's preposterous," Crane said. "You're saying God had—what, literal children?"

"Not in the traditional sense," Poole said. "He's said to have given his blood to a worthy Elonni. It made the man stronger, fiercer. That man's descendants are supposed to be the families we consider the Old Names today."

"All that rot about the Old Names," Crane muttered. "It's utter rubbish. Nobody puts stock in that anymore."

"You say that, Chancellor," Isobel said. "And yet most of your government is held by those with an Old Name."

"That's—well. I'll admit the prestige plays a role. But they made me Chancellor. And Kimberly—"

"When's the last time you heard from Kimberly?" Poole said.

Crane opened his mouth; shut it. "He hasn't answered any of my calls in the past day. But I imagine he's busy, as the Elder of Information, given the, er, state of things."

"Or he's run off because he's afraid," Poole said.

"Or he's dead," Isobel added.

Crane rubbed circles into his temple. "I should have known this was nothing but a conspiracy. You've wasted enough of my time."

"My grandfather was in it," Isobel said as the Chancellor began to rise. "Sannus Eyreh. He was one of them. I never fully understood what it was all about, but I knew it was dangerous. It's why I became a Huntress so young—to get away."

She looked now at Poole, eyebrows raised. He sighed.

"My father was part of it."

"You?" Crane chuckled. "Of all the—*you*? You don't even believe in God."

"I never said the message sank in. I left home at sixteen. Became someone else."

"Well." Crane cleared his throat. "I'm sorry both of you had such...tumultuous childhoods. But you've given me no reason to see this little group as a threat, let alone to the level you claim. I believe I would know if my Elders were members of such a society."

"It's not some social club," Poole said. "They wouldn't exactly advertise, especially to an outsider. But they'd gladly let you think you were running the government while they worked in secret."

"The Elderon has done nothing that I haven't approved of. We work quite well together."

"Do you? Do you really want a teenage girl put to death for a power she didn't know she had? Did you really want to drive werewolves and vampires to extinction?"

"I trust my Elders. And Lacey isn't being put to *death*. She'll have a trial same as anyone."

"For what crime?"

"Her powers are dangerous," Crane said, sitting straighter. "Look what her father did!"

"Her father. She's not him." Poole leaned forward, elbows resting on his knees. "Let me ask you: When you became Chancellor fifteen years ago, who was it who put you on to Will? Who told you that a no-name Elonni with a single spell book could bring down the entire Elderon?"

"Cavalier Lately. He was a brilliant Commander. He discovered William and his band of rebels and took care of them."

"Don't you find it odd that he took an old fireside story so literally? Most people believed the Nine were a myth, yet here he comes, telling you it's all true. Why did you believe him?"

"Well, I— It's a good thing I did. We'd be under a monarchy right now if we'd lost the war."

"But what convinced you?"

"He seemed confidant. I trusted him. What of it?"

"Sannus Eyreh were the ones who destroyed the Ruined Queen. They're the ones who founded the Elderon five hundred years ago. They're the only ones who'd have known that Will's power was even possible."

Crane rubbed his forehead, his arthritic fingers trembling. "I've heard enough. You have no evidence. This is all speculation."

Isobel stepped forward, her eye a hard glass shard. "You remember what I told you back at the palace. What Ryder did to me."

"Yes. And he'll be reprimanded accordingly." He looked away from her. "I'm sorry for the trouble he gave you, but it doesn't mean he belongs to some cult."

Poole rose and went to his desk. He stooped to drag out the briefcase he'd kicked under it.

"They have a book," he said, unbuckling the case and lifting out the *Malus Vylarus*. He held it carefully, the old pages feeling like little more than dust between his fingers. "This is the book they use as scripture. As if the Amerand weren't bad enough."

Crane took the offered text hesitantly. He turned back the cover with a hooked finger. "I'm afraid I can't read Annanym."

"That first page is their creed. 'Might, sight, and wisdom. With these devices, we shall halt the very motion of the sun.'" Poole turned to the next page for the Chancellor. "And a line of ascension. The purest families are at the top. Stone. Fairborn."

"I see." Crane shook his head. "But you see, there's a problem right there. So many of these family lines have ended. The Stones, the Fairborns, the Fryers..."

"The Fairborns?" Isobel titled her head. "You think Mortimer Fairborn is dead?"

"He is," Crane said.

"Chancellor—I just saw him tonight. He's the one who stopped Ryder, who got me out of Haylock. And that right there should tell you something. When have you known a Huntsman to go against his Commander? Mortimer can defy Ryder because in Sannus Eyreh—the thing that really matters to them—Mortimer outranks Ryder."

"You saw him? You're sure?"

"I think I'd remember him," Isobel said. She pointed to her mask. "He's the one who ruined my face."

Poole looked sadly at the woman, familiar words echoing in his mind. She met his gaze and smirked.

"One eye to see truth," she recited, "the other to blot out darkness. He did the same thing to his own son."

"His *son?*" Crane said.

"You wouldn't know about him. Mortimer detracted and had a child with a witch. But he rejoined Sannus Eyreh. He still hunts, but I suppose that's work he's doing for the cult, if you thought he was dead all this time."

"I didn't know. Truly." He handed the book back to Poole in a hurried movement. "But that doesn't mean you're right about my Elders."

"Hi. Albion?" Aeyrin rose from the couch now and stood before the Chancellor, steeling herself with a breath. "My name's Aeyrin Falk. Will's wife."

Crane looked coolly at Poole, then back to Aeyrin. "Forgive me, ma'am. I was under the impression you were dead."

"Sorry about that, but it seemed you were rather eager to have me arrested all those years ago."

He winced. "Yes, well. I suppose it wasn't fair to assume you had anything to do with your husband's deviancy."

She somehow managed a polite smile. "Anyway. Albion. My daughter and I have spent our entire lives hidden away. We've spent the last fifteen years in peace. And yet at the merest whisper of rebel activity, your Watchmen went after her. I condemn what my husband did. But Lacey isn't like Will. And if your forces hadn't gone after her, she wouldn't be with the very people who want to turn her into a weapon. We just want our lives back." She looked at Poole. "But if Sol is right, then there won't be mercy for her. They'll kill her just because of her bloodline. So, I just want to ask you one thing, as a mother. Can you promise my daughter a fair trial, based on her actions, not on what she is?"

Crane stared ahead for a moment. "No. It's already decided. She'll be given a binding potion—a strong one. It...it makes people mad. Destroys their bodies. But you have to understand—"

"I don't have to understand anything," Aeyrin said. "You need to do the right thing."

"I'm... I'm only trying to keep the realm safe."

"You're only protecting Sannus Eyreh," Aeyrin said.

"I—I can't believe this. If any of what you say is true, then..."

"Then you've been deceived," Poole said. "This runs deeper than you know. Sannus Eyreh have always been bent on domination, on taking back the throne, and then on controlling the Elderon. They've whispered into the ears of kings for centuries. You're not the first they've tricked."

"I'll think on this," Crane said at last. He rose and started toward the door, his frail body shaking with his steps. Poole followed him to the foyer, unsure if anything would truly change—but they'd tried. That was all there was to do now.

Crane placed his hand on the doorknob and seemed about to go, but he turned back to Poole. "Absolom I—I am sorry, you know. For what I did to her."

Poole looked away from him. "Just make right what you can. You might consider lifting the ban on Elonni-human marriage, too, y'know."

Crane gave him a wobbly smile. "I take it you have someone in mind?"

"'Night, Albion."

The Chancellor nodded. "Goodbye."

LATER THAT NIGHT, Crane set his tea aside and sighed. An unexpected ice storm had taken the capital, and frozen rain sleeted against the window, stuck to it, and to the pavements below. He was cold. And—why?—he was afraid.

This was a night for dark things. His fingers drummed on the arm of his chair. This was a night he hoped to pass in peace.

Sleep. After all that he'd heard tonight, rest is what he needed.

"Elise, be a dear, bring me a draught of sleeping potion."

His handmaid moved from her stationary place by the wall, soundless but for the whisper of her skirts. She returned moments later with a stoppered vial.

He might have worried she'd poisoned it, but there was nothing in her soft brown eyes to suggest animosity. She simply regarded him as though he were nothing; he expected she thought him unworthy to kill—the Chancellor, unworthy of death. Is that how lost his influence was? Even servants and townspeople thought him a mere figure, incapable.

But if Poole was correct...then wasn't he?

"Thank you," he said, and took the vial. He poured a small amount into his tea and drank. He left the vial sitting on the end table, beneath the lamp, casting a glassy blue shadow.

He was soon asleep, but only just. His consciousness flickered: One moment he knew he was only a man reclined in a chair; the next he was bound in chains, gutted, while masks hovered above him, faceless and bloody; the next he thought he flew across the sky and touched the hand of Elrosh himself.

A crash at the door startled him from his thin veil of unconsciousness. Elise, by the window, jolted to attention like a deer face-to-face with a hunter. She ducked behind a writing desk and met Crane's eyes across the room, questioning.

The door opened. Crane tensed when a familiar, bulky figure slipped into the dark. Surely this was a dream. Surely...

"Chancellor," Ryder Lately said.

"Get out," Crane said. "I'm too tired for company."

Two blunt figures appeared behind him, and Crane frowned. Mathias Bromley, he had suspected might come—but Gordon Priestley...he'd truly thought they were friends.

"You too?" His voice shook.

Mathias and Gordon looked at each other and regarded him without apology.

"The realm is desperate, Albion," Gordon wheezed. "The time has come for a return to the old ways. You are very good at keeping things the same...but we don't need stagnation; we need a renewal."

"I've never—I've done all I could."

"I know, my old friend. God will forgive your inadequacy. Not all are equipped to carry his kingdom."

Ryder's smile flashed white in the darkness. "What did you and Poole talk about?"

Crane went cold with anger. "He was right, wasn't he? You all think you're sons of God? That you can just kill and control anyone you please?"

"People need to be guided to the truth," Ryder said quietly, closing his fists. "And the truth is, they should worship what we are."

"You're disgusting," Crane said. "Pathetic."

"God has the power to heal all," Gordon said.

"And yet here we are. A broken world." Crane looked to the window, sleet making strange patterns, like faces and spirits, on the glass. "What do you suppose God is waiting for?"

"Faith," Gordon said. "Why should he aid the faithless?"

"Why should the faithless believe in something they'll never see?"

"Albion," Mathias said. "Don't talk that way, not now."

Not so close to death, you mean. Crane wondered what nothingness would feel like—nothing, of course. He would be nothing.

"Go on, then."

Ryder stood in front of him, drew a knife, and pointed it at the end table. "Drink it."

Crane looked at the vial.

"Ah. A suicide. Good story."

"It's that or my blade on your throat. And I won't make it easy."

"Then I shall." Crane took the vial and drank down the whole thing.

"God be with you," Gordon said.

Crane managed a last, wry look at the pontiff. His eyes flashed back to Ryder as the Commander grabbed Elise by the wrist and dragged her from her hiding spot behind the writing table. She screamed, trying pitifully to tear herself away from the Commander.

"Actually, you know what makes a better story?" Ryder said.

He aimed his pistol at the girl's temple and fired. She dropped. Blood ran from the bullet hole in her head, pooling across the marble floors. It crawled closer and dampened Crane's slippers.

"Murder-suicide," Ryder said. "Discontented servant poisons her master then blows her own head off? The press would eat the story up. Too bad Law isn't around to write it."

"No," Crane said weakly. He curled his toes as Elise's blood soaked closer, coating his skin.

"Let's go," Ryder said.

Crane heard footsteps, a door shutting. He heard Elise scream in his memory, the gunfire. His last conscious moments, a nightmare. At some point he fell asleep. And then...

ALARMS SANG THROUGH the city, and Poole awoke instantly, Aeyrin curled against his side. He threw off the bedcovers and slipped away from her.

"Sol?"

He threw back the curtains, expecting to see fire, riots in the street, crumbling buildings.

But no—there was no fire on the air, no dust and debris, no screams. And the alarm, what he'd mistaken for an alarm in his daze, was a brass band, just now passing beneath his window, dressed all in black and scraping out a rusty rendition of the realm's anthem. It was barely early morning, and the sky was a twilit blue. Still, even in the dim lantern-light of the street, it was impossible to miss the portrait the band leader held in place of the realm's flag: Albion Crane's face stared out over the street, austere in black-and-white.

They'd woken the city to tell them the news, the news that couldn't wait.

Chancellor Albion Crane was dead.

36

GAMAULT CASTLE

-*Theopolis*-

THIN BEAMS OF morning light broke apart the twilight, culled from the horizon and scattered across the clouds. It was a beautiful day. How strange that the world should wake happily after such a night.

Poole paced his study, his mind dragged from one thought to the next. Law had gone away—willingly, Poole hoped. Crane was dead. Sannus Eyreh were moving faster than he'd predicted. They were ready this time.

Which would mean, of course, that their Patriarch was back.

"Sol?" Aeyrin stepped into his study, her hand hovering by the door as though she had meant to knock. He blinked and managed a smile for her, hoping he looked reassuring, knowing he'd failed.

"This is bad, isn't it?" She sank down into his desk chair, head in her hands. He tipped her chin up and bent to kiss her.

"Yes," he said. "It's horrible."

"At least you're being honest."

Isobel strolled into the study then, covering a yawn, her yellow hair tangled from sleep. "Did anybody else hear a parade going through the streets, or have I lost my mind?"

Poole ran a hand down his face. "Yes. It was Crane's memorial march."

The sleepiness left her eyes with a blink. "Crane is dead?" Poole nodded.

"We need to go," she said. "Leave the city."

"I can't," Poole said. "Delilah St. Luke put a curse on me. Part of my house arrest. If I step foot outside for too long, I'll die." He looked down at Aeyrin. "But she's right. About leaving the city. You two should go."

"No," Aeyrin said slowly, "we shouldn't. Not without you."

"We can't help him if they kill us too," Isobel said. Aeyrin looked at the younger woman, venom in her eyes. Isobel only shrugged. "I'm right, aren't I? With your connection to William, and now to Poole, they'll absolutely want you dead. Or, worse, they'll use you against him."

"She's right," Poole said. "And it would work, too." He looked at Aeyrin. "You understand, right? If they had you...if they threatened you in any way...I'd be useless. I'd do anything to get you back."

Aeyrin looked away, her lips twisted. Isobel seemed to take this as concession.

"Pack only what you need. I'll be ready in five minutes." She left the room, her blond hair whipping behind her.

Aeyrin sighed, dragging her hand through her hair. "We don't know that they'll come for you."

"Love, I—I'm sorry."

She glanced up. "Why are you apologizing now?"

"Because...you've been through enough. And I keep dragging you back into this world."

"Sol, *they're* doing this. They killed Will. They threatened Lacey. You're doing your best. And yes, you've made mistakes, but... I don't blame you."

"Maybe you should."

"Oh, stop brooding." She smiled and rose, pulling him down into a kiss. "You'll be all right, won't you?"

"Of course." He smiled. "They might not even bother with me."

They both knew it was a lie, a paltry assurance. But he couldn't help saying it, just to see her faint smile one more time.

"All right," Isobel said from the doorway, a rucksack over one shoulder. "Ready?"

Aeyrin nodded. "I don't need to take anything."

"My fulcan is on the roof." The Huntress looked now at Poole. "Good luck, then."

"Take care of her." Poole turned back to Aeyrin and kissed her forehead. "Be careful."

"*You* be careful." She kissed him, for what he hoped wasn't the last time, yet he found himself memorizing her, the feel of her lips and the brush of her hand down his cheek, as though he'd need it later, when the worst happened.

She turned toward the door. Poole took a breath.

"Wait. Aeyrin?"

She looked back.

Part of him wanted to save it, to say it when he saw her again, as though it could guarantee they'd meet after all this had passed. But he wasn't one for fate or promises of control. He knew he might never get the chance. "I love you."

She knew what his saying it now meant, too. Tears clouded her eyes, but she smiled them away. "Love you, too."

Isobel rolled her eyes. "Obviously we'll rescue you if anything happens."

Poole laughed. "Right. Thanks."

"Come on." Isobel nodded toward the door, and Aeyrin followed, glancing back only once. Was she trying to memorize him, too? He watched her until she was gone, and stared at the place she had been until the front door closed softly on their departure.

It was only a few minutes later that the door opened again, violently, with a bang and the rustle of hurried feet.

They'd come.

ISOBEL DRAGGED AEYRIN into the space between Poole's row house and the next, the narrow alley tidy and bare but for a neat line of rubbish bins. The two women crouched beside the bins, listening.

They'd barely left the stoop when Isobel heard the ordered march of feet and knew the Watchmen had come. She tuned her ears now to the murmured voices, one distinct among them—the arrogant, sneering commands of Ryder Lately telling his men to halt.

A hard, wooden banging followed. "Open up in the name of the realm."

Isobel bit down on her cheek. She hated that voice. Everything about him repulsed her, more so when the Commander was trying to impress with his clout. As bad as Mortimer was—and he was, by all accounts, the worst thing

313

about her past, the lowest, darkest memory she possessed—she'd enjoyed watching the stronger Elonni toss Ryder around like a limp doll. Her old Hunting partner had been a monster, but Ryder was once her fiancé. That seemed worse, somehow.

Poole's voice drifted from the stoop, bored. "I expected you much earlier."

"Absolom Poole," Ryder said, and Isobel could see his face, the sneer on his ugly, blunt features. "You're under arrest for high treason and murder."

Aeyrin looked up at that and began to rise. Isobel grabbed her by the wrist and pulled her back down.

"You can't help him," she said, her voice below a whisper.

"What do they mean, murder?"

"They'll say anything," Isobel said, though she did find it odd. High treason itself carried a death sentence. Tacking a murder charge on—it seemed pointed. There was a reason. But she wasn't about to go poking around for it.

"We need to go."

Aeyrin shook her head. "I want to hear it."

Isobel raised an eyebrow, but didn't ask for an explanation. She didn't need one. When you loved somebody, you did insane things. You put yourself through hell. She knew even now that Jade must be going mad, staring into one of her crystal balls, trying to pull any shred of Isobel's location from the rocks. What had Nathy told her? That she was dead?

I'll be home soon.

"I haven't murdered anyone," Poole was saying. Isobel forced herself to focus. If one thing went wrong, if Aeyrin made a single noise that attracted the Watchmen, she needed to be ready.

"You have," Ryder replied. There was the sound of metal, chains across the smooth steps of the stoop. "The evidence is in your own home. Isn't it?"

"You can't mean—"

"The cericide? That's exactly what I mean. Search the house, gents."

Boots scraped across pavement and clomped up the steps. Isobel heard Ryder's faint laughter beneath the sound.

"I take it you've hidden your whore somewhere else?"

"Shut up," Poole said, his voice low and dark with a threat.

"I'll find her, you know. Don't look so alarmed, Poole. I wouldn't kill her. I find beautiful women are more useful while they're alive."

The sound of bone snapping followed close behind the Commander's words. Isobel covered her mouth, burying a pleased laugh that threatened to erupt.

Aeyrin sighed. "He punched him, didn't he?"

Isobel risked a glance outside the alley. Ryder stood at the bottom of the steps, clutching at his nose, blood welling between his fingers. Poole shook out his wrist even as three Watchmen descended on him, dragging his arms together and chaining him.

"He's a southpaw," she observed, leaning back into the alley.

Aeyrin held her forehead in her hand. "He's always got to make it worse, hasn't he?"

"I think it's sweet."

They waited until the marching feet receded, until the alley had been quiet for a long while. Isobel rose first and brought her fingers to her lips, whistling for her fulcan. The bird appeared over the roof of Poole's house, lowering itself gently to the road.

"We've got to save him," Aeyrin said. "You've been to Haylock. Can you break in?"

"They won't take him to Haylock," Isobel said, reassuring the fulcan with a few sift strokes above the eye. "He's Elonni, and he's been accused of high treason."

"Then where are they taking him?"

Isobel cast her eyes to the East. She couldn't see over the roofs, but its presence was always there, a bloody shard of history staring down at the city.

"Gamault Castle. They'll want to execute him on Redlawn."

POOLE'S HANDS LEFT prints in the damp, dirty floor as he pushed himself up and turned to his jailer.

"Gamault Castle?"

Ryder smirked. "I reckon it's overkill. Old man like you... But Haylock's been busy with all the nocturnes not following curfew. And to be honest, I prefer to keep a close, personal eye on you."

"I can see that." Poole stared at the Commander's broken nose, the bruise spreading along his right eye. He partly regretted the action—it can't have helped his case. Ryder had certainly taken his time summoning an Allied mage to lift the curse Delilah had put on Poole, leaving him in twisting agony for hours.

But the memory of Ryder's bone cracking under his knuckles was just too satisfying. And the prick had deserved it.

"So. What happens now?"

"You wait here," Ryder said. "While I hunt down your whore and her little monster."

"I thought you'd learned your lesson," Poole said.

"Maybe it's time you learned yours." Ryder left the tower cell he'd dropped Poole into and slammed the heavy door behind him. A single barred window let Poole see out. Ryder stared out at him, a smile on his flat lips. "You're too obvious, Poole. If you'd just kept your feelings to yourself, we might never have bothered with her. Now? I'm going to enjoy breaking every one of her tiny, fragile bones. After my men are done with her, of course."

Poole rushed the door like he might pass right through it, crushing the handle beneath his fingers. Ryder took a small step back.

"Temper," Ryder said.

"You're one to talk." Poole pulled his hand away. The doorknob was warped where his fingers had gripped it.

"Don't worry so much, old man. You'll be long dead before we take care of her anyway."

The lanterns lighting the dim, musty corridor behind the Commander flickered out. Their glass shattered. The Commander swore.

"Hey, Vesper, get back here," he called down the corridor. He flicked a lighter, and the miniature flame barely lit one half of his face. He smirked, triumph in a single pale blue eye.

"It's a shame you had to be so sentimental about the whole thing. You get it, right? If you'd just let her go and left her alone, we never would have found her."

Poole breathed slowly through his nose. A shadow emerged from the darkness, a Watchman with a wary look in his eye.

"What happened to the lights?"

"How should I know?" Ryder said. "Watch him, will you? Make sure he's comfortable." With a final smirk, Ryder walked off, his footsteps muffled in the muck.

"Sorry about that," Poole said, and the lanterns reformed, glass clicking back together, their fires bursting back to life. The Watchman looked from the renewed glow to Poole, smiling in his tower cell.

"So." Poole looked around the empty tower room. "Care for a game of cards?"

The Watchman backed away and posted himself against the wall, eyes flickering occasionally to the reformed lanterns. Poole sighed and wandered to the center of the tower.

The castle. It was reserved for Elonni who'd committed unforgivable crimes: assassinations, treason, heresy. He'd done nothing to deserve this high, frigid cell. He wasn't even a proper heretic. He hadn't deviated from the realm's religion; he'd abandoned it.

But they would *say* he'd committed treason, *say* he was a heretic. They'd called him a murderer, and maybe they weren't wrong. He'd killed someone, but it hadn't felt like murder then. It had seemed a mercy.

He hadn't been ready to believe what the package had meant, the bottle of cericide and the syringe. But this extra charge, this accusation of murder. It was for him only. It didn't affect his sentence—he'd die either way—but it let him know that Sannus Eyreh had a Patriarch, and Patriarch knew.

Only the guilty run from God.

At last, he couldn't run anymore. He regarded the metallic door, the bars on the window. Iyrel. It couldn't hurt him. That didn't mean there weren't things in here that could.

The castle had been the seat of the monarchy for thousands of years. The iyrel was only its defense against the nocturne kinds. Rumors spoke of ways in which the Ruined Queen had fortified the place against the Elonni she sought to overthrow. Secret veins of demon-bone interlaced with the old stone. Ritual traps set by her warlock advisor to hold an

317

Elonni paralyzed in place. He wondered if this tower was one of her old traps for his kind. The irony would at least be amusing—he was trying to help her descendant, after all.

"Letter for you."

He turned back to the door. The Watchman on the other side of the bars was a different man than his original guard, and he wore a thin, smug smile as he held a small parchment square out to Poole through the bars. Poole took it, unfolded it. The note was only one sentence, and it cooled his blood.

And ye shall reap what ye have sown.

37

THE BOY WITH A BROKEN WING

-Fryer's Grove-

DAWN CAME AS a surprise. Nathy looked up from the pages of the *Malus Vylarus* Alastair had transcribed the night before, squinting against the daylight caught behind the curtains. He hadn't felt the time passing. The only thing that distinguished a single hour of the night was Lacey showing up at his door.

He dragged his hands down his face, his calloused palms catching against his unshaved jaw. He needed to stop, catch a few hours' sleep.

But there was a girl in his bed. And she wasn't someone he could cuddle up next to.

Lacey made a soft sleep sound, and Nathy turned. Her eyes squinted against some dream. She'd left room for him on the bed, and those bare inches of blanket had laughed at him all night while he stooped over the *Malus*, doing something with his brain other than thinking about sharing a bed with a soft-skinned girl with hair he could tangle his fingers in and—

"Fuck." He slapped himself hard.

Lacey shifted in the bed, waking. "Nathy?"

"Hey," he said.

"Did you sleep?"

"Nah."

He picked up the last page the monk had finished. Alastair's handwriting was neat, educated, while Nathy's notes were sharp scrawls in the margins. He hardly remembered writing anything. He really did need to sleep...

But he only gathered the pages together and tried to shuffle them back into order. Alastair had marked the pages numerically, and still Nathy had managed to miss a few. He paused at a page without any notes and began to read.

"So," Lacey said, before he could finish a single sentence. "Um. About why I came over last night."

His heartrate picked up when he remembered her wide eyes, her bitten lips, her messy hair. He really was a horrible person.

"I found a note last night," she said. "It looks like it was written by Latrice. I—think she wanted me to find it."

It took his mind too long to catch up. "Oh. Huh."

"What?"

"Nothing. Ah...what'd it say?" He tried to refocus on the page in his hands.

"Something about a teacher," she said. "And...are you all right?"

Was he? He read the first paragraph of Alastair's translation, missed its meaning, read it again, knowing he needed to take it in even as something in him blocked its absorption. He blinked a few times and forced himself to focus.

Let the Son who betrays his Blood be Marked, but do not spill of his Blood, for it is the Blood of Elrosh. Rather banish him, and cut his wings, and let the Mark upon him be punishment all his days.

"Nathy? Hey." Lacey's hand came to rest over his, and when he didn't respond, moved toward the page and took it gently from his loose fingers. She read through the passage, seemed to understand. Her eyes met his across the short space.

"It can't be," he said. He took the *Malus* page back from her, scanning it idly, but his mind was elsewhere—spinning, begging a connection to be made.

A night fifteen years past. Ruark...and Mortimer. They'd taken the sword, and Mortimer had placed it in the corner of Nathy's eye.

The cut—the absence of pain as it was being done, and the fire the blade left in its wake as the blood poured out and his senses caught up.

"Nathy?"

The words. Their softness, a reverence for damnation. *One eye to see the truth, the other to blot out darkness.*

And when his eye was done, ruined, the sword came down on his wing. *You don't deserve to fly.*

Let this mark be upon you.

"Nathy? Are you all right?"

The basement—the house in Denmoor. *Join me.* A pain above his heart. Nathy clutched at the ruined skin of his chest—one eye to see...the other...

You're an abomination.

The knives. The whips. *Let's see what will make you bleed.* The words muttered over a little boy's body—a little boy Nathy barely recognized, because he refused to remember how weak he'd once been.

This is your blood, sacred yet tainted. We'll cleanse it of the witch's stain.

Nathy scrambled to his feet. He heard Lacey speaking, but her voice was only a murmur, wordless, and he was numb.

A copy of the *Malus Vylarus* on the kitchen table. *Let's not tell your mother, shall we?*

What is that?

It's the book of your forefathers. You were destined for great things. But you were also destined for great evil. I can save you. Let me save you.

"Nathy!" Lacey's hand on his stirred him; he looked at her.

"I think I underestimated my old man," he said.

"W-what?"

"He had this book. He read it to me. He used to... Everything he did to me... He was trying to fix me." He collapsed against the wall and rested his forehead on his knees; he wouldn't let her see him fight back tears. It had been fifteen years, but now, with these violent words, the old wound had been ripped open, fresher, and bleeding harder. "He was trying to get me ready. To be a part of this. And when I took my mom's side... Fuck!" The word ripped through clenched teeth. He felt Lacey tense beside him, but then, surprising him, she moved closer.

"D'you...want me to leave?" she said softly.

"No. Stay." He peeked up at her. "Please?"

"'Course. I'm not going anywhere."

Nathy nodded, needing her and not knowing why. "I remember everything."

"What do you mean?"

"When I first came here, Flynn...he wanted to know everything about my dad. What he did, what he was like. I said I couldn't remember. I said there was nothing to tell. Because I didn't want to think about it anymore. What it meant.

"But I know why. He was trying to get the magic out of me. Trying to purify my blood."

Lacey bit down on her lower lip. "That's... reprehensible."

Nathy snorted. "Good word." He looked down at the floor. "All this time, y'know, I just thought he wanted me dead. But even this..." He touched the scar on his face. "And my wing... Was his way of fixing me."

"There's nothing to fix."

"There might be now. I'm just like him."

She gave him a stern look. "How?"

He pushed himself to his feet. "Did you forget who I was? I'm the one who kidnapped you and dragged you thousands of miles from home just for a paycheck, remember?"

"You also stayed and helped me."

He rolled his eyes and turned away, but she wrapped her arms around his waist and held him there. Her grip was surprisingly strong, her presence at his back warm and painfully right. "I know what you're trying to do," she said. "But this broody, emotionally repressed nonsense doesn't fool me."

"Let me go."

She did. Maybe it was something in his voice. Maybe she just didn't want to push him. But he couldn't think about anything to do with her too long. She was beginning to be...complicated.

"You need to understand something," he said. "I'm just like him. He made me. All this?"—he pointed to the scars— "This was... I was his project. He wanted me to be a killer. He got one."

"Nathy." She took his hand. "Listen. You're not thinking clearly. Maybe you don't make the best choices. But you're not like him."

"I'm a murderer."

"Murderers don't fall in love with lost girls," she said "They don't save them, either."

322

She actually stomped her foot. "Stop *torturing* yourself over her. She wouldn't want that."

He gave her a bare smile. "I always knew she'd be gone one day, y'know. So it's on me. For keeping her around when I knew it would only destroy her."

"How could you know that?"

"Because." He tilted her chin up and held her gaze to his. Her eyes were the green of a tentative spring, grass just freed of winter's ice. "I don't win in the end."

"Wh—what?"

"I'm the thing heroes like you are supposed to slay."

"Sannus Eyreh think I'm the monster."

"You." He actually smiled now. It was so ridiculous, this big-eyed girl with her too-serious glare. He couldn't picture it. Even with the strongest powers known to any nation in the world...she was just so fucking *good*.

"You're wasting your time," he said, but his hand moved to cup her cheek. He shouldn't even think of this. He shouldn't let himself notice her eyelashes, or her chapped lips parting in surprise. He shouldn't think of how she could disappear in his arms.

He took one step closer, and that's all he needed to be flush with her, her small figure shadowed against his. She stayed perfectly still, eyes wide. He leaned in. She tipped her face towards his...interesting, that.

But his lips skimmed her jaw and pressed against her ear. "You're sweet, kid. Watch it doesn't get you killed."

He felt her heartbeat at her throat. It was all he could do not to kiss her there, drag the kiss to her open lips. Something had come over him, some certifiable insanity, because he wanted this strange girl. He wanted to press her into his bed right now. He'd had lovers since Artemis, but he'd never made it a point to remember their names, much less stay long enough to feel...*this*, whatever the fuck this was.

"Nathy." He didn't know what was in her voice—fear? Want? Either one meant he needed to stop.

He took her by the shoulders and gently pushed her back. "You should go."

She blinked. Her cheeks and neck were flushed. "But—"

"I know what you're trying to do. And it's pointless."

323

"But, I— Nathy—"

"Just go. I need to be alone."

She backed away, and Nathy felt colder, emptier. He almost asked her to stay, so fierce was the reality of her absence. What was happening to him?

She stopped at the threshold. "I'll be in the library, all right? Come find me when you feel up to it."

At once he wanted to tell her to give up, and not to go. So he said nothing, and she let the door fall shut behind her.

LACEY TOOK THE lift to the second floor, ignoring Jack's muttering about her tithe of a few strands of her own hair. She walked toward the library, numb but for her heart, which hurt in a way she couldn't explain. Nathy's sorrow had shaken her. His near-kiss had stunned her. How badly she'd wanted it—well, she didn't want to unpack that right now.

It didn't make sense. This wasn't the Nathy she'd come to expect. Maybe Jade had turned something loose in his soul after all.

Or *she* had. Why had she asked him to bring up Artemis? Had it only brought up worse, darker memories?

"Lacey."

She turned at the sound of Alice's voice. "Oh, hi."

The girl stood at the end of the corridor, twisting her hands together. "I need you to come with me. It's important."

"What happened?" Lacey took a step closer to the younger girl. Alice's eyes were wide, wet, flicking now and then over her shoulder. She bit down on her already chapped lips. "Alice. What is it?"

"I found something." Alice nodded back toward the lift. "Come on. I'll show you."

LACEY FOLLOWED BEHIND Alice in the green light of the woods, rain trickling through the branches. She ducked her head against a sudden increase in the rain. They went deeper into the trees' dense covering and walked along the forest path, water squelching beneath the thick of fallen leaves. The air was icy, but not quite freezing, and the rain falling from the branches above hit their skin like knifepoints.

A few miles into the forest, the sound of waves rushing at rock echoed like a growl down a long passage. Lacey jogged ahead and, passing through a cluster of trees, found herself suddenly standing on the brink of the ocean, a hundred feet below. It licked at the steep gray slate of the cliff, hungry and roiling and, farther out, crested into great black waves like the humps of a sea monster. Lacey stared at the horizon, where the twisting gray of the cloudy sky met the impenetrable blackness of sea.

Alice stopped beside her, the wind twisting her hair all around her face. She smiled.

"Amazing, isn't it?"

"It's perfect," Lacey said.

The ocean by Theopolis was calm and blue, a shipping port with lively white schooners and raucous fishermen ambling along the docks. This ocean looked vicious and hungry, like it would suck you under if you even dipped a toe in its icy depths. But nobody could get into the water, not unless they jumped, in which case they were more in danger of being impaled by the jagged rocks sprouting from the shallows. There was the merest fingernail of sandy coast and no harbor, only this force of nature, unfit for life. This place would rip something as weak as flesh apart. She felt like she was on the shore of the universe, staring into the heart of a galaxy.

"It's beautiful," Lacey said, stilled by the snarling waves below.

"My wife thought so, too."

Lacey spun. "Your..."

Alice's smile was bent, cruel. And not hers.

"Donoveir." Lacey backed away, only to feel the absence of ground behind her like a force. She halted on the edge of the cliff, tensing her muscles.

Alice stepped closer, slowly, her eyes fixed on Lacey. "I brought her here our first day as a married couple. She loved the ocean. I could see it in her eyes, though. The way she looked at the waves like they might carry her away. She didn't love me. But, then again, I didn't need her love. I had her. A perfect young bride to carry on my name. My first wife had failed to give me children. But Latrice—two sons, and so quickly."

Alice shook her head, looking down the sheer side of the cliff, and the rocks below. "What a terrible waste."

"You tried to kill them," Lacey said.

"Because they were tainted with her blood. I always knew the Ruined Queen's spawn were out there somewhere. But to realize it was my own wife? Such a cruel irony. And yet, I like to believe God chose me to destroy her."

"You failed," Lacey said. "My father survived."

"I will not fail again. Believe me." Alice laughed. "Don't look so frightened. Death isn't such a terrible thing."

Lacey forced a smile, burying her fear as far down as it would go. "You're going to push me off the cliffs, too? You do know I can fly."

"I'm well aware." Alice took a deep breath through her nose. "At last, I can do this final thing for my Patriarch."

"Who's that? Your leader?" Lacey shook her head. "No matter what you do, he would hate you. He'd be disgusted. Not only were you married to Latrice—you fathered her children. Your precious Old Name is mine, too. Your legacy is ruined."

"You're not *mine*," Alice snarled, closing in closer. Lacey flinched, unable to step back even as her body screamed at her to escape. "My wife was not only a monster, but a whore. My name died with me. And hers will die with you."

Alice's eyes fluttered and her body fell back as a cold gust flew from her chest and collided with Lacey. Lacey's feet slipped, gravel spitting up from the cliff. She called for her wings, and they materialized in weak flickers of light. But before she could beat against the air, everything went dark.

SHE HIT THE water and her breath left her, sucked away by the cold. The beating waves resisted her kicks and flails and pulled her down. A rough jerk of the water tossed her to the surface, and she coughed up a mouthful of water.

She tried to swim, though she hardly could. They didn't have access to the ocean in Hollows Edge. She fought clumsily in the water, her wings weighing her down. She tried to call them in, but her energy was sapped. She grasped a rock, held tight—and another wave ripped her away and pulled her down.

A breathless ache put all other thoughts and fears aside; she needed air. She struggled toward the surface but—where was it? The water was rough, murky, tossing her about. Every direction looked the same, black and warped.

She was trapped in the ocean's bowels, and she would die. She'd escaped Theopolis only to sink to the bottom of the sea. Breathlessness tore at her lungs like a wound. She gasped against the pain, and salt water rushed her lungs like a punch.

Her hand reached up. Her fingers broke the glassy surface, but she was falling away from it. Her eyes fought to stay open as she tried to choke up the water in her lungs, as she drifted farther from the world, farther from life.

A hand reached down and closed over hers, but she knew it wasn't real. It was a dream, a final hope, conjured by a dying brain in a body sinking down, down...

SHE HACKED WATER, her chest in agony. Her eyes blinked opened. She felt sand, rough and cold against her skin, sticking to her. Her gaze was turned toward the black horizon line, toward the raging sea. Her eyes shut.

"Lacey?"

She'd never heard such urgency in his voice, and it filled her with the warmth the ocean had stolen from her body. She turned her head toward him and peeled her eyes open; they filled with the hidden sunlight and his eyes, darker than the sea.

"Lacey." Nathy's voice was tight. Pained. He helped her into a sitting position and leaned her into him. "I thought I'd lost you."

"Hm. Sorry. I can't swim."

"I noticed." His voice caught. "Don't scare me like that again."

"Right." Her voice sounded like gravel. "My fault."

"I didn't mean—"

She elbowed his side. "I'm just teasing. How'd you know to look for me?"

"I tried to find you in the library. Poe said he saw you and Alice heading into the forest. I—I just had a feeling something was wrong."

Lacey twisted to face him. "Wait. How did you get down here?"

"I jumped," he said, as though it were obvious.

"Oh, my God. Nathy, it's a hundred feet at least! Are you okay?"

He shrugged. "I thought I'd broken my leg, but I swam out to you all right, so..."

She got to her knees, turned his face to hers, and kissed him. He tasted like salt and sweat, his mouth surprisingly gentle on hers as he parted her lips and deepened their kiss. He wound his hand in her hair as his lips moved against hers. She was icy and damp from the ocean, but his arms around her were warm. She tangled her fingers in his hair and his hands moved to grip her waist. His tongue ran along her lower lip, and his fingers teased the buttons of her shirt. She pressed herself against him, hollow and hoping this madness would fill her. The sound of waves harmonized with the blood crashing through her skull. But then he tensed against her. His hands went still on her body and he pulled away.

"Let's not do this," he said, his chest heaving.

She blinked a few times, coming back to herself. "I-I'm sorry. I don't know why I—"

"Forget it. Never happened."

She looked into the darkness of his eyes; they matched the sea beside them, roiling and bottomless.

"Oh. Okay." She started to rise, but he caught her hand and brought her back.

"Lacey. It's not like that. I could be crazy for you," he said, almost to himself. "If I let myself."

She almost smiled. "Why don't you?"

He held her face in one hand and ran his thumb along her cheekbone, smiling. "Remember? I don't win in the end."

She tried to diminish that impossible space between them, but he stopped her, his fingers trailing across her lips before they could meet his. "Do me a favor?"

She nodded.

He grinned. "Don't tell Saxon."

38

BORROWED FLESH AND BONE

-*Fryer's Grove*-

L ACEY MANAGED TO fly both of them back up the cliff. They collapsed at the top, Lacey shaky from the effort. Nathy scrambled up and cast his eyes around the area.

"Shit."

"What's wrong?" Lacey looked up.

"Alice. I left her right here. She was passed out."

"Do you think she's still possessed?"

"Probably. Donoveir has latched himself on. We'll need to exorcise her."

Lacey got to her feet. "How do we do that?"

"Ideally, we'd have Jade do it. But we might not have time to wait. Poe can probably manage."

"Go get him. I'll look for her."

"Kid—no. I'm not leaving you in a forest with the angry spirit that just tried to kill you. You get Poe. I'll find Alice. I promise."

She tugged on a damp strand of hair. "*Okay* just—don't get killed."

"It's cute when you worry."

"Don't ruin it."

He smirked. "Stay on the path."

She nodded, and then she ran, following the beaten track through the forest until the groves materialized, and the great black house beyond them. She ran in through the side door, stumbling through the mudroom and into the corridor beyond.

"Poe!" She cast about, unsure where to begin. She ran at last to the lift.

"Jack. Have you dropped Poe off recently?"

The brownie sniffed. "Hello to you, too."

"Hello, Jack. Please, it's important, Alice is—"

"What? What have you done to Mistress Alice?"

"Nothing! But she's in danger and only Poe can help her."

"Second floor. Get in." The lift rattled up as soon as she stepped inside. "No charge this time, but in the future, I want better tithes. What use have I got for your hair?"

"Agreed," Lacey said, and rushed from the lift the moment it stopped.

She found Poe and Alastair in the library, side by side on one of the big couches, reading from the same book. Alastair reached to turn a page, but Poe pushed his hand away, then held it.

"I'm not done yet."

Alastair smiled, his cheeks flushed. "Sorry."

Lacey cleared her throat. "Hi. Sorry. Poe?"

Poe beamed. "Lacey!" But his face fell at her expression. "What's wrong?"

"It's Alice." She took a steadying breath. "We went to the cliffs together, but she was possessed by Donoveir, and he made me fall, but then Nathy saved me, and Alice had fainted, but when we got back up she was gone, and now Nathy's looking for her, but she's still possessed probably and she needs an exorcism, but Jade's not here so we need you to do it if you can."

Poe blinked. Alastair's jaw hung wide.

"*Possessed?*"

"It's because she hasn't learned to control her power," Poe said. "I knew this might happen. Right. Let's go." He rose. Alastair set the book aside and took his hand.

"I'm coming with you, then."

Poe's smile trembled. "Thanks. But... Look, I've never done an exorcism. I don't have the necessary materials, and—"

"I do," Lacey said, remembering the bag of goods Jade had given her. "I'll meet you in the garden." She left the boys in the library and ran for the narrow staircase beside the lift. She hauled herself to the fifth floor, breathless by the time she reached her door. The bag still sat there, limp and showing the tops of jars and bundles of incense.

The loose trousers and tunic Jade had given her rested on top. Lacey took the opportunity to shed her soaked skirt and blouse and change into the dry, freeing outfit. Then, she grabbed the bag and went to the window looking down onto the garden. She pried it open and jumped out, her wings carrying her down.

LACEY WALKED A little ways ahead, weaving between the trees, listening, trying to see through the dim light and the rising fog. But without the house to anchor her to a single place, she began to feel afraid. They were lost in a forest inhabited by the deadly unknown.

The sea roared far away. She stumbled on unseen fallen logs, tangled in thorns and crawling plants. A creature jumped from the dark and stood before her, invisible but for two sharp red eyes. It gave off a low growl and hurried on.

"Nathy!" Poe called, and sent up a light from the end of his wand. They'd been signaling since they'd entered the forest, and yet there was no sign of Nathy or Alice.

"Could he have gone back to the house with her?" Alastair said. "It's been awhile."

Lacey wished Jade were here. Maybe she could track Alice or Nathy. Without her power, they were forced to wander. Lacey didn't know how long the forest went on, if there was ever a break in this dense unknowable place.

"Wait." Poe stepped forward, his eyes searching between the trees. He turned to Lacey. "Do you hear that?"

She shook her head. "What is it?"

"Crying."

"Alice?"

"No." Poe reached out toward the nearest tree, resting his palm against the bark. "It's coming from the other side."

A shudder crawled up Lacey's spine. "Is it Latrice?"

"I don't think so. It's so many voices. Besides, she never leaves the house."

"About that. When Alice was...possessed. Donoveir was talking, going on and on. Like he was still aware, still himself. The times I've seen Latrice, she can only say the same words over and over. And she always looks the way she did when she died."

"Possession gives spirits a means to live again," Poe said. "They borrow our flesh and bone and use it as though it were their own. He could communicate so well because...he was literally draining Alice's life to do it. Necromancers can die from being possessed." He looked off to the side. "Most spirits can't possess anyone. Only the cruelest, darkest souls can invade a living body. Your grandmother's ghost—it's just a bit of her. A shadow of her memory. Her last moment of agony."

"But because Donoveir was such a monster in life..."

"He became a monster in death. But he must have died tragically and suddenly, too. That's what makes a ghost—a violent end."

Lacey looked around. "Who's crying out here, Poe?"

"I...think more people died in this forest than we could ever know."

Alastair took Poe's hands in his. "You don't have to listen."

"It doesn't bother me," Poe said, shaking his head. "Someone ought to hear their stories."

Lacey shook her head. "I almost can't believe it's real. Ghosts. An...afterlife."

"It isn't an afterlife." Poe's eyes were hard. "It's a curse. They're held in their last moments or their worst memory. They're barely conscious of the outside world. Unless something shakes them out of it. Like Latrice. She always used to walk the halls, reliving her death. Until you came. Now, she cries over you. She knows you're hers. And she's sorry for what you'll have to do."

"Can't they ever...move on?"

"We can help them fade. Leave the world. But I don't know where they go. If anywhere." Poe waved a hand. "But I guess, after a life like Latrice's, you realize death isn't the thing to fear."

They stood in a mournful silence. Poe swiped at a few stray tears. Lacey wondered how loud the crying was, how painful to bear. She was about to suggest they turn back when a red flare burst over the trees, in the direction of the cliffs.

"It's Nathy." She ran toward the light, the others following close behind.

ALASTAIR KEPT HOLD of Poe's hand as they rushed through the forest, sightless, senseless, in the humming, roaring night. Everything seemed to fade together, trees and undergrowth and stones. They walked with no real direction until the sound of the sea was strong, close.

They stopped at the jagged drop of the cliff, the black waters and skeletal white rock below like a gaping, hungry mouth. Lacey seemed transfixed, her eyes lowered on the deadly drop. Alastair's stomach twisted at the sight of the murderous sea below, the ripping waves like gnashing teeth.

He looked farther down the jagged rock wall and felt both the elevation of relief and a plunge of fear when he spotted Nathy and Alice ahead. Nathy kneeled beside a long stone slab at the precipice of the cliff. Alice lay before him, still and paler than ever.

"Over here," he said, tugging Poe along. Lacey tore her gaze from the rocks and followed.

Poe rushed forward and placed a hand over his sister's heart. He shut his eyes, breathing slowly through his mouth.

"Donoveir has a powerful grip on her. This won't be easy." He rose and nodded toward the stone. "Lift her up there."

Nathy scooped Alice up like she was a weightless doll and placed her on the long, flat stone. Its markings stood out, weathered but clear. Old Lyvian runes and some sort of goddess in repose, her head titled back to face the sky.

"What is this place?" Lacey said.

"Old sacrificial site," Nathy said. "The Lyvian death cults used to come here to...you get it."

Poe twisted his hands together in a gesture reminiscent of his sister. He turned toward Alastair. "Look, um. You might not...I know you're an Elonni monk. And that you probably don't approve of magic and all that. And this is...dark. So if you don't like me after this, I'll understand."

Only days ago, the idea of witnessing something like this—of being party to it, no less—would have filled Alastair with the deepest dread of damnation. Now, he couldn't manage to care. He only wanted that tortured look to leave

Poe's eyes forever. He smiled softly. "Save your sister. I'll only like you all the more."

Poe nodded and turned back to Alice. "Lacey? If you'd light the sage. Alastair...would you make a salt ring around the stone?"

Alastair reached into the bag and brought out two jars of salt. Lacey snapped her fingers and lit the few bundles of sage. As Alastair made the ring, carefully making a circle around the stone, he watched Alice. She twitched occasionally, moaning, her eyes fluttering open and then squeezing shut.

"Will she be all right?" Alastair asked, closing off the salt circle.

Poe cracked his knuckles, then spread his hands wide. "I hope so. Everyone take some sage. It will protect you. A little."

Alastair took two from Lacey and handed one to Poe. "Be careful."

Poe smiled, then turned back to Alice. "Sister Lilith, lend me your wandering soul, and guide me back whence I go." He looked at Nathy. "When Donoveir comes out, he'll go straight for Lacey. I'll try to banish him, but..."

"Go ahead," Lacey said. "I'll be fine." She took a deep breath. Her wings unfolded.

"One evil spirit against three Old Name Elonni?" Nathy smirked, his own black wings growing from shadow. "Good luck to him, I guess."

Alastair focused his own power into the Elonni prayer—"*Hallas Elroi.*" His mousy wings, so unfamiliar from disuse, felt like dust clouding at his back. But then they became a reassuring weight, a brush of feathers. His celestial power trickled through his veins like a promise.

He could do this.

"Necropola, grant me passage to this soul," Poe said. "Give me claws to tear its bonds to this innocent life."

He began to speak another language, what Alastair thought was Lyvian. Alice twitched on the stone slab, then sat up. Her eyes went wide, her mouth locked in a grimace. Poe's chanting grew louder, the words sharp yet songlike in their intensity.

Alice screamed in a voice not her own, but a man's deep snarl. "Get away from me, filthy warlock."

Poe placed his hand over Alice's heart. "Necropola, free this girl, your servant in death."

Alice bucked on the slab and flung her arm, catching a fistful of Poe's hair. In his shock, Poe dropped his sage, steadying himself with the hand locked over Alice's heart. "I see what she knows, warlock. The things you've done."

Poe tried to pull away, but Alice's grip was strong, intensified by the spirit within her. "You went along with everything they did. *Morturi Nox.* You bled innocents on rocks and dashed their brains. Until one day, you turned the knife on your own father."

"Necropola! Free this girl, your servant—"

"All so you could be free. But you'll never be free, child of shadow. Weak, pathetic little killer. You'll never—"

Poe grabbed his sister's throat, his other hand still over her heart. "Shut up, Donoveir." He ripped his hand back, and Alice screamed again, this time in the shrill soprano of a frightened girl. Poe stumbled back, a dark, swirling mass clutched in his hand. The thing writhed and grew, struggling toward Poe.

Lacey moved to help, but Alastair was already acting, his heart compelling him forward while his mind screamed at the danger. *Sanat,* he thought, and bright beams of light emanated from his fingers. He dragged the shadow off Poe and stumbled back, the mass now writhing atop him. It leaked into his consciousness, its darkness snaking like tendrils through his thoughts.

What's this? Donoveir whispered into his mind. *A monk who loves a warlock? I'll enjoy ripping your soul apart, fallen angel.*

Alastair pushed against the spirit with all the power of his light, but his hands trembled. His light flickered. Donoveir laughed into his thoughts.

"Necropola!" Poe's voice overtook the spirit's laughter, stronger than its hate. "Take back this spirit. Cast it into your world." He touched the spirit, and all at once, it began to dissolve. The scent of sage curled around them, the tang of salt bit the air. A scream ripped through the forest, Donoveir's last pathetic moan fading into the damp, cold night.

Poe dropped to his knees, his breathing ragged. "Alastair?"

Alastair pushed himself onto his elbows. "I'm fine. You?"

Poe grinned. "Never better." He lunged forward and pinned Alastair to the grass. Their kiss began tentatively, then grew softer and deeper. Alastair's wings twitched against his back. The kiss was strange, intense, like a bolt of lightning slicing through his stomach and leaving its light behind. Poe's tongue skimmed his and he felt suddenly out of his mind with this need, this ache. All was noiseless, sightless nonexistence apart from the singular desire to never be away from this perfect man.

Too soon, Poe broke away, his pierced lip curved in a smile. "Thanks for the help, by the way."

Alastair blushed, sitting up. "You're welcome." He looked over at Lacey and Nathy, who were suddenly very interested in the bark of the trees and the various plants shooting up from the ground.

"We're done," Poe called to them.

They meandered back as though nothing of interest had just happened. "So," Lacey said. "Is Alice all right?"

Poe nodded. "She'll be okay. She'll need a lot more of that recovery potion Saxon made, though."

"Let's get back." Nathy scooped Alice into his arms and led the way back through the forest. All the while they walked, Alastair held Poe's hand, intent on never letting go.

39

FIRE

A HEAVY RAIN was falling by the time they emerged from the forest, the dense, dark pines giving way to the neat apple trees of the groves. They crept inside through the mudroom, Nathy breaking off from the rest to carry Alice to the infirmary.

"Who's for coffee?" Poe said as they emerged into the corridor. He flung open a narrow door which led into a large kitchen with a stone floor and a heavy wooden table. A large fireplace overtook the far end of the room, big enough for several cooking pots.

"I'm starving, actually," Lacey said while Poe set up a kettle. She found a sack of potatoes on the counter and not much else. It would do.

While the potatoes baked in the oven, and the three friends sat over fresh mugs of coffee, soaking in the kitchen's close warmth, footsteps pounded overhead. A clamor like many falling objects rattled the ceiling.

"What room is right above us?" Lacey asked.

"The study." Poe shrugged. "Probably just Flynn."

She nodded and took a scalding swing of coffee. "Rotten day."

The boys nodded. An intense banging took up above.

"D'you think he's all right?" Lacey said. She rose. "I'm going to see what he's doing."

She grabbed an apple off the counter for Jack and rode the lift up. The ruckus was louder now, and she jogged toward the study, a sense of dread slithering in her stomach. The door was cracked slightly open, and she pushed into the room.

Flynn stood by the desk, tearing books from the shelves behind and flinging them to the ground. Spits of fire fell from his fingers and he worked, barely glancing at titles before throwing them aside. Some of the books smoldered, victims of his uncontained fire.

"Flynn? Flynn, stop." She ran across the room and grabbed his wrist. Fire shot up his arm and she quickly jumped back, her hand tingling from the heat.

"Lacey! I'm so sorry."

"I'm—fine." She looked at her palm. The flesh was pink, hot, but unharmed. "What are you doing?"

Chest heaving, he turned back on the shelves. "I need the Book. We need it."

"I agree. But you know it's not here."

"Maybe he hid it."

"Why would Will hide the Book from you?"

"If he's like her— If he changed his mind."

"What are you talking about?"

He stopped tearing at the shelves, his shoulders slumping. "Your power is great, if fully realized. Not many people are prepared to carry such a burden." He looked over his shoulder at her. "Every Rite you perform—it changes you. The Ruined Queen wasn't a leader, she wasn't a savior. She was a weapon."

I cannot be your weapon. Lacey reached into her pocket and produced the crumpled diary page. "Flynn. I found something, in Latrice's study. A letter she wrote before she died." She pressed it into his trembling hands. "She had a teacher."

Flynn scanned the contents quickly, then closed the parchment into his fist. Flames curled around his fingers, black ash eating into the page until it was gone.

Lacey balked, watching the ash drift to the floor. "Why— why would you that?"

"There are secrets in this house, Lacey. And more than one liar."

She shook her head. "You think I'm lying?"

"No. But you're too eager to believe things are as they seem."

She backed away from him, never letting her eyes leave the fire still twisting around his knuckles. "Flynn...you're scaring me. Put your fire away."

"It can't hurt you," he said, almost to himself. His eyes snapped to hers. "How powerful can his potion really be?" The flames curling around his hand grew, snaking up into a twister of snapping reds and orange, embers crackling along the edges.

Lacey jumped aside as the twister spiraled toward her. With a snap of his wrist, he redirected it, sending it back at her. It grew as it moved, sucking the flames from the fireplace and the wicks of the chandelier. She took cover behind a chair, but a moment later it rocked, struck by the tornado. She crawled away and ran to the window.

She punched out the glass without even thinking, feeling nothing from the shards of glass embedded in her knuckles. Heat licked at her back and she turned on instinct. The tornado barreled toward her.

She put her hands out and shut her eyes. A pleasant warmth, like summer's kiss, ran along her palms, up her arms. She peeled her eyes open to find the tornado at bay, twisting before her but no longer in pursuit. She knew what to do without knowing why. She curled her fingers in and pulled the flame into her body, where it rushed her blood like a stiff drink.

"Remarkable," Flynn said.

"Are you insane?" Lacey stormed toward him. "You could have killed me!"

Flynn smirked. "And yet you're very much alive."

She teetered on her feet, rage and adrenaline making her unsteady. "How did I do that? I haven't done the Ferno Rite yet."

"No, you haven't."

"Lacey!" Saxon ran into the study, halting when he saw the look on her face. "Lace? What happened?"

"He's insane," she said, pointing to Flynn. "And I'm leaving."

"You can't escape this," Flynn said.

"I'm not going to fight for you!" Lacey shouted. "You think you're noble just because you're trying to stand against the Elderon? You're just as bad as they are."

"That's hardly fair."

"You're the reason my father is dead," she said, quieter now, and yet this time Flynn reacted, his calm exterior melting into despair.

"I did everything I could for him."

"Like you did everything you could for Artemis? For Nathy? All you've done is ruin people's lives." She grabbed Saxon's hand. "Come on. We're going home."

"We are?"

Flynn shot his arm out, flames flying across the room and covering the door. Lacey brushed them away with the wave of her hand.

Saxon stared. "How...the hell..."

She opened the door and dragged Saxon through. "I'll explain on the train."

LACEY LOOKED AROUND Latrice's bedroom one last time. She had expected to feel something, had almost believed Latrice would show up to see her off. But there was nothing. Only a feeling of something settled. Maybe Latrice was glad to see her go. She'd be safer now, anyway.

"Goodbye, Grandma." She walked out into the corridor. Saxon stood there, leaning against the wall, wearing a clean suit and overcoat.

"Are you sure?" he asked.

Lacey nodded. "Flynn's mental. I have to get out of here."

Saxon bit the inside of his cheek, looking away from her. "What about Nathy?"

She hoped her face wasn't as red as it felt. "What about him?"

He shrugged. "It seemed like you two were becoming friends. Don't you want to say goodbye? And what about Marshall?"

Lacey tugged a note from her pocket. "I'm leaving them this. If they want to go, they can. But we need to get out of here before Flynn goes off on me again."

"Right." Saxon started toward the lift, but Lacey grabbed his wrist.

"Let's actually go through the window."

He sighed. "You're going to carry me again, aren't you?"

"Last time. Promise."

He followed her into the bedroom. "Bloody Elonni."

341

She dropped the note on the dresser, hoping Nathy would look for her here, hoping he could understand. He knew what Flynn was like—he had to believe her.

She looked back out the door, her heart like lead in her chest. "Bye, Nathy," she whispered.

"Lace?" Saxon waited at the window.

She turned toward him, and away from Fryer's Grove.

THERE WAS ANGER—and then there was rage. Nathy felt he knew the fine distinction between the two. Anger was a weak response, a wounded heart throwing stones at perceived injustice. Rage—that was fire, ice, and power. Rage got things done. He preferred it.

He tore Flynn's door off its hinges and threw it down the corridor. The jagged guts of the old house peeked through the exposed wall like the edges of a wound. Flynn looked up from sprinkling something into his goldfish bowl, his eyes wide.

"Have I done something wrong?"

"You tried to *burn her*?" The books along the walls trembled in their shelves. Nathy didn't know what he was doing, or how, just that some power was moving out of him and infecting the world, making it afraid. Good. "You threw a tornado of fire at her just to see what would happen?"

"She was quite fine when it was all said and done," Flynn said, his hands raised. He centered himself behind the desk—as though that could protect him. With a jerk of his neck, Nathy sent the desk through the wall like a train on its tracks. Plaster drifted through the new opening in the wall, dusting the floor.

"If you don't mind me asking," Flynn said, his throat bobbing. "How are you doing that?"

Nathy smiled. "Doing what?" The books fell from their shelves, fluttering like felled birds to the ground. The window behind Flynn shook in its frame, then shattered.

Flynn scooped up his goldfish bowl before shards of glass could puncture the strange creature inside. "I know you're angry. But you must let me explain."

"Explain. That you drove Lacey back to Theopolis. That she's with Saxon, the person who sees no reason *not* to deliver her to the Elderon. Or that you sent Artemis to her death. That you've never in your life taken responsibility for your own pathetic decisions."

"I sent Artemis because you were too valuable," Flynn said.

Nathy cocked his head to the side. "What did you say?"

"Nathy—you're the Sage. You are the heir to the Rite that will give Lacey her powers of magic. Your mother worked with us, she performed the Rite on Will. But Ruark killed her, and without you, there's no one who can finish the spell."

"You're telling me," Nathy said slowly, "that my girlfriend died in my place because you needed me for your fucking ritual."

Flynn winced. "I wouldn't put it that way myself, but..."

"Put down the goldfish so I can kill you."

"Nathy, you're as good as my son."

"Stop saying that."

"I raised you! I love you!"

"Raised me?" Nathy laughed. "You used me. All this time, you kept me around because you needed another pawn in your game. If you loved me, you would have told me."

"I couldn't."

"Why?"

"Because you're also a Fairborn." Flynn shut his eyes. "I didn't know how much you remembered. How badly he'd gotten to you. Any day, you might have left us for Sannus Eyreh. I had to protect the Nine. I had to know you were one of us before I told you what was happening."

"You knew." Nathy's power felt like a torrent rushing his blood, like lightning trying to break free of the sky. "You knew about Sannus Eyreh? About my father?"

"Yes. But I wanted you to grow up a normal child. To make the choice yourself. Your father wanted to indoctrinate you. I could have raised you as an acolyte of the Nine, but I needed to know you wanted to be one of us. For our safety, and for your sanity. You deserve to choose your path."

"You're really going to try to spin this so you're the good guy? The loving, understanding father?" Nathy stepped closer, holding his rage close to his heart. "I already have a father. And gods know I don't need another one."

He turned away, stepping over the fallen books and the rubble of the torn-off door.

"You're leaving?" Flynn said.

"Obviously."

He charged toward the lift, only to be drawn up short as Poe and Alastair exited. They shrank away from him.

"What happened?" Poe said. "We heard banging and shouting..."

"Move," Nathy said.

"Don't talk to him that way," Alastair said. Nathy levelled a glare at the monk, surprised to find Alastair staring defiantly back. "What's got you so worked up?"

"Nothing. Lacey's gone." He found her crumpled note in his pocket and shoved it into Alastair's hand. "She wrote a bit for you, too."

Alastair scanned the note quickly, then looked up at Poe. "Flynn tried to set her on fire, it seems."

"Hm." Poe nodded. "That's why Latrice is angry, I suppose."

"I really do need the lift," Nathy said.

"Right," Alastair said. "We've got to go find her."

"You do what you want." Nathy moved toward the stairs. "I'm getting back to work."

"Work?" Alastair said.

Poe sighed. "Nathy, assassinating someone never makes you feel better. You know that."

Alastair paled. "Who's he going to kill?"

Nathy didn't hear the rest of their conversation. He took the stairs to the fourth floor. He'd get his weapons and he'd be gone, like he should have been days ago. He'd been an idiot to stay, to start thinking— No. He wouldn't even go there.

Lacey was gone. He couldn't let her matter now.

A CIRCLE OF clients sat in Jade's sitting room when Nathy barged in. They all looked up from their prayerful contemplation of a crystal ball. Jade rolled her eyes and unfolded herself from the couch, where she had been reciting a Lyvian chant.

"I'm in the middle of a summoning," she said.

"I need to know if you've found Ruark," he said. The circle of clients looked up at him as though he'd been summoned from the netherworld. He wondered how wild he looked, how demonic his intent must be that it showed so clearly.

"What happened?" Jade said softly. She reached out toward his heart, but he caught her wrist.

"I don't have time," he said.

"Your aura is different." Bizarrely, she smiled. "You're in love again."

"No," he said. "I just want to kill someone very badly. I can see how you'd get the two confused. Where is he?"

She tugged her hand away, lips twisted in disapproval, but went to her cabinet and retrieved a sheaf of parchment. She handed it to him.

"He's holed up in Wit's End. But you know, killing him won't make you happy. Your heart wants something else."

"I'll log that away." He shoved the parchment into his pocket and waved to the gawping group. "Enjoy your séance."

"It's a *summoning*," Jade called after him as he slammed the door.

He walked farther down the street, the houses moving at a blur, his mind twisting with anger and rage and he didn't know what else. He chose not to wonder.

Jade was wrong. He just needed to get back on track. He'd let Flynn and Lacey distract him long enough.

It was time he took out Ruark.

40

CALVARY

THE TRAIN SLOWED, jerking the carriages and banging Lacey's head into the window. She woke, rubbing the sore patch of skin at her forehead.

"Our stop," Saxon said. He took her hand and tugged her from the bench.

Lacey looked out the window, at the expanse of dying winter grass beyond the station platform. "We're not in Theopolis yet."

"I know. But my house is outside the city."

Lacey raised an eyebrow. "Why?"

"It wouldn't fit anywhere else," Saxon muttered. They left their carriage and followed a small stream of disembarking passengers. Wind gusted across the platform, cutting into Lacey's clothes. For once, Lacey missed the heavy wool clothes of Hollows Edge. The loose trousers and tunic she wore weren't meant for icy climates.

Saxon walked to the information counter and asked for a driver. A moment later, they were being ushered to a sleek white auto.

"Are you sure it's safe at your house?" Lacey said. She was beginning to regret her rash decision. Theopolis felt close, a looming threat, a monster under the bed waiting to gobble her while she slept.

"Of course." He opened the auto's door for her, then slid in after she'd settled. "Even if what you say about the Old Names is true, my family are mages. We'd never be let into a cult bent on destroying magic, would we?"

"I suppose not." Lacey shuddered when her shoulder bumped the auto window. "You don't believe me, do you?"

"It's not that I don't believe you," he said on a sigh. "But the evidence you've got is shaky. An old book, Nathy's scars—

346

pretty far-fetched to take all that and say the Elderon have been infiltrated by a cult."

She looked out the window. "You weren't there."

The auto zoomed across the countryside, the night-soaked landscape dark but for the distant glimmer of lights on the far horizon. Theopolis.

"I might have been there," Saxon said a moment later. "But you were always off alone with Nathy."

She flushed. "We weren't *alone*. Alastair and Poe were there, too."

"So, double dates?"

"Don't be an ass. You could have come along with us, but you were too busy burning to do anything useful."

If he had a response to that, he kept it to himself. The auto drove on several more miles before turning off onto a flagstone driveway lined with cherry trees, their branches bare in the winter cold.

Ahead loomed what Lacey could hardly call a house— even *mansion* seemed too tame a word, for the structure rising before them shadowed the mass of Fryer's Grove. This place rose up seven stories and stretched wide down its corner of the countryside. A massive gable rose above the front doors, and turrets jutted from various corners of the house. Tall hedges rose along the sides of the house and crawled back into an expansive garden that seemed to have no end. As the auto halted before the gate to be let in, Lacey turned to Saxon.

"You live here?"

He nodded.

"Just you and your family?"

"And the servants."

Lacey slumped back against the window. "Oh, of course. The servants."

The auto circled around a massive fountain in the center of the courtyard and let them out before the front door. Wide, sweeping steps led up to front doors a giant could easily walk through.

"This is mental," Lacey said.

Saxon took her hand and led her up the stairs, his eyes downcast. "I know it's a bit much."

"A *bit*?"

"All right, it's extravagant. But you should see the places the Old Names live in."

Strangely, Saxon knocked. Lacey couldn't understand not being able to walk through one's own front door freely, yet the place did exude a sort of presence, an insistence on respect and authority that her little farmhouse in Hollows Edge could never have.

A young woman dressed in a long black dress, her hair tight in a bun, answered. "Master St. Luke?"

"Evening," he said. "If you could let my parents know I'm back?"

The maid bowed and hurried off. Saxon waved Lacey inside ahead of him. Lacey stepped tentatively through the door and stared around, jaw slack. The room was marble from floor to ceiling, lined with columns and dotted by elegantly carved sconces flickering candlelight at them. All around were paintings, some huge, others miniscule, of landscapes and faces and battles from ancient lore. Busts glared at them in between every nook, and the sightless eyes of statues looked out over the expanse. A great marble statue of a goddess resided in the very center of the room: She held her hands to her heart and seemed to weep.

"Welcome to Calvary," Saxon said.

"Bloody hell."

Saxon flinched a smile. "This is just the foyer. Wait till you see the actual art room. Or the ballroom, the dining room, the... Oh. Hi, Dad."

Dr. St Luke stepped into the foyer, hands behind his back, his spine stiff and his shoulders broad. He was dressed in a dark blue suit, a red cravat tight at his throat. His smile was faint and embarrassed. "Saxon. You're back. And Lacey. Good to see you again."

"Yeah. Hi." She crossed her arms.

"I didn't know if you'd be here," Saxon said carefully.

"Yes, well." The physician fiddled with his cuffs. "Commander Lately saw no reason to charge me in the end."

Saxon glared down at the marbled floor. "Right. Course not."

"Well." Dr. St. Luke didn't seem keen to meet Lacey's eyes. "I wish that I could welcome you to my home under more pleasant circumstances." He shrugged. "But at any rate, make yourself comfortable. Take any room you like. Have you had dinner?"

Lacey perked up. "What have you got?"

"Anything you like. Our chef has studied the culinary traditions of Iymar, Fesspire, Sumri—"

"One of each," Lacey said. She put a hand to her stomach. "I feel like I haven't eaten since the festival."

The doctor smiled. "I'll let him know." He nodded once to Saxon and departed, his shoes clicking across the foyer, echoing against the high walls.

Saxon chewed his lip for a moment, glaring after his father. "I can't believe that bloody coward."

"As long as the bloody coward feeds me, we're fine." She looked up at the sound of footsteps descending the great double staircase at the back of the room. A tall, beautiful woman in a midnight-blue gown stepped into the foyer. Her golden hair was wound in an elegant braided twist that left soft curls of hair framing her delicate oval face.

"Saxon. I can't believe you've returned so quickly."

Saxon stiffened, moving slightly closer to Lacey. "Hi, Mum."

"This must be Lacey." The woman reached her hands out as though to take Lacey's, then drew them back to her chest. "So...good to meet you." Her dark eyes roved Lacey's face, then her clothes. "My, my. Let's get you a room, shall we, dear? I'll have the servants bring you a change of clothes as well."

"I've got it, Mum," Saxon said. "Lacey wants a tour first."

"And dinner," Lacey reminded him, her stomach burning in agreement.

Dame St. Luke's smile was a mangled, unhappy thing, yet it seemed trapped upon her face like a bit of rot clinging to a tree. "Of course. But do hurry. Ambassador Kragen is coming by within the hour."

Saxon's jaw tightened. "Why is he coming here?"

"Well, all the Allies are in a bit of a state, you know."

"I don't know," Saxon said.

"Didn't you hear?" Dame St. Luke blinked. "Albion Crane has died."

Lacey's jaw dropped. "He died? How?"

"Seems he was murdered by his servant girl. Nasty little thing, she was."

"Who reported the death?" Lacey asked.

Dame St. Luke wrinkled her nose. "What an odd thing to say, dear."

"It isn't, though. Someone found him. Who was it?"

"I believe," Dame St. Luke said tersely, "it was the Commander."

"Oh." Lacey smiled as though unbothered, but her gut forgot its hunger and sank into frenzied terror. Crane was one of the Elders without an Old Name. One of those Sannus Eyreh might have been happy to dispose of. If he was dead, it was because he wasn't playing along, or at least had tried to change the game.

Saxon touched his hand to the small of her back, startling her from her thoughts. "We'll be going now. Goodnight, Mum."

Dame St. Luke nodded curtly, her smile still stuck in place. Lacey let Saxon guide her toward the stairs, trying not to wonder what Albion Crane's death meant.

"Ready to tour a patently ridiculous mansion?" Saxon said.

Lacey managed a smile, nodded. "I'm so ready to hate you for this."

THE GREAT MARBLED interior of Calvary wound endlessly in great corridors and wide, sparse rooms. The deliberate lack of homey trappings left the eye to wander across the great architecture and intricate design of the house. What items were displayed in the mansion ranged from the banal—an entire room with only a few tables set up with chess boards—to ridiculous opulence.

"The artefact room," Saxon said, gesturing Lacey into a wide hall that seemed to belong in the Theopoline Museum. Old sets of armor, stone tablets inscribed with Annanym, and a gold sarcophagus surrounded by stone lions featured prominently under beams of electric lights.

Lacey gaped at an illuminated, scribed copy of the Amerand, then turned to Saxon with a glare.

"What?" he said.

"This belongs in a museum," she said.

"Probably."

She walked to the sarcophagus, pointing. "Is there still a dead person in there?"

"There'd better be, or Dad paid too much for it."

She shook her head. "You're all the worst."

He shrugged. "I know. Come on."

He led her to the third floor, but Lacey was already tired from the first two. "Saxon? Is this how all Allies live?"

"No. But Dad gets paid well for his...work. With Haylock."

"What does he do for Haylock?"

"Well. That binding potion that you took? He makes it in stronger doses. Some of the more dangerous criminals in Haylock are given a dose. It—it annihilates their powers. Forever."

"He takes people's magic away?" Her fingernails dug into her palms. "And it's the same potion he was giving me?"

"They're dangerous people, Lace."

"Are they?"

They passed a ballroom that could have contained Lacey's house in Hollows Edge five times over. She was done with the pretty trappings of this place, though.

"Why didn't he give the stronger dose to me?" Lacey said as they wound back toward the stairs. "Why bother dosing me every year?"

"There are side effects," Saxon said. "Destroying a person's magic can hurt their mind and body, too. Some of the guards call Dad's potion 'liquid lobotomies.'"

She found there was nothing satisfactory to say to that. Something so awful seemed beyond words. They walked up the many flights of stairs until they reached the seventh floor.

"It's just bedrooms, mostly," Saxon said. Lacey snorted.

"In case you need to harbor an entire country of refugees?"

Saxon didn't respond. He led her down one of the many wide corridors and stopped at a set of mahogany double doors set into a carved archway. Inside was a cavernous room with bookshelves lining one wall and a long oak table against the wall opposite. Shelves with every kind of scientific instrument—beakers and measuring jars, sharp steel utensils, a series of microscopes—floated above the table. The back

351

wall was dominated by a wide window with heavy sapphire curtains held back to reveal a view of the garden maze below. A huge bed sat in the center of everything, its covers the same deep blue as the curtains.

"Bloody hell," Lacey said. "That is, ah...that's a big bed. Is it...?"

"Mine, yeah."

They looked at each other. Lacey cleared her throat.

"It's nice," she said, walking away.

"You can take your pick of the guest rooms," Saxon said when he'd caught up to her. He opened a door at random. "This one's nice, if you aren't opposed to a taxidermy centaur watching you sleep."

"I happen to be very opposed to that."

He smiled and stopped at a door farther along the corridor. "You'll like this one. No dead things on the walls."

The room was many times bigger than any Lacey had slept in before, its walls purple-red and its carpet a deep cerulean. A bed that could hold five people comfortably sat in the corner, and a purple tea table and chairs stood a little ways from it. An elegant phonograph sat across from the bed along the opposite wall.

"This'll do." Lacey turned in the doorway, keeping him out in the corridor. "Well... See you at dinner?"

"Lace... Look, I can tell you're still angry with me."

She leaned against the doorframe, arms crossed. "I am. A little."

He hesitated, his eyes sharp as glass on hers. "I just...keep thinking if I apologize enough, you'll forgive me."

She reached for the door, ready to shut him out, but he planted his palm against it.

"Wait. I was going to say that I realized I was wrong. Apologizing isn't enough. So I'll be honest. And if you still can't stand to be around me, I'll understand."

"I'm listening."

"Okay," Saxon said. "I should have told you about all of it—the bane, the potion. I know it was wrong to keep that from you. I didn't fully understand what Dr. Poole and my father were doing." He sighed. "As far as the bane goes...I thought you'd hate me. And I couldn't stand that. But hiding things from you hasn't really worked out for me. So I've got one more thing to tell you."

She took a deep breath. "Okay."

"About Nathy. The reason I hated him so much... We were best friends in school. And even after my mum pulled me out, we stayed in touch. I learned about a year ago what sort of business he'd gone into."

"Assassinations?"

"Yeah. And...there was somebody I wanted gone."

Lacey leaned forward. "Who?"

His eyes flicked down the corridor. "Ambassador Kragen."

"Oh, my God. Why?"

"There aren't many Allies, you know. So all the families are close. And, like the Old Names, we tend to intermarry when it's possible. Kragen's third wife had just died when my sister turned fifteen. Marrying age." His jaw flexed. "Serendipity, wasn't it? My mother arranged the whole thing. And my father was so wrapped up in his work, he didn't bother to ask questions."

He took a long, shaky breath. "Sophie wasn't happy, but she was brave. She always told me to make the best of things. But then we learned there are things you can't wring an ounce of goodness from."

Lacey pressed her lips together, waiting for the end, though she'd already guessed.

"Kragen couldn't wait for the wedding night," Saxon said. "He left her lying in the garden. Used magic to keep her from— from saying what had happened. But we all knew.

"Mum decided she'd have to go ahead with the wedding anyway. And Dad, he's never stood up to her in his life. Sophie didn't want to live like that. Not after she saw what he was.

"So, she poisoned herself. She didn't die, but her mind was gone after that. Kragen didn't want a 'damaged' wife, so he called off the wedding. Mum blamed Dad for ruining the family prospects, Dad blamed Mum for destroying his favorite child. And... my sister was gone. I was just a kid. I barely understood what had happened.

"But watching my sister suffer all these years... When I found out what Nathy was doing, I asked him to help. I told him he could name his price. He took the money and ran off."

"Oh, my God."

"I know," Saxon said. "I know that doesn't make me any better than a murderer, and you probably think I'm a terrible person, but—"

"That bastard."

Saxon blinked. "Who, Kragen?"

"Well, yes, obviously him. But Nathy—he wouldn't kill him? What was it, he didn't want to risk killing an ambassador? What a twat."

"You're mad...at Nathy?"

"Next time I see him..." She huffed. "We're going to get you the assassination you paid for." She slipped out of the room, starting back down the corridor. "I'll do it myself if I have to."

"Lace. It's okay." He tugged her back and held her against his chest. "I've talked to him. I know why he didn't do it. He didn't want me to have someone's death over my head."

Lacey thought back to Nathy's words the night before—he thought of himself as a murderer. He didn't want to put that on anybody else. Maybe he could barely stand to do it himself anymore.

She looked up at Saxon, their faces close. "You thought I wouldn't like you anymore because you wanted Kragen dead?"

He nodded.

She stood on her toes and kissed him. "You really don't know me at all, mate."

He blinked down at her. "You never cease to surprise me."

She shrugged. He pulled her tighter against his chest.

"You know," he said, his voice low, "my bed is more comfortable. Than the one in there."

Lacey swallowed. "Is it, now?"

"Mm-hm." He ran his thumb across her lower lip. "Plenty of space. If you want space."

"And if I don't?"

"All the better." He pressed her against the wall and kissed her, his hands wandering, muscles tensed. This wasn't like their other kisses. She could feel it in the heat of his hands as they sought bare skin. This was only a prelude. A promise.

"M-ma'am?"

Saxon pulled away at the frightened squeak of the voice. A blushing servant girl held a dress box up. "D-Dame St. Luke sent me up. To—to prepare Miss Barker for dinner?"

"Lovely timing, Mum," Saxon muttered. He tipped Lacey's chin up. His lips brushed hers when he said, "Stay with me tonight."

She nodded. His smile met hers in one last, lingering kiss.

He sauntered off down the hall, giving the poor servant girl a salute as he passed. Her eyes trailed after him as he vanished into his bedroom.

"Sorry," Lacey said.

The girl looked back at Lacey. Her shyness seemed to vanish as soon as Saxon was out of sight. "Gods, you are *so* lucky."

Lacey thought the heat of her face might leave an actual burn. "I—suppose I am."

The servant girl smiled. "Let's get you freshened up, then. Sounds like you'll want to look your best tonight."

Lacey covered her face in her hands and blindly followed the girl into her borrowed room.

41

THE DINNER GUEST

-Calvary, Theopolis-

THE SERVANT GIRL drew a bath and left Lacey with a basket of soaps, vials of shampoo, and a few sprigs of lavender—"To relax you," she said with a wink. Lacey was only too happy to bury her head beneath the hot, bubbly bathwater.

After the bath, the girl drew a slinky red dress from the box she'd brought up. It was a modern fashion, sleeveless with a slick V line, beads clattering at the hem which only just hung past her knees. The girl did up the zipper and turned Lacey toward a mirror. She stared at herself, blinking. She still didn't look like she belonged in such clothes—her hair was still too stringy, her face and shoulders too thin. And yet something had changed. Her eyes were brighter and focused forward, not cast down. She met her gaze in the glass and smiled.

"I'll put your hair up, too," the girl said. "Master St. Luke won't want to wait till after dinner when he sees you."

"I—I certainly *hope* he can," she said, feeling as though Alastair had suddenly taken possession of her body.

The girl giggled and fixed Lacey's hair with a few quick, expert moves. She settled the updo with a glittering gold headband, a single gold feather poking out near her ear.

"Anything else, my lady?" the servant girl asked, stepping away.

My lady. She wanted to tell the girl not to call her that, that it wasn't right. Yet her reflection still wore that thin smile. Her ancestors had carried titles and worn gowns. They'd been royalty.

She blinked, and her reflection no longer smiled. She turned toward the maid. "No. Thanks, though. I'm...not used to dresses."

The maid bobbed her head once and said nothing, merely moved toward the door and exited quietly. Saxon leaned into the room.

"The dress suits you," he said with a smile.

It suited some part of her, maybe. But she'd never be that girl.

"I'm starving," she said, and took his waiting hand.

They made the long descent to the first floor, Saxon leading the way through the impenetrable system of corridors and grand staircases. Lacey hadn't thought a house could be so complicated. She felt as lost as she had in the forest at Fryer's Grove. Though each room was distinct, the opulence blended together, twisting into one grand, beautiful maze.

When they finally arrived, the scent of cooked food knifed through Lacey's stomach like pain. She barely registered the high-arched ceiling, the tapestries on the walls, the gilt dining chairs and polished silverware. Her eyes landed on three fat turkeys and cared for nothing else.

Dr. St. Luke sat at the head of the table, his wife to his right. Sitting beside Dame St. Luke was a younger woman, a few years older than Saxon. She was beautiful, possibly the most beautiful person Lacey had ever seen. Her curled brown hair fell along her face, and her gas-fire blue eyes were sleepy, lost. Her full, curving figure lent further beauty to the jeweled sapphire dress she wore.

The woman looked up and a big, childish smile glowed when she saw Saxon. "Little brother is back."

"Sophie," Saxon said, his voice soft, yet roughened by sadness.

"You brought a stranger." She sank down in her seat, eyes flicking from Lacey to her hands, picking at the tablecloth. "Stranger, stranger, stranger. Bad people I don't know."

"Enough," Dame St. Luke said, slapping her daughter's wrist. "This is Lacey. Our...guest."

Dr. St. Luke took a healthy swig of wine. His wife's eyes cut to him.

"Darling, would it be possible for you to refrain until our guests arrive?"

He refilled his glass. "Of course, my dear."

Saxon took the seat beside his father, Lacey next to him. Sophie stared across the table at Lacey, blinking every few seconds.

"Hi," Lacey said. "I love your dress."

A small smile pinched the corner of Sophie's mouth. "You're nicer than the other strangers Saxon brings home."

Saxon choked a little on the wine he'd been drinking. Lacey cut him a look.

"Sophie, really," Dame St. Luke said. "I'm sure Lacey doesn't care to hear all about that."

"No, no, I'm interested." Lacey grinned at Saxon. "Very."

Saxon's cheeks were nearly the same deep shade as his wine. "I don't—she's not—"

"Lacey," Dame St. Luke cut off her son's sputtering. "Do tell us what it's like in your village. Hollows-something? It must be dreadfully interesting."

"Dreadful, yes," Lacey said.

Across the table, Sophie giggled. "Mother doesn't like you, stranger."

"Nonsense," Dame St. Luke said.

Lacey didn't care if Dame St. Luke wanted her beheaded at this point—she just wanted a hot meal, and she was prepared to sit through any family drama to get it.

A person Lacey assumed was a butler stepped into the dining room and bowed. "Ambassador Kragen," he announced, and stepped aside to admit the vulture-like man Lacey had seen at the festival. Saxon tensed, and Lacey took his hand without thinking about it. The action wasn't lost on Dame St. Luke; her eyes snapped to her son with a cold fury that Lacey felt in her bones.

"Sebastian," Kragen said, nodding. "And Delilah. Radiant as ever." He walked along the table, stopping before Sophie. "My dear Sophie. You're looking well."

"No," Sophie said, her eyes on the empty plate before her.

"I'm sorry?"

"Go away."

"Sophie," Dame St. Luke said through a fracturing smile. "Be *polite*."

"Make him go away." Sophie's voice grew louder. Her fingers curled into the tablecloth. "Make him go away."

"Is something the matter?" Kragen touched her shoulder. Sophie buried her face on the table and wrapped her arms around her head.

Her voice drifted from the table, muffled: "Stranger, stranger, stranger. Bad people I don't know."

Kragen didn't remove his hand. "What on earth is the matter, Miss Sophie?"

"Why don't you get your hand off her?" Lacey said. "Seems pretty obvious *you're* what's bothering her."

The ambassador swung his eyes to Lacey like she was carrion, and he was hungry. "I remember you. You were with our young Master St. Luke at the festival." He dragged his fingers slowly from Sophie's shoulder, then took the seat beside her. "Lacey Barker, isn't it?"

"It's Falk-Barker, actually."

"My mistake." He smiled. "Absolom Poole is your godfather, is that right?"

"Yeah."

He nodded, his thin mouth turning down with effort. "My condolences."

She sat up straighter. "What do you mean?"

"Well, they've taken him to Gamault Castle." He looked down the table at Delilah. "High treason, wasn't it?"

Dame St. Luke looked into Lacey's eyes as she said, "Yes, I believe it was."

"Indeed." Kragen folded his hands under his chin. "Apparently new evidence has arisen that he was involved with those rebels during the War of Teeth. Terrible shame. Not," he said, looking at Lacey, "that any of this reflects poorly on you."

Lacey turned to Saxon, whose own pale, slack look must have reflected her own. "When is his trial?" Saxon said.

"There won't be a trial," Dr. St. Luke said, his eyes hard on the glass of wine before him. "High treason is an Arkrytian offense." His eyes met Lacey's only briefly. "His execution is set for tomorrow night."

"Execution?" Lacey rose from the table. "They're *killing him*?"

"A shame," Kragen said. "But necessary."

Lacey glared down at the ambassador. "You're in on it, too, aren't you? Sannus Eyreh."

He tilted his head. "I'm afraid I don't know what you mean."

"Lace." Saxon tried to take her hand, but she pulled it back.

"No. I'm done." She knocked into her chair as she left, her steps uneven with the rage and fear coursing through her body. Dr. Poole—he was going to die. Her godfather. No—he was her real father, more than Will ever was. She might not share blood with him, but he'd been there through everything. He'd tried to protect her from both Flynn and the Elderon.

And now, he'd be killed for his efforts.

She ran through the corridors, lost but unwilling to stay here a moment longer. Dr. Poole was at the castle—so, she'd go get him. She'd fight through the guards, she'd rip the bricks from the building's walls, she'd do whatever she had to. But Dr. Poole was not dying.

She turned a corner and stopped at the sight of a figure standing mere feet from her. Ambassador Kragen peered down his beaklike nose, his smile limp, cruel.

"It's rude to leave a table like that, dear girl."

She turned, ready to run back down the corridor the way she had come. But Kragen was there, too, shaking his head. She moved to duck into the nearest doorway, a conservatory with instruments lined along the walls, the muted room somber in the its silence. But...no. Kragen rose from behind the grand piano like a musician ready to take his bow.

"Is something the matter?" he said, his voice before her, behind her, to every side, chorusing on itself.

She spun in the doorway, but he stood before her; no matter which way she turned, his presence erupted like a sprouting mushroom.

"How are you doing that?" she said.

"I'm not. It's all in your head, dear. Magic doesn't always require a twisting of nature's ways—sometimes, all it needs is a weak mind to prey upon."

Weak. Lacey looked between the many manifestations of Kragen circling her in the room, heat pulsing from her palms. "We'll see how weak I am."

Fire sprayed from both her hands, crawling out into the corridor and throughout the conservatory. Kragen's doppelgangers vanished in plumes of smoke, and his laughter drifted away with them.

Then, there was screaming.

Lacey ran back into the corridor and stared through the flames, hardly believing it. Saxon stood pressed against the wall, helpless to the fire beating closer to him and crawling up his trouser leg. Lacey ripped the flames back, uncoiling them from their grip on Saxon. She drew them in, letting them die in a warm haze beneath her skin. Saxon collapsed against the wall. The scent of cooked flesh hung on the air.

She ran toward him. "Saxon! Are you all right?"

"Am I all right?" he said through his teeth, hands hovering above his charred skin. "What the hell *was* that?"

Tears fractured her vision as she stared down at the damage she'd done, the meat of his muscle red and hot through his singed clothes. "I didn't see you. I—I was aiming for Kragen."

"Kragen? What are you on about? Kragen is downstairs with my parents." He gritted his teeth against a scream, straining with pain. "Since when can you use fire magic, Lacey?"

"I...I don't know. I don't know how I'm doing it."

He tore at his trousers, and bits of skin came away from his leg along with the charred fabric. Lacey stared, wide-eyed and trembling.

"Can you heal it?"

He ignored the question. "You did one of the Rites, didn't you?"

"*No.* We never had the Book, Saxon. I don't know where I got the fire from."

He's still here.

Flynn's face flashed across her memory. The way he'd thrown the flames at her as though certain she would manage them. Donoveir's voice in Alice's throat: *You're not mine.* And the letter...Flynn had destroyed it after Lacey told him...

She had a teacher.

She gasped. Saxon glanced up, his hair sticking in the sweat along his face. "What?"

"N-nothing. It's impossible. Come on." She tried to offer Saxon a hand up, but he shook his head.

"I'll manage on my own," he said.

"Saxon, I wasn't *trying* to hurt you."

His jaw clenched, and he wouldn't meet her eyes. Though he wouldn't say it, she knew what he was thinking. He'd never wanted her to be more than a weak little human with the pretty trappings of an Elonni. This—her fire, her potential beyond even that—it was too much. He couldn't love her like this.

Fire flickered under her skin, wanting out. "Fine. Bye, then."

"Where are you going?" he asked wearily.

"I'm going to help my godfather. Then I'm going to find my mum and—and we're leaving. We're leaving the realm."

"Lace." Saxon ground his teeth, his eyes still focused away from hers. "You can't just leave. You're out of control."

"I'm *what*?"

"You have no idea how to handle this power. What's going to stop you from hurting someone else?"

She took a slow step closer to him. "You want me to let the Elderon, what—bind me up again?" Even as she said it, flames licked down her forearms, like the tongues of snakes seeking prey. She took a breath, bringing the fire back beneath her skin. "I'll learn how to control it."

"What if it's too late by then?"

Footsteps clattered farther down the corridor. Lacey looked once more at Saxon.

"I'm sorry I hurt you. But I—I have to go. Goodbye."

"Lacey, *don't*."

She didn't listen; she ran. She pounded down the corridor, fire falling from her skin the more she hurt, the more she wished she could stay with him. But it didn't matter. His part in her life had been sweet, reassuring—but never made to last.

She stopped at the first window she saw and sent a burst of flame through the glass. Shards from the window burst out onto the garden below, and the metal frame folded against the inferno. She jumped through the wide space and let her wings catch her on her way down.

42

THE POTION

-Calvary, Theopolis-

SAXON DIDN'T HEAR the footsteps until they were upon him, and didn't bother looking up until he was wrenched to his feet. He choked on a scream as his weight fell onto his burned leg.

"Where is she?"

Saxon shoved Kragen off him, stumbling with the action. He caught himself against the wall, breathing hard. "What do you care?"

The ambassador's withered features twisted in contempt. "Stupid boy. You had one task, one simple task, and you failed."

"I said I'd bring her back. I never said I'd force her to stay."

"Yes. And look what she's done to you." Kragen sneered. "I do hope the pleasure she brought you was worth that."

Saxon forced himself away from the wall, steadying himself despite the searing pain in his leg. "Watch yourself, ambassador."

Kragen laughed outright. He was frail, but only in body. The elder wizard's magic was superior, far beyond anything an Ally ought to know. Saxon could throw a punch, but he'd likely be dead before his fist found purchase on that smug, wilting smile.

"You threaten me, little boy? Because of you, a dangerous monster is loose in our city. Because you—"

"That's quite enough, Eadred."

Saxon barely spared a glance for his father. How long had he stood there, watching? And why, even now, did he do nothing?

"My apologizes, Sebastian." Kragen swept his birdlike gaze to Saxon's father and nodded. "If you'll excuse me, I think I'll make a few calls."

Saxon waited until the ambassador was gone from the corridor to look his father in the eye. "How do you do it?"

"What's that?" Sebastian said, exhaustion—or worse, boredom—in his tone.

"How do you stand in the same room as him? Eat at the same table?" Saxon curled his fingers into his palm, relishing the bite of his nails against flesh. "Rather—how do you call yourself a father when you let him...when Sophie..."

Anger muted him, and his father's resilient apathy told him it was pointless to go on. He pushed past Sebastian, knocking into him. It was a pathetic gesture, and Saxon felt again like a stupid boy, begging to know why his sister was broken, demanding to know why no one could do anything.

He'd nearly escaped when his father's voice called him back, and, like a child hoping for answers, he stopped and looked over his shoulder. His father hadn't moved and still faced away from him, but his voice carried, broken yet sure.

"There's a difference," Sebastian said, "between living, and living with yourself." He turned to face Saxon, something nearly alive flickering in his pale blue eyes. "If there's a point to my life anymore, Saxon, you're it. I lost your sister. But I can do what needs to be done to protect you."

"What does that mean?" Saxon said, spitting the words.

"It means that I'll do worse things—horrible things, if I have to—if it means you're safe." He reached into his suit pocket and produced a cigarette case. "I think your mother wanted to see you," he said, lighting up, and turned away, as though nothing important had been said.

"OH, SWEETHEART. COME right in."

Saxon shut the door to his mother's study and leaned against it, arms crossed. She didn't look up from the letter she was writing. She had changed from her evening gown into a crisp powder-blue suit, and her long blond hair was organized in an elegant braided bun.

"Well, sit down," she said, still not looking up. "I hate it when you hover like that."

Saxon stepped further into the study, his right leg giving a little to the pain. The ache of the fire still burned in his muscle, and he'd been too furious with his father to think of asking for a potion.

There was the pain in his heart, too, but he was sure there was no cure for that.

His mother's study was a cozy room bathed in the artificial warmth of electric lights. There was no desk; a tea table and two narrow-legged chairs, set up neatly under a wide window, took the place of a workspace. An armchair sat in the farthest corner with a knitted blue blanket thrown over its back. A small bookshelf stood by the wall to Saxon's left. Rather than books, it was packed with flowers in vases and their most recent family portrait: Mum sat in a wingback chair with her husband and son on either side. Saxon thought his smile in the photo was tolerating, maybe a bit amused. His father, meanwhile, had barely managed to smirk for the camera. He looked like he would rather be a hundred other places.

And Sophie, sitting at her mother's feet with her legs tucked under herself: radiant, blue-eyed, with curling dark hair and a faraway smile. There was something in her expression that let you know she wasn't quite there—not detached, like Dad, but...gone. Saxon stared at her, his father's words from all those years ago rushing back: *She won't be the same.*

Delilah finished off her letter with a flourish and folded it twice into a neat square. She plucked her wand from the tabletop and tapped the letter once. It curled in on itself as though consumed by flame, though there was no fire, and vanished.

"Who are you writing to?" Saxon asked.

"Hm?" She blinked at him, then smiled. "Oh, Saxon. I'd nearly forgotten. Here." She pushed a long, thin box across the tea table. "A new wand. Ryder told me yours was destroyed."

Saxon peeked in the box—a long, shimmering black wand glinted up at him. Its handle twisted elegantly to a knob, and a Wynish carving stood out along the stem.

"Thanks," he said, and shut the box. "But why do I need this?"

"Well, dear, you *were* just attacked. Best to have some means of defense. Even if you're out of practice."

Saxon stowed the wand in his inner jacket pocket, ignoring the jibe. He'd taken too much after his father, especially in his aptitude for magic. Delilah was possibly the best spellcaster in Theopolis; the fact that her son couldn't manage much more than elementary attempts at magic had to grate.

He took a step toward the table, halted by a jolt of pain. Delilah's eyes snapped to his leg.

"You're limping," she said, and rose from the table. She went to her cabinet and plucked out a small vial filled with some sunshine-yellow substance. "Drink this."

He took it from her fingers. "What is it?"

"For the pain," she said, examining the ends of her nails too intently. "I know how you get when you're...under duress."

"Right." He handed it back. "Or it's a truth potion."

She looked up sharply.

"Potions are the one thing I'm good at," he reminded her. "Anyway, it's not necessary. I'll tell you anything you need to know."

Delilah smirked. "My goodness, Saxon—how quickly you've abandoned your scruples."

"I haven't. The Nine are insane. They've got to be stopped." He took a breath against the agony in his leg. "They'll turn her into a monster otherwise."

"How many Rites has Flynn performed on her?"

"None. So she says. But I don't think she knows what's really going on. Somehow, Flynn gave her his powers. He wants to use her. Even if it kills her."

"Then we've got to take her new powers away. More than that: We've got to do something to make her...unappealing to them."

"A binding potion," he said.

"It's the only way. Other than killing her, of course." This she said almost wistfully.

Saxon's jaw locked against the things he wished he could say to his mother. He chose a diplomatic route. "Can't you just go after Flynn? Lacey's gone. She's leaving the realm. Just—let her live her life. She's not the problem here."

"They'll stop at nothing, dear. It's best to take care of the problem at the roots. Wouldn't you agree?"

"I don't, actually."

"Darling, she set you on fire."

He shrugged. "I've had worse dates."

Delilah blinked at him for a moment, frightfully silent. "You really think you can get whatever you want, don't you?"

He shrugged. "I get that from you." He turned, but felt himself suddenly locked by thin, cold fingers around his bones and every nerve. He was forced back to facing his mother. She released him from the spell with a drop of her hand.

"Don't walk away from me," she said. "You think I'm a fool. Or, if not a fool...well, a bitch, am I right?" She laughed. "Don't worry, darling. I'm quite used to the accusation. With it comes the implication that I'm far too emotionally involved to get anything done properly. Yes, I'm passionate, but easy to trick. Easy to lie to because I'm so *eager* to believe that I can trust my only son. Is that what you think, sweetheart?"

"Mum, I don't—"

"Saxon. You St. Luke men all have the same problem—you can't lie." She stood very close to him and looked almost lovingly at his face. "You have the exact same tell as your father, did you know that? You look to the left—but only for a second—and make sure you look me in the eye while you actually speak the lie. Very clever. I'm sure it works on Lacey."

"Leave her out of—"

Delilah raised her hand, silencing him. "I see right through you, darling—a poor, poor fool with everything to lose." She smirked. "But sweetheart, if you're going to play this game, you've got to bring more to the table than a big heart and stupid dreams. You think you can help her—you think you'll be her hero—but you know that's not how this ends." She stepped back and smiled. "She'll hate you no matter what you do. So, do what's best for her—and for everyone in the realm."

She reached behind one of the photos on her bookshelf, her hand coming away clutching a vial of bright green potion. Saxon knew it immediately; it had been brewing in his father's laboratory all those days ago.

"We need you, Saxon," Delilah said. "Do this one last thing. Protect the realm. And save Lacey from herself."

Saxon's hand twitched at his side, ready both to reach for the potion and to strike it from his mother's hand. Lacey was dangerous—he knew that now. And yet... "I can't do that to her," he said, remembering how she'd reacted to the news of the potion. How she'd looked at him as though he were a monster. "It's got to be her choice."

"You only say that because you want to preserve the possibility that she could love you. But dear, the pretty face you're so obsessed with is a mask. And when that falls away, you'll see the monster waiting within her. I hope it's not too late by that point."

"How would I even get it to her?" Saxon said. "I've no idea where she's going."

Delilah nodded toward the door, and it slid open, admitting a tall, broad man about Sebastian's age. He wore a simple dark suit, faded at the elbows and creased. Dirt crusted at the beds of his nails, and his old face was worn, but smiling. He looked like nobody, like a village preacher. Yet Saxon knew he was Elonni, and that he was important. The man wore his aura like a coat, and even Saxon could feel it crawling through the room, owning it.

"She'll seek the Book," the man said. "And I happen to know where it hides."

Saxon shook his head. "Sorry, who are you?"

"Just call me Amnon," the man said, offering his hand. "I'm here to help."

"I don't make it a point to trust random strangers," Saxon said.

The man smiled. "Smart boy. Practical." He stepped further into Delilah's study and his eyes fixed on the grim family portrait, the pretense somehow more painful when displayed for a stranger.

"I wish I could say I was there all those years ago," the man went on. "But I wasn't. I followed my calling, a noble calling, I thought. But..." He shook his head. "In war, there are often two forces of evil. And when that's the case, men like not to take sides. But you've got to ask yourself: Is one side more deadly than the other?"

Saxon sighed. "You mean the Nine."

"Everyone lost someone in the War of Teeth. But only the Nine threatened to take everything." He fixed his gaze on Saxon. "Lacey isn't the perpetrator. She's the weapon. This is your only chance to help her."

Something in the man's smile, or his gaze, made Saxon nod his head. He could help Lacey. He could save her. She might hate him. But at least she'd be free of the Nine, of her own dark power.

"All right. I'll try."

Amnon's kind smile inched up. "Excellent."

"My son's not very good with magic," Delilah said, leaning forward too eagerly. Saxon shot her a dull look, and she stared unapologetically back. "Well, you aren't. And after all that schooling you went through. Honestly."

"Well," the man said. "Let's see if we can't rectify that." He took Saxon's hand in both of his. Something sharp and hot bristled between their skin, uncomfortable and yet strangely assuring.

"*Daerad*," Amnon said, and Saxon crumpled, his hand trapped but the rest of his body twisting, reeling from the pain that seemed to burst from his own veins and fill his body like blood. He had no voice for screaming, no way of opening his eyes to beg the man to stop this with a look. But as quickly as the shock had come, it faded, and Saxon found himself somehow still on his feet, his skin crackling, his heart pounding.

"You've got a lot of potential," the man said.

"T-thanks." Saxon rubbed a hand down his arm, trying to flatten the raised hairs there. Whatever Amnon had done, it had worked. Saxon felt electric, like the smallest movement might send a spell flying.

His mother pressed the binding potion into his hand. "Thank you for cooperating, darling." She returned to her tea table and nodded to the door. "You may go."

Saxon left the room, careful not to slam the door. Mum hated when he slammed doors. And for some reason, that stopped him doing it.

43

THE BLOOD OF ELROSH

-Gamult Castle, Theopolis-

LITTLE MOONLIGHT EVER made it into the tower. The sole window was high on the wall and barred, its view blocked by the weathered edge of a neighboring tower. It had been only a day since Poole's arrest, yet isolation had already taken its steady toll on his mind. Here, the price was not only hunger and cold, but madness at the loss of time and sense of place. The sun had only set once—or had it? Had the days thickened into one? Had he been here a week, perhaps? It felt like so much longer. It scared him that perhaps less time had passed, and his meager estimate was too much.

Eternity had never appealed to him. His father's stories of immortal life and the pale, endless corridors of some distant heavenly realm struck not awe, but fear, into his young mind. Because time and life were only precious when spent, and the promise of more and more cheapened the days one had to live.

This frozen cell felt like his childish imagining of heaven—endless, boring, permanent. So, he was almost grateful when the long wooden door opened, and Commander Lately stood on the other side, looking far too pleased to be delivering any good news.

"Get up, old man."

Poole pushed himself to his feet, though the manacles around his wrists and ankles made it rather awkward.

"Ready to die?" Ryder said, his smile fixed and hungry.

"That's a really stupid question, you know."

Ryder crossed the tower cell calmly, swinging a set of keys. He unchained Poole, taking his time, humming off-tune all the while.

"I've yet to meet the man who wants me dead," Poole said.

"Patriarch has more important concerns."

"Well, now I'm offended." Poole rubbed the sore, broken skin of his wrist when the manacle fell away. "Who is he these days?"

"He prefers to remain anonymous."

"But, as you've said, I'm about to die. I'm sure I won't get a chance to tell anyone."

"He's far and above you. You don't deserve to know his name."

Poole sighed. "It's Amnon, isn't it?"

Ryder crushed his fingers into Poole's windpipe. The force sent the back of his head into the tower wall.

"It's not," Ryder snarled, "your concern."

Poole smirked. "Knew it."

"Killing you will be my greatest pleasure yet."

"Then get on with it."

Ryder tied Poole's wrists and shoved him forward, toward the tower door. A procession of Watchmen waited on the steps leading into the castle's bowels. They drew weapons and walked ahead of Poole and Ryder, leading the way into the cold, dry night, and the execution grounds beyond.

Redlawn—a gory nickname granted to what had once been a leisurely stretch of green between the castle walls. The old monarchs had taken to hosting their executions there, dyeing the grass red with men's lives. It had since been paved with flagstones, smooth and colorless under the moonlight. But the place's history hummed under their feet. How many people had lost head and blood and heartbeat right where Poole now stood?

A scaffold was set up in the center of Redlawn, with a simple wood block and basket set upon it. No executioner in sight—of course Ryder intended to do the honors himself.

The Watchmen gathered around the scaffold in a circle. Ryder jerked Poole forward, bringing him up the wooden steps.

"I'd read you your sentencing," Ryder said. "But it seems pointless."

"Agreed."

"Kneel."

Poole complied. The music of a sharp blade played in his ear. He took a deep breath. This would certainly be interesting, whatever happened.

What happened was not what he'd expected. A caw like the crushing beat of thunder roared over the courtyard. A fulcan swooped overhead, and Isobel leapt from its back, landing between the circled Watchmen and the scaffold.

"Ryder," she said. "Let the professor go."

The fulcan circled back, lower to the ground, and Aeyrin jumped off, a simple, rusty shotgun slung across her back. The huge bird settled behind her, looming as though in protection.

"Aeyrin." Poole began to rise, his heart beating hard in his throat. She couldn't be here, she couldn't risk it. She had no idea he couldn't—

Ryder grabbed him by his hair and drew his sword across Poole's throat, digging the blade in hard, breaking veins like little bits of string.

There was weightlessness—euphoria. A feeling like contentment settled in his stomach as he began to fall back— and then pain knifed through his stomach. It was cold and crawling and final, like every channel of his body—blood and bone and nerve—had focused on this one spot and would pour everything he used to be into awareness of this pain until he faded. He hit the scaffold, his hand going instinctively to his neck. It came back bright red and wet. His stomach pulsed with pain, and it finally made sense when he caught a broken glance of the demon-bone knife still stuck in him.

"Kill the Huntress," Ryder called to his Watchmen. "Leave the human for me."

No. Not her. Poole tried to cry out but found his throat useless for making any noise other than a distressed gurgle. He rolled onto his side, dragging himself forward across the scaffold. Swords rang, so near, and yet they sounded far away, nothing next to the rushing torrent of blood in his head. A stranger sound—the clatter and blast of a shotgun. Ryder's voice above the din.

"You'll pay for that, bitch."

Poole lifted his head toward the scene below the scaffold, his vision coming in and out of focus. Ryder's body rippled in rage as he lifted Aeyrin by the neck and threw her against the ground like a toy he'd grown frustrated with. He picked up the shotgun and bent its barrel over his knee.

"You're nothing without that, are you?" He threw the ruined weapon aside. Metal ground against brick as it skidded away.

Aeyrin tried to rise, but Ryder kicked her down. Distantly, Poole wondered how many humans could take such a beating from an Elonni and live. Everything inside her must be mush. But she kept pushing against Ryder and he kept punishing her with kicks. At last, he knelt before her and laced his fingers around her throat.

Poole listened to the death of her screams, the last embers of breath on her lips, unable to do anything but stumble and, at last, fall off the scaffold, useless.

And then—a burst of light, like the sun falling to earth. The fireball broke the courtyard open, flinging bricks and rubble. Poole was certain death had managed to claim him. Surely this was his mind's last mad conjuring before he faded away.

"Dr. Poole?" The voice above him was like Aeyrin's, only sharper, younger. "H-hang on. Don't die, all right?"

"Die?" he said. It sounded like a promise, like something he wouldn't mind at all. Aeyrin's death—that he couldn't take.

"Please hang on." Lacey rose and turned away. "Hey! *Get away from my mother!*"

Another crash of flames rocked the ground. Ryder stumbled away from Aeyrin as a cord of fire chased him across the courtyard like a biting snake. Lacey, her ruddy wings extended, flew after him.

Poole pulled the knife from his stomach and rose, stumbling, to fall mere feet from where Aeyrin lay, purple rings around her neck, blood on her lips. Her eyes met his and he reached for her with the hand still gripping the knife. "Take it," he said. Her fingers brushed his, and the world seemed to fade, like sudden, needful sleep.

AEYRIN WATCHED HIS eyes fade to unawareness. Her fingers gripped the knife blade, cutting into her flesh, and though she was distantly aware of the pain, it seemed a mere echo next to the tearing of her heart.

"No. Sol...come back..."

A girl's scream rang out close by—Aeyrin almost believed it was her own, but her voice seemed to have died on those last hopeless words.

Ryder stalked back over and kicked Poole's side. There was no resistance, no twitch of life, and he laughed. Aeyrin twisted the knife into her palm.

"Poor bastard." Ryder knelt beside Aeyrin. "Poor *you*. Seems like everyone you love dies." He dragged a finger under her chin. "Don't worry. Your daughter is next. But I'll make it quick."

Aeyrin jammed the knife into his side; blood flowed down her wrist. Ryder roared and fell back from her, white with pain. A circle of fire ignited around him, a burning, narrowing prison cell.

"Mum?"

Aeyrin pushed herself up onto her elbows. "*Lacey?*"

Her daughter knelt beside her, sweaty and dirty, but alive. Blood darkened the hair at her temple, red on red. Aeyrin reached out, but Lacey inched away.

"It's fine. Just a cut."

Relief warred with grief. She'd lost Sol only moments ago, yet here was Lacey, *safe*. Well...safe, but twisting with flames, her eyes reflecting the fire across her skin.

Lacey followed her mother's stare. "Um, don't panic, all right, but I can use fire magic. And I can't control it at the moment, so..."

Isobel limped over, tying off a makeshift tourniquet across her bicep with her teeth. "Aeyrin? Is he...?"

Aeyrin dared take her eyes away from Lacey and scrambled over to Sol. She pushed his hair, heavy with sweat and blood, from his eyes. Eyes that stared without comprehension.

"No," she said weakly.

"He can't be..." Lacey slumped down beside Aeyrin. "I thought—"

Her eyes darkened as they rose to the wheel of fire. The Commander snarled like a wounded beast in a trap. Her jaw clenched, and the fire moved in closer.

"Lacey." Isobel held up her hand. "Wait."

Lacey stopped pushing the flames closer, letting their hot breath hover close to the Commander without burning him.

Ryder spat into the flames. "What's wrong, Ingrid? Don't want to watch me die?"

Isobel smiled. "Oh, sweetie. No. I just want to be the one to kill you."

On the last word, Lacey dropped the flames, and Isobel grabbed the Commander by his hair. She pressed a blade into his neck and dragged it hard through flesh and artery; the blood behind his skin released like a broken dam. She kicked his chest, and he fell back, his eyes sightless on the sky above. Lacey dragged the flames back up and let them eat over his body, charring his clothes, his flesh, every little bit of matter that used to be Commander Ryder Lately.

Aeyrin stared down at Sol. The wounds in his neck and stomach yawned, impossibly huge and bright. She buried her face in his chest and let herself cry. She ignored the stench of blood and dirt and the feeling of torn skin. She could almost pretend they were lying beside each other in bed. Her imagination, torturing her, made her feel his arm curl around her waist, made her feel him turn towards her. She opened her eyes to find his own wide and...moving across her face, alive, studying her like she was a work of art.

She shot up. "Sol!"

"Hey, gorgeous," he said. His voice was like gravel under tires. "Come here often?"

"Holy gods!" Lacey scrambled back, fire twisting along her arms. Isobel took a step back, her hand hovering uncertainly over her knife. Aeyrin didn't care how he was back—he was *back*. She threw her arms around his neck as he tried to sit up.

"Ow," he said. She let go.

"I thought you were dead!"

"No. Bit of a sore throat."

She punched his arm. "You *ass*, you scared me to death." She sobbed once, but it somehow became a laugh.

"It'll take more than that to kill me," he said with a humorless smile. He took her hand and pressed it to the wound at his stomach. She drew her hand back, afraid to hurt him, but...the wound had gone, leaving only shiny pink skin like a scar. His neck, too, which had gaped like a second mouth, was sealed tight, only a thin line marking where he'd been cut.

"How did you...?" She looked into his eyes. "Sol?"

"Family curse," he said. Isobel stood above them, and her lips parted.

"Oh my God," she said. "You're...*Trueborn*."

"Trueborn?" Aeyrin said.

"He's..." Isobel waved her hands. "*Immortal*. The descendant of the first true king. The literal son of God."

Aeyrin felt the bizarre urge to laugh. "That's a bit ironic."

Lacey was shaking her head, still wrapped in flame. "When you say immortal..."

"'No weapon of man, nor fang of beast, nor age of the earth may render the flesh from thy bones,'" Isobel recited.

"My dad had that stitched into a throw pillow," Sol said. He rose and took Aeyrin's hands, lifting her with him.

Lacey looked up at him, her fire flickering to a calm. "But how? You're not..."

"I should explain," Sol said. He sighed. "My name was once Absolom Stone. And my father was the Patriarch of Sannus Eyreh."

376

44

RETRIBUTION

-*The Eastern*-

THE STREETS OF the Eastern were empty, quiet. So changed from the way the place had been before the Watchmen's rampage. The usually busy streets were crowded only with evidence of lives ruined in moments—snapped wands, lost shoes; broken windows and hanging doors. A torn fairy's wing lay soaking in a gutter, a glimmer against the brutal streets. Nathy paused beside a still, lumpy form lying half-off the pavement. The Watchmen couldn't even clean up the fucking bodies.

He knelt beside the dead woman, her face sunken and sallow in death. Her brittle fingers still clutched a wand. Death's rigor had already let her go, and now she moldered here like forgotten rubbish. He moved her hands over her heart, the wand centered between them.

"Go with the Sisters," he said. He rose, leaving the woman behind.

All this destruction, just to find one girl. Lacey would hate it—blame herself, probably.

Lacey...

No. It wasn't worth his time, thinking of her. She was with Saxon—who, yes, was an idiot, but Lacey could take care of herself. She'd gone with him. So?

When everything had gone wrong, she'd run off with Saxon, not Nathy, and what else did he expect? It's not like he'd offered. Not like he'd tried with her at all. He didn't want to try, even. He didn't...

She'd been a daydream, pointless and brief, like lighting a candle just because the light is pretty. He'd get over it. He wasn't any good for her, anyway.

But he could do the one thing he was good at.

ROSELYN RUARK FELL back against the pillows, a contented tilt to his lips. Times were hard—weren't they always? But it was the little things that got him through. He reached for the girl beside him, but she was already out of bed, on the other side of the room, hands shaking as she slipped on the torn remains of her dress.

"What's your problem?" he asked, genuinely curious.

She glared through her matted blond hair, green eyes sharp—hungry—and caked with black makeup and glitter. His girls dressed up just so they could dress down. But their faces were always perfect, dark messes.

He sat forward and watched her shake like a junkie. "Are you mad at me?" he said. "What did I do?"

"Fuck you."

He rolled his eyes. "Come on, Artemis. Don't be like that. Here I thought you were starting to like me."

She raked her hair back with red-painted fingernails like drops of blood, her eyes turned away from him. "Give it to me," she said. "I'm dying."

"Say sorry for being a bitch."

She breathed a small, shaky laugh, shook her head. "I'm sorry, Roz."

"All right," he sighed. "I can't stay mad at you."

She crossed the room, each step a stumble, a shake of her pale, narrow body. She crawled across the bed and curled against him, and he wrapped one arm around her. She grabbed his right wrist and bit into it. He felt the flash of weakness as his blood left him, but he wouldn't trade this. Watching her do it made him need her back. She licked his skin, catching the weak streams of blood from the wounds.

"Better?" he said.

She nodded, but with the hunger in her eyes gone, he could see what had been beneath—hate. Ruark thought he knew what that was about. He slapped her.

"What the hell, Roz?" She held the side of her face, fangs barred. He wrapped a hand around her throat and shoved her down into the mattress.

"You're ungrateful, you know that? I could have just killed you—but I made you better. Stronger than you could ever be. Yet you still look at me like *I'm* the bad guy?"

"Roz," she choked out, her fingers scrabbling at his hand.

"They abandoned you," he said, pressing his fingernails into the soft skin of her throat. "Flynn sacrificed you. And Nathy?" He squeezed his grip tighter. "You think he'd even want you like this? You're a lot more work than you're worth."

He reached into the bedside table, keeping his other hand around her throat, and brought out the dull iyrel knife he always kept there.

Her eyes swerved to the blade. "No, Roz, please."

He pressed the blade flat against her chest and she screamed, wrenching up but finding no escape, trapped beneath him. The iyrel snaked across her skin, burning thin black lines like veins around her collarbones.

"Tell you what," he said, pulling the knife back for a second. "I'm gonna kill Nathy myself. And I'm gonna make you watch. I'm going to carve him into a thousand pieces; maybe you can have his blood, whatever's left."

"Roz," she snarled, the beast rising to the surface.

"Yes, Artemis?"

"There's someone at the door."

"Yeah, I'm sure—"

He heard it then, too: Footsteps. His old instinct as a Huntsman never died, and he sensed this approach, the malice at his back. He grinned.

"Idiot."

NATHY'S HAND HOVERED over the doorknob. He'd waited a long time to kill Ruark. He just hoped it was as fun as he imagined.

He threw the door wide and just missed the knife careening toward him. It stuck in the wall by his head.

Ruark sat on the rumpled bed, legs crossed, smiling. He wore only trousers. Though thin, his chest was tight with hard muscle and flecked with scars. A length of gauze was wrapped around his midsection from where Nathy had stabbed him during their last encounter. The small room smelled of blood and sweat and sex.

"Hope your girlfriend's gone," Nathy said. "I'd hate to drag anyone else into this."

"Please, come in," Ruark said. His smile flashed. "How's the wing?"

Nathy grabbed him by the hair and threw him to the hardwood floor.

"Ah. Temper. Has anyone told you you're exactly like your father?"

"Believe it or not—" Nathy stepped down, hard, and felt the sudden, crumbling snap of bone beneath his foot. "You're not the first person to say that."

Ruark screamed through his teeth and cradled his shattered wrist. "You've got issues, kid."

Nathy kneeled before him and smiled. "You're right. I do. Fortunately, this is the perfect outlet." He twirled a knife between his fingers. "Where would you like it? Me, I was thinking I'd stab you through your eye, but I'm open to suggestions."

"If I die, Lacey dies."

Nathy dropped the knife, and Ruark swiped for it. He kicked Nathy back and used the momentum to launch to his feet.

Ruark considered the knife now clutched in his palm. "I knew that would get you. You're funny, Nathy. You want to kill me for what I did to your last girlfriend." He knelt, digging his knee into Nathy's stomach, and pressed the knife to his neck. "But here you are, already mad for another girl."

"Fuck off," Nathy said, his voice strained by the pressure of the blade at his throat.

"See? Right there." Ruark dragged the blade slowly, drawing a thin line of blood. "It's all in your face. I could tell, y'know? The way you tried to protect her—hopeless romantic, aren't we, kiddo?"

Nathy shoved Ruark off; the momentum sent the blade deeper into his throat, but the pain was temporary, easy to forget next to the flaring rage in his heart. He drew his sword.

"I should have started with this," he said, and swung the blade. Ruark ducked aside easily.

"Come on, Nathy, when has that ever worked?" Ruark listed his head. "You know, that's why you could never kill me. You're stronger—I won't say you aren't. But you're too...angry. It makes you useless."

"Thanks for the advice." Nathy swung out at the showman again; once more, he dodged easily.

"Now this is pathetic. And to think, the time you're wasting here when that sweet little mutt is being sent away to—" He drew his finger across his throat. "She won't be so cute without a head."

"What are you talking about?" Nathy said through his teeth.

"Delilah St. Luke has her. Which makes this her last night on earth. Unless you hear me out." Ruark shrugged. "Look, kiddo, I know it's hard to take, but I'm the one holding the strings here."

"I know who you work for," Nathy said. "You're just a shill for Sannus Eyreh."

"Exactly!" Ruark tossed his hands. "Thank you! Not as stupid as I thought. I work for them—but I'm not *one* of them. All that Old Name, Elonni supremacy shit? Not my tune. They just happen to pay rather well for what I do best."

"Murdering nocturnes."

"Pays the rent." Ruark shook his head. "Don't get self-righteous with me, kiddo. We're in the same line of work. And it just so happens I'm interested in taking you on as a client."

Nathy ground his teeth. He wanted to kill him, wanted to swing his sword until a blow struck, but found himself saying, "Talk, then."

"There's the idiot I know and love." Ruark hopped onto the bed, crossed his legs, and grinned. "You gonna sit nicely and listen?"

"Yeah, Roz," Nathy said. "Get on with it."

"Drop your weapon first."

Nathy stabbed the blade into the mattress an inch from Ruark's knee. "Happy?"

"Ecstatic." Ruark smiled. "The Elderon and I have a...mutually beneficial relationship. Hunters, we're not the best loved of the military. Too wild for their liking. All these years, I've bought my right to live with other people's secrets.

Those prudes would've shut my show down in an instant if I didn't know so much—and oh, what I know."

"So far you haven't said a goddamn thing that makes not killing you worth it," Nathy said.

"Patience, jackass. Normally it's pretty ordinary stuff. One of 'em's a paedo, another is fucking hookers. Boring. But here I come upon a fun little fact from my old hunting partner."

Nathy quirked an eyebrow.

"When Mort left it all behind to be with your mom, he tells me if I want to make a good living, I ought to know that the Pontiff himself is in a cult. A cult replete with torture and murder, no less. And then, wouldn't you know, the Justice is in it too, and the Commander. Easy money. Those poor fools let me do anything just to keep their secret. Yeah, the Elders are powerful, but if ordinary people knew? Hell, even Elonni would revolt, then.

"But the day your dad had an attack of conscious and went scrambling back to his cult, I found a better way to make money. Do what *they* want. Guard a sword. Make sure someone goes missing. Slice up a few faces." His eyes landed on Nathy's scar. "Of course, Mort usually wanted to do that part. He thought it was so fun."

"So, you're a mercenary for Sannus Eyreh," Nathy said. "I don't understand why I'm not killing you right now."

"Kid—what've I been saying this whole time? I don't have a dog in this fight. I go where the money goes. I side with the best value every time. Right now, you're holding the cards. I know I can't fight you. You're powerful, you're pissed off, and you're not gonna stop hunting me until you're satisfied. Right?"

Nathy let out a sudden, hard breath. "You want me to spare you? For what?"

"First of all, your sword back. Your mom and the Nine were going to use it to kill the Patriarch of Sannus Eyreh. Which is why she gave it to you. Mort was on to her; she knew she didn't have much time left. So she gave it to you to keep out of their hands until you could deliver it safely to Will Barker."

"My mom wanted Will Barker to have the sword?"

"She thought he was still alive," Ruark said. "Your poor mother had no idea she was sending you off to fight for a lost cause. Tragic."

382

"Why did they need that sword, though? What was the point?"

"You really don't know anything, huh? Kid, that sword is the only thing that can kill Patriarch. All that shit about their bloodline coming from Elrosh? It's true. And the truest of Trueborns is as good as immortal. You could stab him in the heart with an ordinary sword and he'd just heal right up."

"But that's only the Stones," Nathy said. "They're all dead."

"Yeah, no they aren't." Ruark smirked. "Solomon got his, that's for sure. Hacked to pieces with the only sword that could kill him. His sons, too. Most of them. One was already dead. And one slipped away."

"How do you know this?"

"Because I know who killed them," Ruark said slowly, as though Nathy were too stupid to follow along. "Piece it together, come on. Who last had the sword?"

Nathy's blood went cold.

"And who had a nice promotion waiting in the wings if all the Stones were dead?"

"Shit," Nathy said. "My father killed an entire family...so he could rule over a cult."

"He had his reasons. Namely, saving you. Sannus Eyreh wouldn't exactly let you in given you're a bastardized mutt, no offense. But if Mort was Patriarch? Hey, maybe his freak kid could have a place of honor after all."

"You're trying to say he murdered eight people for me?"

"He's a thoughtful one, ain't he?"

Nathy raked a hand through his hair. "You realize you've just told me what I want to know? What's your reason for me not killing you now?"

Ruark leaned forward, a grin splitting his face. "You're gonna need an insider to fight this war. I know where and when Patriarch plans to strike. I know *how* he plans to strike. He's knocked every player off the board—Poole's in Gamault, Crane's under a fresh layer of dirt, and Lacey is in the hands of Sannus Eyreh's dogs—all planned by a guy who knows his enemies better than they know themselves. And if you want to stop him from killing Lacey the same way your mom died, you'll need to let me go—so I can help you."

"D'you know how long I've waited to kill you? And you want me to throw that away on the possibility that you're telling the truth?"

"Do you want to take the chance that I'm not? You don't want another dead girlfriend on your hands."

Nathy punched the showman, relishing the feel of bone and blood on his knuckles. He threw himself on top of Ruark before the man could struggle up. But Ruark had his knife, and it dug into Nathy's bicep with hot, ripping pain. Ruark's fist collided with Nathy's good eye, momentarily blinding him, but his instincts were better than his sight. He landed his own blow, knocking Ruark off the bed, where he crashed against the ground. He grabbed the showman by the throat.

Revenge is a boy's game.

Isobel's words cut through the blind rage working through him. Why was he killing Ruark? Because of Artemis. Artemis and no other reason. But Artemis was dead.

Lacey was still alive. He could give her a life, the thing he'd let slip from Artemis. If he'd just let this go...

Nathy threw Ruark down. "Fine."

"What was that, kiddo?"

"I said, *fine.* You help me stop these lunatics, and I'll let you live."

"And never, ever kill me. I don't want you turning around the minute Patriarch is gone and knifing me."

Nathy pulled out his wand. "We'll take a blood oath. If either of us ever goes back on our word—"

"We'll drop dead on the spot." Ruark grinned, hair caught in the blood of his lips. "I like you, kiddo. Hey, fix my fucking wrist while you've got that out."

Nathy sneered and shot a spell at Ruark's broken bone. The showman winced.

"Did you have to make it hurt?"

"Yes, asshole. Gimme that." Nathy held out his hand. Ruark slapped the knife into it, and Nathy slit a long vertical cut down his left forearm.

"I'll let you do the honors." Nathy handed the knife back and Ruark copied his action. The stink of blood hung heavy on the air.

Nathy held out his bloody arm. "Shake on it."

384

As soon as Ruark's hand clasped Nathy's, Nathy took his wand and pressed its tip to their joined hands.

"Fansi lotym myn septu, mose loto mose."

My word is my life, and his word his.

The wand glowed a faint, smog-like black, and tendrils of darkness curled around their joined hands. They crept up both men's arms and wound around the wounds like a stitching. When the smog had gone, their wounds had sealed, leaving identical long black scars.

"Ladies will love this," Ruark said, examining his.

"You're sick, y'know." Nathy pocketed his wand. "Where's the sword?"

Ruark turned toward an overflowing trunk in the corner of the room. Nathy's wound flashed through his body in nauseous waves, but he stayed on is feet, scanning the room for possible unpleasant surprises. Everywhere he smelled blood, and it reminded him of the one thing he wished he could forget—Artemis's body, cold and torn, the stench of battle soaked into her clothes.

He would never close the wound she left, not even with Lacey. And now Lacey had left her own gash, and she didn't even know it. He hadn't known it until now, when he'd given up everything he'd wanted to save her.

A faint sound like a muffled cry came from the coat closet beside the bed. Nathy glanced over at Ruark, still cursing and shuffling through the contents of the trunk. He crept closer to the closet, his hand extended. He gripped the doorknob.

"Found it," Ruark called. "Hey, hands off. Private property."

Nathy jerked his head at the closet. "You got someone in there?"

"Rats. This place is a dive. Here." He tossed the sword; Nathy caught it by the hilt. The blade was at least five feet long, heavy and glowing with a strange energy. He turned the blade, hunting for the inscription he knew was there: *To bend the knee of God.*

This was it. This was what he'd wasted too many thoughts and lives for.

He looked up. Ruark was grinning. He should have been a grinning corpse.

"So. Where to, mate?"

Nathy curled his lip. "Come on. Jackass."

"I missed working side by side with a Fairborn," Ruark said. Nathy's fist curled. *You can't kill him, you can't kill him.*

He had lost his chance forever, his opportunity to be baptized in his enemy's blood, to take communion of dead flesh and feel the sanctity of vengeance.

For a girl.

So much for retribution.

45

THE PROFESSOR'S TALE

-Ashborn-

ISOBEL'S FULCAN SOARED high above Theopolis, the city a mere scattering of golden light and white stone. Lacey shivered against the icy air. She hadn't had a chance to grab a coat while fleeing Calvary, and the wind tore right through the elegant dress she wore. She thought suddenly of Saxon, of his eyes falling on her. Of the way he'd looked, one moment, like he could love her. And then...

She shook her head. She was leaving him behind for good now.

Soon they were flying over the country estates thrown wide over the low hills beyond the city. They flew too fast and too high for her to pick out which one was Calvary. She hoped he was safe there, that his mother and Kragen didn't believe he had let her escape. One look at his burnt leg ought to convince them.

Isobel steered the fulcan down to the outskirts of a small town. She slipped off the neck of the great bird gracefully, and Dr. Poole and Aeyrin followed. Lacey, still shaking, remained on the bird's back.

"Lacey?" Aeyrin reached out her hand to help her down. Lacey didn't take it.

"Is it safe here?" she said, her voice shuddering with more than cold.

Isobel nodded. "It's a human town; nobody will bother you. We aren't staying long, besides."

Lacey let her mother help her down from the fulcan. The four of them walked silently into town, Isobel leading the way. The streets were narrow, the shops stout brick structures flickering with candlelight. Isobel stopped at a tavern on the street corner and they shuffled inside.

"Well," Dr. Poole said, "I could use a drink."

Isobel nodded absently. "I'll see about rooms."

Lacey and Aeyrin were left standing by the door. Aeyrin, tentatively, put a hand on Lacey's shoulder.

"Are you all right?"

"I'm not dead," Lacey said. "So, there's that."

"What happened while you were gone?"

Lacey shook her head. "Later. I'm still processing Dr. Poole resurrecting from the dead."

"That is...a lot to take in." Aeyrin shuttled her toward a small, cozy lounge area with a long couch and several worn armchairs. "Come on. We'll try to relax a moment, yeah?"

Lacey sank numbly onto the couch; Aeyrin sat beside her, throwing occasional, worried glances at her.

"I'm fine," Lacey said.

"I know." Aeyrin patted her leg. Dr. Poole arrived, holding a generous glass of whiskey and a pint of beer.

"Here you are." He held out the beer toward Aeyrin, but Lacey took it and allowed herself a hearty swig before relinquishing it to her mother.

"So," she said as Dr. Poole took one of the chairs across from them. "You're a divine being. That's gotta sting."

He smirked. "Shut it. The only divine thing about me is my charm and dashing good looks."

Lacey and Aeyrin stared at him, unresponsive.

"Right. Not funny." Dr. Poole sipped his drink.

Lacey took a deep breath and leaned forward. "You're a Stone."

"Right."

"Which means your family are the leaders of Sannus Eyreh."

Dr. Poole's gaze whipped to hers. "How do you know about them?"

"We found their book," Lacey said. "In this ruined old house down by Fryer's Grove. The *Malus Vylarus.*"

Dr. Poole's jaw clenched. "They had a meeting house there. One of the locations they'd go to for their—*rituals.*"

"Rituals?"

"They would capture nocturnes and...sacrifice them. Sometimes torture them for information first. They were always looking for—well, I take it you know about the Ruined Queen by now?"

"Flynn was very informative, yes." She looked away from him. "Were you ever a part of it?"

"I was inducted into it, as all children of Old Names are. But no, I never participated." Dr. Poole tipped his drink side to side, watching the ice move. "I always hated my father, what he stood for. But I think maybe I would've been just like him, if not for my mother."

"Your mother?" Aeyrin said softly.

"She never wanted anything to do with him and his bloody cult. But the Old Names always intermarry, and she was a Sanso. She had no choice. She was my father's third wife. He must have always been a cruel man, but by then... By then, he was only a monster." He shut his eyes and clenched his fist. "And after years of his abuse, she just wanted to die. I helped her. One injection of Cericide and she just...fell asleep." He met Aeyrin's gaze. "That package you were told to give me? It held the same bottle of Cericide and the syringe I used."

"Is that what the Commander meant?" Aeyrin said. "When he said you were a murderer?"

"Yes." Dr. Poole swallowed. He pulled up his right sleeve and displayed the scar Lacey knew was there but had nearly forgotten. "My father branded me as a traitor. An enemy of God. I was the Seventh Son, the destined traitor."

"Destined?"

"The first Son of God had seven sons," Dr. Poole said. "His youngest betrayed him, according to the old legends. Now, any seventh son born to an Old Name family is regarded as cursed. If he'd known my mother was pregnant with another son, he would have killed her. He would have liked to kill me after I was born, but there's a sacred law in the *Malus Vylarus*. Killing a Son of God is akin to spilling the blood of Elrosh himself. It's a cardinal sin. The most he could do was mark me and banish me."

"What happened to your family?" Lacey asked. "I heard all the Stones were dead."

"They are—or, I thought they were. After I was banished, I changed my name and enrolled in university. I didn't hear of them again until just before the war, when the entire capital was in a panic because the oldest of the Old Names had been wiped out. My father and my five half-brothers were found with their throats slit in the family estate."

"But how?" Lacey said. "I just saw you with your throat slit and you popped right back up."

"There's one weapon that can kill us," Dr. Poole said. "A sacred sword forged by the first Trueborn. Its blade is the only thing that can end our lives."

"The first Trueborn made a sword that could kill him?"

"He had a little more sense than his descendants," Dr. Poole said. "He knew that absolute power can't be controlled. He sought to temper his own kind. That sword was passed down in my family for millennia. My father never let it out of his sight." He shrugged. "Until, apparently, he did. Someone killed them with it. When I heard what had happened, I went back to the estate. The sword was gone."

"The..." Lacey blinked. "Oh, my God, I know who took it." She met his waiting gaze. "Mortimer Fairborn. I met his son, Nathy, and...well, it's complicated, because Nathy is half-mage, and his father was horrible to him. But he also wanted him in Sannus Eyreh, I suppose. But Nathy's mother—she stole the sword and gave it to Nathy. But then Nathy's father stole it back."

"Who has it now?" Dr. Poole asked levelly, though Lacey could hear the strain in his voice.

"Roselyn Ruark."

"That's unfortunate," Dr. Poole said. "We could really use that sword."

"But why?" Lacey said. "All your family is dead, and the other Old Names aren't immortal—are they?"

"They're not," he said, his eyes shifting away. "But the problem is, my entire family isn't dead."

Lacey and Aeyrin leaned forward, waiting. Dr. Poole took a long drink from his glass.

"My father and five half-brothers were found in the estate. But that leaves one more brother. My mother's other son."

"He wasn't with them?" Aeyrin said.

Dr. Poole shook his head. "He'd gone away not long after I was banished to be a missionary abroad. I've always kept my ear to the ground, waiting to hear he's returned. But there was never any sign. Until you gave me that package," he told Aeyrin.

Her mouth dropped open. "*That*—that was your brother?"

"Who else would know about it? I was never charged with killing my mother. Only Amnon knew. And he hated me for it.

"Amnon was never meant to be Patriarch. My eldest half-brother, Arctan, was being groomed for it. Amnon, for all his faults, never seemed the type. I almost can't believe he's taken it on. Suppose it's some sense of duty he has to Sannus Eyreh."

Lacey sank back against the couch. "So we're fighting your brother. And Nathy's father."

"*You're* not fighting anyone," Aeyrin said. "We just got you back."

"Your mother is right," Dr. Poole said. "You're safe now, away from the Nine and Sannus Eyreh. I'll get both of you far away from here."

"You're coming, too," Aeyrin said, sitting up straighter. "If your brother has been threatening you, you need to leave as well. We can all go." She smiled faintly, hesitantly, as though she couldn't believe it, but sorely wanted to.

Dr. Poole rubbed the back of his neck, trying to bury his own smile. Lacey looked between the two of them.

"Wait...are you...?"

They looked at each other.

"Ha." Lacey smirked. "Knew it."

"Right, well." Aeyrin cleared her throat. "After your father left to join the Nine... You wouldn't remember this, but you and I lived in Theopolis for a time. With Sol."

It didn't surprise Lacey. It didn't even sting. Will had never deserved Aeyrin. But still, she needed to know.

"What exactly happened with Dad?" Lacey said. "And please, don't try to hide it anymore. I get why you hid me away, I get that you were both afraid. But I had a right to know."

Aeyrin looked down. "You're right. You did."

Dr. Poole took a swig of his drink. "Suppose we should have known you'd figure it out one day. You know we only wanted to protect you."

"You're not the only one," Lacey muttered. Then, stronger: "But I deserve to know who and what I am. And all Flynn told me about my dad was this ridiculous hero legend. Somehow, I don't think that's the whole story."

Dr. Poole and Aeyrin exchanged glances. They seemed to silently communicate something. At last, Aeyrin looked at Lacey. "What do you want to know?"

"How did he find out about what he was?"

Aeyrin's shoulders slumped, as though the memory weighed on her. "He always knew who his father was. He was raised by his uncle, his mother's brother. And he told your dad what had happened. Not that he needed to. Will remembered Donoveir." Her eyes shone with a deep sadness. "He told me his father had murdered his mother, but he didn't know why. It always plagued him. Donoveir was an Old Name, but Will never wanted anything to do with it. He hated the Elonni elite. So, when he was conscripted into the army...he was just so angry."

Dr. Poole leaned forward, his depleted drink held between his hands. "That's when he went back to Fryer's Grove. He was stationed in Denmoor—it wasn't far. He found Flynn there. I hadn't heard from him in months myself, but he wrote me after that. Said he'd found something that would change the course of the war. For the nocturnes."

"He was given a temporary leave," Aeyrin said. "But when he came home, he was entirely different. Still so angry, yet hopeful. But...it scared me. He talked about having power, about some book his mother had left him. He...told me he'd done something. A series of rituals. And there were more he needed to do."

"The Rites," Lacey said. "If someone like Dad—like me—has the Book of the Nine, we can get stronger. Borrow nocturne powers."

Aeyrin nodded. "That explains it, then."

"Explains what?"

"He..." She looked at Dr. Poole. He picked up the sentence for her.

"He tried to do a ritual on you. Brought one of the heirs over to do a Rite."

"When I caught them doing that to you," Aeyrin said, "I grabbed you. But—look, he was completely changed by then,

392

But...perhaps the weight of the world is a little much for you to bear alone."

"Mum wants us to run," Lacey said.

"She's a good mother, then."

"Right. But...my father started something. Maybe it needs to be finished."

Isobel raised an eyebrow.

"I keep thinking about Nathy," Lacey said. "What his father did to him. What Sannus Eyreh has done to everyone. My father was too broken for this. I'm not."

"Will Barker was a warrior, sweetie. You don't have to like him, but don't think a level head makes you a match for his legacy."

"I'm not saying it does." Lacey sat up straighter. "I don't know if I can do this. But I can't just run away."

Isobel took a sip of her wine, her beautiful red lips turned in a smile. "And how can I help?"

Lacey looked back toward the lounge. Her mother and Dr. Poole were happy at last. They wouldn't understand why she was leaving now. But they'd be back together soon. She hoped they knew that. She turned back to Isobel. "Can you get me back to Fryer's Grove?"

"I can." Isobel rested her chin on her palm. "Indulge me: What made you change your mind?"

"I haven't. Not yet. But...I need to talk to my grandfather."

46

THE LONG LIFE OF ANTENOR FLYNN

-Fryer's Grove-

THE FULCAN LANDED in the courtyard of Fryer's Grove in the early morning a day later. Dawn waxed across the horizon, pinkish light peeling back the safety and secrecy of night. Isobel dismounted, graceful as ever. Lacey, cold and sore from riding upon the great bird for so many hours, nearly collapsed when her feet touched solid ground.

"All right there?" Isobel said.

Lacey steeled herself and nodded. Together they walked toward the house. Before they'd even made it to the porch, the doors flew wide, and Alastair ran toward her.

"Lacey! Where have you been?" He dragged her into a surprisingly strong hug. "It's been days."

She peeled away a little, looking curiously into his gray eyes. "I left a note."

Alastair tossed his hands. "I never saw it. First you and Saxon vanish, then Nathy—"

"Nathy left?"

Isobel cut in. "Where is he? Did he say where he was going?"

"He just got back." Alastair shook his head. "Lacey, it's— it's mental. You've got to come talk sense into him."

Isobel and Lacey looked at each other, then ran toward the house, Alastair trailing behind.

"Second-floor study," Alastair called, and the three of them piled into the lift. Alastair dropped a stale biscuit to the floor for Jack.

They rushed toward the study, Isobel leading the way and throwing the door wide. The room was much changed from Lacey's last visit—most notably due to a trail of rubble across the hardwood, leading back to a crumbly hole in the wall adjacent to Flynn's room.

"What the...?" Lacey looked from the wall to the opposite side of the room. The tenants of Fryer's Grove all hovered around the grand desk in the corner—Alice sitting on its edge, Poe leaning against the window, and Jade, yelling at the person sitting behind the desk.

Nathy had his feet kicked up on the scarred wood, seemingly unbothered as she berated him.

"You've put everyone in danger," Jade said. "If I'd have known *this* is what you had in mind—!"

Isobel halted in the middle of the study. "Jade?"

Jade turned. The anger on her face dissolved, leaving a wide grin and sparkling eyes. "Izzy! You're—I *knew* you were alive!"

Jade ran to Isobel, who caught her, and then they were entangled in a kiss.

"Don't you ever fucking scare me like that again," Jade said.

Isobel sighed. "I—"

"Shut up." Jade pulled her back in

Nathy rose from the desk, eyes on Lacey. She looked away, thinking suddenly of their kiss, and of Saxon. She blushed.

"You're the first girl I stormed a mansion for, and you weren't even there to be rescued."

"You went to Calvary? Was Saxon—"

"No one was home," he cut in, his eyes falling away.

"Um. Thank you. For trying."

He shrugged and looked quickly at the hole in the wall, then back at her. "Why did you come back?"

"Ah...should I not have?"

Isobel and Jade broke apart, and now, Isobel looked at Nathy. "She's doing the right thing, Nathaniel. She's going to help us fight Sannus Eyreh."

Jade glared at her cousin. "Oh, well *he* thinks he's already got that figured out."

"I do," Nathy said.

"What do you mean?" Lacey said, walking up to the desk. "Where did you—" Her words died as her eyes fell on him. "What happened?"

His left forearm was wrapped from wrist to elbow in white gauze, yet there seemed to be no blood. He smirked. "You should see the other guy."

"*Who?*"

"Me."

Lacey turned to the source of the voice and stepped back at the sight of the lean figure lounging by the fireplace. Roselyn Ruark's eye was shadowed with bruises, his nose broken, but otherwise, he seemed his old, aggrandized self.

Isobel drew her knife. Lacey called her fire to her hands.

"Calm down, ladies." Ruark gazed at Lacey, eyes flickering with amusement and dislike. "I'm not here to cause trouble."

Lacey turned slowly back to Nathy, afraid to take her eyes off Ruark. "What happened to killing him?"

"Change of plans. He's helping us."

"Are you insane?" Isobel said. "Nathy, this thing—"

"Is the worst person in the eleven continents? Yeah. That's why he's helping us. Horrible people with morals are always problem. Horrible people with none come in handy once in a while."

Ruark threw up his hands with a small *what-can-you-do* smile.

"I told him this was insane," Jade said.

Isobel looked at her. "Can you read his intent?"

"I—yes." Jade bit the inside of her cheek. "It's not malicious. But that doesn't mean we should trust him."

"I tend to agree." Isobel twisted her knife between her fingers, eyes on Ruark.

Lacey drew her fire back and turned to Nathy. "You know he killed my father, right?"

"It wasn't like I *wanted* to," Ruark said. "I had a job; I did it."

Lacey shot a burst of fire at his feet. He jumped back just in time.

"I'm not saying any of us have to like him," Nathy said.

Lacey crossed her arms, listing her head. "And what about Artemis?"

Nathy's eyes flicked away. "She's dead," he said. "Turns out dead people don't want or need your help."

"Are you all right?" Lacey said tentatively.

"Never better." He walked around his desk and stopped, eyes on Ruark. "Head out. And don't fuck this up."

Ruark's eyes flicked to Nathy's bandaged forearm and then to his eyes. "I don't think that's an option. Don't worry, Fairborn, you'll get what you want out of this. Got the sword?"

Nathy nodded once and unsheathed a blade at his back. The metal gleamed a strange, sunny orange. A set of Annanym was carved just below the hilt.

"Good luck, then." Ruark grinned. "Don't lose that, okay, kiddo?" He saluted with two fingers and left the study.

Everybody turned their eyes to Nathy. Isobel spoke first. "What makes you think you can trust him? *Roselyn Ruark?* Nathy, he—"

"I know what he did, I know what he is, and I know what I'm doing," Nathy said, turning the hilt of the sword in his palm.

"What's that then?" Lacey said, nodding to the new weapon.

"The sword my mother wanted me to have," he said. "It's the only thing that can kill Sannus Eyreh's Patriarch."

"You got it back." Lacey eyed the sword, its strange glow like sunlight trapped in the metal. "Dr. Poole told me about that."

Nathy raised an eyebrow. "What would he know about it?"

"Oh—right. Dr. Poole is actually Solomon Stone's son. He's on our side," she said hurriedly. "But apparently his brother is the new Patriarch."

Nathy nodded. "Good to know."

"So, what's your plan, then?" Isobel said, crossing her arms. "What can Ruark do for us that we can't do ourselves?"

"He was working for them," Nathy said, sheathing the blade. "And they think he's still working for them."

"How do you know he's not?" Lacey said.

"We have an understanding."

"What does that mean?"

"It means we're all set for the upcoming battle, and you need to leave."

Lacey's head snapped back in surprise. "Me? I thought I was the secret weapon."

"No, this is the secret weapon," he said, jerking his thumb toward the sword at his back. "You're their target. And don't take offense, but you're not ready to fight anybody."

"Excuse *me*, but I can set anybody I want to on fire."

He blinked. "Sorry?"

"I'm part Ferno. It's why Flynn was throwing fire at me. He knew I wouldn't actually get hurt. He was trying to drag my powers back out. It worked."

"She's not half bad," Isobel said.

Nathy shook himself. "This is weird. Okay. Even so. You're exactly who they're after. I'd rather you not be here."

"Nathy." Lacey took a step closer to him, their eyes locked. "I am *doing this*. I'm going to get the Book, I'm going to perform whatever Rites I can, and I'm going to destroy these lunatics before they hurt anybody else I care about. I'd rather you helped me, but if you're going to be a prat, I'll gladly leave you out."

He considered her for a long moment, eyes narrowed. "You can really set people on fire?"

"Care for a demonstration?"

"I'm good." He smiled. "And fine. You're in."

"Good. Now." She took a deep breath. "We need to talk to Flynn."

THEY LEFT THE study for the room next door. Lacey steeled her nerves and knocked, pushing the door wide after a long, silent moment had passed.

Flynn sat at his cluttered desk, head in his hands, golden hair leaking between his fingers. He peeked up at them as they entered and sighed.

"I thought you wouldn't come back."

Nathy eyed the desk. "See you got that back."

"You scuffed the floor," Flynn said dully.

"Oops."

Lacey sat on a stack of books and Nathy leaned against a bookshelf, his shoulders tense despite his light tone. He didn't meet Flynn's questioning gaze, and, at last, Flynn turned back to Lacey.

"Lacey, I'm—"

"My grandfather. I know."

Nathy's jaw dropped; he stared at Flynn. "What is she talking about?"

Lacey swallowed. "Your father wasn't the Ferno Olgarth Fryer brought from Sumri—it was you. You were the teacher Latrice talked about in that letter." Lacey worked the thick bronze ring she had found in Latrice's room from her finger. "You gave her this." She placed the ring on the desk, where it glowed against the detritus. "You knew what she was when you saw the Book. And you wanted her to unlock her powers. You were the Ferno Heir, so you were the perfect person to guide her."

Flynn smiled faintly. "I wouldn't say perfect."

"You?" Nathy began to shake but controlled himself, tensing. "How? There's no way you're old enough—"

"I was thirty-nine when she came here," Flynn said. His eyes never left Lacey's. "If I'd let nature take its course, yes, I'd be quite dead. But as I'm sure you've figured out, we Fernos are adept at potions." He extracted a small vial from his desk and handed it to Lacey. "I take that every day. It's popularly known as the elixir of life. It keeps me from aging. But technically I'm, gods, what is it now...? Ninety-eight, I believe."

"You look good," Lacey said with a smirk. She returned the vial to his extended hand, and he slipped it into his pocket. "So. Why keep yourself alive?"

"Revenge is a powerful motivator," he said with a smile to Nathy, who looked away. "I was torn from my home, forced to serve a vile family for two generations. And then that monster killed the woman I loved. And his little cult, they stood for everything I hate. As far as I knew, I was the last Ferno heir. The end of the line. If we were to have any hope of seeing the Ruined Queen's heir back on the throne, I needed to stay alive until it happened."

"So..." Lacey met his eyes, searching for any hint of dishonesty. "You didn't know my father was your son?"

"Not until he returned here." Flynn stared off at his bookshelves, his eyes lost. "I'll admit, I wanted little to do with Latrice's children. I hardly interacted with them. And, if she knew Will was mine, she never told me. But...there he was.

Right in front of me. Latrice's son, with the power of fire. I suppose it's not surprising."

"But you saved him," Lacey said. "When Donoveir tried to kill him—it was you, wasn't it, who pulled him out of the water?"

"Very astute." He shrugged. "I was trying to preserve the Monarch's bloodline. I would have saved both boys if I could. Besides, I didn't want to watch innocent children die for his madness. Even if I believed them to be Donoveir's." His gaze flicked to Nathy. "Did you get your sword back?"

Nathy's hand traced the sword's hilt, numb.

"It's the only thing that can kill Patriarch," Flynn said. He smiled at Lacey. "And you are the only one who can stop this madness." He reached into his desk and extracted a small jar. Inside was a yellowed and rot-edged paper, rolled tight and nestled beneath the cork. He tapped the paper out and smoothed it on his desk. Lacey faced it toward herself so she might read it. It was written in Sumrian

"It's a page from the Book. My Rite as Firekeeper to pass on to the Ruined Queen's descendant. I performed it on Latrice, and then on your father." He nodded to Nathy. "And he is your Sage, the mage heir."

Lacey turned to Nathy, blinking. "Did you know?"

"He just told me," Nathy said, his voice low. "Sorry, kid, but I don't actually know how to help you."

"You'll find your way." Flynn tapped the page between them. "We all have one. And with the eight Rites and the Book, you'll be able to stop Sannus Eyreh."

"I don't understand," Lacey said. "If you loved Latrice so much, why did you use her?"

"I didn't use her," Flynn said, his voice low, angry.

"She said as much in her letter. 'I cannot be your weapon.' You just wanted her powers."

"I loved that girl," he said, leaning forward so quickly Lacey jerked back, thinking for a moment he would hurt her. "Not merely for what she was. We were both prisoners here. We needed each other."

He leaned back in his chair, eyes on the ceiling, as though he were watching the memories unfold above him. "Olgarth brought me here when I was just a boy. At first, he seemed to

404

have little use for me beyond torment. He wondered what happened when a Ferno touched water. The short answer is, nothing. But we can suffocate, same as anyone. He would take me down to the beach and have his other servants hold me beneath the waves until I flailed. I hoped every day that he would finally just kill me. He never did." He calmed, looked at his hands clasped on the desk. "And so maybe, Lacey, you can understand why I wanted to hurt them back."

She looked down at her hands, her fingers twisted together. He continued.

"When Olgarth died, and Donoveir inherited the house, I hoped things might change. They did—for the worse. Donoveir had peculiar habits, you see. He liked to go into town, find young mages and fairies and elves looking to earn a living with their bodies. He would go into the forest with them and come out alone. It was my job, once a month, to pick the bones from the forest floor and burn them."

His eyes met hers, challenging, but she wouldn't look away. She beat back the horror and sickness and waited. He smiled with raised eyebrows.

"And then Latrice came. I adored that girl the moment she crossed the threshold. Of course, I was terrified to go anywhere near her, because I was sure it would be obvious to anyone how I felt about her. I bullied her maids to favor her, treat her kindly. I gave them gifts I wanted passed on to her. It took me months before I finally spoke to her."

Now he looked away, his face contorted with wretched memory. "He was cruel to her from the beginning. But she endured everything with a strength I've never seen in another person. He would beat her for some insignificant thing, and she would go to the parlor and knit afterwards, as though nothing had happened.

"One night, I made a fire and brought her tea and...we just talked. For hours. Donoveir never missed her once he was done with her; nobody noticed us."

He sighed. "I know...I know I changed her. In some ways for the better, but in many ways for the worse. But things were good for so long... She seemed happy when we were together."

"What changed?" Lacey said.

"I told her I was the Firekeeper. She knew of her heritage, what the Book meant for her. But she had never imagined awakening the powers. I suggested that it was time—that the both of us had suffered enough under Elonni rule.

"I wanted to find the other heirs, to bring them to her. I wanted to change things. She did, too. We thought it would be a revolution. Payment, for the blood of my people, for every young woman forced into a loveless marriage. We were going to restore the rightful heir to the throne—the Ruined Queen's line would rule again.

"I left for a time. I escaped so I might find the others. I rallied the mage, werewolf, and vampire Heirs. I was gone for a little less than a year. But when I came back, things were worse. *She* was worse. Dark, distant. At times it was like I'd never been gone, and others...I didn't recognize the girl I loved. She distrusted me. She pushed me away.

"Mere days before her death, she hid the Book; I never knew where. She told me she wouldn't help us, that I couldn't use her. We fought." He put his face in his hands. "I called her a traitor. How could she choose them, those monsters, over me? Us." He dropped his hands on the desk. "And she said I'd done her worse than Donoveir. At least she knew what sort of monster he was. I was a wolf in sheep's clothing. I had—*pretended*. I was a liar. I never loved her. The same things you said."

Lacey dropped her eyes from the fire in his. "I'm sorry. I shouldn't have said that. I didn't know..."

"It's fine. You weren't there. *She* should have known. She must have known I loved her...."

"It's hard to believe anyone can love you," Lacey said softly, "when you hate yourself."

"What d'you mean, kid?" Nathy said.

"Just... She went through so much. You don't get out of that believing you're worth anything but what people can take from you."

Flynn rested his forehead on his palm, suddenly tired. "What I did, Lacey, I did because I wanted to free her and everyone like her. But she only saw manipulation. And I can't blame her for that. We—the Nine—did need her. We wanted her to be a part of it. But she never knew kindness or goodness. She thought she'd be a tool, a weapon.

"And...she thought we'd taken things too far. The Nine talked about annihilation, the levelling of all Elonni. Maybe we were too extreme. She wouldn't risk an innocent life. She always told me they weren't all bad. And usually, I laughed at her. I said, 'Look what they've done to you, to my people.' I suppose I lacked nuance. She didn't want to take sides. She didn't want to rule. She just wanted to stop being in pain."

Lacey thought of her grandmother, a girl barely older than she was now—so destroyed by cruelty, and yet being asked so much. "How did Donoveir discover what she was?"

"He found the Book. He'd become suspicious of her, believed she was hiding something. She was so lost, so tired of it all... Normally, she was careful. But he found the Book just resting beneath her pillow. He recognized it. Sannus Eyreh had been hunting the descendants of the Ruined Queen for centuries. And here she was, his own wife.

"And Donoveir, he couldn't bear the—the *shame*, I suppose, of being married to what he considered the greatest atrocity to ever to walk the earth. Had his fellow Sons of God discovered the truth, they'd have killed her *and* him—or, at least, set fire to his flesh to burn the stain of having known Latrice. So, he decided the only thing to do was kill her. I wasn't living in the house anymore—I might have stopped him otherwise. By the time I arrived, hoping to talk, to make amends, she was dead, and Donoveir was on his way to the cliffs with the boys. I chased him. I managed to save Will. Diomedes was already gone."

Lacey looked away, remembering the tiny graves—her father's, empty. But that other little boy... It was too horrible to think of.

Flynn went on, weary now. "Donoveir confessed the moment the Dark Guard showed up. He was proud of it. Of course, given his status, he spent a very short time in prison. I needed only to wait.

"When he returned here," he said, in a darkly detached tone, "I cut him to pieces while he was still alive. I could have just burned him to death, but that seemed too simple, after what he'd done. I soldered each wound so he wouldn't bleed out. I wanted him to feel pain worse than Latrice ever had. Of course, that was impossible. He'd destroyed her. Nothing could hurt worse than every breath of her life."

"Damn," Nathy said. "And I thought I had issues."

Flynn's laugh cut the air and died on a sigh.

Lacey shut her eyes, but that didn't stop the tears from falling. "I know why you did it," she said. "Sometimes I want to kill them, too." She met Flynn's eyes. "I want to help you stop Sannus Eyreh. But we're doing it my way. We're not going to start a bloody war, or kill innocent people, or punish the Allies—we're only going after the Old Names. And once they're gone, that's it."

"You understand," Flynn said, "that killing the Old Names destroys the Elderon as we know it. You plan to leave the realm without any leadership?"

"I'm not a princess," Lacey said. "And I won't be a queen. Whatever happens—I don't have any right to rule."

"Anarchy sounds good to me," Nathy said.

She shot him a look. "There are senators and ambassadors," she said. "And Elder Law. Not to mention the Allies—well, the ones not helping Sannus Eyreh. They'll work something out."

"You're destined for the throne," Flynn told her, folding his hands neatly on the desk.

Lacey clenched her jaw; he would never truly understand. But she didn't have time to debate him. "Let's just focus on getting the Book back, shall we?"

"I've no idea what your father did with it, Lacey," Flynn said. "We've searched everywhere he ever went."

"He always kept it with him, didn't he? It seems obvious, then. It's in the place where he died. Stranger's Pass."

He frowned. "We searched there, too. It wasn't there."

"How did my dad find the Book? You said Latrice hid it."

"He...found it here. In the house." Flynn twisted his lips, thinking. "I'd searched for it for decades, and he found it within a day."

"Because she didn't want *you* to find it," Lacey said. "She only wanted her son to have it if he wanted it. I have a feeling my dad did the same thing. He always meant for me, and me alone, to find it." She sat up straighter. "So, let's go get it."

Flynn looked at Nathy, who shrugged.

"Whatever. Count me in."

Flynn smiled, looking for the moment like his old manic self. He lifted a shattered teapot, no more than its handle and base intact, and toasted it. "To freedom."

Lacey sighed. "Right. To freedom."

47

STRANGER'S PASS

-Stranger's Pass-

OUSES ROSE FROM the snow, half-buried, ruined, and deserted. Nobody had touched this ground since the snow fell. Likely, nobody had been here for years. The three intruders to this wasteland carved a long, lonely path with their feet as they walked through the ruined town. A church bell tolled in the wind, echoing from its crumbled stone tower across the perfect mounds of snow.

Lacey glanced up at Nathy, but his eyes were ahead, locked on the gray line of the horizon. Flynn's bronze skin and golden hair glowed, stark against the landscape. His fire eyes warmed Lacey when he smiled back at her. Nathy could have dissolved into the landscape, darkly contrary, a shadow on the ice.

"Do you remember it?" Flynn said.

"No." Lacey looked around. Everything was indistinct. Even if there was a landscape, a sculpture, a shop window locked in her memory from long ago, she couldn't have identified it from these ruins. She tried to pick out her first memory, and she thought it was of a bright road, her mother crying, and a door opening...Dr. Poole reaching out...

"It's like it never happened," Lacey said. "Like he never existed."

Flynn looked away. "I wish you could remember him. And not just the stories."

"But the stories are true," Lacey said. The wind hit her, sharp and sudden. "He left us. He hurt my mum."

"I know."

"Are you saying I should forget that?"

"No. But we're all monsters. Some of us have just learned to hide it. The way others learn to hide their humanity." He looked back at Nathy.

Nathy smirked. "I kill people, Flynn. That's all."

"Ha! So that's the idea?" His eyes darted to Lacey and back. "You're hoping she'll see the blood on your hands and forget you've got a heart of your own."

Nathy and Lacey exchanged a brief look, which he ended. "I think you're poeticizing."

Flynn shrugged.

They came to a skeletal neighborhood. Stark fences jutted from the yards like dead hands reaching, guarding ruined, vacant houses that sank like skeletons in the snow.

"What happened to this place?" Lacey asked. "Why is it abandoned?"

"It was one of the last stands in the War of Teeth," Flynn told her. "After they came for Will, the Elonni overtook it as a stronghold against the wolves—it cut Mondberg off from the clearest path toward Theopolis. The wolves attacked, regardless. It was a massacre." He let his eyes linger on a home with smashed windows and a caved-in porch. "The wolves were all but annihilated. The human inhabitants, too."

Lacey wondered what ghosts roamed here. She walked a little closer to Nathy and was grateful when he didn't move away.

"Are you okay?" she asked.

"Fine."

She stared up at his scarred face. "Really?"

His eyes turned up and he let out a breath. "When you left..."

"Yeah?"

"Why'd you go with Saxon?" He lowered his voice, not meeting her eye. "I mean, I get it. But I would have helped you."

Lacey looked quickly down. "Oh."

"Don't—don't worry about it."

"I didn't think—"

"It's fine." He shrugged, smiling. "I figured you two would find your way back to each other."

"It wasn't..." But she stopped herself. She hadn't even thought to tell Nathy about what Flynn had done. The moment she'd realized she needed to leave, she'd gone to Saxon. But she managed to ruin even that.

"I don't think Saxon cares for me much anymore," Lacey said instead.

411

"What makes you say that?"

"I set him on fire. On accident."

Nathy's mouth twitched. "That's—" He coughed. "Don't feel too bad."

"You're laughing."

"Am not."

Flynn paused in the street, eyebrows raised, and they waked toward him, silent. They turned into the ruined remains of lawn, its fence bowed away on one half. The door hung off its hinges on the porch. Something about it whispered in Lacey's memories but vanished like a breeze when she tried to hold it. She followed Flynn into the dark and cold interior of the home. Though the wind could no longer reach them here, Lacey shivered. Even Nathy seemed stilled by the descending sadness of the place.

It was a home in ruins, lent to chaos and destroyed. Overturned furniture, desks with their drawers ripped open and dangling on the hinges. A writing desk smashed to scraps of wood. There were toys, too, many of them, all for a little girl. A dollhouse. A rocking horse. Moldering coloring pages. Lacey's mind reached toward the items, trying to associate them with herself, her life, but the most she conjured was a faint, soft feeling, of her hand on the rocking horse's face, her fingers prodding the marble eyes.

But where was her dad? Where was Will? The books on the shelf were her mother's, surely, all intellectual pursuits which someone with Will's harried mind could never enjoy. The home was bare of whatever made Will a man, a person, and she was beginning to wonder if he had ever been more than a story, at first a pleasant lie and then a cruel legacy.

"Let's check upstairs," Lacey said. She led them up a creaking staircase. The hall at the top was still more cluttered, and snow covered the end of the corridor, dumped in through an open window. Something snapped beneath Lacey's foot and she looked down to see a toy Watchman, a single wing broken off, its sword snapped in two. She picked it up, studied it, and something rushed back to her like a wave crashing to shore.

"This was my dad's," she said. "This was one of his only toys when he was little. He wouldn't let anybody touch it. He got so mad when I...when I broke its wing."

Flynn put a hand on her shoulder, but she couldn't bear to look up at him. She set the ruined figurine back on the floor and walked on, pulled to the end of the corridor.

She opened the last door she came to. Beyond it lay a study, its window shattered, the portraits on the walls knocked to the floor. Lacey's eyes flitted to two things—the desk, upon which sat a candle with a fluttering blue flame; and a large crusted bloodstain staining the wood before the cold stone fireplace.

She backed into Nathy, her hand to her mouth. It was her father's blood—it had to be. Until know his death had been an intellectual fact, like knowing a date in history, or the name of an old king. But here was visceral evidence of the pain he'd endured, the essence of his life soaking into old wood.

Nathy held her shoulders, and when she began to shake, turned her toward him and held her head to his chest. She gritted her teeth against the growing lump in her throat.

"How peculiar," Flynn said.

"Flynn?" Nathy said. "Maybe not now?"

"But...this candle."

Lacey pulled away from Nathy and turned toward the desk. "What about it?" she said, her voice thick.

"It was burning when we first searched the house, too. Fifteen years ago."

Lacey stepped closer to desk. The blue candle flame danced and seemed to grow larger the longer Lacey stood there, staring at it. It reached toward her, hot tendrils crawling along the air. She reached her hand out and touched the wisp of blue flame.

It wrapped around her fingers and hand, crawled up her arm. Distantly, Nathy's voice called out as the fire twined around her shoulders and plunged into her heart.

THE PEOPLE OF Stranger's Pass knew what to do when the wolves poured from the forest and took the streets. They knew the alarm screaming through the street was not a joke.

The humans' pants and shouts and last goodbyes mingled with the howls coming from the forest, echoing down the streets. Wolf-voices crashed through the town like thunder: fierce, animal, but beneath that, accented with something distinctly human.

A lone Watchman, his wings tight against his back, stood in the street and addressed the crowds thronging around him.

"Everyone, return to your houses, by order of the Watchmen! Lock your doors and guard yourselves with silver." He carried a long blade glittering with moonlight, clutched in his right hand, a deep look carved into his face. A pistol hung from a holster at his side, and his fingers twitched above the handle.

William Barker blended in, pushing through the crowds. Most people stopped at closed doors, yanked against the locks and cried to be let in. Will tried the occasional door to match the frantic movements of the humans around him, but at each locked door he glanced over his shoulder and sped on. They would find him soon. Perspective needled him: *You're out of time.*

A few people ran to the scattered houses beyond the village square. Will followed them, but as soon as he broke into a jog it happened: A huge black shape crossed in front of him, eclipsing his escape. The wolf dragged its feet and glared with long, yellow eyes. Will froze. He watched the unmoving creature, and it issued a deep growl.

Will lifted his hands. "Ragnok—listen to me—"

A gunshot snapped by Will's ear. He spun to see the Watchman, wings unfurled, weapon raised, running toward the wolf. The beast, its left flank smoldering from the silver bullet, snarled and lunged. Its front claw sunk into Will's left shoulder and pinned him beneath its weight.

He peeled his eyes open. Above him was only the darkness of the wolf.

"We're on the same side," Will said through his teeth.

The wolf reared his head, fangs barred, and aimed its jaws toward Will's throat.

More gunshots—the Watchman was close now, firing into the wolf's wide, hairy flank. The creature howled and stepped back. Will felt the tear in his flesh fully now, blood hurrying from his veins. His vision swam as he forced himself to sit up. Before he was ready, the wolf righted itself and lunged, but it careened over Will and crashed into the Watchman, who had been trying to reload his gun.

Will heard the tearing of flesh and the man's mangled screams. A bloody cough and a plea: "You...Elonni! Hel—"

Will didn't turn around to look and did a fair job of ignoring the damp thudding noises of dismemberment—he'd become something of an expert in identifying lost causes.

"Was that necessary?" he said when the sounds of slow, methodical chewing had ceased.

"They've killed enough of my people," a rough human voice answered. "It feels good to kill one of them."

Will pushed himself to standing with his uninjured arm and faced Ragnok, now dressed in human skin, naked, fresh blood staining his teeth and beard.

"I know. But—"

"They've died for you," Ragnok interrupted. His long auburn hair hung down to his waist in thick, greasy clumps; it swayed around him as he approached Will. "I thought you said this was our time."

Will bit the inside of his cheek. "I thought it was."

Ragnok barred his human teeth in a wolfish sneer. "My people are nearly gone. You mean to tell me we wasted our lives for nothing?"

"Not nothing," Will said. "There's still time. And even if I don't make it—there's another way."

"Your little girl is gone, is she not?"

Will sighed. "We always find our way to the Book. She won't be able to help it. I couldn't."

Ragnok shook his head, smiling. "I think I might miss you, Barker. If you insist on continuing this, do so at your peril." His lips spread wider, blood making his grin manic. "My pack and I are going to have one last meal. Don't count on me for anything in the future."

His skin seemed to shred away, thick, mangy fur bursting between the seams, and he was a beast again. With a final snarl, he turned and barreled back into the town square.

Will turned and ran toward the neighborhood. The screams and the sirens faded to background noise, the cries of the humans died down. The wolves barked, far away. His shoulder throbbed; his steps turned to a lurching here-and-there of the feet. But he breathed slowly through his mouth and focused on the slice of orange moon over the distant roofs.

He only stopped when the town thinned away and unfolded onto a spread of houses scattered on unkempt lawns. Fences jutted from the high grass like crooked teeth. Fog lay across the roofs and all the windows were dark.

He stopped at a faded green house with a porch and a large overgrown garden. Its oak double doors were marked with graffiti, their windows cracked. The fence surrounding the property, cast out of cold, winking iyrel, sunk into the earth. Will forced away the memories the ruined house held for him.

He climbed over the fence, flinching at the deep burn of the toxic metal on his flesh, and jogged to the house, checking over his bloodied shoulder with every bound. He heard nothing, saw no one—but that didn't mean anything. The porch creaked under his feet and the door groaned as he cracked it open, just wide enough to fit himself through.

The house was the way he remembered. Clean, smooth. Right angles leading to ordered, square rooms. The books were where Aeyrin had left them—her copy of *The Knowable* still dog-eared and spread on the coffee table like a bird in flight, awaiting the perusal of an intelligent eye. Toys were laid out as if they'd only just been played with. Had it truly been a year? He thought he could smell Aeyrin's perfume, hear their daughter laugh. He took the flight of stairs at the end of the hall.

Upstairs, on the top floor, the decay of the house was more obvious. A window at the end of the hall had been left open, and dead leaves and twigs lay scattered on the moldy carpet. The hallway sharpened as he walked, becoming more and more cluttered with unwanted furniture, boxes of toys...a little tin figurine of a Watchman, its painted eyes worn away, plastic sword still in its frozen hands...a limp doll with red

416

yarn hair. He picked up the ragged thing and it lolled in his hands, its sewn eyes blankly regarding his profile. Lacey had always loved this doll. Why hadn't they taken it with them?

He cried, hard and unexpectedly, as everything he'd lost ripped through him, dug into his skin and blood like a parasite and left him hollow. This was it—a feeling worse than nothingness, something he dreaded worse than the unknown awaiting him at the end of this hall. The realization of what his life would never be, of what his family still could be if only there were an antidote for the poison he was to them.

He wiped his eyes and clutched the doll. Renewed, he turned into the last room. The study. The room was lined with bookshelves and occupied by a large desk pushed against a picture window. A cold, ash-clouded fireplace sat below an old portrait of his uncle, and Will stooped by it.

He passed his hand over the brittle remains of burnt logs. A fire popped into the grate, huge and crackling, as though it had been burning a while. He pulled three things from his bag—a book, a letter, and a candle—and set them on the floor before him. He stumbled to a knee. Blood flowed from his shoulder and black edged into his vision.

"*Thaiya longen intoten,*" he said.

The candle sprouted a small, blue flame; the crackle of the friendly fire reminded him, unwantedly, of them, and the brief years when they had been a family. He picked up the candle and touched its flame to a corner of the letter. Immediately it was covered in flames, but it did not burn away. It simply flared, bright white, imprinting a shimmering after-image when Will closed his eyes. He held it and was not burned, and set the letter into the larger fire burning in the grate. The flames shot up with blue streaks.

"*Thaiya mogen fyototen,*" he said, and touched the blue flame of the candle to the Book. It, too, burned without being consumed. He dropped the Book into the fire, which glowed bluer still.

"*Ay myamin tuthon.*"

The flame crawled from the wick, slipping down the wax, seeking something living. It wound around Will's wrist, curled slowly up his forearm. He shut his eyes and gritted his teeth. Though he felt no pain, the slinking flame now working

417

its way into his mind stung with an unfamiliar sensation—not pain, but as far from pleasure as anything could be.

The flame retracted, content, and flickered on its wick. Will stood with the candle and set it on the desk. The blue flame glowed, and would until Lacey came for it.

Downstairs, a crash resounded as the front door flew from its hinges. Will clutched the ragged doll in his hand.

"Good luck, Lacey."

He thrust the doll into the fire. It sat between the book and letter, its comic face smiling through the flames. As he moved his hand from the fire, it fizzled and went back to orange. Its glow faded until nothing remained but a scattering of ash, the items inside gone.

Footsteps marched on the stairs. Will stood. He felt bloodless, cold. He looked at the candle flickering on the desk. "*Aya yanamin methon,*" he said, waving his hand over the flame. It jumped as his hand passed it, but otherwise there was no sign anything remarkable had happened.

The footsteps crowded in the hall, and now he could hear voices. They were close.

He wanted Aeyrin to be his last thought, and she would be, but he thought of his old friend, too. Sol would never forgive him; yet he'd gotten exactly what he wanted most.

"Take care of her, you bastard." Will smiled and shut his eyes. He had to believe she was happy now.

"Aeyrin." Her name stuck in his throat. "I'm so sorry. I love you."

The men who wanted him dead crashed closer. "He's been here! This way!"

He pictured her face...she had eyes the color of photographs. Their daughter, with his hair and eyes, but Aeyrin's smile—her heart. "I ruined everything," he said, his last confession. Here at the end of all things, that was the one thing in life he was decidedly set on, and it might as well be the last thing he said.

He sat on the floor and waited to be killed.

48

THE BOOK OF THE NINE

-Stranger's Pass-

LACEY DROPPED TO her knees as the candleflame released her and her father's memory gave way to her own consciousness. She held her head, dizzy, and looked up to find Nathy and Flynn hovering over her. Flynn's hair was whiter, graying as though he had begun to age. And the loss in his eyes only made him seem older, burdened.

"What happened?" he said.

"I...saw into my dad's mind. His memory. He trapped it in that candleflame." She looked now to the fireplace. "It's in there—the Book."

Lacey crawled to the fireplace, her palms cold against the hearth, her heart chilled by the bloodstain, and took a deep breath. "*Ryum ectes totum.*"

A huge fire burst into the grate, shuddering and twisting in its fury. Lacey sat back as the tongues of flame spat out first a letter, then a book and, finally, a small, ragged thing of red yarn. She picked up the last item, and this time, memory swept through her with violence.

This had been her favorite toy. She slept with it in her bed...down the hall from Dad's study, to the left. She used to bury her head in the red yarn hair and smell the mustiness of it. Mum used to ruffle her hair and say, "My two ginger girls."

Dad bought it for her, at the travelling market. He'd gotten it instead of a tool he'd needed to fix the roof. "All that can wait," he'd said. "You deserve to have something nice."

"Lacey?" Nathy sat on the floor beside her and took the doll from her numb hands, turned it over in his. "Was this yours?"

She nodded. "My dad gave it to me."

He set the doll back in her hands, then picked up the Book, which she hadn't the energy to consider.

"This is it, Lacey." He held it in his palm, and the Book fell open along a crease of missing pages, seemingly torn from their place.

"The missing Rites," he said.

Flynn scrambled for something in his pocket. He unfolded a dirty sheet of paper, and set it on the open Book. The tiny fibers of the detached page reached to one of the torn edges left in the Book and reattached themselves with a rapid stitching.

"One down, seven to go," Nathy said.

"Not quite." Flynn knelt with them, the effort creasing his forehead and adding a pinch to his mouth. He'd seemed so lithe not hours ago. But now, looking at him, Lacey could swear he seemed ten years older.

Flynn took her hand in his, the one on which she wore the bronze ring. Consulting the book, he began to speak in Sumrian. Lacey didn't know a word of his language, and yet, despite its unfamiliarity, something deep in her mind understood the words.

I, the Firekeeper of the Ferno Kind, swear fealty to my Queen, to the cause of justice and equality. I offer my life to her services and pledge the ability of my kind to her uses. May this Book be her instrument, and this Rite her power.

Flames reached from his hands to hers, overtaking her entire body in seconds. She sucked in a breath, suddenly overwhelmed by the sensation—warm, perfect, crisp fire rushing around her, enclosing her in a heated embrace.

"Flynn," Nathy said, worry and warning both in his tone.

"She's fine," Flynn said.

The fire seemed to burrow into Lacey's chest. She rocked forward, pain arching along her spine. Her wings unfolded without her command and curled around her body, golden with flame and great with power.

This—this was how it felt. To be strong. Lacey found herself smiling as the flames cooled to a pleasant breeze, her hellish cocoon so beautiful and right.

At once, the fire dispelled, leaving Lacey shaking from the cold of the room. She looked between the two men.

"The Rite is complete," Flynn said.

"Do you...feel any different?" Nathy said.

"Stronger," Lacey said, still smiling. She caught his expression and frowned. "What's wrong?"

"Well," Nathy said, shrugging. "For a while there your hair was white and you had fire running out of yours eyes."

"I did?" She touched her face. "Is it gone?"

"Yeah, you're..." He reached out and pinched a lock of her hair between his fingers. "You."

"Okay. We should go." She got to her feet, Nathy rising with her. She scanned the room until she found an old bag with a frayed strap lying amongst the other junk. She shoved the Book and the doll inside and slung it over her shoulder.

Flynn smiled at her and pushed her hair behind her ear. "I'm proud of you, darling."

She chewed her lower lip. "Don't be. I haven't done anything."

"You have," Flynn said. "More than you realize."

They crept back into the hall, but Lacey stopped, frowning. "D'you hear something?"

Nathy put a hand on her shoulder. "Someone's here." He looked around and tugged her down the corridor, Flynn following.

"You think..." Lacey's breath caught. "Sannus Eyreh?"

"I don't know." Nathy pulled her into a cluttered sitting room crowded with furniture and a sense of life gone by. Flynn peered around the doorway and swore, slamming them inside the room.

"What?" Nathy said.

Fires crept across Flynn's skin. Nathy drew his wand and aimed it at the door just before it burst open.

"Lacey." Saxon's eyes met Flynn's, challenging, unafraid, and Flynn stared right back as though he'd like nothing more than to set fire to the younger man. Saxon tore his gaze away and looked at Lacey. "Get away from him."

Nathy stepped forward, his hand tight around Lacey's. "What's the problem, Saxophone?"

"Take your hand off her," Saxon said. He drew his own wand, and sparks shot around his hand like lightning in the clouds. Lacey pulled away from Nathy and walked to the center of the room, in between the two men, their tension knifing through her.

"Saxon, what's going on?" she said. "Why are you here?"

"They're using you, Lacey," Saxon said. "They just want that bloody Book."

Lacey put a protective hand over the satchel, reassured by the Book's hard corners beneath her fingers. "You don't know what you're talking about."

"They want to slaughter people, Lace. Every Elonni and Ally out there."

"It's good to know you're as bloody stupid as ever," Flynn snarled. His flames beat like waves across his skin. Lacey had never seen such hatred in his eyes. She looked over her shoulder at Nathy, but he seemed just as lost.

"He's one of them too, Lacey." Saxon stepped forward, the force of his ready magic pulsing on the air.

"So I'm the bad guy now?" Nathy smirked. "Come on, Saxon, we were almost friends again."

"Maybe." Saxon's jaw tightened. "That's why I hate to do this."

He launched the spell before Lacey could do anything. Nathy took the blast to the chest and flew back. He crumpled against the far wall.

"Where'd you learn that?" Nathy said, pushing himself up onto his elbows.

Saxon aimed his wand again.

"Saxon, stop it!" Lacey tried to grab his hand, but he moved too quickly and deflected a blast of fire barreling his way. Flynn was pure flame and rage. And he was too fast. Flynn lit the room with a rushing inferno, a wall of fire heading straight for Saxon. Lacey rushed at the flame with her own, beating it back and dissipating the fire. Smoking scorch marks lined the wood floor. Saxon stood behind Lacey, his breathing uneven.

"Lacey," Flynn said. "What are you doing?"

"We're not enemies," Lacey said, glaring at both men. "Sannus Eyreh are the enemy."

"Sannus Eyreh are just a story, Lacey." Saxon shook, still tense from the firefight. "They made up this conspiracy to convince you to fight for them."

"A story?" Nathy said, getting back to his feet. "You think I'm making this up?" He pointed to the scar across his eye. "Pretty elaborate hoax."

"You're obsessed with revenge," Saxon said. "You just want to hurt people because you can't deal with your own shit."

Nathy cocked his head. "You think?" His wings materialized, black feathers falling around him. He didn't move, didn't even have to lift a hand, and the wall behind Saxon began to crumble, the roof cracking. Saxon turned just as the brick and dust burst out, caving in around him.

Lacey tackled Saxon to the ground, her own body pummeled by the detritus falling around her, her wings extending and hovering above them like an umbrella. The house groaned once it was over, shifting dangerously beneath their feet.

"Lacey!" Nathy was above her, tearing bricks and rubble off her and lifting her up. She spat a mouthful of ground plaster.

"What *was* that?" Lacey said.

Nathy's hands fell away from her. "I-I don't know. I'm—" His words cut off as Saxon rose, wand in hand.

"You could have killed her," he said, his voice low and shaking with rage.

"Saxon, stop." Lacey stood between them, hands extending to either one.

"I'm trying to help you!" he shouted.

"How are you helping me?" Lacey said. *You're destroying me.* She loved these three shattered, contrary men. She couldn't watch them tear away at each other.

Saxon took a tentative step closer, stowing his wand. "Please, Lacey. I just want to help you. I love you."

Lacey flinched. Nathy's energy changed beside her, twisting in rage and pain, but she hardly registered him as Saxon walked nearer, took her face in his hand, and kissed her. She let him have her for this one moment, the pulse of her heart and the fire in her skin. But then he pulled away, too soon, and he didn't meet her eyes.

"I'm sorry, love."

He reached into his pocket, and his hand flew to her neck. A small, hot pain blossomed in her throat. She couldn't understand what he'd done until his hand came away, clutching a syringe, the feeble remains of a green potion settled at the tip.

All at once, her energy drained. Her wings receded in a flash of light. She tipped forward into his arms.

Fire, she told herself. But her call went unheeded. Not so much as an ember crossed her skin.

"What have you done?" Flynn roared, charging toward Saxon, fire in each hand. But he was blown back across the room by a force of light from the doorway.

"Oh, good. You found her." An older man with distinguished features and bright, clever eyes stood in the doorway. He smiled at them in turn. "Thank you, Saxon."

Lacey's voice was feeble when she said, "What did you do to me?"

Saxon held her tight against his chest. "I'm sorry. I had to."

She tried to push away from him, but even her pathetic human strength wouldn't answer her. She managed to turn her head. Nathy stared down at her brokenly.

"Bring her here," the newcomer said. Lacey twisted to face him, and her heart jolted as she recognized him.

He'd been in her village—the new preacher, borrowed, she had thought, for the last rites of a slain man. His lips had led the people of Hollows Edge in a hymn while blood soaked the snow. He'd talked to her, kindly yet darkly—*Better hope they don't find what's in your heart, girl.*

"Who are you?" she said, her voice barely a breath.

He bowed his head to her, a hand over his heart. "Amnon Stone, my lady."

Patriarch. Dr. Poole's brother. The monster who was hunting her had her at last. And the boy Lacey loved was leading her right to him.

Saxon brought her before Patriarch; her steps faltered, her entire body failing her as she crossed the room. She glanced toward Flynn, unconscious against the far wall. Nathy rushed toward the man, but Patriarch merely held up his hand. Nathy froze in place, the surprise on his face shifting into agony as Patriarch's fingers curled into a fist. Nathy's hands scrabbled at his heart, blood slowly draining from his face.

Lacey found a meager store of strength to take a breath and yell, "Stop! Please, *please* don't hurt him."

Patriarch eased his invisible grasp and looked down at Lacey, his smile sweet and amused. "You're fond of the inbreed?"

"You have me," she said. "I'm the one you want."

"I'm afraid I can't let the heirs go, my dear girl."

Lacey pushed away from Saxon, unsteady on her feet, and turned to Nathy. She eyed the collapsed wall behind him. He must have understood her intent, because he shook his head.

"Kid, I'm not leaving you."

"You have to." She let the bag fall from her shoulder and kicked it to him. It skidded to a halt before him, and his hands closed around it. Their eyes met.

"Run," she said.

He locked his jaw, looked away, his eyes shining with tears. And then, the house began to tilt. The walls cracked; the floor buckled. The house shook, roaring on weakened foundations, and a fissure ran across the floor between Lacey and Nathy.

"Kid?"

She looked at him across the split in the floor.

He smiled. "See you soon."

She tried to reach across to him, but the split floor threw her back into Saxon's grip. Nathy crossed the other half of the room and swung the still-unconscious Flynn over his shoulder. The roof buckled above them and a wall of debris rained down, blotting out her view of Nathy and Flynn.

Patriarch snarled. He grabbed Saxon and Lacey and spread his wings toward the yawning roof. They broke through the rubble and flew a few yards before touching down on the street below. Lacey's old house, the place she could hardly remember, sank into the earth, nothing but a ruin now.

"You." Patriarch shoved Saxon forward. "Find them. They can't have escaped that."

Saxon started forward, stepping into the rubble of the house. He paused for a moment, his eyes hard on something. Lacey's heart sank as Saxon picked his way back across the yard.

"Well?" Patriarch said.

"I found traces of a portal," Saxon said. "They escaped."

"That's impossible." Patriarch's fist tightened on Lacey arm as he dragged her closer. "I suppose you think that was clever?"

"Amnon—*hey*." Saxon reached out for Lacey, but Patriarch flung his arm out, catching Saxon in the stomach. Saxon skidded several yards away, groaning.

"I will hunt the Nine," Patriarch said, "long after you're dead. You've only bought them a few hours more of life."

"That's enough to stop you," she said.

He smacked her, twisting her vision and sending a jolt of pain down her neck.

"It's time I destroyed you." He dragged her across the snowy street to where Saxon knelt, blood on his lips. "And you can watch."

He grabbed Saxon by the hair and dragged him close. Light encircled them, churning and bright, and suddenly, they were moving, the world beneath their feet falling away as they took to the air, moving at an impossible speed.

49

SONS OF GOD

-Fallow Wood-

LACEY OPENED HER eyes, her body sore and bruised. She lay on her side in a familiar forest, the sound of a river licking at its bank nearby. Saxon lay a few feet away, moonlight lying in broken shapes across his pale face.

"Saxon." Lacey wanted to reach out for him, but her body wouldn't respond. She felt weaker with every minute the binding potion crawled through her veins.

"You idiot," she whispered. Her breath stirred a dead leaf.

"My lady?"

Lacey twisted her head and found Patriarch looming above her. He wore a heavy white cloak, its hem and cuffs embroidered with golden Annanym. His features were stern, blockish, with none of the easy angles of his brother's face. But their eyes were the same dark hazel, Patriarch's now glinting with moonlight.

Lacey let her head fall back to the forest floor. She knew that beyond the trees stood the old, ruined house.

"Why haven't you bothered killing me?" she said.

"You must be dealt with appropriately," he said with an air of practicality. "I must wash your stain from the Earth."

"So, there's a ceremony involved?" Lacey sighed. "Of course."

He kicked her ribs, and she buried a scream.

Saxon stirred at the sound of whimpering and pushed himself up. His eyes first went to Lacey, and he scrambled toward her. But before he could reach her, his gaze flicked to Patriarch. His mouth curled in a snarl.

"What is this? Where are we?"

Patriarch listed his head; he looked almost sorry. "Dear boy, are you actually that daft?"

"You—you've all been lying to me."

"Yes," Patriarch said, nodding. "I know you so badly wanted to play the hero, but alas, you are the fool."

Saxon reached out and touched Lacey's arm. "Can you move?"

She managed a withering glare. "No, Saxon, I can't move. And why is that, d'you think?"

"Lace." He seemed to choke on her name. "I'm so sorry. I thought I was helping you." He got to his feet and lifted her with him. Her legs failed her and she had no choice but to let him hold her up. She gritted her teeth, wishing she could tear away from him. To let her fire go and burn this lost part of the forest away.

"Please, come with me," Patriarch said.

"No." Saxon tightened his arms around Lacey. Patriarch sighed, tipping his head back. He didn't seem to do anything, but suddenly, Saxon dropped her and staggered back, holding his head and gritting his teeth. Blood trickled from the corners of his mouth, his nose.

"*Stop*," Lacey said to Patriarch. Then, to Saxon: "Just do what he wants."

Saxon gasped as the pain apparently left him.

"Good," Patriarch said. "Now, come along."

Saxon lifted Lacey, his arms around her back and under her knees. He followed Patriarch across a little stone bridge above the river. The familiar bulk of the ruined house loomed against the hard wall of the forest. The water wheel, still during Lacey's last visit, now turned, stirring the river with the gentle sounds of woodwork and water.

The front door opened slowly, and a familiar, stooped figure stepped out. "My king," Father Priestley wheezed. He had exchanged his gilded vestments for a white robe like Patriarch's, its heavy fabric drooping around his shriveled body.

"Gordon." Patriarch nodded. "Are we prepared?"

"Yes, my king." His eyes fell on Lacey, limp and useless in Saxon's arms. He frowned. "I'm afraid the rumors are true. Ryder Lately is dead."

Patriarch bowed his head. "A link in our chain has been cut. He was the last of his name. We will honor his memory." He turned his head toward Lacey. "Once our enemy is dead."

Father Priestley opened the door wider. Lacey thought they would be led inside, but instead, a throng of other white-robed men emerged, funneling through the doorway. They arranged themselves in a semicircle around Patriarch. One stout, round man Lacey recognized as Justice Bromley. She scanned the other faces, stopping when recognition shocked her gut.

A tall man with a sharp jaw and high cheekbones stood centered between the others, a bored smile on his lips and contempt in his blue eyes. He was pale and blond, but unmistakably Nathy's father. He caught her gaze and his smile grew, losing its irony and twisting with real mirth. His fingers curled around the hood of his robe and he drew it up, darkening his eyes and leaving only that long, cruel grin.

"My Sons," Patriarch said. "The time has come to put an end to the line of the Ruined Queen."

The gathered men said, together, "*Hallas.*"

Patriarch turned and blinked in surprise, as though he had forgotten Saxon was still with them. "Oh, yes. Fairborn? Take the girl."

Mortimer broke away from the ranks. Saxon tightened his hold on Lacey and backed away, but Mortimer was faster and unburdened. He tore Lacey from Saxon's arms, holding her carelessly by one arm. She buried a scream as her shoulder popped out of place, pain knifing through her bones and muscle.

"Are you keeping that one?" Mortimer said, nodding to Saxon.

"Hm? Oh, no, I'm done with him." Patriarch waved his hand dismissively. Mortimer dropped Lacey and drew a sword from beneath his robes.

"Better if you hold still," he said to Saxon, smiling.

Saxon's eyes were on the blade, fixated, his body useless as Mortimer planted his feet and drew the blade up. Lacey stared as a band of moonlight caught the metal. Only hours ago, she'd thought Saxon was safe. Gone from her life, and from danger. And now, he was standing beneath a blade. He met her eyes across the short distance and gave her a weary smile.

"I'm sorry, Lace. I love you."

She shook her head, refusing to accept what was about to happen, and found herself screaming: "Patriarch tried to kill your son!"

Mortimer lowered his sword. He looked over his shoulder. "Say again, princess?"

Lacey shuddered; even their voices, the rich mine of contempt running beneath every syllable, were the same. "Patriarch tried to kill Nathy. I know you don't want him dead. So how can you do the bidding of someone who wants to murder your only child?"

He spun in one quick, easy motion, and lifted her chin with the tip of his blade. "You've got courage." He applied pressure on the hilt, bringing the point of the sword harder against her skin. "You and Nathy are close?"

"Yes," she said, straining against the blade. "And he told me about you."

"Stay on task, Fairborn," Patriarch said.

Mortimer cocked his head, regarding his leader with cool amusement. "I'd like to hear what the lady has to say. Sir."

Another man in the semicircle broke away. "My king. If he's not going to kill the boy, I'd be glad to." His voice was reedy and groveling. Familiar.

Mortimer smirked. "Always the sniveling wastrel, aren't we, Eadred?"

Lacey tensed. *Kragen.* She flicked her eyes back to Mortimer. "It must bother you that they let *him* in—a warlock. Yet they want to kill Nathy for his magic. At least he's an Old Name."

"Fairborn." Patriarch took a step forward. "Do not listen to the enemy's lies. She means to tempt you from the righteous path. I'd hate to see you go down that road again."

Mortimer released the blade from Lacey's throat. "Of course."

He turned back to Saxon and raised the blade. Saxon shut his eyes.

Lacey dug her fingers into the dirt, begging her powers to return—to save him. She gritted her teeth, tears clinging to her eyelashes.

And then, inexplicably, a wall of fire split the forest floor between Saxon and Mortimer. Lacey looked down at her own hands, still useless and shaking with weakness.

Her gaze snapped to the sky, where a fulcan hovered above. Nathy and Flynn dropped down from the back of the great bird, and it flew off, back in the direction of Fryer's Grove.

Flynn cast the fire away as he approached. Saxon stumbled away from the extended sword, but Mortimer's attention was no longer on him. He stared now at his son. Nathy drew the strange, glowing blade and knocked his father's sword aside.

"Leave the idiot alone," Nathy said.

Patriarch stepped forward, his eyes fixed solely on the blade. "Deumsyth."

Nathy didn't take his eyes off his father. "Get away from her," he said.

Mortimer sheathed his sword and held his hands up. "I have no intention of fighting you, son."

Nathy pressed the blade to his father's chest, pushing him farther back. "I'm not your son. Not anymore."

"Fairborn." Patriarch seemed calm, but tension ran along his jaw, cinching his eyes. "How exactly did your bastard come into possession of my sword?"

"Dunno, sir." Mortimer smirked. "Ask him."

Patriarch stormed forward, grabbing Lacey by the neck as he went. His fingers circled her throat, pressing. "Give the sword to me, inbreed."

Nathy aimed the blade at Patriarch. "Why should I?"

Patriarch drew an iyrel dagger from his robes and pressed it to the hollow of Lacey's throat. She gasped at the stinging pain of the metal. "Because I can kill her before you make a single move."

Flynn shot a stream of fire their way. It engulfed Lacey and Patriarch, tickling her skin like a breeze. Patriarch, too, seemed unmoved by the coursing flames. They died, and he stood unharmed. The other robed men surged forward now, and two each held back Flynn and Saxon. The rest hovered behind Patriarch.

431

"Yes," Patriarch said dryly. "In anticipation of battling two Fernos, I asked Eadred to enchant our robes. I'm afraid your fire is useless." He dug the blade harder into Lacey's throat, drawing blood and a gasp from her throat. The agony of the poison metal redoubled the pain of her broken skin. "And you've only angered me."

He threw Lacey down and stomped his foot down on her injured shoulder. This time, a scream broke free as her bones fragmented and pierced her skin. He knelt and stabbed the iyrel blade into her broken shoulder. She didn't know if she made a sound, or if she merely lost consciousness as he twisted the blade back and forth in the meat of her muscle. When she came to, when the pain fully washed through her body, she gasped, tasting bile. Her vision fragmented at the edges.

There were screams that were not hers. Lacey opened her eyes to find Nathy on his knees, locked, apparently, by the power Patriarch's mere gaze exerted. Patriarch dragged his hand up through the air, and Nathy rose like a marionette, the sword's hilt still clutched in his hand.

"Give me the sword," Patriarch said. "She dies either way. But perhaps you'd like to watch her suffer?"

"Stop," Nathy said. He dropped the sword. Patriarch sent Nathy bucking back to the ground, a smile on his flat lips.

"Deumsyth. The God-Slayer. At last." He picked up the blade and looked briefly at Mortimer. "The last time I saw this sword, it hung in my father's study. A symbol of our immortality. Our control over our own deaths. It seems a miracle it's found its way back to me."

Nathy rose unsteadily and scrambled toward Lacey. He gently lifted her from the ground. "Kid?"

"You should have kept the sword," she said.

He rose, bringing her to her feet with him. "I'd rather have you, honestly."

She fell against his chest, dizzy and nauseous. "We can't win now," she said.

"You could never win," Patriarch said. "If you'd please." He nodded toward the thick of the forest. The men holding Flynn and Saxon dragged them forward. Mortimer grabbed Nathy's arm and pulled him along. Lacey stumbled, but Nathy's grip kept her upright.

They filed through the trees and into a clearing. It was filled with moonlight, bright and bare as a stage. In its center grew a white thorn tree, the topmost boughs splayed across the sky and splitting the moonlight into ragged fingers, its roots risen and clawed like the foot of some great beast. Manacles hung from the lower branches. The strange duel-eyed symbol that Nathy had scarred onto his chest had been burned into the grass. A dull golden goblet the size of a small bowl sat in the eye's center. It was filled with a dark clotted liquid that gave off a sharp iron stench. Blood.

Flynn and Saxon were forced to their knees and abandoned. Mortimer simply let go of Nathy and joined the other men forming rank around the eye, backed by the growth of the white thorn tree. Only Patriarch stayed with his prisoners. His eyes glimmered, a smirk on his lips like this was all an amusing practical joke, and Lacey the silly girl who'd stumbled down here.

"Welcome, my lady, to slaughter." He bowed his head, and when he lifted it again, his eyes were wild, hungry.

She still found it difficult even to keep her footing; she had no idea how she could fight him now. Nathy pushed her behind him and faced Patriarch.

"How about you leave her alone?" he said. "Saxon's already eliminated her powers. What's the point of killing her now?"

"Her ability is in her blood," Patriarch said. "She will spread the disease of what she is into further generations. I have a chance to destroy that. Along with the rest of you."

"I think you'll find I'm hard to kill," Nathy said, and cocked his head. "Unlike your family. Someone really pruned the family branch there, didn't they?"

Patriarch shoved him back so hard Nathy fell into Flynn, but he smoothed his complexion with a sudden expert calm and addressed them like a judge before his defendants.

"The Lady of Ruin, the Sage, and the Firekeeper. Servants of the Nine and traitors to Elrosh. You have done more damage to the world than can ever be repaired. There is only one way to atone for a crime so many generations deep."

"Don't hurt them," Flynn said, stepping forward. "It's my fault, I did this. I brought them into it."

"We'll surely kill you as well," Patriarch said, amused.

Flynn spread his arms, blocking Lacey and Nathy. "I'm begging you. I'll do anything. They're my family."

Nathy laughed shortly. "Come on, Flynn. If he kills you, he's killing me too." Nathy's black eyes darted to Patriarch's. "I don't want to live if people have to die for me."

"You two seem to...want death," Patriarch said. "You're not afraid of it." His eyes flickered to Lacey. "So you die first."

Nathy sprang. Saxon launched off the ground and started forward with murder in his eyes. But neither of them got to Patriarch. With a lazy wave of his hand he sent both men flying. They cracked against trees on opposite sides of the clearing and crumpled like bags of bones.

"I grow weary of this." Patriarch turned away from them and started toward the white thorn tree. "You know what to do."

The robed men stepped forward and drew swords in synchrony. Lacey's eyes met Flynn's. Not far away, Nathy and Saxon lay, unconscious.

"Don't let him hurt them," Lacey said.

Flynn's expression fissured. "I'm sorry, Lacey. I'm so sorry."

One of Patriarch's men gripped Lacey's arm and dragged her toward the tree. She glanced up into his hood and frowned. The narrow bend of his jaw, the small lips, were familiar.

"*You.*"

Roselyn Ruark shushed her. "You any good at escape acts?"

"No," she said through her teeth.

"That's a shame. Just trust me."

"Won't he notice you're not...one of them?"

Ruark subtly shook his head. "I killed Almer Eshel and took his robes. He wasn't important. Nobody's even talked to me. Almost feel sorry for the bastard, now..."

Lacey flicked her eyes to the other robed men; they stood in their circle chanting, hands placed together in prayer. "You'd better have a plan."

"I always have a plan."

He stopped at the tree and fixed the manacles around her wrists. With a longer length of chain acting as a pulley, he lifted her up until she hung in agony off the ground, dangling against the spidery white tree. Her destroyed shoulder seemed to draw every ache in the rest of her body toward itself, radiating pain stronger and brighter. Her teeth worked her lower lip as she tried to swallow her tears and the desire to scream.

Patriarch stood in the center of the eyes burned onto the ground, holding the goblet, raised as though in a toast. His men closed around him and continued their low chant, their voices rumbling like thunder far away. Patriarch's voice lifted above theirs, clear and strong.

"The Blood of Elrosh shall strengthen thee and bring Righteousness to thy task." At the close of these words, Patriarch brought the rim of the goblet to his lips, and drank the blood. The thick, dark liquid fell into his mouth and ran down his chin, leaving dark splashes on his white robes.

The men broke their circle around him and Patriarch stepped forward, a hunter's smile on his blood-stained lips. He stopped before Lacey, Deumsyth clutched in his hand.

"I banish you to the pit, Ruined One."

He lifted the blade.

"Amnon!"

Dr. Poole stood at the edge of the clearing, his hazel eyes bright in the dark, his wings spread, ready for flight. In his hand was a long sword. His hair was a mess, hanging in his eyes, his suit rumpled. A scar still circled his throat from where it had been slit.

He walked forward, between Patriarch's men. Lacey wanted to cry out for him to stop, yet none of the men made a move to hurt him. They seemed strangely reverent, *afraid*. Only Patriarch remained calm.

"Well. The Seventh Son returns." Patriarch spun, cloak swirling behind him, and walked toward Dr. Poole. "Are you here to atone?"

"Not quite." Dr. Poole smirked, his eyes narrowed in hatred. "Didn't realize you were in town, Amnon."

"I assume you received my messages?"

"Nice of you to write." Dr. Poole tightened his grip on his sword. "Now. Get away from my goddaughter."

Patriarch chuckled. "I'm afraid I can't see any reason to do that, Absolom."

The trees beyond the clearing shuddered then, and two giants broke through the branches and onto the clearing. Other, smaller figures emerged from the trees, too: A woman with two heads, clutching a wand in each hand; a girl with goat horns bearing a bow and quiver; a cyclops holding two clubs, his solitary eye narrowed in determination; and others, many strange and frightening and yet, to Lacey, miraculous. The members of Ruark's Troubled Troupe spread out around the clearing. And, with them, Isobel and Jade, swords in their hands and bows at their backs.

"Well," Dr. Poole said. "Perhaps because you're outnumbered?"

Patriarch sneered. "I'm a god, little brother."

"Right, well." Dr. Poole crossed blades with Patriarch, shoving him back. "So am I."

50

SACRIFICE

-Fallor Wood-

PATRIARCH SNARLED AND twisted his blade down, breaking free from Dr. Poole's hold. "Kill them all!" he shouted to his men, and there was a frenzy of motion to obey. Swords were drawn, and the hooded men descended on Ruark's troupe.

Ruark broke away from Patriarch's men and rushed to the tree. In one quick motion, he tugged the chain and Lacey dropped back to earth. He undid the manacles from her wrists and hauled her to her feet.

"Time to go, ginger."

He dragged her across the clearing, Lacey faltering in her damaged state. She scanned the battlefield, heart in her throat. By the tree line, Nathy launched himself at his father, tackling him. His expression twisted in rage, black eyes wide, and he no longer looked like the boy Lacey had kissed by the sea cliffs. He looked like a demon, an avenging angel. He wrenched his father up and punched him; his fist came away red with the man's blood.

Not far from Nathy, Saxon drew his wand and launched bright spells, backing away as they were deflected off the blades of approaching men. He managed to get one spell through and knocked one of Patriarch's men to the ground. Father Priestley wheezed and clutched at his chest while Saxon stared on, eyes wide.

Flynn circled himself in flame and launched the fire toward an oncoming horde of five men. They were staid for a moment, but the flames seemed to slide from their cloaks thanks to Kragen's spell work.

"We have to help them," Lacey said as Ruark weaved through the surging bodies.

Ruark only laughed. She looked back at the tree. Dr. Poole dueled one-on-one with Patriarch—clearly losing. He had no practice wielding a weapon and was on a weak defense.

"Let me go!" Lacey said, tugging against Ruark's grip.

"Roz!" It was Nathy, wielding a sword taken from one of Patriarch's men. Mortimer stood nearby, bloody and slick with sweat, breathing hard. He looked up, honing in on his old hunting partner.

"Get her out of here," Nathy said, and before anyone could act, he swung out at his father. Mortimer scrambled back, weakly meeting the blow with his own sword. Nathy moved like an expert and swung the blade without mercy. Fighting to kill. Meanwhile, Mortimer stayed on the defensive. He didn't try for killing blows, he didn't take advantage of Nathy's distracted rage. He merely blocked with his sword and tried to stay alive.

"You heard the man." Ruark picked Lacey up and threw her over his shoulder.

"Are you insane? Put me down!"

"Um, no." Ruark slinked through the rage of fighting bodies and slipped into the thick of the trees. With the noise of the battle a distant rumble, he dropped Lacey to the forest floor. She got to her feet and tried to run back. Ruark pushed her back down.

"I'm not leaving them!"

"Look, ginger, your boyfriend's doing you a favor. No offense, but you're a little, ah...can I say pathetic without you having one of your adorable little fits?"

She charged for the clearing. Ruark caught her around her waist and his fingers bit into her arms.

"I take it that's a no. Fine. He said I'd probably have to drag you out screaming." Ruark had only just finished speaking when Saxon burst from the clearing.

"Oh, fucking brilliant," Ruark said, and collapsed against a nearby tree as a spell smacked him in a blinding blast of red. Lacey scrambled up and Saxon grabbed her hand.

"I'm on your side, pretty boy," Ruark said, rising and holding his side where the spell hit. His shirt beneath the cloak smoked ruddily. "Nathy asked me to save his damsel."

"You're dressed like they are," Saxon said.

"Wow, look who passed primary school. It's called a disguise, you sophomoric twat."

"Why are you—" But Saxon didn't get to ask his question. A spell hit Lacey squarely between the shoulders and she dropped. The last she heard before the soft ring of final, fading pain was Saxon screaming her name.

SAXON KNELT BESIDE Lacey, between her and her attacker—Kragen, his beak nose trailing blood, a papery smile on his lips.

"Dear boy. I thought you'd learned something from this experience." He clucked his tongue. "Evidentially not."

Ruark stepped forward, but Saxon rose and held out his arm. "Guard Lacey. I'll handle him."

Saxon threw a spell at Kragen, which the other warlock deflected with his own wand, a bored smile curling his mouth. He launched another, and another, each one beaten away by lazy flicks of Kragen's wand.

"You've got to practice more, son. An Ally's life isn't all idle talk and parties. You'll have to learn to take a life someday." Kragen launched one of Saxon's spells back at him; it threw Saxon to the ground, pain gripping his chest. Kragen stood over him. "It's in our nature to kill...only to be killed."

"That's a pathetic way to live," Saxon said.

"Pathetic? No, no. You're pathetic, with your meager attempts at heroism. The sweet little rage you hold so close to your heart." Kragen grinned, his lips chapped and flimsy. "I see how you look at me. How badly you wish you could destroy me. But you're angry over nothing."

"My sister is not nothing," Saxon said.

"I saw something I wanted," Kragen said. "I took it. You're only outraged because you lack the strength to do so yourself."

Saxon left his wand on the floor and charged the ambassador. He knocked him down and pummeled his face, relishing the hot blood on his knuckles. Each strike was a moment of rage from the past, long suppressed and finally free because now, without the cover of propriety, they could

439

both be who they truly were—Kragen, a monster, and Saxon...he didn't know what he was. Furious. Murderous.

"You destroyed her," Saxon said with another punch. "She was a child."

Kragen laughed, bubbling blood, which he spit in Saxon's face.

"Come now, boy. You can't fix her by killing me," Kragen said. His fingers gripped Saxon's hair and held their faces close. "And you can't stop what you'll become. You only hate me because of how much we have in common."

"I'm nothing like you," Saxon snarled.

"Tell that to yourself when you're forcing your wife on her back to give yourself pleasure, children, control." Kragen grinned bloody teeth. "It's a hunger, and you can't fight it. You'll fall farther than any of us because of how high you've elevated yourself. At least I know what I am. You—"

Saxon dug his fingers into the ambassador's throat. "You don't get to talk anymore."

Kragen laughed, and Saxon punched him again and again until his knuckles were raw, until Kragen's face was a bloody pulp. He rose when the man went limp.

Ruark wandered over and whistled. "Shit. I underestimated you."

"What," Saxon said, his arm numb, his mind ringing.

"You just beat a man to death. Kudos."

"He's not dead," Saxon said in the same detached tone.

"Yeah. He is." Ruark shook his head. "Warlocks, I'll never understand you people."

Saxon dropped to Lacey's side, but she was already rising, forcing herself up despite a deadly pallor to her skin. Her eyes landed on Kragen's body.

"Who..." She took Saxon's hand, still smeared with blood and spit and everything else that had burst from Kragen's face.

"Gods. Saxon." She looked into his face.

"I guess I got carried away," he said. He wiped his knuckles on his trousers.

She shook her head. "You had to."

"I didn't. Not really."

She touched his cheek and turned his gaze toward hers. "Are you all right?"

440

He sighed. "Nathy was right. I don't feel better." He shut his eyes. "Lace. I—"

"Don't." She dropped her hand from his face. "You can apologize when we're not fighting a cult."

"Speaking of," Ruark said. "It's time I got you out of here."

"No," Lacey said. "I'm not going anywhere."

"You can't fight," Saxon said.

"Nobody else is dying for me!" Lacey said. "I'm tired of this—this bullshit. Patriarch wants me. Not Nathy, not Dr. Poole. They're not going to get killed over me."

"Lace—your powers are gone," Saxon said.

"Then somebody give me a goddamn sword."

"Your arm's broken!"

She shoved him away with her good arm, drew the sword from beneath Ruark's robes, and stormed back toward the battle unfolding beyond. She stumbled once, her feet still unsure beneath her, but she caught herself against the nearest tree and kept going.

"Your girlfriend is persistent," Ruark said.

Saxon shut his eyes, his hand against his forehead. "Yeah."

"Kinda...sexy. It almost makes up for her being ginger."

"Honestly, Ruark? Fuck you." Saxon ran after Lacey, his wand clutched in his hand.

THE SMELL OF cooked flesh choked the air, and Poole saw from the corner of his eye that Flynn had managed to rip the cloak off one of Amnon's men who now writhed, burning, by the tree line. His fire twisted around as the giants and the members of Ruark's troupe teamed up on the many robed men scattered across the clearing.

Poole ducked as Amnon swung the sword again. His chest ached; his lungs burned. His throat was dry from every hard breath.

He feinted to the side, but clumsily, and Amnon grinned. "Tired, Absolom? I suppose now you must regret spending your life with your nose in a book. Perhaps you could have learned to defend yourself."

"Surprisingly," Poole said, "I didn't anticipate dueling anyone to the death in my lifetime."

"Didn't Father teach us always to expect the unexpected?"

"All I remember him telling me was that the sun revolved around the earth—which he seemed to think was flat. Stopped listening to his 'lessons' about then." He breathed hard, and Amnon seemed to be giving him a moment to recover, watching him with amusement.

"I'd hoped you'd come," Amnon said. "I meant for you to. Of course, this would have been far less messy had you stayed away, but I've dreamt of the opportunity to kill you."

"You didn't tell Ryder who I was," Poole said. "Why?"

"He was a brute. Useless, ultimately. Father's dream was to see our purity restored. I've no time for casual monsters." Amnon chuckled. "He must have been surprised when his execution went so poorly."

"It's just a game to you?" Poole took a hard breath. "You're just picking who deserves to live now, even among your own followers?"

"I have high standards. Many of the Old Names are so far from Elrosh's blood, they barely qualify as his Sons. But I will bring Father's vision to pass."

Poole swung his sword, and it was knocked from his hand by Amnon's lazy parry.

"Now that was sad," Amnon said. "You're hardly the worthy opponent I'd hoped. Almost makes this whole affair rather boring."

Poole dived for the sword, but Amnon kicked him back. Amnon picked up the sword and threw it behind him, far out of reach.

"You are truly so—"

An arrow flew across the clearing and buried itself in Amnon's back. A snarl, half amusement and half disgust, came to his lips.

Isobel ran across the clearing and skidded to Poole's side. She pulled him up and offered him a sheathed blade. "Though you might need some help."

"You weren't wrong."

She grinned. "I dunno. Looks like you've done pretty handily." She regarded Amnon, one hand on her hip. "Mind if I take a swing?"

"Having a woman fight your battles?" Amnon grinned madly.

"I don't mind. Better than dying." Poole looked at Isobel. "Is Aeyrin all right?"

Isobel barely nodded. "She's safe. Get down!" She pushed Poole aside just as Mortimer swung his sword at them. Isobel drew two knives from their scabbards and met the blow with crossed blades.

"Jackass," she said.

Mortimer's face was cold, mocking. "Izzy. Good to see you."

"You too." She sliced at him. Poole backed away, eyes scanning the fray, as the two Hunters battled in a musical furor of blades. Nathy ran up, his eyes on his father.

"Coward," he said. His eyes moved to the tree line where Lacey had vanished.

"Is she safe?" Poole asked.

Nathy nodded. "You're the godfather?"

Poole raised an eyebrow. "And you're the...?"

"Don't worry about it." Nathy grinned.

Poole gripped his sword tighter and faced his brother, who regarded the battlefield with a look of mild disappointment.

"This is rather a waste," he said.

"You could stop it," Poole told him.

Patriarch smiled. "I meant on your part."

Before Poole was ready, they were dueling again. He blocked the descending strikes just in time, too close for comfort. His brother danced before him, expertly slicing the air; his blade caught Poole's arm and cut deep.

Poole grinned through the pain. "You're pretty good, for an old man."

Amnon smiled. "Do you see now, little brother, that you cannot rely on the wisdom of man?"

"Warfare isn't the wisdom of man?" Poole laughed. "By all accounts it was our first invention." He jumped back as the blade swung for his stomach. Strangely, the cut on his arm didn't heal—he felt the pain more harshly as it gaped, open and bleeding.

443

"You got Dad's sword back, I see."

Amnon inclined his head. "Deumsyth. The God-Slayer." He twisted the hilt in his hand and considered the blade lovingly. "He always intended I have it. He said I may need to kill you someday."

"He always did like you better."

Amnon flashed toward him, knocking him to the ground. The blade pressed into his throat, burning, worse than demon-bone, worse than anything.

Amnon's eyes glittered, hungry, alive. The look of sanctification. Of a god regarding man. "I send you back to the devil, Seventh Son."

Poole took a deep breath. But the blow didn't come. Amnon lurched forward, blood pooling in his mouth. Nathy stood behind him and ripped back his own sword, bloody to the hilt.

Amnon stumbled up and turned toward Nathy. Poole stared at the wound, deep in his brother's back, but swiftly sealing shut.

"That," Amnon said, "was very stupid."

Nathy's look of cool amusement broke when a scream rattled across the clearing—Lacey. Poole scanned the crowds and found Lacey pinned beneath one of Patriarch's men, Saxon unconscious a few feet from her.

Nathy turned, a snarl on his lips.

Amnon twisted Deumsyth in his hand.

"Nathy!" Poole shouted, but his warning came too late. Amnon stuck his sword through Nathy's back, just below his heart.

"No!" The scream roared from an unexpected corner. Mortimer ran toward Patriarch; Isobel stared after in horror. "You bastard! You promised me!"

"Stand down, Fairborn," Patriarch said, turning back to Poole. "It is not for man to know the ways of God."

Mortimer stared at his son, his pale faced drained of any color. Nathy was kneeling on the ground, holding his chest in surprise. Flynn's fire died and he stood very still; his eyes on Nathy were like the last embers of a fire, black flecked with merest gold. Lacey threw her attacker off with a sudden burst of strength. She ran across the clearing, her right arm twisted strangely against her side.

She dropped to her knees before Nathy, staring at him, and he stared back. Of all the people in the clearing, Nathy seemed able only to look at her.

"Hey, kid," he said with hardly any voice. Lacey reached out to touch his face, but before she could, Nathy fell to his side, still.

"No," Lacey said. "Nathy! Wake up!"

She sounded like a little girl. Like a child who didn't understand that in this world, there was death, and some things that could never be put back together. Her expression fractured into a look Poole had never seen on his goddaughter's face. She had a hand on Nathy's face, on his neck, like she was looking for a pulse. "Wake up," she said again, weaker. Her hand slipped away.

Patriarch laughed, the sound sharp and wrong in this mournful place. "Like a child crying over her dog. It's really rather touching."

Poole swore fire flickered in Lacey's eyes, like a spark between flint and stone. Lacey snatched the bloody sword from Nathy's hand and aimed it at Patriarch, arm shaking. Patriarch sputtered laughter.

"R-really? You—you want to fight me, little girl? Oh, dear. Well. It would be rude of me to deny such a worthy adversary."

"Lacey," Poole said. He got to his feet slowly. "Lacey, get away from him."

She merely shook her head. There were tears in her eyes, but the set of her jaw was determined, and the shaking in her arm wasn't from fear—it came from rage, a rage that sparked in her eyes like green fire.

"Are we really doing this?" Patriarch said, almost bored.

Lacey held her chin high, levelling him with her eyes. "I am the heir to the Ruined Queen's throne. Your sworn enemy. If you want to fight anyone, it might as well be me."

LACEY SWUNG THE sword. Patriarch stepped aside as though dodging a bit of rubbish in the street rather than a blade. She knew she couldn't hurt him. Even Nathy couldn't. And now he was...

Rather than think it, she chose to feel it, in the deep, hollow place that had once been her heart. The happiness that had soured to grief. She thought of Nathy's smile, his tears, the way his lips had fit against hers when they kissed.

He hadn't been evil, or worthless, or cruel. He was *good*. And she'd—she'd loved him in some way. He'd given her things other people wanted to take away.

Saxon had drained her powers away—but what was his pathetic little potion to her? Her powers went beyond magic, beyond gods. And they were hers. She was the Ruined Queen's descendant.

Patriarch believed she was the most dangerous creature in the realm. Well, what sort of monster could be defeated so easily?

She was more than anybody had guessed. Not a nocturne or an Elonni or a human. She was Ruin.

And she would destroy this pitiful man.

"*Hallas Elroi*," she said, and her wings unfolded, but not in a gentle burst of light and feathers. Her wings were like flame, and they consumed her, coursing along her body so hot that even she felt dizzied by the flame.

Fire twisted around her unbroken arm, and she aimed for the one part of Patriarch not protected by his cloak—his face.

He clawed at his eyes as the inferno hit, burying his face at last into his sleeve to dampen the flames.

She dropped her arm. Patriarch snarled. Her flames had made quick work of his flesh, eating away at his skin and eyes. But soon, his ruined mouth flipped into a smile. "Haven't you been paying attention, child?"

Even as he spoke, his skin reformed, smoothing away the burns into nothing but the shimmery newness of healed skin.

He could only be killed—only be wounded—by the sword in his hand.

He grinned. "Yes, my lady, I am immune to anything you can offer—especially one so weak as yourself. You have only completed one Rite. Without all of them, you haven't any hope of defeating me. You can burn the world and everything in it. But I will remain."

"We'll see," she said.

He swung the blade and Lacey, unthinking, reached out. Her left hand caught the broad side of the blade, her fingers and thumb digging in to the sharp ends. She pushed all her fire to her arm, her hand, gritting her teeth and screaming as the heat overtook her. It was too much, even for her. She felt her skin melting, sticking to the metal the tighter she gripped it. But then, there was a slight give. She pushed herself harder, pouring heat and rage into the act. The blade glowed a brighter orange where she held it, like a sword right out of the forge. The top half of the blade bent and finally tumbled over her hand, where it landed by her feet.

She ripped her palm from the blade, barely reacting as her melted skin stayed behind. She grabbed the broken half of the sword and took a step back. Patriarch stared at the ruined remains of Deumsyth.

"Remarkable," he said, breathless. "Truly. The magic of every lowly kind in one stupid, worthless little girl."

Lacey held the shard of blade in her burnt, bloody palm. "I'm not worthless."

She moved forward and stabbed the fragment of blade into his chest. Patriarch staggered back, and Lacey drew the blade away. She'd missed his heart, but still, he was wounded, the gash bleeding freely between his fingers.

He glanced around the clearing, his eyes wild. "I'm afraid this hasn't gone at all the way I'd hoped. I'm graceful enough to accept defeat when I see it. When the Elrosh sees fit, he will deal justly with you. And I will be his vessel." He looked at his men left standing. Only seven marched forward, heads low. The others remained motionless in the clearing. Kragen lay dead beyond the trees.

Mortimer stayed where he was, eyes on his slain son, tears gripping the edges of his eyes.

"Fairborn!" Patriarch barked.

Mortimer shook his head. "I'm done with you, old fool." Mortimer threw off his white cloak and spread his wings; they were white like moonlight, and they caught the air. He flew away over the treetops.

Patriarch watched Mortimer go with a dark smile. "I'm sure we'll meet again. Come. Let's away." He and his remaining men huddled together. Patriarch raised up his hand and there was a crash like thunder and the flash of lightning. The men vanished where they had stood, leaving only trails of smoke behind.

NATHY LAY IN the grass only feet away, and the sight of him in a pool of blood finished what resolve Lacey had. She dropped to her knees and crawled to him. Flynn was already there, coaxing the sweaty hair from Nathy's face.

Lacey brushed her knuckles along Nathy's jaw. "Nathy," she said. She wrapped her arms around the boy lying in his blood, the boy who made her heart beat too fast, the boy with a broken wing. Flynn's hands stroked her hair as she sobbed, doing nothing to comfort her.

"Lacey. Sweetheart. Look at me."

She shook her head, face buried against Nathy's neck.

"He'll be fine. Lacey. I already saved him."

She looked up, her eyes out of focus from the tears clouding them. "What?"

"While you fought Patriarch, I gave Nathy the last gift I could afford." He reached forward and folded something into Lacey's palm. She blinked, and a clear, empty vial came into focus.

"Flynn..." Their eyes met, his dimming with age as it continued steadily to overtake his body.

"I skipped my dose today," he said, "because I feared someone...worthier might need it." He placed his hand on Nathy's chest.

"Flynn." Lacey gasped, relieved and horrified at once. "How much..." She swallowed. "How much time do you have left? Can we still—if we get you back to the house—"

He shook his head, white hair brushing his wrinkled forehead. "I was doomed from the moment I missed my dose. My body is aging rapidly. No amount of elixir can save me now. It can heal any wound, keep you eternally young, even save you from the brink of death." His hand moved to Nathy's face. "But it can't help me. Not anymore."

"Uh."

448

"Nathy!" Lacey cried. She put a hand on his face, and his good eye flickered open and shut.

"Hey, kid," he mumbled. "Sorry."

Flynn grinned. His skin looked looser, his hair whiter still, like he'd aged thirty years since they'd left Fryer's Grove. Nathy eyed him blearily.

"Flynn?" His voice was rough. "What'd you do to yourself?" Understanding seemed to hit him. He touched his chest and, finding no wound there, pushed himself up. "You didn't. Flynn."

Flynn smiled his old smile, the erratic grin of a man nearing a discovery. "I think I've lived long enough."

Nathy's jaw locked. "What about the Nine?"

"I started this for love—but it just became revenge." He turned to Lacey and took her hand. "The woman I love is dead. Destroying Sannus Eyreh won't bring her back." He rested his hand on Nathy's face. "And nothing will right the world. Just these little things...they have to be enough. I would rather leave the world with a man like you in it than live in one without you."

Nathy shook his head again. "All right. Then what about me? You're my—" He exhaled sharply, jaw working. "You're my *father*. You can't go."

"And you're my son. But you can't hold on to me forever, just as I can't hold onto what used to be. The time for being selfish is over—for both of us."

Nathy ground his teeth, grabbed fistfuls of his hair and seemed to dissolve, hunched over himself as though this reality were a physical assault, and he, helpless to do anything but endure it. Lacey tried to reach for him, but Flynn grabbed her hand.

She stared into his urgent eyes, and he spoke in a low voice. "Lacey, the Nine—I'm leaving it up to you. Whatever you...whatever you believe is best." He rubbed the bronze ring around her finger. Before her eyes, his hair whitened still further and thinned. "You're the Firekeeper now. And the Monarch. Don't let anyone choose for you. But Lacey—it's dangerous. They're dangerous. Please, my girl, just be careful."

She nodded, not knowing what else to do as she watched Flynn—her grandfather—turn white and wrinkled before her eyes. Nathy uncurled himself and scrambled to his knees. Just as Flynn began to fall back, Nathy caught him.

"We'll get you back to the house," he said. "You've got more of the potion there."

Flynn, aging with every moment, smiled up at him. "It's time I went, Nathy. The world has enough bitter old men."

"I need you," Nathy said through his teeth. "I—I don't know what to do."

"No one does." Flynn grinned, and Lacey tried not to react as his teeth fell loose from his gums. He shrunk, shriveled, skin edging closer to bone with every breath.

Nathy rose, jaw set and eyebrows knotted. He carried Flynn as far as the edge of the clearing before he stopped and set the frail man down. He sat with his forehead to his knees. Lacey ran to him. She didn't want to look at Flynn's body, unmoving on the cold ground, his flame-colored eyes turned to dead coals. She put a hand on Nathy's shoulder; he brushed it off.

"I'm fine."

"Nathy..."

He rose, picked up Flynn's body, and walked through the thick of the trees. She caught flickers of their forms as they moved farther away, shadows in the moonlight, and soon the living man, and the dead, were out of sight.

Lacey didn't move until she felt fingers brush her cheek. She took Saxon's hand and let him pull her into an embrace. Dr. Poole stood behind them, watching her, and she pulled away from Saxon and ran to him. Then, she cried. She let the knife-like pain of her heart become unbearable, she let her mind betray her demand for calm and pride. She felt the weight of generations in her hand now, in the tiny bronze ring around her finger.

"Can we go home?" she said, and her godfather held her tighter.

"Anything you want, Red. Anything."

THE COST OF LOVE

THE SUN BURST through the misty sky, dyeing the clouds a pure, new-day yellow. Through the window, everything looked warped, twisted strangely, even the sun, even the good things. Maybe that's what Fryer's Grove did to everything—manipulated it into something not quite right.

Lacey turned away from the window and looked around Flynn's study. Flynn's pet fish bobbed in his bowl, a dull look in his eyes. She sat in the floral chair and stared across at the stack of books, the place she had always sat when she came here, to talk to Flynn...her grandfather.

Her family, her blood, had been so close. And she'd let it all slip away.

Her nerves jumped and she could no longer sit. She rose abruptly, pain slicing through her splinted and bandaged arm. She walked to the bookshelf where she found a distraction—something was missing. A long, narrow strip of dustless shelf told her what had been taken: the picture Flynn had so cherished, of himself and Nathy as a young boy.

Nathy...she saw his lost black eyes in everything, in each twisted reflection. She went to the window and looked down at the graveyard below. How many times had Flynn looked out this window, to the ground where his only love lay buried, her headstone a weak reminder of her life? Now he was buried, too.

Nathy stood by Latrice's grave, pushing dirt over the new resident of the cold ground. He'd buried Flynn beside her. Exactly where he'd have liked to go.

"Lacey?"

She froze. Saxon. She couldn't see him. Not now. She'd avoided him since that deadly night in the forest, and he'd let her. They seemed to silently agree: This had gone too far. Loving him—trusting him—had killed Flynn. It had cost everything.

He put a hand on her shoulder and turned her toward him. One look and she realized how badly she'd missed the blue of his eyes and the way they gazed at her.

"Hey," Saxon said.

She brushed his hand away. "Is that all you have to say?"

His smile was weak and dredged up all the misery inside him, surfacing in his eyes. "No, but it's a start."

She walked around him, out of the office, the now-sacred space of Flynn's memory. She felt intrusive; maybe the ghosts of Fryer's Grove wanted to be alone. Together at last.

But they weren't. Ghosts were only mockeries of their former selves. Flynn was gone—his love, his laughter, his brilliant mind. Darkness and dust alone remained. She stopped in the corridor and gritted her teeth. Her eyes burned; her throat ached. But she wouldn't cry in front of him.

Saxon was right behind her, but he didn't touch her this time.

"Lace. Love, I'm—"

"Don't say you're sorry," she said through her teeth. She turned on him, tears fracturing her vision. "Sorry doesn't mean anything. It doesn't fix anything."

"I know, but—"

"You ruined everything, Saxon," she said. Her eyes fell away from his and she added, softly, "I ruined everything. Because of you."

There was a long, aching silence, filled with nothing but their heartbeats and Lacey's shaky breathing. Saxon stood like a statue, watching her with a frown, like he might fight what she said, deny her this painful truth. But his expression broke and morphed into agony.

"I was an idiot," he said, and the hatred, the loathing in his voice made her look up. The tears never fell, but she saw them, sharp distortions in his eyes. "A bloody idiot. I always knew I was. I trusted the wrong people. Because I thought"—his voice caught—"because I thought I was protecting you."

She didn't flinch away from his hand as it cupped her face; his watery eyes took hold of hers and she couldn't break their connection.

"Turns out I was the thing destroying you. And all along...you were trying to save me. From loving you too much. I should have let you."

"We're bad for each other," Lacey whispered.

"I know." He kissed her and Lacey felt a powerful, displaced joy amidst the ache in her chest and the pain in her body. "And that doesn't change a goddamn thing. I love you, Lacey."

"You can't," she said, instead of telling him the truth, that she loved him too.

"I can't do a lot of things," he said. "But the only person who can stop me now is you. I may have to give you up...but I'm done lying to myself."

Breath wouldn't come, and Lacey thought she might suffocate before she could stop him from ruining them both. She swallowed and found her feeble, tear-choked voice.

"I know how this ends," she said. Nathy's eyes flashed in her memory, back when he was happy and sad at the same time, when he had her in his arms and they were on the brink of breaking down for each other. He'd been right all along. He was pragmatic, after all. Reality always beat ideals. "Nobody wins in the end."

Strangely, Saxon smiled. "So what do we do until the end?"

She blinked. "I...we just..."

He raised an eyebrow, smirking.

She pulled him down to her and their kiss filled her with that familiar happy madness, the thrill of rule-breaking, and the release of just...letting go. Of ignoring the future and the present and being somewhere else, if only for a second.

Until she remembered what they'd done, and how every kiss would be haunted by ghosts, every moment in his bed bought with the blood of another man.

She pulled away, unable to look at him. "I'm not racing to a dead end," she said.

He shut his eyes. "Lacey—"

"You lied to me. You knew what I was all along, and you just...you delivered us right into his hands. You told him where we were, you took my powers—and I want—" She clenched her jaw. "I want to forgive you. But if I do, I'll always wonder. Whose side you're on. When you'll stop being on mine. How many more people will die. Because I know I'll choose you every time if we let this happen."

She turned away from him, from the ghosts, the memories and mistakes, all burned together, all accusing. She knew now his eyes would haunt her, too. Blue, the color of sorrow, of lost love. They would stare beside Nathy's, shadow-black, the color of vacancy and secrets.

"Lacey..."

But he didn't chase her this time. Once was enough.

"SORRY TO INTERRUPT."

Alastair and Poe jumped apart. They'd been tangled together, snogging on one of the many worn couches in the library, and Lacey felt strange and intrusive. But she needed her friend just now. She needed to talk to someone.

"I'll, ah..." Poe bit his lip, stifling a small laugh. "I'll catch you later," he finally said, kissing Alastair in a way that made Lacey look at her shoes. She took Poe's vacated seat and smirked.

"Glad to see things are going well."

Alastair narrowed his eyes. "This had better be good."

"It's not." Lacey twisted her hands. "I—I know you weren't there. But I just...wanted to hear it from you. Did I—was I wrong?"

Alastair smiled sadly and put an arm around her shoulder, like he knew she was about to cry. She hid her face against his shoulder. "You couldn't have known Saxon would betray you. You were trying to help."

"I just—" She sniffled. "I feel like I killed Flynn. Like he's dead because of me. And Nathy...I took that away from him. I took the only person who—who could be his father."

"No, Lacey. Patriarch did that."

"But I fell for it." Lacey released a sob, bit her lip to keep more from coming. "I knew Saxon was there to... But I couldn't believe he'd actually do that. Take my powers. I walked right into it."

"You love him," Alastair said softly, his eyes kind. The judgement had worn away, softened perhaps by Alastair's own love. "It's not your fault. It's his, certainly."

She shook her head, her hand pressed against her forehead. "But Nathy... He's the one who lost everything. My stupid mistake cost him the one person he cared about."

"He's got you," Alastair said.

"Me." She spat the word. "He hates me now."

"I doubt that," Alastair said. "Look, I don't like to pry into people's lives, which is why I never said anything, but... Honestly, Lacey, have you noticed the way he is with you?"

His words sent another fissure through her composure, breaking off another piece of her heart. He was right. Nathy did care for her. And she'd broken him. A man who did his best to hide his feelings and still ended up destroyed by them.

Alastair squeezed Lacey's shoulders. "What about Saxon? You two are—"

"No," Lacey said. "We're not. I don't think I could ever trust him again. Besides, it's..." Pointless. The word had begun to lose its sting. It felt like a familiar truth by now.

Alastair looked down, suddenly tense. "I wanted to say... I talked to Saxon after you all got back. He said he recognized one of Patriarch's men. It was my father. And I thought, well, I ought to apologize—"

"He's not your problem, Alastair." She took his hand and squeezed it.

"He's my family."

"You can choose a new family, you know. You've got me. And Poe, obviously. Maybe Alice?"

Alastair snorted. "I think she's coming around to me, yeah."

Lacey found herself smiling. "See? You're all set. You'll be staying here, then?"

He nodded. "Doubt the monastery would take me back, anyway."

"You lot had better visit me sometime."

"Course." He grinned. "You'll be moving to Theopolis, then?"

"Yeah. Dr. Poole is moving us in straightaway. He's already worked it out for me to start at his university next term."

"Lacey—that's brilliant. What'll you study?"

"Naturalism. It's Dr. Poole's subject. Might have a knack for it."

"You'll do great."

The library doors opened then, and Alice ran up and threw her arms around Lacey. Lacey winced as the younger girl's arm buried into her shoulder.

"Ow."

"Oops. Sorry." Alice grinned. "Well, how's it feel to be a hero?"

"I'm not a hero," Lacey said.

"Don't be modest. Jade told us all about how you flamed out and melted that sword." She grabbed for Lacey's hands. She'd taken a potion for the burns, but the skin was still shiny and raw, concealed under thick bandages. "Wicked," Alice said.

Poe peeled his sister away. "Leave her alone, Alice." He smiled down at Lacey. "All right there?"

Lacey shrugged.

"Latrice has stopped crying for you," Poe said. "The house is...happy."

"It is?" Lacey said.

"Yeah. Latrice, y'know, she's not alone anymore over there."

Tears, this time not borne of misery, rimmed her eyes. "That's good to know. Thanks, Poe."

"Are you really leaving?" Alice said. "Why can't you move in here?"

Lacey smiled. "Don't think my mum would like that very much. Speaking of." She rose. "I ought to get ready."

Alastair nodded. Alice wrapped her arms around Lacey's waist.

"You actually turned out all right," Alice said.

Lacey hugged the girl with her good arm. "You, too."

When Alice broke away, Poe kissed Lacey on the cheek. "Take care, all right?"

She left her friends in the library, their goodbyes heavy and warm in her heart. She wished that was it—the last she'd have to say farewell for a while. But there was one last person she needed to see.

RAIN PATTERED THE nearly frozen grass as Lacey walked across the garden. She found him outside by the groves, chopping wide stumps of logs into manageable bits of firewood. His shaggy black hair hung in his face and, despite the cold and damp, he wore only trousers and a dirt-stained white shirt. His left arm was still wrapped, but his other wounds were bare, fresh red scars across his copper skin. He heard her approaching and looked up. A dark look crossed his face but quickly faded into sorrow.

"Leaving already?"

She stopped beside the woodpile. "Yeah."

"Too bad." He set his axe aside and sat on the cutting stump. "You gonna miss it?"

She nodded. "Well. I'll miss all of you."

"Hm." He met her eyes briefly, then looked down. "At least you got people going with you."

"Nathy, I'm so sorry," she blurted. "I—I can't even imagine—"

"No, you can't. You're right. So don't try."

She let the sting dig into her; she thought she deserved it.

"I just want you...to not hate me," she said quietly.

His laugh was a single, hard breath. "Yeah? For what? Not your fault it all went to hell."

"It feels that way."

His dark eyes met hers and she felt a slithering, cold misery in the pit of her stomach. "Why've you been avoiding me?"

"W-what?"

"You only just now came to see me. We've been back for days and you can barely look at me. I wanted to—I *needed* you, but you've just been holed up all this time—"

"I didn't know what to say."

"And you still don't, apparently."

She looked at her feet. "What do you want me to say?"

He shrugged and looked away. "Nothing. I'm just...I'm angry. I just need to be angry."

457

She let silence fall between them for a long time before she found the courage to speak again.

"Nathy?"

His eyes darted to hers; he looked almost eager.

"I'm sorry. This is all my fault."

He watched her, jaw locked, and a muscle jumped in his cheek. "Some of it is. The rest...guess I only have myself to blame." Something changed in his expression with such violence it made Lacey step back. He grabbed the axe and threw it into the forest, where it broke in two against a distant tree.

"Nathy—"

"Flynn shouldn't have died for me! What's my fucking life worth?" He stopped, his chest heaving. He didn't look at her; he wasn't talking to her. Veins stood out on his arms as he clenched his fists. "I'm just a killer. Just another worthless animal."

"Don't say that," Lacey said, too afraid to speak any louder, though she doubted he heard her. He didn't acknowledge her if he did.

"I'm the reason they died," he said. "They all died for me. And what've I done?" He kicked the woodpile and it scattered.

Lacey fought the tug in her bones commanding her to run. She stared at him as he breathed heavily, palms against the cutting stump, bent in half. His hair hung, hiding his eyes. She slipped beneath his arm so she was between him and the stump, trapped between his arms, and stared up at him. He backed away only an inch before returning, and took her face in his hands. He brought her close, so near she felt his breath on her lips, every agonized pant. As their lips touched, an unnamed feeling shuddered through her, something that was desire and terror both.

"I've lost everyone," he said.

"No," she said. "I'm still here."

He pressed his lips to hers, hard and unyielding. She stifled a weak gasp and he stilled, lips parted on hers. She saw the flash of his black eyes as they opened and closed.

"Keep going," Lacey whispered.

Nathy kissed her again, gently now, and for a moment, long and final, his touch was forgiving.

But then he pulled away and dropped his hands with such abruptness that Lacey felt like she'd fallen from a great height.

"Nathy..."

He shook his head, and her words died. She wasn't even sure what she'd meant to say.

"I can't love you," Nathy said now.

Lacey pressed her lips together. Her eyes burned, so she turned her gaze away. "I know."

"It's not..." He sighed. "Don't miss your train, okay?"

Before she could generate a reply, say anything to make him stay, he walked into the forest, his muscles tense through his shirt.

"Wait! Nathy!" She started after him, but her energy left her as though she'd had her powers ripped away once more. Everything in her quieted. Her blood hummed in her head, beat dully in her heart.

She dropped into the grass, amidst the scattered logs. Their scent, the pleasant tang of freshly cut wood, crept into her memory and locked with this moment. She knew every time she encountered that scent, she would think of Nathy, walking away.

I can't love you.

"But I love you," she whispered to no one.

She heard footsteps by the forest's edge and her head snapped up, but there was no one there. Only a single black feather resting amongst the leaves.

A feather from a broken wing.

TO BE CONTINUED...

ACKNOWLEDGEMENTS

I STARTED THIS book at a kitchen table in Colorado in 2014. I'd just graduated from college and had no idea what I was doing. But there was a girl with wings who'd lived rent free in my head for years, and she finally started whispering her story.

Seven years and change have passed, and here we finally are. There were so many times when I believed this book wouldn't happen. I trunked it three times, revised it...eight, nine times? It outlived the laptop I typed those first words on.

This book feels like a miracle, but really, it was a war. And I had a small but fierce army at my side.

Mom, who read the very first pages of my terrible first draft and was willing to read the many iterations I churned out over the years. You caught the typos I was too frazzled to see, and you said it was good when I wanted to set it on fire.

Dad, who believed in me and saw my potential when I couldn't. You've always known I was capable of more than I could imagine.

My brother, Eric, who gave me place to stay during a pandemic and listened to me talk about imaginary people like they were real. I apologize if the sword fights are terrible.

My dog, Hermione. I started writing again after she came into my life, and she pulled me out of the dark more times than I care to admit.

Kathryn, for listening, and encouraging me throughout my quest.

Dr. Hanna, if you're still out there. Sorry this book took so long, and I hope you don't spot any egregious errors.

Grandma Lois, who passed writing down to me. I wish you could have read this.

And every family member and friend who encouraged me, even if it was only a few words. There were so many times when I might have given up if not for a perfectly timed encouragement, and you're all heroes on my strange little quest.

Thank you, thank you, *thank you.*

E.R. GRIFFIN IS an author and veterinary assistant. She has an obsession for hardcover books, all things Legend of Zelda, and international travel. Her short story "What She Left Behind" appeared in the anthology *Betty Bites Back: Stories to Scare the Patriarchy*, edited by Demitria Lunetta, Mindy McGinnis, and Kate Karyus Quinn. *The Queen of Ruin* is her first novel. You can possibly find her on Instagram @egregiouserrrors. She lives in Maryland with her dog, Hermione, a cocker spaniel with an insatiable appetite.